six kinds of crazy
by becka drum

to all of the people who still talk to me
even though I'm six kinds of crazy
especially Brad
who took it so far that he married me
and Sara
for sharing her awesomeness

Evansgate Tour Schedule

St 9/22 – San Francisco
M 9/24 – Los Angeles
W 9/26 – Seattle
F 9/28 – Portland
Sn 9/30 – Denver
Tu 10/2 – Calgary
F 10/5 – Omaha
M 10/8 – Salt Lake City
Th 10/11 – Las Vegas
F 10/12 – Las Vegas
St 10/13 – Las Vegas
Tu 10/16 – Santa Fe
Th 10/18 – San Diego
St 10/20 – Phoenix
W 10/24 – Indianapolis
Th 10/25 – Detroit
St 10/27 – Chicago
Sn 10/28 – St Louis
Tu 10/30 – Little Rock
Th 11/1 – New Orleans
M 11/12 – Virginia Beach
            (Hampton Roads)
W 11/14 – Houston
Th 11/15 – Dallas
St 11/17 – Washington DC
Sn 11/18 – Baltimore
Tu 11/20 – Philadelphia
Th 11/22 – New York City
F 11/23 – New York City
St 11/24 – New York City
Tu 11/27 – Boston
Th 11/29 – Pittsburgh
St 12/1 – Charlotte
M 12/3 – Atlanta
W 12/5 – Jacksonville
Th 12/6 – Miami

Chapter 1

I don't normally go to concerts. It sounds stupid, but music is really personal for me and I don't feel like sharing the experience with a crowd of strangers. My sister knows this, of course, but she begged me to make an exception. Allison promised that this show would be worth the breach of personal policy and she was really excited to be able to take me.

Except, of course, she isn't here.

I look around warily as I open the door of a coffee shop crammed between a diner and a laundromat. Tables are scattered around, as well as overstuffed chairs and couches. The walls are covered in eclectic artwork, some of which seems to be for sale. The place is long, with different levels that require one or two stairs to move between. A sign on the window says that they have live music every Saturday night, but I can't figure out where anyone would play. Plus, it's a Tuesday. Maybe Allison made a mistake.

My favorite band of all times, Evansgate, is kind of a big name to be playing in a coffee shop. Although I've never been to one of their concerts, I've seen pictures of them performing in front of thousands of people, on a huge stage covered with sound equipment and lights everywhere. What would they be doing playing in a place like this?

I glance down at the ticket I'm holding before I remember there is no helpful information on it. I lean back and look to either side, but most of the places are closed for the night. With a shrug, I step inside. Yup, it's a coffee shop. What am I supposed to do with a ticket? Even as the thought is passing through my head, a bouncer guy stops me. This is the weirdest coffee shop I've ever been in. I've never been to one that needed a bouncer before. The man is huge, but not fat, just very tall and built like an NFL linebacker. He puts his hand out, palm forward, to stop me, like his very presence wouldn't be enough. "I'm sorry, but Toddies is closed tonight for a private event."

Well, that explains the ticket. I pull mine out and give it to the man. He looks at it closely and then allows me in. There are not very many people inside, maybe 20, maybe less. I'm still not sure where Evansgate would even play. I don't see a stage or anything. The people are milling around, looking at the artwork or just sitting and drinking coffee. Two people are sitting at a table playing a board game, backgammon I see when I walk by. It looks like a regular night in a coffee shop.

I wander past the coffee counter towards the back. The place is actually shaped like an L and I can see a tiny stage that is set around the corner, not visible from the front. It looks like something that would host poetry readings and open mic nights.

Microphones and instruments are set up, but not what I would have expected for an Evansgate concert. A keyboard, a guitar, a bass, and drums accounts for all of the band members, but the guitar is acoustic and it doesn't even look like a full set of drums. The bass and keyboard are plugged into tiny speakers. Four stools are set around the stage.

I walk back to the counter and order a latte – when in Rome and all that. I go right back to the stage area, even though no one else is back there, and claim a giant armchair right next to the stage. It doesn't look like they're expecting the crowd to be on their feet, so I feel confident that I couldn't get a better view.

I sink back into the chair and wonder how I got myself into this. Going to a concert is bad enough, but alone? I actually feel nervous, which is stupid. I wonder how Allison even found out about this. I don't see any advertisements that say that Evansgate will be playing.

But with my sister, it's usually better not to ask. Allison lives in Dallas where she has some high profile, high power, super secret government-type job that requires a lot of travel. Even though we talk a lot and are pretty close, I have no idea what she does. She can't talk about it, so I try hard to never bring it up. Whatever it is that she does, though, allows us to see more of each other than we would otherwise.

I live just outside of Richmond, Virginia – which is a long way from Dallas. But Allison has to come to Washington D.C. often for work – which is *not* a long way. When she is here during the summer, I take advantage of the opportunity to spend some time with her.

And yet, here I am, sitting in a coffee shop in Washington D.C., by myself. I stifle a laugh. Being alone is the story of my life. My husband, Sam, travels almost all of the time for work. But thinking about Sam brings a queasy feeling to my stomach, so I quickly cast my mind around for something else.

People are starting to wander towards the stage now and I know they are looking at me. I'm sure they're wondering what I'm doing sitting here by myself. How did Allison talk me into this?

My sister is really quite pretty. She is tall, like me, only not *too* tall – unlike me. She has dark blue eyes, that almost look black in the wrong light and long, long almost-blond brown hair that she always wears up. Allison is the kind of person who is used to getting her way.

She is extremely persuasive and had that look on her face that is hard to say no to.

"I know how much you love Evansgate, and I'm telling you: this isn't something you're going to want to miss. Go, have fun. We'll meet back up later. Please? I'll feel better knowing that I'm not leaving you to absolute boredom because I got called into another meeting." Her argument was hard to refute, and I should have expected it. She usually gets called into meetings at the last second.

"I don't know much fun it will be without you."

"You can handle it, I'm sure. Just be safe, okay?"

"I can handle it."

She laughed and gave me both of the tickets. "Don't you want to keep one just in case you can come later?" I asked her.

She reluctantly tucked one ticket back into her bag. "I really don't see that happening, so don't get your hopes up."

I look down at my ticket again. It doesn't look like a normal concert ticket; it hasn't been mass printed by Ticketmaster, that's for sure. There isn't even a seat assignment on it, which I thought was odd when she gave it to me, but now I understand.

"Where am I supposed to go?" I asked her.

Allison gave me explicit directions to a place called Toddies (because she knew better than to expect my sense of direction to get me there) and headed off, presumably to a meeting, as I called out, "Go save the world!" to her retreating back.

Don't get me wrong. I'm looking forward to seeing Evansgate, especially this close, but I still wish she was here. I shift in my seat and look at my watch. I'm trying to check out my fellow concert goers without being too obvious. A lot of them seem to know each other. I sink further back into the comfy chair to wait.

And then, there is Evansgate. They are walking right past me, so close I could reach out and touch them. I purposely took a seat stage right because that is where the bass is set up and I wanted to sit closest to Chris Eck. I should be embarrassed to admit it, but I have a huge crush on him – as does every other female in America. I could say that he is hot, amazingly so, but there really just aren't words to accurately describe his looks. He is more than hot, more than gorgeous, more than any word I could try to use. He is really tall; I would say 6'5" at the very least with dark, almost black, hair and ice blue eyes. He has perfectly straight white teeth (good teeth are important to me). Allison and I call him "The List Man" sometimes because once we wrote lists of men we would make our husbands let us sleep with, in the unlikely

3

event that an opportunity presented itself, and Chris Eck was the only guy I could come up with to put on mine.

The guys file onto the stage. Drew Holst plays the guitar. Drew has hair so light it is almost white and he wears it really short on the sides, longer on top where it is tousled into a messy style. I would almost describe him as heavy set, but it could be because Short Mark is thin in the extreme, and comparatively, Drew is much bigger. Mark Evans is the lead singer and he also plays the keyboard. He has dark brown hair and brown eyes. He has a baby face which makes him cute, but he is really short – or at least short for a guy, definitely shorter than me. And standing next to Chris, he looks even shorter. I call him Short Mark because I have to have a way to differentiate between the two Marks to myself. The drummer is named Mark Cannadiak. I don't know how to pronounce that so I just refer to him as Blond Mark. He has dirty blond hair (surprise) with light blue eyes, and a bit of baby face, too. He is also really thin, almost gangly because he is tall as well.

Short Mark steps up to the mic and greets us, really calmly and quietly. "Hey, guys, thanks for coming out to listen. It's been a really long time since we played like this; I hope you enjoy hearing it as much as we are going to enjoy playing it."

It seems almost like a jam session with friends. The music sounds very different than it does on their albums: quiet, clean, and really mellow. I love it. I can't believe Allison is missing this.

Before long, I'm mouthing the words. I just can't help it. It's one of the reasons that I don't really like going to concerts – I always sing along, but at least I'm not singing out loud.

It's a very weird talent of mine, if it can be called a talent. I only have to hear a song once and I know all of the words, and I know them forever. It's like having a photographic memory, only it's music. Well, I can't just *hear* it, I have to *listen* to it and I've learned that if I don't like the song, I *can't* learn the words. I've tried, but my brain must shut out what it doesn't like. Also, it's not always easy to understand what someone is singing. But if I look up the lyrics and read them while I listen, it works just as well.

At first I try to hold my hand over my mouth, and I try to make it look as natural as I can. But it isn't possible to make that look normal, so in the end I just give up. A few times, Short Mark looks at me and smiles. A lot of their songs have really fast, complicated lyrics. Being able to sing very fast is one of the things Mark Evans is known for. But the hardest song by far is "Yesterday's News". Sometimes I'm surprised he can even keep the words straight.

4

Short Mark pauses the show for a moment while he takes a drink of what appears to be coffee. It's such a normal thing to do that it almost seems out of place. He smiles and says thank you when there is quiet applause. "We haven't played this one in while, so I hope that I can get it right, but it's always been one of my favorites." He turns back to the rest of the guys and says, "'Yesterday's News'?"

When he turns back, he looks at me and smiles, almost smirks. He is trying to trip me up; I'm sure of it. He doesn't look away from me for the whole song, and I can tell by the look on his face that he is impressed. I keep up with him word for word. At the end, I wink.

Okay, I'm flirting with the lead singer of Evansgate, and even if I do really only have eyes for the bassist I'm aware of how awesome this is. But really, who is going to give up the opportunity to flirt with Eddie Vedder at a Pearl Jam concert, even if they really love Jeff Ament?

The other members of the audience are looking at me now too and I'm officially embarrassed. I slide around in my seat so that I'm completely facing the band and no one in the audience can see my face. A prickle in my ears tells me that a lot of them are still looking at the back of my head, but at least I don't have to see them staring.

I'm now directly facing Chris, and he isn't more than five feet away. He smiles at me and I can feel my heart squeeze. Wow, he is gorgeous.

They play for longer than I expect. Unfortunately coffee goes straight through me and finally I can't stand it any longer. Now I regret sitting in front because that means I have to walk past everyone to get to the restroom. I know I'm not the only one who has gotten up during the show, but I still feel like I have a spotlight trained on me as I pick my way through the seats.

I'm bummed when I get out of the bathroom because the show is over. A lot of people have stepped up to the stage and are talking to the guys. I decide it's best to just make my escape. I don't really want to face any of these people now that I've embarrassed myself so fully.

On the sidewalk, I take out my phone and turn it back on. I call Allison but she doesn't answer. I leave her a message telling her that I'm about to go underground to take the Metro back to our hotel and I'll see her there. I hate taking the Metro by myself, especially at night. But tonight I'm grateful that it's unusually crowded. It's easier to blend in and not feel like a target when you can hide in plain sight.

It isn't a long walk from the Metro station to our hotel and I'm grateful for that too. I could have called the hotel for the shuttle to come and pick me up, but I thought it was a little ridiculous to have them drive less than half a mile. Allison still isn't back from her meeting when I get in, and I fall asleep before she comes.

Chapter 2

I wake up to the sound of Allison's alarm. She groans as she rolls out of bed and heads to the shower. I get up and put on some coffee in the little pot in our room. Allison and I always bring our own so that we don't have to drink the garbage that the hotel provides, but we also don't want to have to leave to get something good. I fix her cup and set it on the vanity counter for her when I hear the shower turn off. Then I climb back into bed with my own.

"Thanks," Allison says the second she steps out of the bathroom and sees her cup. "I love it when I travel with you."

"Why? Because I make you coffee?"

"Yes. You have no idea how nice it is to find it ready and waiting."

She's right. I don't. "I don't mind making it for you. You're paying for my room and all."

"Not me, Baby Girl."

I shrug. "Close enough."

"So – how was the concert?!"

"It was amazing. I can't believe you missed it! How did you even find out about that?"

"Do you remember Maria?" I nod. Maria was Allison's neighbor when she lived in DC. "Her cousin, or something, knew about it and offered her tickets. When she heard I was going to be in town she offered them to me because she couldn't go."

"Lucky me!"

"I'm glad you had fun. Me? Not so much." Allison pretends to pout. "Ah, work. I have to go downtown today. If you come into the city I'll meet you for lunch."

Our hotel is in Pentagon City because Allison is spending most of her time at the Pentagon for this trip.

"When are you leaving?"

"Soon. Why?"

"Let me see if I can get ready fast enough and I will ride in with you."

"What will you do?"

"The weather is supposed to be gorgeous. I'll mess around on the Mall, take in a museum, I don't know. Tourist stuff."

"Okay. Hurry up."

I rush through a shower. Allison is still putting on her make-up when I get out. I throw on some clothes and dry my hair as quickly as I can. I skip make-up because she is already waiting for me. I grab my shoulder bag instead of just a purse and jam some stuff in it, like sunscreen and a book, as well as my wallet and phone.

"I'm ready."

We grab bagels from the breakfast bar to eat on our way. The Metro is very crowded with people heading into work this morning. I'm glad I finished my bagel while we were waiting for our train because we are standing and it's nice to be able to hold on.

When we change trains, we split up. "Call me about lunch," I tell her.

"Will do. Be safe today."

"Yes ma'am. Now go save the world." She hates it when I say that. But, really. I don't have any idea what she *is* doing, so why can't I just assume she is saving the world?

I take the Metro to the Smithsonian stop and come up the stairs right into the Mall. I was right, the weather is amazing. It's *almost* chilly in my shorts and tank top, but I know it will heat up soon and I will be grateful that I'm wearing them. I can't believe how nice it is for late June. I inhale deeply and look up at the sky.

I wish I had put a towel in my bag so that I could just lie on the grass and watch the fleecy clouds go by. I consider finding a place to buy one. I spin in a slow circle trying to decide if there is anywhere close enough. It's too early for the museums to be open, but I might be able to find something in a gift shop in one of them a little later. Or I maybe I'll just lie in the grass somewhere. It's wet now, but it will dry out soon.

There is always something happening on the Mall, and today I see that a big area down by the monuments and Reflecting Pool is cordoned off with yellow caution tape. There are a couple of trailers parked there and people with cameras. I hate it when big pieces are closed to the public because I feel like it ruins the view. But I start in that direction anyway because I figure the best sights are that way. It's early, so there are not a lot of tourists out yet and I can appreciate the Reflecting Pool and Lincoln Memorial by myself. It's hard to tell from here, but it looks like the yellow tape might impede that slightly, but I'll make the best of it.

I walk to the Washington Monument and take a few minutes to look up and marvel at its height. I always do, and maybe someday it will stop surprising me, but every time I am shocked at how tall it seems when you're standing at the base. The yellow tape is blocking off most of the space between the Monument and Reflecting Pool, as well as the whole area to the right of the Pool, so I walk down the left side. I meander really slowly, even though I would really like to see the Lincoln Memorial before it gets crowded. I hate how many people clog that place up.

I'm watching some swans on the water when someone grabs my hand from behind. I jump in surprise and whirl around to find myself face to face with Chris Eck. My brain jams and I can't speak. Why is he here? Why did he stop me?

In a rush, last night floods back into my mind. I made them mad – or something – and he is going to tell me to stay away from their concerts forever.

"I thought that was you!" he exclaims. "You are the girl from the show last night, right? Or am I about to be really embarrassed?"

"No. I mean, yes, I am, I was there last night. And I'm so sorry. I know I shouldn't have been singing along, but it's just so hard not to."

"Don't apologize! I thought it was great! But why did you run out?"

"I don't know. It seemed like the thing to do at the time."

He laughs. "I really wanted to meet you. I was disappointed that you left. I can't believe you're here!"

I don't know what to say to that, so I just nod.

"Evans really wanted to talk to you, too. Are you busy? Are you going somewhere?"

"Just to visit President Lincoln."

"Would you come over and meet the guys?"

A chance to meet Evansgate. My brain is still a few beats behind, but it's starting to catch up. I'm talking to Chris Eck! I try to control my face so that I don't grin like a maniac. "Um, yeah. I can do that."

We walk back around the Pool. "I'm Chris, by the way."

"Uh, I know your name."

"This is the part where you tell me yours."

"It's Sara."

"Sara, it is very nice to meet you," he says, sticking out his hand. I can't believe I'm shaking Chris Eck's hand. I take a mental deep breath and force myself to calm down. He's just a guy. Unbelievably good looking, but still just a guy.

When we get to the yellow tape, Chris lifts it up for me to duck under. We walk towards the trailers. Short Mark is talking to someone wearing headphones around his neck and holding a clipboard. He puts his hand up to interrupt the guy when he sees me. He smiles and says something else, then comes towards us.

Chris is telling me that they're recording a video for the new album that they're working on. "It's called *Saving the World*."

"Hey! My sister does that!"

"Does what? Save the world?"

"Yeah."

"What does she do, work for Greenpeace or something?"

"No, not Greenpeace."

"Then what does she do?"

I shrug. "I don't know." I add "obviously" with my tone.

He is struggling not to laugh at me as Short Mark reaches us. "Well, hello."

"Hi." Brilliant, Sara.

Chris saves me though. "Do you know his name too?"

"Yeah, I'm pretty sure I've got it."

"Evans, this is Sara."

Short Mark sticks his hand out. "It's nice to meet you." This is a perfectly normal exchange, I have to remind myself. "Do you out sing everyone when you go to their concerts?"

"No. Only the weak ones."

"I'm weak, huh?"

I have to laugh. "I wouldn't say I 'out sung' you."

"I would. I think you might know the words better than I do."

"You have the advantage of having written them, of course."

"Remembering them all isn't always easy though. I was glad you knew all of 'Yesterday's News', because there were a couple of times I think I would have messed up without you to follow."

"You weren't actually following me, were you?"

"A couple of times. I haven't played that song in a long time. It's always easier to follow someone's lead than to just sing it outright. I'm not going to lie; I was kind of testing you with that one."

"I figured as much. But I'm sorry to tell you that there isn't a song you play that I don't know all the words to."

"Not one? I'm flattered you think enough of our music to learn all of the lyrics."

He doesn't need to know that I don't have to do anything to learn them. Let him be flattered.

Drew has come over now. "So it was her?" he says to Chris.

"Yup. This is Sara."

"Hi, Sara," Drew says sticking his hand out.

"Hi, Drew."

"That was impressive last night. I don't even know all the words

10

to 'Yesterday's News'."

Short Mark nudges me. "I should keep you around. You know, just in case I need help remembering my lines."

I feel comfortable agreeing because I know that he's not serious. "Sure. What do they call that person who stands there and whispers to actors on stage when they forget their lines?"

Drew guesses, "A cue person?"

"No, I'm pretty sure they have an actual title. Prompter!" I jab my finger in the air as I remember.

"Memory like a vault, this one," Short Mark says. "Now that we know your title, you can tour with us, right?" He gestures around, to include the guys standing there.

"Where's Blond Mark? He might want a say in this." And then I realize what I said. I clap my hand over my mouth. "I mean – I mean the other Mark? Where's the other Mark?"

But the damage is done. The guys are laughing.

Short Mark gives me a shrewd look. "Blond Mark, eh? What do you call me? Please say it's better than 'Brunette Mark'."

"Ah, nothing. I just call you Mark. Mark and Blond Mark, that's it." I've always been a terrible liar.

"I don't believe you. Come on! What do you call him? Please tell us!" Chris is practically begging.

Oh, why not? I'm never going to see them again. "Short Mark. I call you Short Mark. But I don't mean – it's just I can say Evans, but I don't – I..." I stutter.

Drew and Chris are howling with laughter. "That's awesome!"

"I'd rather be short than be known as 'Blond Mark' – that just sounds like the punch line to a joke." And just then, Blond Mark comes around the corner of a trailer. "Hey, Blondie!" Short Mark calls out.

"I feel as though I have missed the funny part of that joke, Evans," Blond Mark says. But he is already laughing.

"Blond Mark, I'd like you to meet Shorty – I mean, Sara." He is laughing. "She's our new friend."

Blond Mark smiles at me. "You don't seem very short. But don't mind him. He has a bit of a complex about his height." That sends them over the top. Chris has tears running down his face and Drew is struggling for breath, they're both laughing so hard.

I smile at Blond Mark. "It's nice to meet you."

He smiles at me and shakes my hand. "I saw you at the concert last night. Where did you go? Eck really wanted to meet you."

Chris stops laughing suddenly. "Yeah, I really did. You never did tell me why you left."

Suddenly the guy wearing headphones is yelling at them. "Cannadiak!" (Oh, so that's how you say it!) "I told you to round them up! Let's go!"

"Well," I say. "It was really nice to meet all of you. Have fun, recording your video. Or would it be 'good luck'?"

Chris grabs my hand. I know, *swoon*. "You don't have to go! I mean, unless you have to go. You could stay and hang out with us. Or did you have an actual appointment with President Lincoln? Because you really shouldn't keep that man waiting."

"Nope, I've got a lot of nothing to do today." I can cancel lunch with Allison.

"Excellent!" He takes off when Headphones Guy starts yelling at him again.

I'm not sure where to go, but I feel like there's a good chance I could get in trouble for being here. I decide to get outside the yellow tape at least.

But as I duck under, I hear Chris yell my name. When I look up, he is running over. "Seriously? You're ditching us again?"

"Oh, no, not really. I just didn't know where to go. I don't want to be in the way. And I was afraid I would get in trouble because I assume I'm not really allowed on that side of the tape."

"Come here, please?" How do I say no to Chris Eck? I duck back under the tape. I follow him around to the other side of the trailer. "Tom?" he calls out.

A man, maybe in his fifties, with graying hair turns around. "Yeah?"

"I'd like you to meet my friend, Sara. She's going to hang around today. Can you help her out?" Then to me, "Sara, this is Tom Cleary, our manager. He'll keep you out of trouble." With another smile, Chris jogs off again.

"Hello, Sara. It's nice to meet you."

"Um, yes. You too."

"The key to staying out of trouble with the director is to stay as close to the trailers as possible. That way you know you aren't in the shot, no matter where the camera is pointing."

"Oh, that's easy enough."

"Come on, let's get comfortable."

He grabs two folding chairs and takes them back around to the front side of the trailer. We sit down and watch the guys horse around in front of the cameras.

"I know they look like idiots now, but this video is going to have some special effects and it will look better when those are in."

"Oh." I don't know what else to say.

"So, Sara. Do you live in DC?"

"No, I live just outside of Richmond."

"What brings you to our nation's capital?"

"I'm visiting my sister."

"Where does she live? I used to live in Arlington."

"She lives in Dallas." I laugh at the expression on his face. "She is here for work, and whenever she makes it to DC, I figure I can drive the two hours to see her."

"I assume she is working now?" I nod. "What do you do with your time when she is at work?"

"Um, wander around the city. Pretend to be a tourist. You know, watch major musicians record their latest video. Same old, same old."

He laughs. "How often does she come to DC?"

"A lot, actually. Maybe once every couple of months or so."

"Do you take time off of work to come?"

"Not in the summer. I'm a teacher, and I appreciate the distraction of a trip to DC."

He smiles. "What do you teach?"

"High school chemistry."

"That sounds like it could get frustrating. I'm glad you get your summers off."

"I am too, except I get bored. So how did you get hooked up with Evansgate?"

He smiles. "A friend of a friend. But that's what everyone says in this business."

Tom and I fall silent as we watch the guys work on their video. There must be a lot of special effects coming because it seems really weird; you can tell there is something missing. I can't make sense of anything they're doing. Tom's cell phone goes off and he looks at it, and then hops up. "Sorry, Sara, but I have to go take this. Just stay by the trailers, okay?"

Chapter 3

I glance at my watch as Tom walks away. It's already after 11, so I should probably let Allison know that I'm canceling on her.

To Allison:
Going to have to cancel our lunch. Talk soon. xoxo

She cancels on me so often that I don't even feel guilty. I drop my phone in my lap because I'm sure she's going to text me back. I wonder how long the guys are going to be. I'm starting to get bored. I glance down when my phone buzzes. Allison was quick.

From Allison:
I'm glad this means you won't be mad when I have to cancel lunch today. Swamped! What is it that you are doing that could be more interesting than spending time with your sister?

Perfect! But, I don't know what to tell Allison. For some reason, I feel weird telling her the truth. My fingers hover over my phone.

Before I can decide what to text her, the guys start back towards me. I stand up and push my phone into my pocket. "All done?" I call out.

"No way, sweetheart," Chris returns. He says "sweetheart" kind of funny, like a mobster from the twenties or something. "We're just on a break. Come on," he says, taking my hand, "this is the part where they feed us."

I have no intention of eating their food, but I follow them around the trailer anyway. In between the two trailers someone has set up quite a spread. It was clearly catered by some upscale restaurant or something. I think I was expecting a giant sub or pizza, but this is gourmet. There are sandwiches, but they're on artisan breads. There's hummus with pita chips, fresh chunky salsa with blue corn tortillas, and a spinach-looking dip with bagel chips. There's a beautiful salad, fresh fruit, and an assortment of cheese and crackers.

A lot of people are already loading plates (the real deal, no paper here) and wandering off to sit on the grass. I stop, but Chris tugs on my arm. "Come on, let's eat."

"Oh, no. This food isn't for me."

"Seriously? Do you have any idea how much of this is going to go to waste? Do my heart some good and save something from the trash can."

I laugh. "I really don't feel right eating, but thank you for the offer."

"I'm not taking no for an answer."

For some reason the idea of sitting down and eating with these guys seems really intimidating. I shake my head. Chris sighs dramatically and heads over to the table. I sit down in the soft grass and then lie back to soak up some sun. Short Mark comes over with his plate of food and sits down next to me. I'm looking up at him and I realize he's kind of gross.

"You know, your hair could stand to be washed."

"I have an image to uphold – I have to exude cool. I wouldn't want to wash any of my coolness away."

"It's possible to be cool and clean at the same time. I know. I've seen it done."

He laughs. "We're supposed to be gross for the video. It's manufactured by the makeup people. You know, clean dirt."

"Oh, that makes me feel better."

"You really should eat, Shorty."

I sit up. "I can't, Short Mark. I don't feel right eating your food."

He laughs. "Are you always going to call me that?" A little thrill runs through me at the thought of seeing them again sometime.

"Are you always going to call me Shorty?"

"Probably."

"Then, yup."

"Okay, but you have to call Cannadiak 'Blond Mark' all the time to be fair."

"Oh, definitely. One just doesn't work without the other."

Blond Mark comes over with Drew right behind him. "Not eating, Sara?"

"That food is not for me. You guys enjoy though."

"Don't be stupid. There is so much, you could eat four or five times and no one would notice."

Short Mark pokes me. "Yeah, and it's for you if I say it's for you." He looks at me pointedly. "It's for you."

I laugh. "Really, I'm fine."

Chris returns with two plates of food. "I told you I wasn't taking no for an answer." He sets one of them down in front of me then pulls a napkin and fork out of his pocket. Then, he pulls out a bottle of water.

"How big are your pockets?"

"Big enough. Now eat."

"You're a butthead, did you know that?" I ask Chris.

He laughs. "Did you really just call me a butthead?" I nod. "Sweetheart," he says in that same way as before, "I would have been a butthead if I sat down and ate lunch in front of you without getting you any."

Short Mark sticks his fork in the air. "I agree. Although, I also agree with your assessment, Shorty. He is a butthead." Chris throws a chip at him. "See? Butthead."

"Okay, fine. I give up." The food does look delicious, so I eat.

The guys ask me a bunch of questions and I have pretty much the same conversation with them that I had with Tom a couple of hours ago.

"So how long are you in town?" I ask them, anxious to get the conversation away from myself.

Short Mark answers first. "It depends on if we can get everything we need today. Once we finish the video, we'll probably stay for a couple of days and do the tourist thing." I nod. "How about you? When are you going home?"

"I haven't decided yet. Allison – my sister – is going to be here until at least Wednesday of next week."

We're finishing up lunch while we talk and Short Mark has somehow ended up sitting on my napkin. "Um, Short Mark? Could you scoot so I can retrieve my napkin, please?"

The guys burst out laughing again. "Evans, I think that is what I'm going to start calling you," Blond Mark says.

"Okay," I say, "but just be warned that I'm calling you Blond Mark."

Chris and Drew are rolling again. Chris sits up suddenly and grabs my hand again. "Marry me. Please?"

"Um, I can't. I have a personal policy to only marry people if I know their whole name. And, I feel as though you should be warned, I'm six kinds of crazy. Oh, and I probably should have mentioned this first: I'm already married."

Chris glances at my left hand. "Married. Of course. I should have guessed."

The situation is so ludicrous that I can hardly stop myself from laughing out loud. "Six kinds of crazy, honey. You don't want to marry me." I can't believe I'm even having this conversation with Chris Eck.

Someone comes over to us. "Guys, we'll be doing the song for a while after lunch." There are two guys behind him carrying guitar cases. Well, I assume one of them has Chris's bass. I'm not sure why they brought them over here though.

Drew opens his case and takes out his guitar. He starts plucking the strings. Ah, he's tuning it. Then he starts playing Van Morrison's "Days Like This". I can barely hear it because it's an electric guitar and he doesn't have it plugged into anything. I'm lying back in the grass again with my eyes closed. It's like I don't have any control over myself. The words just come out. I'm singing really softly though. I trail off because a shadow suddenly falls on me and I can feel someone's eyes. Short Mark is leaning over me, blocking my view of the sun. "Sorry," I mumble.

"You know Van Morrison too?" he asks.

"Um, yeah."

Chris has his bass out now. I assume he was tuning it. He starts playing "Into the Mystic" and Short Mark is watching me very carefully. I sing, off key, I'm sure, but Chris plays the whole song so I keep going.

Short Mark grabs Drew's guitar and starts "Brown Eyed Girl". I only sing the first couple of lines, and then I jab him in the belly. "That's not much of a test. Look at me, I have brown eyes, I have a dad. Did you really think I wouldn't know that one?"

Before he can say anything Headphones Guy comes over and yells at them to get a move on. "We're running out of daylight here!"

We all look up at the sky. The sun isn't even directly overhead yet. "Yeah," I murmur, "I hate how early it gets dark in the summer."

The guys all laugh and start to get up. Chris is the last one to walk away. He turns back and says, "Christopher Thomas Eck." And then follows the other guys.

Chris takes his bass and Drew has his guitar. But, Blond Mark's drums are already set up a little ways away, with Short Mark's keyboard in front of them. There are a few mics set up too, and cords lying on the ground. I watch as Drew and Chris walk over and plug their instruments in without having to ask. Someone gives the guys ear pieces.

They start playing, but the only thing I can hear is the drums. The cords from all of the instruments run into a sound board, there are no speakers. I'm guessing the guys can hear through their ear pieces. Headphones Guy is wearing his headphones, of course, and a couple of other people are too.

There are other things to watch now too. A group of people are building a backdrop of sorts using wood and metal plates. It's not completely solid and I can tell they are placing it specifically to have the Lincoln Memorial peeking through. I am amazed how fast they put it together.

They must sing through the song a lot because they are playing for more than 20 minutes. As soon as they stop a bunch of people rush in and start grabbing things: the sound board, cords and cables, the mics, Short Mark's keyboard, several people are grabbing the drums.

They carry them over to another spot so that the Lincoln Memorial is behind them and quickly reassemble everything. Then the guys start again. It's the same thing over and over. They move so the Washington Monument is behind them, the backdrop, the White House. I'm assuming they're playing the same song over and over. I wonder if they're getting bored. I am.

At some point, I notice my phone is buzzing in my pocket. Oops! I forgot to text Allison back. There are several texts from her.

From Allison:
What are you doing with yourself? I promised Dad I would keep you out of trouble. Ha!
2 hours ago

From Allison:
What? Was my joke offensive?
2 hours ago

From Allison:
You've never ignored me this long. WHAT ARE YOU DOING?
1 hour ago

From Allison:
Sara! I will make a call if I need to. WHERE ARE YOU?
15 minutes ago

From Allison:
I am giving you exactly 10 minutes and then I am calling someone to find your body.
1 minute ago

Thank heavens I looked now! I know my sister well enough to know that wasn't a bluff.

I don't exactly expect that to be enough. Of course, she texts me back almost immediately – as fast as she could type out the message, I'm sure.

From Allison:

I probably won't be around for dinner. I'm sorry this week has been such a bust. I'll make it up to you. Will you be okay without me?

Hm, would it offend her if I told her the truth? Probably.

To Allison:

I'll be fine. Save the world.

For once I'm glad that she has so much work. They're moving all the stuff again, and Chris comes over to me. "Whatcha doin'?"

"Texting my sister. We were supposed to have lunch today, but she couldn't. Now she just told me that she won't be around for dinner." I exhale loudly. I shrug my shoulders and put a smile on my face. "I love ordering room service."

"You have been sitting around here all day, doing nothing – did you think I asked you to just for the sake of making you bored? When I'm done, I'll take you out for dinner, okay?"

"You don't have to do that! I'll be fine. And I've had a lot of fun today. It's been quite a learning experience."

"You can only learn so much and then it just gets boring. I wanted you to stay today so that you'd be around when I was done. Please hang out with me some more."

"Okay. It's not like I have any better offers." I wink.

"Well, if you can lower yourself to my level for the evening, I would appreciate it."

"I can probably handle that."

Am I flirting with Chris Eck? More importantly, is he flirting with me? He knows I'm married. Plus, I'm me. Why would Chris Eck be interested in me? But why *did* he ask me to hang out here all day? Dozens of questions are buzzing around in my mind.

The guys start playing their song again; they're in front of the White House now. I'm still standing in front of a trailer, but I've moved around to the back side of the other one so that I can see them. I sit down on the ground with my back against the trailer and lean my head back. I lied. I am so bored.

I sit up straight with a jolt. He's a rock star, and a gorgeous one at that. He has girls throwing themselves at him all the time. He probably has a girl in every port. Is that what I am? His girl of the hour? He knows I'm married, but I *have* been flirting with him. I've probably given him the impression that I'm perfectly willing to cheat on my husband with him. I'm sure he's slept with tons of married women; that probably doesn't bother him at all.

But I'm still kind of stuck on one thing. Why would he be interested in me? He could get any girl he wanted, I'm sure of that. I can't imagine that he wouldn't go for someone beautiful. It's not that I think I'm ugly; I'm just not beautiful by anyone's definition. I'm way too tall: 5'11¾". I'm not fat but I don't have a killer body or anything. I have fairly thick brown hair that falls just past my shoulders and is perfectly straight no matter what I do to it. It's pretty enough, I guess, but it's *brown*. Top it all off with brown eyes and you get a perfectly average looking individual.

But guys don't always care. I heard once that guys think about sex every seven seconds or something. I'm guessing if that's true it doesn't matter what she looks like, any girl would do – especially if you have the means to get them. And Chris Eck has that. Maybe it's just my quirky little ability to sing all their songs that got him interested enough to look at me and then he just assumed that we'd have sex because all girls do.

They're finished now and heading my way. All four of them are coming, so I'm guessing they're done with this phase of the process. Short Mark is talking. "We'll still have to do it in the studio, but I feel like we got enough to work with."

Chris smiles at me, but I can't bring myself to smile back. I have to go now, because I am *not* willing to cheat on my husband, no matter what impression I might have given him. "We get another break for a little while," he tells me. "Do you want to go visit President Lincoln?"

The other guys have gone into one of the trailers. It's starting to get hot and I assume they are air conditioned.

"Um, no thanks. It's too late. That place gets crazy crowded."

"Oh! I'm so sorry. I should have let you go this morning."

"It's totally fine, I've been there dozens of times. There will be more opportunities, I'm sure. It's no big deal, really." Stop talking, Sara! "But, um, I am going to go ahead and take off now. It was really nice meeting you all. Thanks for letting me hang around and watch all day. Oh! And thanks for lunch! It was really good."

Chris's brow furrows. "I thought we were going to do dinner."

"Uh, yeah, I'm sorry. I just don't think that would be a good idea."

"Why not?"

"Because I'm married. So, I'm just going to go. But thanks again. It was really fun!"

I turn to walk away, but Chris grabs my hand. "Please go to dinner with me. I wanted to actually talk to you, but I really didn't get a chance, obviously."

"No thanks. Besides, you'll probably still be taping."

"Then we'll do dessert, or a drink, or something later."

"Chris, it really isn't a good idea."

"Because you're married? What difference does that make?"

"It makes all the difference!"

"Don't you have any guy friends?"

"Of course I do!"

"So what's the problem?"

"I'm not going to have sex with you!" I blurt out.

He laughs. He *laughs*. "I wasn't expecting you to. You're married."

"Yeah, I'm sure that matters to a guy like you."

"What kind of guy would that be?"

"You're a famous rock star. You probably have a different girl every night of the week."

"Ouch. Sara, that is genuinely offensive, you know."

"Come on, Chris. It's common knowledge that you guys move through women like people go through gum."

He looks at me and very quietly says, "I don't."

I'm starting to feel really bad. "You don't?"

"Nope. Sorry to burst your bubble, but we're not like that. I don't have a girlfriend, but I still don't run around." I am completely confident that he is telling me the truth.

"Oh God. I am so sorry." I can feel the blush creep up my cheeks.

He smiles. "No problem, it's a normal assumption, I'm sure."

"No, really that was awful. I'm sorry. So sorry."

"Well, you're totally forgiven. Are we back on for dinner or whatever? As *friends*?"

I nod meekly. "But you have to let me buy it to make up for that."

"Don't be ridiculous! I owe you for making you sit around by yourself all day."

I'm still totally embarrassed. "I'm so sorry, Chris. I –"

But he cuts me off. "It's fine. We're going to be great friends. Now what should we do for the rest of my break?"

"How long do you get?"

"Probably not very, why?"

I walk out from between the trailers and look around. There's an ice cream cart vendor at the base of the Washington Monument. Perfect. I grab Chris's hand. "Come on. I'm going to get you ice cream."

He smiles at me. "Okay. Lead the way."

We sit on the edge of the sidewalk and eat our ice cream. It is getting hot, and the ice cream is melting, so we have to eat it quickly. That's probably for the best, since he doesn't have very long before he has to go back to recording.

"How much more do you have to do?"

"I don't really know. I just go where they tell me to when they tell me."

"Well, you should get back before Headphones Guy comes yelling."

Chris snorts. "Did you just call him 'Headphones Guy'? I don't think I want to know what you call me behind my back!"

I blush, which I know is a mistake, but I can't help it. I look at my shoes, but now I have stirred his curiosity and Chris doesn't feel like letting it go. He asks. He smiles. He pouts. But then he grabs my hand, pulls my chin up with his other hand, looks me square in the eye, and says, "Please. I really want to know."

Well, crap. "We call you 'The List Man'." As if he's going to let it go at that. He raises his eyebrows. "Um, you know. *The List*." He shakes his head. "The list of people you can sleep with without your spouse getting upset?"

Now he smiles. "Does that mean I'm on your list?"

Oh, why not? It's not like I'm ever going to see him again. And, at least I'll be able to say I lived this day to its utmost. "You *are* my list." I blush again.

"But, just to clarify, you are not going to have sex with me."

I shove him. "No! People make those lists as a joke. The opportunity never actually presents itself."

"Oh, I see. Well, come on. Let's go back."

Headphones Guy is already yelling. I can see the other three guys coming out of the trailer. Short Mark is looking around and he smiles when he sees us. "Come on! We might be able to get this finished today!"

It's after three, so I'm pretty sure dinner is out. They have shifted everything and now they are taping with the White House behind them. The guys are back to running and jumping, with something clearly missing from the scene. It must take a lot of editing to make these things viewable.

I feel like we ate an early lunch, and even with the ice cream I'm really starting to get hungry around six. They guys have to be starving. And exhausted. They have been running around for hours.

Suddenly Headphones Guy calls out, "That's it! Great job everyone!"

They're done? It looks like we'll be doing dinner after all. Chris comes jogging up to me. "Are you ready for dinner?"

"Sure! Where do you want to go?"

He smiles. "I don't know much about DC, actually. Do you have any suggestions?"

"Hm. Do you like milkshakes?" Chris nods, still smiling. Have I mentioned how amazing his smile is? "I know a great place right up Independence." I point to Independence Avenue across the mall. "It's close enough that we can walk."

"Okay. Great! Let me get cleaned up a little and then we'll go."

He goes into a trailer and I plop back down in a patch of grass for about 15 minutes. He comes back out and we say good-bye to the other guys. Short Mark gives me a big hug and a kiss on the cheek. "See you later, Shorty. It was fun." I don't actually think that I'll ever see him again, but I nod.

Chapter 4

Chris and I cut across the mall, and I'm worried about how far we have already walked. Just to get to the end of the Mall and past the Smithsonians, we've probably already gone about a mile. I don't think it's very far up Independence, but he has got to be exhausted. At the end of the mall, Independence goes uphill. I forgot that. Chris is holding up remarkably well, so I decide to push my luck. "Come on slow poke!" I start to run up the hill. I flip around and run backwards so I can see him. I hold my hands out, "Come on!"

His face breaks into a huge grin and he takes off. I thought I would have no problem beating him; he's supposed to be tired, but he catches me quickly. I turn back around and put on a spurt of speed, but it's no good. He is a lot faster than me.

He turns back, laughing. "Come on slow poke!"

Once I start laughing, I'm done for. The hill is really steep and it's hard enough to run up it without losing breath to laughing. I stop and bend over, gasping for air. Chris walks back down to me.

"Do you need a break, *slow poke*?"

"Apparently. You're in much better shape than I am."

We walk the rest of the way and now I'm too tired to talk so we're quiet. It's much further to Pennsylvania Avenue than I remember, but we get there.

We stand in line to order at my favorite little diner in DC and for some reason I'm suddenly tongue-tied. I don't know what to say anymore. I almost feel like we're on a date. Chris is studying the menu hanging over the grill like there is going to be a test on it. I don't even have to look. I always get exactly the same thing: a fried egg burger and their famous fries. But, for somewhere to look, I'll study it too, I guess.

I'm not even sure I can eat anything at this point. I was starving a little bit ago, but I don't feel even a little bit hungry now. It's been replaced by nervousness.

Chris turns to me. "Well, what's good?"

"Everything. But I always get an egg burger. And their fries are fantastic."

"Okay. But I don't like eggs, so that's out for me."

When we get to the register, Chris starts to order a burger for me, but I stop him right away. My stomach is so full of butterflies nothing else is going to fit. "I'll just have a small order of fries."

"Are you sure?" I nod. "I don't think you eat enough." He turns back to the girl at the counter. "Okay, I guess we'll have some fries." He orders a cheeseburger, a vanilla milkshake and a couple of beers. It's dinner time, so of course the place is packed. We take our buzzer and our beers upstairs to find a table.

"Of course I have to talk about the singing thing," he starts. "Do you only do us and Van Morrison – or do you have a larger repertoire?"

"Oh." How do I say this without sounding like a freak? "I, um, know the words to every song I've ever heard."

"No way."

"Yeah, I'm a little like Rain Man."

"That might be the coolest thing I've ever heard. *Every* song? Like every every?"

This is probably going to lead to some sort of test. "Well, that kind of depends. I have to *like* it and actually, genuinely *listen* to it. I don't know. Maybe it takes two or three times before the words stick." I know that's not true – as long as I listen once I've got it, but it sounds a little bit better that way, right?

I don't think I could even explain the look on Chris's face. He kind of looks impressed, but also I can tell he doesn't believe me. (No one ever does.) "The liking it bit – is that really essential?"

"Actually yes. I don't know why exactly. Maybe my brain just tunes out the stuff it doesn't like."

"And you can recognize them by the music? The opening chords?"

"Well, yes. Not all of them, maybe, but most."

"You know I'm going to have to test this."

I figured we were headed in this direction. "Everyone always does. But shouldn't I be the one who is all awestruck and stuff? You're the famous guy – and in my fave band and everything."

The people at the table next us have clearly been listening to us and now they are staring at Chris, trying to figure out who he is, I'm guessing. Chris notices. "Ah, famous. No one knows who *I* am, sweetheart. It's Evans most people recognize." Just then our buzzer goes off and Chris jumps up. "Be right back."

As soon as he walks away, the guy at the next table leans over. "Who is he?"

I don't know what to say to that. "Excuse me?" Maybe if I act offended he will realize that was really rude.

"Who is he? Is he really someone famous?"

"Clearly not. You don't know who he is."

I turn my head away because I don't want to be having this

conversation, but the guy grabs my arm. "No. I'm serious. I heard you talking. I want to know who he is."

The girl sharing his table looks just as eager, and not at all embarrassed for the way her boyfriend is behaving. Maybe she put him up to it. I would be mortified if anyone I was with acted like this.

"Maybe you shouldn't listen in to other people's conversations. Then it wouldn't be an issue for you." I turn my head again and try to pull my arm out of his grasp, because he is still holding it. But he pulls me closer to him. "Seriously, guy. Let me go." I'm really starting to get uncomfortable. I know I'm in a restaurant full of people so he couldn't really do anything, but he is making me nervous.

"Just tell me who he is and I will leave you alone."

Yes. Definitely getting nervous. "And then what? What are you going to say to him? If you are just going to drop it, why do you even need to know?"

He squeezes my arm tighter. "Why does that matter to you? Just tell me."

"Ow! You're hurting me!" But suddenly, he's not. I jump back in surprise because someone has grabbed *him* and pulled him away.

"I think you should probably go now," Chris tells him. Wow. He can be intimidating if he wants to. He's got the height and he's not a scrawny, stretched out stick figure either – clearly the man has seen the inside of a gym. Yum. I mean: I'm married. I am married and he is a famous rock star who could have anyone and I don't stand a chance. And, I'm married.

The guy doesn't really seem interested in leaving though. I'm actually kind of impressed that he's not running away; he is clearly very confident in his ability to defend himself. I can see that Chris is getting angry. "Would you like me to teach you a lesson about keeping your hands to yourself, or are you just going to leave?"

The guy sneers at Chris. "Bring it."

Oh, great. We have attracted the attention of a couple of Capitol policemen who were probably enjoying their dinner break. "Is there a problem here?"

Chris turns towards the cop and the girl at the table yells, "Evansgate! He's in Evansgate!" I mean, *yells*. The entire upstairs of the restaurant has frozen and turned in our direction. I feel like melting through the floor. I can't even look up at Chris.

"No officer, there is no problem – as long as this guy leaves now. I wouldn't mind him apologizing to my friend for hurting her, either."

I'm staring at the floor, and slouching down as far as I can in the seat, but I can tell it's a policeman who says, "What happened, young lady?" Crap. Is he talking to me?

"Sara?" Chris asks.

I look up. "Nothing. Nothing happened."

The girl is still really excited. She has been using her phone to look up more information on Chris apparently. "He is! He is in Evansgate! His name is Chris Eck!" Is she completely unaware of the fact that there are policemen involved? "Will you sign something?!"

Chris ignores her. "I'm not sure exactly what happened, but when I came up the stairs, he was pulling on her arm and she was saying that it hurt."

The girl is scrabbling around the table and her bag, looking for something for him to sign, I'm sure. "Can I get a picture with you?!" She jumps up and hands her phone to the jerk.

Still ignoring her, Chris slides closer to me. "Sara? Sara!" he suddenly squawks.

"What?"

"Your arm!" He points to my arm that the guy was grabbing. I don't even have to look down to know that there are bruises already forming.

"I bruise easily."

He immediately squats down next to me. He is squeezing himself between the tables and it can't be comfortable or easy. The girl yanks her phone back and starts taking pictures of Chris – and me.

"Look, let's just go, okay?" I really want to get out of here. I feel like this whole thing is my fault, but I'm not exactly sure how it all went wrong.

But the police are having none of *that*. "Miss? Do you want to press charges for assault?"

Chris's face is very close to mine. "I think you should," he says.

"No, it's fine, really. I just want to go." I look up at the officer. "No. I'm fine."

The policemen look very serious. "Are you sure? I'd be happy to arrest him."

Finally the girl shuts up and looks at her boyfriend. I glance at him too. He is looking quite pale.

"I'm sure." I turn to Chris. "Let's just go, okay?"

"Okay." He stands up and puts his hand under my elbow to help me to my feet. I glance down and see that our food is all over the floor and the milkshake looks like it exploded when it hit. Chris has vanilla milkshake on his pants.

"What happened to our dinner?"

Chris looks down and seems to notice it for the first time. "Oh! Sorry! I just kind of dropped it. Do you want me to go order it again – to go?"

I was hungry, then I wasn't, but now I'm almost sick. "No. Let's just go."

The cops are still talking about arresting the guy. Apparently, even if I don't press charges he has done enough to be in trouble. I'm trying to ignore them and I bend down to pick up some of the mess. Chris scoops my arm up again. "Leave it. The jackass and his girlfriend can clean it up." He looks at the policemen. "Right?"

One of them nods. "Just take her home."

Once we are back downstairs and out on the street, I take a deep breath and realize I feel like crying. Great. That would be lovely. Apparently I haven't embarrassed myself quite enough today, so now I need to go and cry. I'm not a pretty crier. I get all blotchy and make a horrible face. I run my hands through my hair and take another deep breath.

Chris is looking at me like I might break. "Are you okay? I'm so sorry about that. What can I do?"

"Why are you sorry? It's my own stupid fault."

"I highly doubt that. But, just for argument's sake, why don't you tell me what happened?"

It hadn't occurred to me that he might want to know the whole story. I'm not sure that I want to tell him though.

"Sara?"

I look up at him. For a moment I'm distracted by the thought of how nice it is to look *up* at a guy. I mean, Sam is technically taller than me. But I can't wear heels or anything. I can't believe I'm walking down the street with Chris Eck. My dream man. My never-in-a-million-years man. And he's perfect: funny, sweet, a gentleman, and a musician – I've always had a soft spot for musicians. How does this man not have a girlfriend?

"Sara?" Chris interrupts the tangent my thoughts have run off on.

"How tall *are* you?"

He laughs. "I'm 6'7". What about you?"

"I'm 5'11¾"."

He laughs again. "If you were a guy, that would just be six feet."

"Yes, well, I'm a girl and I want to be as short as possible."

He gets serious again. "What happened?"

"Sorry." Better get back on track. "He just asked me who you were when you went downstairs and I didn't tell him. And he got angry." Chris is staring at me. "That's it. End of story."

"That's it?" He doesn't sound like he believes me.

"Yeah. He was listening to our conversation, and he wanted to know if you were really famous, and who you were."

"And you didn't tell him?"

"Why do you sound so surprised? Why would I tell him?"

Chris looks surprised. "Well, for one, he was hurting you in his attempts to get the information. And two, I don't know... Never mind." He looks embarrassed.

"What? What's two?"

"Well, most people we come across can't wait to tell everyone they know that they met us. Facebook, photos on their cell phones, the whole bit. I just thought you might want to... show off."

I smile at him. "Wow. You really think you're something special, don't you?" He looks embarrassed again. "I'm kidding! You are something special, I promise. I am amazed with how my day has turned out. I'm expecting to wake up and find out I was dreaming any second. Trust me. But..." I trail off. "It's not really my place to tell other people about you."

Chris gives me a huge smile again. "Want to go to a club tonight? I have to. But it'd be a lot more fun if you would come with me."

I look down at my clothes. Not exactly clubbing material. Chris follows my gaze. "You look beautiful."

"Right. Either way, I'm not dressed for clubbing."

"That's easy enough to fix. Please come." How do you say no to that?

"Okay. But I'll have to head back to Pentagon City to go to my hotel to change. And, I might have to wear what I wore to the concert last night. I don't think I brought anything else."

He smiles. "That's fine by me. I like that skirt."

We're walking down Independence now and I turn left towards the Capitol South Metro stop. "Where are you going?" he asks me.

"The Metro. I have to go back to my hotel, remember?"

Chris smiles. "Seriously, woman. I'll give you a ride. I have to go back to mine too, but we'll go to yours first." He pulls out his phone and calls Tom. "Hey, man. Can you send a car? I'm... I'm... Sara? Where are we?" He looks around.

"Corner of Independence and First Street. Library of Congress is right there – see?"

"Did you hear that? Independence and First. Library of

Congress. Yeah. Where is everyone else? Okay. I'm taking Sara back to her hotel and then I'll be over there to get ready. Yes. I will. We can. Okay. Thanks." He hangs up and smiles at me again. "Now we wait."

"Hey," I start. "Thanks... for... that back there."

He looks in my eyes for a second before answering. "You're welcome." Then he lightens his tone, "So! You're a teacher. Tell me about high school. How's that go for you?"

We sit on the edge of a jersey wall set up outside the Library of Congress. "It's interesting, I guess. There is always something different going on so it keeps me on my toes."

"I'm not sure that I could deal with teenagers all day, every day. What?" he asks when I start laughing.

"Aren't they kind of your target audience?"

"I guess they kind of are, but that doesn't mean that I have to deal with them."

"I suppose not. But they're not that bad."

"Is it nice to have your summers off and stuff?"

"Well, it gets kind of boring, being alone all the time."

"Why are you alone?"

"Oh, well, Sam travels a lot."

"Sam is your husband?"

"Yeah, and he's gone *all* the time. I only see him for a couple of days here and there."

"Are you serious?" I nod. "That sucks."

"Mostly it's just lonely."

"I can imagine."

While we're talking, a limo pulls up and stops. Chris gets up, like that's our ride.

"What?!" My jaw drops and I stare at him. "You called a limo?!"

Chris already has the door opened and is waving me in. "No. Tom did." The driver has hopped out now and grabs the door from Chris so he can get in. Chris smiles at me. "Sweetheart, you're hanging with famous people, remember? Only the best." I really love his funny way of saying "sweetheart."

The driver looks at Chris. "Where are we headed?" Chris looks at me.

"Pentagon City. Um... I don't know the address." I tell him the name of my hotel.

The driver smiles at me and pulls a cell phone out of his pocket. "That's all right. I can find it." He shuts the door and walks around to the front of the car. We sit there for a few minutes while he works out the location of my hotel.

I look at Chris to distract myself. I don't want to look like an idiot gaping around the limo, because it's pretty impressive inside. "Where are the other guys? Is everyone going tonight?"

"They're at the hotel. I think they're just watching TV or something. Although Evans and Cannadiak – I mean Short Mark and Blond Mark –" he winks at me, "are probably working on some music. But, yes, we're all going. The label gets us to make appearances sometimes. I'm not sure who is making money off of it or how, but we just have to do it."

"I know."

Chris raises his eyebrows. "What do you know?"

"If famous people show up at your place of business, people talk. Then word gets around that Evansgate was at this club and people flock there for the chance to see someone who is someone. They're either thinking that you are coming back or that if one famous person was there, others must go, too – because all famous people know each other."

"How do you know that?"

"I'm a girl. I don't know. I just do."

"Well, I don't know very many famous people."

"Either way, that's just America's mentality."

"Oh. Oh, right."

When we get to my hotel, I decide that I need a shower and the whole bit before I'll be club ready. I ask Chris if he wants to just drop me off, but he decides to come upstairs and hang out while I get ready.

Our room is really pretty nice. It is a big square with one corner blocked out for the bathroom; what's left is shaped like an L. When you come in, there's a big living area, a tiny kitchenette (which is really just a mini fridge, microwave, and coffee pot on a counter), a table, and a desk. The two queen beds are in the other part of the L. There is a very large vanity area that opens to the beds, but you can't see it from the rest of the room. Through the vanity is a tiny little bathroom, just barely big enough for the tub and toilet.

Chris flops down on the couch and turns on the TV while I get in the shower. I shower as quickly as I can, but once I get out, I'm suddenly not sure what to do. Should I go out there in just a towel? I didn't grab any clothes before I came in. I step out of the shower into the vanity area. "Chris?" I call.

"Yeah?"

"I have to get some clothes. Um..."

"I won't look. Much."

"Ha ha. Remember, buck-o, I'm a married woman." I dash out and glance towards the couch. Chris is lying on his back with a pillow over his head. I grab my clothes as fast as I can. What can I say? He complimented the skirt, so I'm definitely wearing that. But I do have another tank top option that is actually better for clubbing than the shirt I wore to the concert.

Whoa. I'm going to a club with one of the hottest bands in the country. Am I really ready for this?

Once I'm safely tucked back behind the wall blocking the vanity from the rest of the room I tell him he can take the pillow off of his face and I throw my clothes on.

"Whew! Good thing. If you had been much slower, I would have suffocated." I come back around the wall to get my hair dryer. He flinches back and throws his hands up. "You didn't warn me you were coming!"

"I'm dressed, you idiot."

He looks up. "Oh. Yes, you are." He comes over, lies on the bed, and proceeds to watch me get ready.

"That's kind of intimidating, you know."

He looks surprised. "Why?"

"No wonder you don't have a girlfriend. This is the part where we try to make ourselves look pretty for your half of the species. It's uncomfortable with an audience."

"Oh. Do you want me to go away?" He starts to get up when the door to the hotel room opens.

Allison gasps, "Oh! I'm so sorry! I must... I must have the wrong room."

I step around the wall. "Nope. How would your key work in the wrong door?"

"Sara! What are you...? Who is this?" She gives me a look that says, "He is not your husband."

"This is my new friend, Chris. I've been hanging out with him today." I give her a meaningful look and she looks at Chris closer. Then she looks back at me, and this time her look clearly says, "Chris ECK?!" I nod. "What are you doing here? I thought you had plans for dinner."

"Oh," she says. "I'm just back for a quick change of clothes and to brush my teeth. What are you doing? Going somewhere?"

"Um, yes. But I don't actually know where. Chris asked me to come out with him and... his friends."

"Okay," Chris cuts in. "We could pretend that you don't know who I am all night. But I saw the look you gave Sara. Let's call a spade a spade. I'm taking Sara out with the rest of Evansgate tonight. We have an appearance to make at a club." He smiles at Allison and I can clearly see her swoon. I mentioned his smile, right?

"Okay. Well, you two have fun." Allison gives me a look as she heads towards the vanity.

Chris nods and says, "Suddenly I feel like I need to see what the hallway looks like again." He hops up and heads out the door.

"OH MY GOD Sara!" Allison yells as soon as the door clicks shut. "Chris Eck?! You've been hanging out with *Evansgate* today?! No wonder you ignored me!"

I look back to the mirror and put on my mascara. "It's not that big of a deal. They're actually really cool and down to earth." I set down my makeup and turn to face her. "Oh – who am I kidding? It's been the best day of my life!"

She giggles. "The List Man! Have you ever actually discussed your list with Sam? Do you get a freebie?"

I swat at her with my hairbrush. "No, you dope. It's totally not like that. Of course. But, oh! I have to tell you what happened!" I tell her the story of the jerk at the restaurant while I finish putting on my make-up.

"Holy crap, Sara! You should have had him arrested!"

"I think they might have arrested him anyway. I don't know. I just wanted to get out of there. It was so embarrassing, Allison. The whole place was staring at us."

While we are talking, Allison has thrown on new clothes and she heads for the door as soon as she is finished with her teeth. "I'm sorry I have to run. I can't wait to hear all about your *whole* day!"

"Don't wait up!" I tell her as she opens the door.

"Have a good time tonight, Baby Girl. Don't do anything I wouldn't do twice." Allison would do anything once.

She laughs as she walks out and Chris comes back in.

"Rea –" He stops cold and stares at me.

"What?" I look down. Nope, wearing skirt, bra on the inside... I glance in the mirror. Everything looks fine there too. "What?"

"Nothing. You just look great. Are you ready?" When I nod, he sticks his arm out for me to take. I grab my phone and wallet and cram them in my pocket – one of the reasons I like this skirt is that it has pockets. Chris sticks his hand out. "May I? I would rather they not disturb the shape of your behind." I try not to consider what that means, but hand him my things.

When we get back in the limo, Chris turns to me and says, "It's a personal policy of mine to only marry people whose full name I already know. I proposed earlier, but I should have gotten your name first." He smiles at me.

"Then maybe I shouldn't tell you. I'm already married, remember?" He just looks at me. "Sara Elizabeth Clarke. That's Sara, no 'H' and Clarke with an 'E'."

After a thoughtful moment he asks, "So Allison is your older sister?"

"Um, yes. Why? Does she look old?"

"No! She just referred to you as 'baby girl' so I assumed she is older."

"Oh. No. I mean, yes. It's just – that's what my mom used to call me. So, sometimes Allison still does."

"Used to?"

"My mom died last year."

Here it comes: that awful look on someone's face when you tell them that someone you loved died. He doesn't disappoint. "I am *so* sorry. I didn't –"

"It's okay. She was very sick. But, she had a good life and she was happy." Time to change the subject. "Do you have any brothers or sisters?"

"Nope. Just me. Good thing too, because I kept my parents very busy!"

"I'm sure you did. Where are you from?"

"I grew up in Oregon."

"So did my husband."

He doesn't look pleased with the coincidence. "That's nice." He doesn't sound like he means it. "Where did you grow up?"

"New York."

"City?"

I shake my head. "Up-state."

"Do you still have family there?"

"My dad."

"Do you ever visit him?"

"Oh, no. I never visit my dad." Heavy on the sarcasm.

"All right, smart ass. You know, not everyone has a good relationship with their parents."

"Good point. But, I do. Why do you ask?"

34

"I like the City. I was just wondering."

"I do too. Where do you live?"

"Officially, in Oregon. Still with my parents. Fantastic, right?"

"*Now* I know why you don't have a girlfriend! How old are you?"

"I'm 31." He sounds kind of defensive. "I stay in LA when we are recording, live on the road when we are touring, and there isn't really a lot of time in between. It doesn't make sense to have my own place when I'm never there to take care of it."

"Fair enough."

"How old are you?"

"You aren't supposed to ask a lady that." I pretend to be offended.

"If you are claiming to be a lady, then you are older than I thought."

"How old does one have to be to be considered a lady?"

"I don't think it's based so much on age as activities. Ladies play bridge and drink tea in dresses manufactured in the early 1950s."

"By that definition, I guess I'm not much of a lady."

"So how old are you?"

"I'm 28."

"Okay, Sara, no 'H', Clarke with an 'E', are you ready to have some fun?"

My stomach drops. Am I really going to do this? "Yup, let's go."

Chapter 5

Thursday morning, while Allison is at work, I email Sam.

> You are not going to believe who I hung out with
> yesterday and last night! I actually met Evansgate! I
> hung out with them all day while they taped a video –
> and then went to a club with them last night! It was
> awesome!
> How's work? When are you coming home?
> Love, Sara

I lay back on the bed and replay last night in my head. My best friend, Matt, would have loved it. That's the kind of thing we always do together, and we do a lot of it. I can't wait to tell *him* what I did yesterday!

There were only a few low points last night. Like... they expected me to dance. I don't dance. It takes rhythm and coordination – two things I am severely lacking. I would say that it was okay because I managed to distract them, but that was kind of the other low point. They had a corner table (*big* table) upstairs roped off for them and that was where I planted myself for the evening. I had a few beers, but since I hadn't eaten dinner, they went straight to my head and I started singing along with the music that the DJ was pumping out. Once they realized that I wasn't exaggerating before, they started requesting all kinds of different songs, and being Evansgate, the DJ played every request. I have a very eclectic taste in music, so I had heard all of it – and of course knew the words. I became the side show entertainment for the night. I was drunk enough, though, that I didn't mind.

It was amazing, really. Everyone knew who they were. I mean, Chris on his own in a tiny little restaurant is one thing. But when the four of them are together, there's no mistaking who they are. And Chris was right. Everyone recognized Short Mark. Of course, sitting at their table meant plenty of people were looking at me. I'm sure they were all wondering who in the world I was, and why a nobody like me would get to sit there, but again, I was drunk enough that I didn't care.

Chris sat next to me all night. He wouldn't even let me go to the bathroom by myself. I mean, he let me go *into* the ladies' room alone, but he waited right outside the door. He told me it was because he had to ward off any crazy guys we might come across. Not that I was complaining.

It was great getting to know the other guys too. Short Mark is really funny, and really easy to talk to. He reminds me a lot of Matt. They both have a lot of dry wit. Blond Mark is the most high maintenance of the group, more worried about his clothes and hair than the other guys. But he's still funny and really nice. Drew is the oldest; the others are all the same age. He is in his mid-thirties, which isn't old, but he seems like an old soul. He is definitely the most grounded of all of them.

Chris told them all the story of the guy at the restaurant, and after that they all seemed to be really protective. I felt like a pet or something. They talked to other people some, but no one else sat at the table with us. They signed a bunch of autographs and had their picture taken with half the people in the club, but they were really cool about it. I think it would make me crazy to have people in my face all the time.

My phone buzzes. It's Allison.

From Allison:
They DID arrest that guy last night! His name is Walter Anderson. But, he's already out on bond until his arraignment.

Whoa. It's so cool having Allison for a sister. I don't even want to know how or why she knows that. I text her back and wander around the hotel room trying to decide what to do. I knew as soon as I got out of the limo last night that nothing would ever live up to my day yesterday and that today was going to totally suck in such stark comparison. Now I have no idea what to do with myself.

I could try heading to the Mall and actually going to a Smithsonian again. The weather is just as beautiful, it is just hotter. I would appreciate the air conditioning in the museums today. But the chance of me going to the Mall and not dwelling on yesterday, and then seriously regretting that it is over, is very slim. Besides, Allison is at the Pentagon today, so if I'm going to have any sort of opportunity of actually seeing her I'll have to stay over here.

I walk to the window where I have a lovely view of the Pentagon. I wonder where Allison is in there. My phone buzzes again. I pull it out – I'm sure it's Allison and glance at it absentmindedly.

From *unknown number*:
I stole your phone number last night. Now I have it

forever. Can we hang out again today? (This is Christopher Thomas Eck.)

Hold the phone! What? When did he get my number?

> To *unknown number*.
> Did you really think I wouldn't know who this is? (from Sara Elizabeth Clarke)

I can't believe this is happening. When I walked away last night, I assumed that was it. I would never see them again – unless it was from the back of a crowded auditorium if I ever went to another concert. I even thought about the fact that we didn't exchange info so there was no chance of ever getting together again.

From *unknown number*:
You didn't answer my question, Sara Elizabeth Clarke.
Can we hang out today?

While I am reading this text, my phone buzzes again. I know it is not another text from Chris because that would have just shown up below the one I was reading. I assume it's Allison, but I glance at it anyway. I don't know the number.

From *unknown number*:
Hi Shorty. Please come out and play with us today.
We need someone to show us the sights.

Short Mark! Well, that at least explains why they would be interested in seeing me again.

> To *unknown number*.
> Okay. What do you want to do?

Almost immediately, my phone buzzes again.

From *unknown number*:
We're downstairs. Are you coming down or are we coming up?

Holy crap! I look around the room frantically. Then I realize what's more important and run to look in the mirror. *Holy crap!* I look exactly like I spent the night at a club. What do I do?

> To *unknown number*.
> I'll come down. Give me a minute.

Before I can even start the rush to attempt to better my appearance, my phone buzzes again.

From *unknown number:*
Too late. On our way up.

Crap crap crap! I start with my hair. At least I had the forethought to wash my face before I went to bed last night, so that isn't completely awful. I yank the brush through while I try to find something better than my holey t-shirt and pj pants. Teeth! Morning breath! More important! I drop everything and grab my toothbrush. I'm still frantically scrubbing when there's a knock at the door. Spit! Rinse!

As I head to the door, I glance down again at my outfit. Not much I can do now.

"Hey, guys! Uh, what are you doing here?"

Blond Mark smiles. (Oh yes, they're all here!) "Eck wanted to see you again." Chris jabs him in the ribs.

"We decided we needed a tour guide for the day." Chris smiles. Swoon.

"Well, clearly you are all earlier risers than me. Um." I glance down again.

Drew smiles and throws his arm around my shoulders. "We're all family, kiddo. No need to impress!" Drew has a wife back in LA, and Blond Mark has a girlfriend. I learned a lot last night.

I drop onto my bed. "Now that you're done with the video, how long are you going to stay in DC? When are you going back to LA?"

Drew and Blond Mark sit on the couch, Short Mark takes the desk chair, and Chris comes and sits next to me on the bed. "We're here... through the weekend?" Chris looks at the other guys as he asks.

Short Mark laughs. "Apparently Shorty, that depends on you. How long are you going to be in town?"

But before I can answer, Drew says, "I'm leaving tomorrow. Bethany will kill me if I don't. But you clowns are welcome to stay as long as you like."

Blond Mark nods. "Yeah, Angie is ready for me to be back in California. I'm leaving tomorrow too."

Chris looks at me. "I don't really have any plans, so I'm pretty flexible. We aren't going to be working next week."

"Allison is definitely leaving on Wednesday. I was at least going to try to stay through the weekend in the hopes that she might get an hour or two off at some point so that we could hang out. But it's summer.

I'm as free as a bird, and my room is paid for."

"Good to see our tax money being put to good use. Can we order some room service?" Short Mark asks loudly.

"Sure," I shoot back. "But I charge a 25% convenience fee on top of their rate."

They all laugh. "Hm," Chris frowns. "That's a little steep. Maybe we should find a restaurant."

I give him a look. "One, I'm hardly dressed for that. Two, I think it would be best if I avoided restaurants with you from now on." As if there was a future for us.

"Maybe you should just let me pick them from now on."

From now on! He said it too! Does this mean I might actually get to see him again?

"Hey! By the way! When did you steal my phone number last night?"

Chris hangs his head guiltily. "I wanted to be able to call you sometime. So I called myself when you were in the bathroom."

"Is that why you wanted to carry my phone?"

"No. I really did not want it to mess up the profile of your butt. I can say that, right? Because we're just friends."

"Yes," says Drew. "As friends, we are all deeply concerned about how Sara's butt looks in that skirt."

What parallel universe have I fallen into? "You know, real friends *are* concerned with that sort of thing. Real friends will tell you when your butt looks big in your jeans. And apparently, when your cell phone is affecting it as well."

Chris rubs my head. "Come on, I'm hungry and I know you're not going to leave without a shower. Move it." He pushes me off of the bed, "Get clean." How does he know that about me?

In the shower I can't help but think about how it feels like I've known Chris all my life. It's just so easy to talk to him. I don't really even know that much about him, but I'm just so comfortable around him. The other guys too. Then I concentrate on taking the fastest shower of my life.

When I get out I don't even dry my hair. I just throw on a sundress and we head out.

We have another amazing day. I'm sure it's nothing special for them, but for me... I can't even put it into words. Even in my own head, I'm speechless. We don't really do much. Just tool around the monuments, act like tourists and stuff. I guess they kind of are tourists. I come up often enough that I don't feel like one anymore. It's the same thing all day though. Someone will recognize Short Mark, and then the others, and then it's pictures, autographs, squeals and swooning. I can't really say much in that department. Every time Chris smiles at me I swoon a little myself. The guys are all so cool about it. I'm really impressed.

Tom meets us for dinner. We eat at their hotel, and no one disturbs us for the meal. Chris assures me that it's different in LA. No one asks for autographs or pictures.

While we're there, Allison texts me and says that she is going to be able to have dinner. (Oops, no need to tell her that I'm already eating.) I hop to my feet and ask where the nearest Metro station is.

"I'm totally kidding!" I say when I see the looks on their faces. "I know you don't know. Don't worry. I do!" I start to collect my stuff and Chris jumps up.

"You're not really going to go, are you?"

"Well, yeah," I tell him. "I haven't seen Allison at all the whole time I've been here. I really should go and spend some time with her while I can."

"Okay." He pushes in his chair.

"Where are you going?" I ask.

"I'm taking you back to your hotel, stupid. You don't really think I'd make you ride the Metro, do you?"

"You're hardly making me. And you're in the middle of your dinner."

He smiles. "I'm getting used to you interrupting my dinner, actually. I don't know what I'll do when I get to eat one without you messing it up."

I've only known him for two days and yet I feel like it's been a lifetime. I feel like I'm used to messing up his dinners. How much am I going to miss it when I can't anymore? I hope none of this is showing on my face.

"Fine. Let's go."

The guys made flight arrangements and are leaving in the morning, so I give them hugs. "Thanks guys – I've had a blast."

"Definitely, Shorty. Can't wait to do it again sometime."

Chris throws his arm around my shoulders as we walk out. "Careful," I tell him. "I bruise easily."

Allison gets the whole night off, which I know means I won't get to see her at all for the rest of the time she is in DC. "Does this mean I should just pack it up and head home tomorrow?"

"Um, probably. Unless, of course, you have a different reason to stay." Her face is screaming, "SPILL IT!"

"What do you want me to say? It's a fairy tale. It's been awesome! They are so much fun, and way more normal than you would expect. And I don't understand why they are so nice to me, so... I don't know. I spent the whole day with them, Al. Just them and me. And, I totally felt like I belonged. Why? They don't know me. But, it doesn't even matter. Because, like all fairy tales, it will end. No one actually lives 'happily ever after' you know. Life just goes back to normal. Only it's much more depressing because you got a glimpse of how fun life could have been if you had been dealt a different hand."

Allison gives me a long look. "How are things with Sam?"

"Sam!" I didn't check my email all day. I pull my phone out to see if he emailed me back. Sure enough –

> That was a lot of !! Does this mean you get free tickets
> to their concerts now? Don't know when I'll be back.
> Busy here.
> Sam

I hand my phone to Allison, which is probably a mistake because she already doesn't like him very much. She makes a face. "I don't like him very much."

"I know. But he's a good man, he really is. I'm very lucky to have him. I love him, Allison."

She makes another face. "If Chris Eck came in here right now and threw himself at your feet, would you leave Sam?"

This is a question that Allison has asked me many times. It was always a joke though, of course. She would ask me why I stay with Sam; I would tell her that I love him; she would ask if I would ever leave him; I would say no, and then she would always say, "If Chris Eck came in here right now and threw himself at your feet, would you leave Sam?" I always said "Of course!" But it doesn't seem funny anymore.

"That's not fair, Allison. It was different when he was a stranger."

"I know. I'm just trying to make a point."

"What is your point?" I ask her petulantly.

"That you need to move on. You can do better than Sam."

"Maybe I don't want to."

Later when we are lying in bed, I say, "Allison? I'm worried that I'm going to be sad when I go back to my regular life. It will seem lonelier now."

"Now? Now that you know Evansgate?"

"It's not just that I know them. It's that I had so much fun. I felt... good. For two whole days I felt great. Now... I'll be sad."

"Why? What has really changed?"

"I've had a taste of what life would be like if I had people to do fun things with all the time. I could totally imagine that being a regular thing. But all I get is two days. A regular two days for them, and they will stand out in my memory as the best two days of my life. And they're gone. Forever, those two days will be behind me."

Allison climbs out of her bed any lays down next to me in mine. "There will be more. Some day you'll look back and *almost* remember those two great days. You'll think, 'I thought those were the best days of my life and it would never get better than that!' But there will be something else that has comes along – two days that are even better." She plays with my hair while she talks.

"Allison? Would you ever cheat on Tom?"

"Do you think Sam is cheating on you?"

"No! Of course not... It's just... You travel a lot. You're away from Tom a lot. Do you think you would ever cheat on him? Do you think he would cheat on you while you're away?"

"I hadn't before now, thanks." I can almost hear her smile. "No, Baby Girl. I don't. But I know why you're asking. You don't have to say it. And it breaks my heart for you. I wish Mom were still alive so she could tell you that she doesn't actually like him anymore. She would feel the same way I do – and you know it. Then you could leave him with no remorse. You can't stay with him just because you think that is what Mom wanted you to do. You still have me. You still have Dad. You're worth more than that, Sara."

She just doesn't understand. Sam and I built a life together. We're just in a bad spot; all couples have them. I open my mouth to defend myself, "I –"

She cuts me off before I have a chance to say anything. "I know. I won't say anything else."

It takes me a long time to fall asleep.

Chapter 6

I wake up when my phone rings. Allison is long gone. I grab my phone and blearily say hello without even looking at the display.

"Sara? Did I wake you up? God, woman! How long do you sleep?"

Chris! "Um, what time is it?"

"A little after noon."

"Oh. I had some trouble sleeping last night. I'm tired. It's summer. That's the beauty of being a teacher. I can sleep as late as I want for two and a half months a year."

"Or a rock star. Only I can sleep as late as I want almost every day."

"Are you rubbing it in on purpose?"

"Yup. What are you doing today?"

"I'm going home, like I thought you were. What are you doing?"

"What?! You said you were staying through the weekend! I wanted to see you. Please, don't go home yet. Let's hang out some more – please?"

"Okay. It's not like I have anything to go home to. But what happened to *you* going home?"

"I was having too much fun with you to go back to LA and do nothing for a week. I thought I would stay a little longer."

"Okay, well, what do you want to do?"

"Anything you want."

Anything I want? I'm still so tired after my lack of sleep last night. I can't imagine tromping around DC right now. "Sleep?"

"Your place or mine, sweetheart?"

"Mine. I'm warm and comfy and I don't want to get up."

"How convenient! I'm downstairs!"

"You can't be serious."

"As a heart attack. I'm on my way up!" He hangs up.

Crap. Do I have to start every morning like this now? I drag myself out of bed and open the door. I prop it a little bit, climb back in bed, and pull the covers over my head. Why don't I care that he is seeing me at my worst? I don't even bother brushing my teeth this morning.

It's not long before he is in my room. He shuts the door and flops down on my bed next to me. "Hello, Sleeping Beauty. Are you in there?"

"I'm here. I'm sleeping, remember? You asked what I wanted to do, I said 'sleep'. Now shut up and close your eyes."

He laughs softly and lies down. I'm still for a very long time, but not asleep. I mean, come on, Chris Eck is lying in bed next to me. What are the chances that I'm actually going to sleep? I know he's just humoring me and has no intention of actually sleeping, but I lie really still to make him think that I am.

This entire situation is so weird. I can't understand how I feel so comfortable with him. We could have been friends for years and it would still be strange to be this completely natural together. I'm not sure Allison and I are even like this.

It's a long time later when I finally roll over. Ironically, Chris is asleep. I decide I might as well brush my teeth. Chris wakes up as I climb out of bed. "Where are you going? I thought we were sleeping today." He is flat on his back with his arms spread out.

"I'm brushing my teeth. And then climbing right back in that bed." Oh, how I want to climb right into those arms. Ah! I can't even believe I thought that! It's just been so long since I've been held by a man. Even when Sam is in town, he is working. And his schedule is so screwed up because his nights and days are backwards. I sleep in an empty bed now. But I miss it. I miss just sleeping with my man. Lying in his arms. Feeling safe and protected. Okay, no rationalizing. I just need to stop thinking these things.

Once I'm sure I have eliminated any trace of morning breath, I head back to the bed and sit down. "What do you want to do today?" I ask him.

"Oh, I want to sleep. That's my favorite thing to do." But he is already starting to sit up.

I hit him with my pillow. "I'm serious. Do you really want to lie around in my bed all day?"

"I could think of worse things."

Suddenly I remember what Allison told me and I grab both of his forearms excitedly. "Oh! I forgot to tell you! His name is Walter Anderson."

"Who?"

"The jerk from the restaurant!"

"How do you know his name?"

"That's not all I know! They *did* arrest him Wednesday night! But apparently he was out on bond by lunchtime on Thursday."

Chris sits bolt upright. "How do you know that?"

"Allison told me, duh."

"What exactly does your sister do for a living?"

"I honestly don't know. But you don't want to get on her bad side."

"Clearly." Chris looks at me for what seems like an eternity, but is probably only 30 seconds or so. "Marry me. Please?" I know he can't be serious, why in the world would he want to marry *me*? But it still stirs an unfamiliar feeling in my middle. Yearning? My life is hard right now. It would be really nice to have something different.

But that's the coward's way out. "Sorry. Not a polygamist. Or is it a bigamist?"

"So... leave him and run away with me."

I look at him closely. His eyes almost look like he is serious. "Please don't say that."

"Why?" His tone is slightly surprised. Could he really not understand why this would be wrong?

"Because I really want to be your friend. But I *am* married, and I can't be your friend if you really want something more. It's not fair to Sam." Why are we having this conversation? It seems way too serious, and so *far-fetched*.

Chris considers that for a bit. "Okay. Fair enough. Be my best friend. Please?"

"Okay!" I look around the room. It's dark because the curtains are still pulled. It's also a bit of a mess. "All right, BFF, what do you want to do today?"

"Today?" Chris looks at his watch. "I think you mean tonight."

I turn to look at the clock on the night stand. Hm. Maybe I *did* fall asleep. I stand up and stretch. "First things first. I'm going to shower."

Sunday morning Chris comes over to our hotel and has breakfast with us.

"What are you two crazy kids going to be doing today?" Allison asks.

"I don't know." I look at Chris.

"I'm just hoping to spend it with your sister."

Allison looks torn between relief and disapproval. "She is married, you know."

Chris nods. "People keep telling me that. I've also heard that you can have people killed. Should I come to you if I would like that rectified?"

Allison starts laughing. "I don't think I can. Or I might have already."

I glare at my sister. "Well, I have just decided that I'm going to take a bus tour of the monuments today. You two have a lovely time at my expense." I can't believe she said that to him. What is he thinking now? My sister just told him that she doesn't like Sam. I can't even look at Chris. I can't look, but I can actually hear the smile in his voice.

"Allison, it was lovely to have breakfast with you this fine morning. Now I have to go see a man about a bus."

I'm a little sad when I realize that Chris and I will part ways soon. I feel like it will be very hard to be apart from him now, even though I've only been with him for such a short time. Okay, I'm a lot sad.

We don't actually take a bus tour, of course. But we do wander around the sights again. It's a little different without the other guys there. For one, no one bothers us much. Of course, people still stare some, but that is just as likely to be because he is 6'7" and *gorgeous* as that they recognize him from the band. Also, it seems a lot more intimate without the other guys clowning around.

We talk without pause all day. It's so easy to talk to him. We get lunch at a cart vendor and sit on a bench to eat. While we eat, we people watch.

Chris clears his throat and he looks so serious that I'm nervous about what he is going to say. I'm not ready for another deep conversation. "You told me that you are crazy. Actually, I believe I was promised six kinds. I've seen very little crazy."

I poke him in the chest. "I've spent every waking minute of the last few days with a complete stranger. That isn't a very rational thing to do."

"Uh, I did that too."

I shrug. "Hey – I said nothing about your mental state. There's plenty of room in crazy town for both of us."

"That's all you got? Really?"

He looks at me expectantly.

"What? It's an expression."

"I've never heard it before."

"It's *my* expression."

"Do you think that person is famous?" Chris asks me in mock seriousness, as he points to a woman in running clothes who obviously thinks very highly of herself. Clearly we are moving on to a new subject.

"Oh yes. I'm sure she is a major star – in her own world at least."

"What about him?" He randomly points into the crowd. "Do you think he is famous?"

"Why would any of these people be famous? And, if they are, wouldn't I know that?"

"Do you think I'm famous?" he counters.

"Well, yes. And I knew who you were when you first stopped me on the Mall that day, if you remember correctly."

"Fair enough. But, the rest of these people don't think I am." He glances around. "It's nice to be with you."

"I know. I'm just really great like that."

He smiles. "And super modest. You really should be careful that you don't drag down your self esteem. I hear a low self esteem can be unhealthy."

"Yes, I'm sure it is. I battle that constantly. You're so right. I don't think nearly highly enough of myself. I'm sure I'm much more awesome than I give myself credit for."

He laughs. "I'll try to stick around to remind you how awesome you are. I would hate for you to suffer from a low self esteem." Now I'm laughing. He pulls out his phone and starts messing around.

"What are you doing?" I ask him. Have we finally run out of things to talk about? Is he bored?

"What?" He looks up like I've distracted him. "Oh, I'm just setting up a reminder to myself to call you at least once a week to remind you that you are awesome. I'm really worried that you might be developing a complex." My heart jumps at the thought of actually being his friend. He stuffs his phone back in his pocket and looks at me more seriously. "What's up with your husband?"

I'm immediately defensive. "What do you mean?"

"What does he do?"

"Oh. He works for an international shipping company."

"In Virginia?"

"Actually, it's in Atlanta. That's where we used to live."

"He doesn't even work in the same state he lives in?" I shake my head and shrug. "What does he do for this shipping company?"

"He's the Director of Internal Communications. Basically, he has to keep all of the offices talking to each other. It's a huge job."

"Why?"

"Because there are offices all over the world. And, as it's a shipping company, things are always going on between them. Sam makes sure they're all speaking the same language. Figuratively! I mean, he doesn't actually speak any other languages; he has to rely on a lot of interpreters. But he gets everyone sharing the same information."

"Why did you move?"

"We wanted to live somewhere that was better for raising kids. When he started traveling more and didn't really work out of the office in Atlanta much, they let us pack up and pick a new place. He works from home now – when he's home." I'm immediately sad, and Chris can tell. We were so excited to start our life in Virginia. It seems like an age ago, and things are so different now.

"What's wrong?" This is not a conversation that I want to have with him. "Do you miss him when he's gone?"

I shake my head at first, because that's not what is making me sad. But then I realize what I've essentially said. "No! That's not what I mean! I mean, of course I miss him when he's gone."

He keeps talking like I haven't said anything, like he understood that when I shook my head I was telling him that wasn't it. "Then what is wrong?" I stare at him for a moment. "What?" he asks.

"Why do I feel like you know me so well?"

"I don't know."

"But you understand what I mean, don't you?"

"Yeah," he says very quietly. "I do. So, what is wrong?"

"You're not going to let it go, are you?" I wrinkle my nose when he shakes his head. "I feel like it's been built up too much now. Let's talk about something else."

"Okay. What do you do when Sam is away?"

"I teach."

"And in the evenings?"

"I grade."

"Sara." He looks at me with a look in his eyes that I can't understand.

"What?"

"Why are you sad?"

"I can't have kids." I blurt it out really quickly. Like taking off a band-aid. The fact that I've told him something that I haven't told anybody, except my sister, strikes me as significant somehow.

Chris throws his arm around my shoulders in a half hug. "I'm not going to say 'I'm sorry.' I know you don't want to hear that." How?! How does he know that? He kisses the top of my head. "So, Ms. Teacher. What do you do when you are not working? Please don't tell me you knit."

"What's wrong with knitting?" I pretend to be offended.

"Nothing. I like a pair of warm socks as much as the next guy.

49

But I have a feeling a really fun person is being caged nightly in the Clarke house."

"Yes. I keep her at bay with knitting needles."

"I thought so. I'll see what I can do to let her out every once in a while." He grabs my hand and pulls me off of the bench.

When I go to sleep Sunday night, my head is full of him.

Chapter 7

Monday morning, Allison is back at work and I am lying in bed wondering if I should call Chris. I really want to show up at his hotel and text him that I am downstairs waiting for him like he did to me, but I don't have the means of making that happen as easily as he does. And with my luck, I would text him and find out that he is waiting downstairs for me at *my* hotel.

I settle for just texting him from my bed.

> To Chris:
> Good morning sunshine. I have no plans today and I was just wondering if we were going to get together at some point.

I don't have to wait long before he responds.

From Chris:
You're up early this morning. And you can stop pretending like there is any chance I have something to do other than follow you around like a lost puppy.

From Chris:
I am at your beck and call, m'lady.

> To Chris:
> What? You're not downstairs waiting for me this morning? I'm disappointed.

I'm just trying to be funny, but immediately, my phone buzzes. Am I really just trying to be funny? I realize that I really do want him here. Let's face it, I tell myself, you're only in DC so you can see him at this point.

From Chris:
Give me 5.

> To Chris:
> I'm getting in the shower. Take longer than 5.

I don't even wait for his response before I hop in the shower. I'm getting better at taking fast showers. Chris has given me a lot of practice in the last few days. As soon as I'm out, I grab my phone.

From Chris:

I am downstairs, imagining you in the shower. Please
don't make me wait down here very long.

How am I supposed to be friends with this guy? I delete his text –
just in case, I tell myself. I don't want anyone (Sam) to see it and get
the wrong idea.

To Chris:
Come on up.

I throw on some clothes and run a brush through my hair. When
he knocks on the door I rush over to open it. Something occurs to me
suddenly. "Hey! That was awfully quick! Were you already
downstairs?"

"Kind of." He smiles.

"What does that mean?"

"I was sick of running back and forth. I moved to a room here.
I'm two floors below you."

"Oh." I don't know what to say to that. I step back to let him into
the room and shut the door behind him. We just stand there and look
at each other for a second.

"My room is bigger," he says.

"Of course it is."

"What do you want to do today?" he asks me.

"Honestly? Nothing. I'm tired of running around. I want to be
lazy."

"You've *been* really lazy, sweetheart. I feel like we've spent a lot of
time asleep."

"It's summer vacation. I'm supposed to be lazy."

"Okay. Come on." He turns to leave.

"Hey! I just said I don't want to do anything!"

"I know," he says. "But my room is bigger. Let's not do it there."

I grab my things and follow him out the door. We walk down two
flights of steps, because waiting for an elevator seems silly, and go into
his room. He's right. It *is* bigger.

"Wow. This place is nice." I look around and sit on the couch.

He opens the fridge and pulls out a bottle of water, which he holds
out to me. I nod and he gives it to me before getting another one.
"Want to watch a movie?" he asks. He uses his foot to push me aside
and then sits down next to me on the couch.

"Okay. What do you want to see?" I don't really feel like watching
a movie, but I don't feel like wandering around DC anymore either. "I

52

know!" I say so suddenly that Chris spills water down his front.

"What?"

"Let's go to my house. Can you do that?"

"I can do anything I want. But isn't your house kind of far?"

"A couple of hours, maybe. I have a car. When are you going back to LA?"

"I don't know. I hadn't booked a flight yet."

"Can you fly out of Richmond? Come stay at my house! Let's do nothing there!"

Chris looks at me for a second before a big smile spreads across his face. "Really? You want me to come to your house?"

"Yes! I'm ready to be at home, but the only reason I'm still here is because I'm having fun with you. Come home with me! It's perfect!"

"Yes, baby girl, I believe it is."

I'm on my way to the door when I whirl back around. "I – what did you call me?" It doesn't sound wrong coming out of his mouth, but it still surprises me to hear him use my nickname, even if he doesn't really know that's what it is.

"I'm sorry. Sara, no 'H' go pack your crap. We're going to your house!"

I want to tell him that I don't care. A lot of people call me that and that wasn't why I was asking. But I'm ready to hit the road. We can have that conversation later. "Pack yours. Meet me downstairs in 15 minutes."

I rush back up to my room. I text Allison first that I'm taking off because I'm sick of the inside of the hotel room.

> To Allison:
> If you can get away for a few minutes, come give me a hug good-bye. If not, mail one. I love you.

I start throwing my crap into my suitcase, but I don't get very far before there's a knock on the door. I'm wondering why she didn't use her key when I throw the door open, expecting to see Allison standing there. "That was fast!" I say. But it's not Allison. "Chris! What are you doing up here? I thought we were going to meet downstairs."

"I was only here last night. I didn't unpack much. It only took me a minute to put it all back in. I'm ready. Let's go!"

I smile at his enthusiasm. "Well, I've got a little more packing than that." Chris sits on the couch and directs me while I rush around throwing things in. As I am zipping up my suitcase, Allison opens the door.

She is clearly surprised to see Chris on the couch. "I thought you were going home?" she asks.

"I am. Chris is going with me. I'm sorry, Ally. But I'm sick of the hotel thing. Chris is just going to fly out of RIC, so I even get company for the drive home." I smile at her, begging with my eyes for her to just let it go.

"Drive safe, Baby Girl. I'm so glad you came up to see me! I'm sorry I had to work so much."

"Well, you are actually here to work, so I think I can forgive you." I throw my arms around her. "I love you, Allison."

"I love you too, Sara." She pulls back and gives me a look with her eyes that says, "I'm glad he's going with you." She probably would have added "DUMP SAM WHEN YOU GET HOME" if she could have.

In the car, I decide to tell Chris the whole story behind "Baby Girl".

"My parents couldn't decide on a name for me when I was born," I start.

"Okay. I'm glad they finally did."

"Yes, smart ass. They did. But on my birth certificate, it says, 'Baby Girl Harris'. They had to wait until the stupid thing came in the mail, and then go to the courthouse to have my name legally changed to 'Sara Elizabeth', but before that I was actually named 'Baby Girl'. My mom never stopped calling me that."

Chris smiles at me. "How did she die?" A lot of people try to avoid the subject of my mother. But I miss her and I like to talk about her. It keeps her alive for me.

"She had cancer. Of course."

"I'm thinking your mom was a bold lady."

"She didn't play bridge, drink tea, or wear dresses manufactured in the early '50s. But, she was bold."

"What did she do?"

"She raised Allison and me. That's it. She married my dad when he was just out of college, and she was just out of high school. I don't think they were married for three months before she got pregnant with Allison."

"How many years are there between you two?"

"Five. I think it would have been too many for us to be close if Mom hadn't been sick."

"I'm not sure if that is terrible or not," Chris says thoughtfully. "I'm glad you have Allison. She seems like a good person."

"You have no idea. She is amazing. I feel bad for her though. My mom was sick for a long time. Allison took care of me and my dad."

"Where did she go to school?"

"Harvard. She is really smart."

"Clearly."

"I think it was a relief for her to get away for school, but she always felt really bad about leaving us." I pause for a second as I think about it. "But Mom was really doing well when Al was at school, actually. She didn't get sick again until it was time for me to go."

"Where did you go?"

"I just went to Syracuse. I needed to stay at home to take care of her so that Dad could work. It was hard even to leave her long enough to go to class sometimes. I was always afraid that I would come back and she would be gone."

"I bet she hated that."

"How did you know that?"

"I don't know. Good guess?"

"Yeah, she hated it. But it was okay. Syracuse is a good school. I got a degree in Chemistry. Then I got a Masters for good measure."

"You mean, so that you could have an excuse to stay at home longer?"

I smile ruefully at him. "Yeah. That's exactly what I mean. Allison was working in DC then, and I knew I couldn't *leave* her. But I also knew she wouldn't let me just stay either."

"So you stayed in school."

"Yup. It turned out to be a good thing."

His sense of what I wanted to talk about has either run out or he is just ready to talk about what *he* wants to talk about. I have a feeling it is the latter. "How did you meet Sam?"

"He was at Syracuse getting his MBA while I was an undergrad."

He looks at me expectantly. "And?"

"And, I don't know. He knew my mom was sick. He was really nice to me. And to her. He would come by the house to see me since he knew I couldn't get out."

"She liked him?"

"Yes, she did." I'm almost defensive again. While she was helping me plan the wedding Mom seemed so *well*. I think it was because she was so happy.

"But your dad and Allison do not?"

"Not especially, no. But it's bigger than that. And I don't really want to talk about it."

Chris puts his hands up in defense of my tone. "Fair enough. When did you get married?"

"Right after I finished my Masters. He was living in the city and he got a job in Atlanta. He wanted me to go with him."

"So you married him."

"Yes, I did. We lived in Atlanta for a little while and then he started to travel more and more with work. When my mom got really sick again, I just moved home for a while. Sam was gone all the time anyway, and my dad really needed me."

"How long?"

"Until she died? I was there for about seven months. Then Sam said that we needed to pick a good spot to raise a family and that was where we would move. I have a friend who had moved down to Richmond to work at MCV – uh, Medical College of Virginia – and he told me that it was great there. So, that was where we moved. I felt really bad leaving my dad, but he's done pretty well."

"What was your mom's name?"

"Betty. Well, Elizabeth, but they called her Betty."

"What's your dad's name?"

"What's yours?"

"Why?" Chris looks puzzled.

"Why do you want to know my dad's name?"

"Why not?"

"It's Joe, my dad is Joe."

"Okay, Sara, no 'H', daughter of Joe and Betty Harris. My name is –"

But I cut him off. "Christopher Thomas Eck, yes I know."

"Son of Andrew and Laura Eck."

"And now we are friends?" I ask him. We have gotten a lot of the preliminary getting to know you stuff out of the way now, haven't we?

"Well, yes. But not just because I know your parents' names. I just have a personal policy to know the names of all my friends' parents." He winks at me.

"Oh, me too. Definitely. Any other personal policies I should know about?"

"Uh, not yet. But they seem to be coming to me on an individual basis. I will let you know if another comes up."

"Thanks."

"What about you? I only know your policy on marriage."

"I also don't go to concerts."

He laughs. "I wouldn't have guessed that, seeing as how I first saw

56

you at a concert."

"It was a one off. But I'm glad I went."

"Me too."

We're quiet for a few miles before Chris turns in his seat to face me. "When did you find out that you can't have kids?"

I deliberately do not turn my head towards him. I look straight at the road when I tell him, "About four months ago."

"What happened?" he asks quietly.

"We moved to Richmond to raise a family. No family was coming. We went to the doctor. No family is coming."

Chris puts his hand on my arm. "It's okay, Sara. I don't care what he says. It's okay."

I jerk the wheel and pull off to the side of I-95. "What did Allison tell you?" There is ice dripping off of my words. He couldn't possibly know that this is the source of struggle for me and Sam. He doesn't even know we are struggling. For all he knows, I'm the most happily married person on the planet.

He puts his hands up in defense again. "Nothing! I... I just... I can't explain it, Sara. I just know that he is being an asshole about this."

My tone is cranky, "How?"

"I don't know. I just do." He suddenly changes to a much brighter tone. "What instruments do I play?"

"What does that have to do with anything?"

"Just answer it. What instruments do I play?"

"The bass."

"Uh, yes, thank you. What else?"

I think for a moment. "The piano and the guitar."

A huge smile breaks over his face and for one second I'm struck dumb. This man is beautiful. There are no other words. I don't understand why he is sitting in my little Mazda with me, but I suddenly feel so grateful to be alive – and with him.

"Yup. How did you know that? Did you read it on Wikipedia?"

"No, I didn't. I don't know. That seemed like the most logical answer."

He nods. "I knew it. We were actually soul mates in our previous lives."

Chris grabs my hand and then pulls me into an awkward hug over the center console. For a moment, a bright, hot fire burns in my belly and I think about what it would be like to be his. He kisses my forehead and says, "Onward, James. Let's go home."

At some point on the way home, we crossed some unseen line and when we get out of the car at my house it is like stepping into a sauna. The only exception is that a sauna is usually a more pleasurable experience.

Chris chokes when he gets out of the car. "Good Lord! Do you live here? Is it like this all the time or did you decide to melt the earth on my account?"

"You think this is bad? You should go to Dallas. Hm. Although, it is really uncomfortable today." I glance at the sky. Searing hot sun? Check! Clouds? Noticeably absent. The air feels heavy. "Well, good grief. Get inside before we suffocate!" Chris grabs our bags out of the trunk and drags them up the steps as I unlock the door. I push the button to let the garage door down and step inside to turn off the alarm. It's not much cooler inside.

"Please don't tell me the AC is broken!" I groan. But when I look at the thermostat, I see that it's just turned up really high. I quickly adjust it and then turn on a ceiling fan. "Let's not go upstairs until after the AC has had some time to cool things off."

"Yes," Chris agrees. "Instead I think I will melt into a puddle of goo right here in your living room. Re-form me when the air has cooled enough for me to hold my shape again." He then proceeds to whip off his shirt and lie flat out on the floor under the fan.

I only thought it was hot before. I'm standing there, with my jaw hanging open, trying to figure out how to work my brain properly when he opens one eye to look at me. "Sorry. But, good Lord, woman, it's hot." He closes his eyes again and just lies there while I ogle him.

I cannot put into words how amazingly good looking this man is. I don't even want to try because I know I will not do him justice. He has *perfect* abs (yup, that's definitely a six-pack) and a beautifully chiseled chest. His arms are very muscular, but not in an *I lift weights in the mirror while I drink my steroids and dream of killing innocent puppies* kind of way. His skin is slightly tanned, and his shorts are hanging low enough that I can see the tan line at his hips. He's not hairless, but the just-right amount on his chest (and belly) is remarkably light, considering how dark the hair on his head is.

"Sara?"

I blink several times very quickly. Then I realize my mouth is still hanging open and I manage to get it closed. "Y–" I croak. I clear my throat. "Yes?"

"Are you okay?" He swings around to a seated position looking very concerned. I wonder what I look like.

"I'm fine." My voice is still kind of croaky.

"Are you sure? What's wrong?" Despite my silent prayers to the contrary, he leaps up and touches my arm. "Sara? Seriously, what is it?"

"Nothing." Damn, still croaky. "Just really hot." I clear my throat two more times. "I can't just whip my shirt off to cool down." I swallow – there, that's better. I even manage to smile.

"Sure you can, sweetheart. I won't peek. Much." He smiles and waggles his eyebrows vaudeville-style at me. The eyebrows fit so well with the way he says "sweetheart" that I almost laugh.

After the AC cools things down a bit, I give Chris the grand tour. My house is pretty big; Sam and I bought it with the hopes of filling it with a family. Downstairs we have a big kitchen with a large area for our table, a formal dining room, a family room, a formal living room, the office, the laundry room, Sam's man cave with a pool table, and a half bathroom. On the second floor there are five bedrooms, including the master, and four bathrooms. The third floor is a loft area and another bedroom with a bathroom. Then we have a three stall garage. Yeah, way too much space considering it's just me most of the time.

The searing heat has brought a tremendous thunderstorm with it Monday night. I should take this moment to admit that I am horribly afraid of thunderstorms. Chris and I fall asleep on the couches downstairs watching a movie, but I wake up when there is a terrible crash of thunder that shakes the walls. I sit bolt upright and cannot quite manage to completely stifle the scream that jumps to my lips. I remember Chris though, and clamp both hands over my mouth.

Not quickly enough. Chris jumps up next to me and throws an arm around my shoulders. "Sara? What's wrong? What's happened?"

I start to laugh at myself but another crash of thunder has me heading for the hills. I leap up and sit back down again with my feet tucked under me. I press my eyes closed and squeak. I open one eye to peek at Chris when I hear him laughing.

"You're afraid of thunderstorms, aren't you?"

"You tell me, long lost soul mate," I snap. "Stop laughing at me!"

Completely serious, he says, "I'm here, Sara. Nothing is going to happen." But a giant crash and simultaneous flash outside make him jump too. "Well, not much." He tugs my hands away from my face. "How do you handle this when you're alone?"

"Not well," I admit. I'm so glad that he is with me for this I could almost cry. I lean into his chest and take a deep breath. His smell is so comforting I find myself sinking deeper. But another crash makes me jump and I leap away when I realize that I'm losing control over my emotions.

"What do you normally do during thunderstorms?" he asks again.

"Call Allison. Or my dad. Watch a movie. Cower under the blanket like the big baby I am."

"Okay." He grabs the remote and restarts the movie we were watching when we fell asleep. Then he pulls a blanket off the back of the couch and holds it up with one hand while inviting me under with the other. "I think we can leave your dad and Allison out of this one, right?" He winks. "Will I be enough?"

I curl up on the couch under his arm and he throws the blanket over me – with only my eyes peeking out. My head is on his thigh and I can smell him. "Yes. We can leave them out." I close my eyes and listen to his even breathing while trying to tune out the sound of the movie. He rests his hand on my back.

"Sara?"

"Yes?" I open my eyes and look up at him.

"I'm glad I'm here."

I smile. "So am I."

Chapter 8

When I wake up, Chris is asleep with one hand still pressed on my back. My head is still on his thigh and the TV is still on. His head is lolled back over the back of the couch. It does not look comfortable. "Chris?" I whisper.

His head snaps up. "What?" He reaches up to rub the back of his neck.

"I'm so sorry!"

"For what?" He genuinely looks confused, like he couldn't fathom a reason that I might feel repentant.

"For making you sleep like that!"

He smiles at me. "It's okay. I don't mind, really." When he sees the look on my face he adds again, "Really." He stands up and stretches. "What's on the agenda today?"

I curl up into a little ball. "I don't know. What do you want to do?"

"Is the pavement going to be boiling again, or did that storm last night knock some of the heat out?"

"I doubt it. It's probably going to be boiling again." I grab the remote and turn on the Weather Channel. Yes – boiling again.

Chris looks at me. "I think I would either like to be inside or wet this day." He smiles. "Or both."

"All right. Pool it is." It's really too hot to eat, plus I don't have much food, so we have OJ and bread with jelly for breakfast. We change into swimsuits. I know I am putting on my skimpiest suit on purpose, but I don't want to think about why that might be. I grab some towels, sunscreen, and water bottles in a cooler. I could walk to the pool, but today it's too hot to even consider, and it's not even 11 yet. Thankfully, the Mazda is in the garage, but getting in after it sits at the pool all day is going to be miserable.

On the drive over I decide to warn Chris. "There is a possibility that I might see a student or two of mine. Actually, I usually do."

"Okay," he says. "I wouldn't mind meeting some of your students."

"They're probably going to know who you are. They are kind of your target audience, remember?"

He smiles. "Mrs. Clarke, are you embarrassed to be seen with me?"

I laugh and grab the bag from the back as I get out. "Yup, that's it. I wouldn't want anyone to get the impression that I know you or anything. Heaven forbid they think I like you enough to want to spend time with you."

As we walk towards the entrance of the pool, Chris walks so close to me I'm having trouble keeping my balance. "Okay," he says. "I'll try to act like I don't know you. Keep a low profile."

"It's probably too hot for people to even come to the pool today. We'll probably have the place to ourselves."

But, I'm wrong. For the first half hour or so, we do have the place to ourselves. Before 12, though, people really start to roll in. And it looks like a lot of them are high school students. As I watch, a DJ comes in with his table and starts to set up in the shade. Ah, yes. "It's the summer kick-off party today," I mutter, mostly to myself. Then louder, to Chris, I say, "It was supposed to be over the weekend, but it got rescheduled when a thunderstorm blew in. I got an email about it, but I completely forgot."

"Oh, you totally knew that before we came," Chris says. "I know you just wanted to show me off to as many people as possible." He winks at me.

"Yup. You're on to me." I hold out my wrists like I'm offering them for handcuffs. "Guilty as charged."

I'm standing in the four foot deep area and Chris is sitting on the side, with his feet in the water next to me. I have my arms on the sidewalk next to him. "Seriously, Chris! This pavement is *hot*! How are you sitting on it?" As I am speaking, a herd of kids heads our way.

"My seat was about to be over-run anyway," he says as he jumps in. When he surfaces, I'm caught again in a moment of complete lust. The man is just amazing. I'm sure my jaw has dropped again. He smiles at me.

That's when I notice that he has an audience. And two of the girls were in my fourth period last year. They're elbowing each other and giggling, eyes completely glued on Chris. He smiles at them and in a fit of giggles they look away – right to me.

"Mrs. Clarke?"

I smile. "Hello, Heather, Rachel. Are you having a nice summer?"

They both nod mutely as Chris slides over and extends his hand. "Hi!" he says brightly. "It's nice to meet you!"

"Girls, this is my friend, Mr. Eck. Chris, this is Heather and Rachel." Heather is giggling again but Rachel is staring at me with her mouth hanging open.

Although they weren't students of mine, I recognize both of the other girls and one of the boys with them. One of the girls is very audibly whispering, "I *told* you it was Chris Eck. I *told* you!"

Rachel swallows twice and then says, "Mrs. Clarke, you know Chris Eck?"

"Yes, I do." What else am I supposed to say?

Chris smiles again. "So how do you like Chemistry? Is Mrs. Clarke a good teacher?"

"Well, they can't exactly say I'm awful while I'm standing here. They might end up with me for AP Chem next year. It's okay, girls. He really is quite normal."

Rachel is making faces like she has a big bubble trapped in her mouth and Heather still has a case of uncontrollable giggles. One of the boys I do not recognize sticks his hand out. "It's really nice to meet you Mr. Eck." He's smiling in a very teenage boy sky high confident kind of way. "Do you know Mark Evans?" Almost immediately the poor kid realizes how stupid that sounded and his smile drops.

"Yes," Chris says dryly. "We've met." Then he laughs and sticks his finger in my arm. "But 'Shorty' here is really one of his best friends."

Heather stops short. "Mrs. Clarke, do you know all of Evansgate?"

"Yes. I do." Still don't know what else to say.

"Wow!" One of the boys says. "Could you get us tickets to one of their concerts?"

"Well, that might be difficult. To start with, they don't play in Richmond. Also, I have a lot of students. How could I decide who to give tickets to fairly?"

Chris looks at me when he says, "Just because we never *have* played in Richmond, doesn't mean we never *will*." I stick my tongue out at him. "But you're right," he adds, "you probably have too many students for me to hand out tickets to them all."

It doesn't take very long for word to spread that Chris Eck of Evansgate is at our pool today. We're both hanging over the side of the pool now, only I'm just standing there while he is signing everything from napkins to skin. He has had his picture taken with about 40 different girls and at least a dozen boys.

I lean over and whisper, "How much do you hate me right now?"

He looks at me, surprised. "Hate you? Why would I – how could I hate you?"

I gesture at the quasi-line forming for an autograph. "Oh, I could think of a reason or two."

"It's a small price to pay to get to spend the day with you." He looks down. "In a bathing suit." He smiles and very slowly returns his gaze to my face, which I'm sure is beet red at the moment.

I duck under the water to think for a second. He knows we can only be friends. He knows that I am married. But it doesn't seem to slow him down at all. Chris flirts with me constantly. And I like it. And that is wrong. And, of course, I flirt with him constantly too. But I don't know what to do about it.

I come up when I run out of air. Chris is still staring at me, and now the line behind him is too. "Sara?" he asks. I look at him. "Do you want to go home now?" I nod mutely.

He turns to everyone standing there and says, "I'm sorry ladies and gentlemen, but it is time for me to go. If you would please excuse me." He hops out of the pool and grabs a towel that he holds out towards me. He is standing there, more perfect than should be possible, dripping all over the sidewalk, just looking at me like it's the most normal thing in the world. I unscramble my brain as quickly as I can and hop out next to him.

"Thanks," I say as I take the towel. "But you have really disappointed your fans." I nod in their general direction.

He leans in very close as he wraps a towel around his waist. "The first thing I had to learn in this business is that you just have to decide when you're done and quit. You can't drag it out or keep telling yourself, 'Well, they're in line. When I get to the end...' because the line will never go away. It's hard, it really is, but sometimes you just have to know when it's time to cut and run."

I stare at him, amazed. "I'm sorry that I brought you here. I'm sorry that I put you in that position and I'm sorry for all of these kids. Let's go home." I grab my bag and start for the exit without ever looking over my shoulder.

I can hear Chris call out, "Thank you! And good night!" before he turns to follow me.

When we get back to the house I grab some clean towels for Chris and then hop in the shower. After I put on some clean, very light weight, clothes, I sit down at my computer. I haven't emailed Sam since Saturday night.

> I'm glad you are having fun in DC – it's nice that you have found something to do while Allison is working. Don't do anything stupid though. Guys like that can be dangerous, Sara. I don't want you to end up in trouble.

I have to go to Singapore for a little while and then I
have a tour in the States for a week or two. I'll come
home first. I need a new suitcase load anyway. I'll let
you know when I'll be flying in. I'll get a car from the
airport.
I love you. Please be safe.
Sam

Well, at least he is being nice again. But I can tell he already
doesn't like Chris and he hasn't even met him yet.

I'm glad you'll be home! I can't wait to see you. Let
me know when you'll get here!
I came back home yesterday. It is so hot here, it is
almost painful. [Might as well get it over with.] Chris
came back with me to hang out here for a little while
before he has to go back to LA. We went to the pool
this morning and you should have seen my students
fawning over him! I think I have definitely won some
points in the cool teacher department. Not much else
going on. I'm going to try to lay low to avoid the
heat. Be safe. I love you. Love, Sara

Chris comes in as I'm finishing. "What are you doing?"

I smile as I hit send. "I'm just emailing Sam. He's coming back to
the states soon."

"That's nice. Does he know that I'm here?"

"Yeah. He told me to be careful because guys like you can be
dangerous."

"Guys like me? What? Guys from Oregon? I heard I had that in
common with him. Is he dangerous?"

"I don't think that was what he was referring to."

Chris's tone is very cool. "Oh, I'm sure it's not." He smiles again
to lighten the mood. "What do you want to do for the rest of the day?"

"My life is very glamorous you know. I had a full day of exciting
things ahead of me. Laundry... scrubbing toilets... grocery shopping.
You know – life."

"Ah, yes. Life. Sounds exciting. Where do we start?"

Chris helps me with my mundane chores for the afternoon. I wash
a load of clothes, and then for good measure, we wash his too. I dust
while he vacuums. And then we go out to the grocery store, seeing as
how I have almost no food.

"Now what?" Chris asks when we finish putting the groceries away.

"I don't know. It's hard to always think of things to do."

He pauses for a moment, thinking. "Why do you teach?" He looks around at my admittedly spacious home. "Do you need the money?"

"No," I almost laugh. "Sam has plenty of that. I just need something to fill my time. It gets lonely around here by myself."

Chris looks sad for a moment. "Why do you do it?"

At first, I'm taken aback by his question. "Do what?"

"Stay here by yourself all the time."

"Uh, because I live here."

"But why do you stay?"

"Because I'm married, and this is our house, and I belong here."

He nods. "That makes sense, I guess. What else do you do?"

"I am in a book club – two actually, a Bunco group, I sponsor SADD and the Science Club at school, volunteer to chaperone all of the dances, and take a cooking class. Oh, and I'm trying to learn to dance."

The longer I talk, the bigger Chris's eyes get. "Wow. You do keep busy. How do you have time to teach anything?"

"All of that only adds up to, maybe, 10 evenings. I mean really, we're talking less than 20 hours a month. And none of it is really ever on the weekends. I usually spend those grading and catching up on the latest blockbusters."

Chris looks sad. "Are you lonely?"

"Sometimes," I admit. "It's a big house. Most of my friends have kids or live hours away, so there isn't usually anyone to do things with. So I just fill my time."

"I really don't want to leave you here. What are the chances you would come to LA with me?"

"Probably not very good. I can't really afford to go gallivanting around the country. Besides, at some point I have to exit this fantasy world and get back to real life."

"Fantasy world?"

"You know..." I stumble. "This." I spread my hands out. "Hanging out and running around with you. You'll have to get back to your life, and I will have to get back to mine."

"What? Waiting around for your husband to come around for a day or two? Sara, like it or not, you are a part of my life now. We are *friends*, and I don't turn my back on friends." He looks at me pensively. "I think you should just quit teaching, but I know you won't do that. But, cut back this fall. Don't take a cooking class. Don't sponsor any clubs at school. Can you do that? Open yourself up a little bit and spend some time with us."

"Us? You mean Evansgate?" He nods. "Chris, you live on the other side of the country."

"Exactly. So, don't fill every second of your days. Leave some time for travel." He smiles. "I'll come here too!" He gets quiet again. "I really don't like the thought of you wandering around this house by yourself all the time. I don't know how Sam sleeps at night."

Friday night Chris gets to meet my best friend. Matt and I have been friends since forever, and he is the person I spend the most time with. Matt, who is thrilled with the opportunity to meet Chris, suggests our usual night out. We are regulars at a bar called Sine's downtown, and that's where we go. We introduce Chris to our favorite bartender and he is cool enough that it earns us a few free drinks. Well, I guess Matt and I get a lot of free drinks, but I'm sure it's nice for him to have a reason to give them to us this time.

Matt is almost exactly my height; I think he might be dead on six feet. He has blond hair and blue eyes, the perfect Aryan complexion. Matt's family is very German – I'm pretty sure his grandparents are still there. It's cool having a friend who speaks another language fluently. He teaches me and Chris a bunch of ways to curse in German. He teaches me all the time, but I can't ever remember anything, something Matt enjoys pointing out. After a while, when our foreign swearing has become loud enough to disturb others, we go home.

After we drop Matt off, Chris turns to me in the car. "That guy is a lot of fun."

"I know. He's my best friend, remember?"

"I thought I was your best friend. You told me we could be best friends."

"Okay, he's my old best friend, and my current second best friend."

"That's better. Do you get to see him a lot?"

"I do. He is pretty much the only one I do anything with."

"Sara, that's kind of sad. What about your other friends?"

"I don't have many. There are a lot of people that I am friendly with, other teachers, people in my book clubs, that kind of thing, but not many that I would consider friends."

"Why not?"

"I don't know. I just don't. I'm sure a therapist would tell you that

I have commitment issues or something like that."

"I see. Well, thank you for admitting me to the exclusive Sara's Club."

"Don't let it go to your head."

Chris stays with me until Sunday, then he flies back to work on the album. I drive him to the airport and come home to my suddenly very depressing, empty house.

Chapter 9

I sit down at the computer. I'm thinking about what Chris said. Could I really do that? But, even if I "leave some time open" I still have to be here during the school year – what am I going to do at night? Granted, sometimes it does commit me for weekends. If I didn't have that, I *would* have more freedom. I growl to myself. It still doesn't seem worth it.

I check my email. There are two from Sam, but first I email Chris.

> Chris
> I can't "cut back" without being too bored. But, it's still summer and I've got nothing now! When's my first trip to LA?
> Love, Sara

Then I read the emails from Sam.

> I'll be home Tuesday afternoon. Do I have a suitcase packed and ready? I'll do a switch. I'll have to fly out to Chicago on Thursday night because I have to be there Friday, and unfortunately, Monday and Tuesday so I'll have to be there over the weekend. But at least I'll be home for the 4th. I'll go straight to NYC from Chicago, but I might be able to come home again on Saturday before I have to go to Atlanta.
> I love you. Sam

The next one came in almost right after the first.

> Is Chris still there?

> Sam,
> No, I drove him to the airport this morning. I can't wait to see you on Tuesday! What time do you think you'll be in? Fly safe. I love you!
> Love, Sara

The thought of being with Sam again seems so foreign that I'm nervous about what I will say to him. And I should explain the suitcase thing. Sam is never in town long, but when he does get a chance, he likes to switch out his suitcase. I will get one freshly packed and ready for him to grab and he will dump the one he had for me to launder and replenish. He gets his clothes cleaned by the hotels where he stays when he is on the road, but I can understand wanting a little variation in wardrobe choices as often as possible. It's something I used to surprise him with, but now I guess he expects it.

On Monday, I clean up a little more to be sure that Sam comes home to a clean house. There really isn't much to do in that department. I keep a clean house anyway, and Chris and I did all of my chores while he was in town. I also pack a fresh suitcase for Sam. I keep a checklist of things that I need to include and I've done it enough times that it doesn't really take me very long. I make a shopping list of travel supplies that he is running low on to pick up the next time I go out.

When I check my email, I find one from Chris.

> Sara,
> Fine, I will share you with the rest of the world during the school year. But I'll take you when I can get you! How about a week from Friday? I miss you already. Life is less fun without you. Evans says, "Hi Shorty."
> Love, Chris

> Chris,
> I can't. Sam is going to be in the states and he might be able to come home that weekend before he goes to Atlanta. Sorry! But that makes me sad. I miss you too. Definitely a lot less fun (and more lonely) without you.
> Tell Short Mark (and Drew and Blond Mark) that I say hello and I miss them too.
> Love, Sara

There's one from Sam too.

> Hopefully I'll be in around 7 pm, but you know how delays can be. I'll text you from LaGuardia if I can.
> Does this mean that I won't get to meet the famous Chris Eck?

I can always tell when Sam is in a bad mood with me because he doesn't sign his emails. And what does he mean by "if I can"? How could he not get a chance to text me during his layover in NYC? I email Chris again.

> Chris,
> Sam wants to know if he will ever get to meet you.

What are the chances that you could come here
again? I'll come to LA next, I promise!
Love, Sara

Well, it looks like I'll have all of Tuesday to kill as well. I was
hoping Sam would get in earlier. He usually starts working around 9
pm every night, so I won't really get to see him at all. But that's the way
these things always seem to work out.

Around lunchtime on Tuesday my phone rings. It's Chris. I
answer it excitedly. "Hi, Chris!"

"Hey, Sara! I miss you so much, it's almost ridiculous."

"I miss you too. Things are so quiet around here. I went to the
grocery store yesterday. I started to feel invisible because I wasn't
being pestered for an autograph."

He laughs – and the very sound makes my toes tingle. I really do
miss him. "I was unaware that people were asking for yours before.
Maybe I was just distracted and didn't notice?"

"You don't realize how much standing with you raises my stock in
the world. But it *is* almost weird to go out and not be stared at. I
thought I would welcome the anonymity of the real world. But I almost
miss the screaming masses." I pause. "But maybe it's just you I miss."

"Sweetheart, I didn't exactly get recognized *every* time we left the
house. That really only happens with Ev – Short Mark." Ha laughs.

"True. But you're so gorgeous that even if they don't know who
you are, people stare. I'm back to being passed over."

Chris pauses a beat before speaking. "You think I'm gorgeous?"

"Please don't act like you don't know that you're a Greek god. But
what's up?"

"I can't call without a reason?"

"I guess. But is there a reason?"

"As it happens, there is. I would love to come back next
weekend." There's a brief scuffle on the line.

"I want to come, too, Shorty."

"Hey, Short Mark! How are you doing?"

"I'm fine. Thanks for returning Eck to us. But next time, I'd like
him back unchanged, please."

"What's that supposed to mean? I didn't change him!"

"Even if you didn't mean to, you did. He's much more boring
now. But you didn't tell me if I would be welcome."

"Of course you are! Then you can monitor any changes for

yourself."

"Ah, I don't know if even *I* would be enough to prevent them." He laughs. "Your BFF wants the phone back now. I'll see you in less than two weeks, Shorty!" There's a muffled exchange.

"Do you have any plans for tomorrow?" Chris asks.

"I don't know. Sam will be here; maybe we'll try to see some fireworks?"

"I suppose that is the normal way to celebrate our nation's birth."

"Are you doing something better?"

"I'm going to book a flight – ouch! Two flights, okay?"

"That's going to take you all day? You must be very slow with a computer."

"Well, I'm sure that the boss will make us work, despite the fact that it's a national holiday."

"You spent too much time with me. I'm sure the band doesn't appreciate you ignoring the album."

"Nobody worked last week, no worries. Evans is just a slave driver when we are working. Ow! What? You are." Short Mark must still be standing there. Then he comes back to me, "We'll take the red-eye out Thursday night, will that work?"

"Anything. Just let me know and I'll come get you at the airport."

"Sara?"

"Yeah?"

"I can't wait. I really miss you."

"Me too. Now get to work on that record. We'll talk soon!"

When I hang up, I'm almost giddy. I glance at the clock. It's about 11 am in Dallas. I call Allison at work.

"Allison Lebeau."

"Hey! It's Sara."

"Hi! What's going on?"

"Nothing. And I mean that. But Sam is coming home tonight for a couple of days." I pause. "And Chris and Short Mark are coming to visit a week from Friday!"

"No! You guys are really good friends now, aren't you?"

"Yup. Are you jealous?"

"Only of the love they are stealing from me."

"As if. No one could compete with my big sister. How are things?"

"Fine. Busy as usual."

"Yeah, I was surprised that you answered the phone."

"I can't really talk long."

"That's okay. I just wanted to say, 'Hi.' And to tell you that I'm in trouble."

"I know, Baby Girl. But it will be okay. This could be a very good thing."

"You probably aren't the person I should talk to about this. You're very biased."

"Everyone is biased against Sam."

"You didn't used to be... You used to like him. He really is a good guy, Allison. It's not his fault. This would be hard on any marriage."

"I know. But things could change if he wanted them to."

"I wasn't talking about the travel."

"I wasn't either. But I have to go. I love you."

"I love you, too."

Things are weird with Sam.

"So, if you do make it back home before Atlanta, you can meet Chris. And Mark Evans too." I'm *trying* to act normal.

Sam looks surprised. "How?"

"They're going to come visit."

"Why?"

"Because they're my friends."

"But you just saw them."

"Yes, but they're my friends. I have fun with them. Besides, I told them you wanted to meet them so they agreed to come in case you could."

"Just like that?"

"Yes. It's the beauty of being a rock star. You can dictate your own schedule, and you have plenty of money to make this sort of thing possible."

"Yes, plenty of money. I don't know how I feel about you spending so much time with them, Sara."

"Why? What's wrong with me spending time with them?"

"They're guys."

"You don't have a problem with Matt."

"That's different. You've known Matt forever. And, you've never been more than friends with him."

"Um, Sam? I've never been 'more than friends' with Chris or Short Mark either."

"But you never wanted to with Matt."

"I don't want to with them either. You're being ridiculous."

"I'm not being ridiculous! You're being disrespectful!"

"You did *not* just say that. Who am I disrespecting?"

"Our marriage."

"Please. I'm the only one participating in this marriage most of the time."

"What's that supposed to mean? This is my *job,* Sara. I do this for us."

"No you don't. If you did anything *for us* it would involve finding a way to be together more than a couple of days here and there."

"I can't believe you are picking a fight with me when I just got home."

"I'm not picking a fight. I'm not the one accusing you of being 'disrespectful'."

"Don't start. Not now. And my travel never bothered you before. Why are you suddenly so upset about it?"

"It has always bothered me. Do you really think I like never seeing you? Never even talking to you? Do you like it?"

"Of course I don't. But it's my job. And I really didn't think you would want to move to Hong Kong or Germany."

"Has that ever been a possibility?"

"It could be."

"Well, why haven't you ever mentioned it?"

"Because I didn't think you would want to."

"But you never even gave me the option. It's a marriage, Sam. You do what you have to. It's life."

"Do you want to move?"

"Not really. But that doesn't mean I won't."

"Look, can we talk about this later?"

I look at the clock. "Let me guess. You have work to do?"

"As a matter of fact, I do. We'll argue later, okay?"

"Sure. I look forward to it." I turn on my heel and march out of the room. I am hoping that Sam follows me to try and make up, but he doesn't. I briefly consider going back in, but decide to text Allison instead.

> To Allison:
> If you're around I would love someone to talk to.
> Fighting with Sam, of course.

I stare at my phone for a while, willing her to answer me. I'm not surprised when she doesn't, but I am really disappointed.

> To Allison:

Around 11 I go into the office. "I'm going to bed, Sam. Are you coming?"

He looks up. "I'm not really tired. I'm still on Singapore time. And I'm in the middle of something."

"Good night, then. I love you."

"I love you, too. And I'm sorry. I should have talked to you about it. But to be honest, I don't think *I* want to move. There may come a day that I have to, but until then, I don't really want to live in another country. I really am sorry, Sara."

"It's okay. Don't stay up all night."

As I climb into my empty bed, I sigh. Nothing changes, even when he's home. I miss Chris. I catch myself thinking that he would never leave me to go to bed by myself every night, when I realize that he would. He is a rock star. He spends a significant portion of his life touring. Well, at least I know it's not something I would want to get into. It would be like getting out of the pot just to land in the fire. I comfort myself with the idea that now I have something to focus on if I ever start to think I might leave Sam because of Chris. I took vows and you don't get to give up just because something that looks like it might be better comes along. Uh, but maybe I'm getting ahead of myself. And I'm sure that he would never be interested, so it's kind of a moot point.

Sam is "still on Singapore time" Wednesday. He goes into our room and goes to bed as soon as I get up. I decide to call Matt to grump.

"Hey, stranger," he greets me.

"Hi."

"You don't sound very festive. It's a holiday, you know. You should be celebrating."

"Celebrating what?"

"That I don't have to work today."

"Good. Let's go do something."

"I thought Sam was home."

"He is. But he is sleeping off his jet lag."

"Oh. Well, I heard about a concert on Brown's Island. Do you want to go, or are you going to embarrass me by singing along with all of the songs?"

"Yes and probably."

He laughs. "I'll pick you up at noon. Wear flame retardant

clothing. I think there is a chance of spontaneous combustion today."

"I'll see what I can do."

When Matt picks me up I am wearing as little clothing as possible to still be seen in public. He whistles when I get in the car. "I think you left some of your clothes in the house."

"I left a lot there. A whole closet full."

"Har har. But seriously, where is my dowdy teacher friend?"

"Did you just call me dowdy?"

"Maybe. You have to admit, you usually dress a little more conservatively."

"Usually I'm worried about running into students."

"But not today?"

"I realized I see them at the pool all the time and I'm wearing a bikini there."

"I hate to point out that that's pretty much what you're wearing right now."

"I know. But they've already seen me in the bikini."

"I hope you don't see any *parents* of your students. They may wonder about the county's hiring policy."

I didn't wake Sam when I left. I figured he needed his sleep. I stuck a note to the fridge telling him that I would be back around dinnertime. I doubt he'll even notice my absence.

The concert isn't half bad. I'm surprised how many people have braved the inferno to see a no-name band. There is a lot of beer being consumed, and I have a feeling that helps. I've only had a couple of beers, and then I switch to water. I'm watching Matt chug beer after beer and I'm thinking that I might need to be able to drive us home.

"Thirsty much?" I ask him.

"No. I'm *hot*."

"Well, I know that. You've always had to beat back the girls with sticks."

"And yet, somehow, you have resisted my wiles all this time."

"What can I say? I've seen you naked."

He grabs his heart like I've shot him. "Oh! That hurts. Why are you so cruel, lovely lady?"

"I have to keep you honest. No one else will. But you know I'm teasing. I've never seen you naked."

"Yeah, you're right. So you don't know what you might be giving up."

Around 3:30, I'm really starting to melt – despite my distinct lack of clothes, and Matt is really quite drunk. "Can we go?" I ask him.

He nods weakly. "I think it would probably be best."

I half haul him back under the railroad tracks to where we parked. I open the doors and step back to let as much heat out as possible before getting into the car. I pull out my phone and call Sam.

"Hey, will you meet me at Matt's?"

"Why?" He sounds very grumpy.

"Because I'm going to drive him home – he's had a little too much to drink. But I don't want to have to return his car later."

He sighs. "I suppose."

"Well, I don't want to put you out or anything."

"It's fine. When?"

"We're leaving Brown's Island now. A half hour?"

"Fine." Sam hangs up without another word.

Matt looks sideways at me. "He's become a real peach, your husband. Do you think we can safely get in yet?" He points to the car.

"I doubt it, but we can try anyway."

I have found the downside to wearing skimpy clothes. The leather in Matt's car scalds my skin wherever it touches. I leap back out of the car, "YOW! That is hot."

"Yes, ma'am, it is. Here, give me the keys and I'll turn on the AC."

I pass the keys through the open door to Matt, who leans over and starts the car. Then he fiddles with the controls and climbs back out. "I might as well get out of the oven too," he says as he leans against the roof. But he immediately jumps back. "That is hot!"

I laugh at him. "I know."

Sam is waiting at Matt's house by the time we get there. "He looks happy," Matt's voice is heavy with sarcasm.

"Yes, it ought to be a pleasant ride home."

I park the car in Matt's garage and then hand him the keys. "But don't go anywhere, got me?"

He salutes. "Yes, ma'am." He comes over to give me a hug. "Don't let him get you down," he whispers in my ear.

"Thanks for the concert. It was fun."

Matt waves as I walk to the car. He hits the button to put the garage door down as soon as I open the passenger door.

"Do you really think that is appropriate attire, Sara?"

"Oh, hello, Sam. I'm glad you're getting back to our time zone."

"I'm serious. Why would you wear that out in public?"

I look down. I'm wearing shorts, but they barely cover my bum. Shorts, technically, but really more like wide underwear. I've paired them with a string bikini top. "Yes, I do. When it's a million degrees outside, one has to dress accordingly."

Sam sneers. "I don't appreciate my wife going out with another guy dressed like a hooker."

"Ha! I'm hardly dressed like a hooker. Pretty much every girl at the concert was dressed very similarly, even some of them that really needed to cover up more." I make a face as I remember some of the gobs of flesh we were forced to look at. "And Matt doesn't count as another guy. He probably could have stood in as one of my bridesmaids."

"He's not gay, Sara."

"I know. But you know there is nothing there." I pause. "Is this about Chris?"

"No," he answers a little too quickly. "This is about you dressing with some decorum."

A lot of choice words leap to mind, but I bite them back and sit in silence the rest of the way home. When we get there, Sam stomps back into the office and I go upstairs.

I look in the mirror for a minute and then pull out my phone. I hold it out as far as I can and I take a picture of myself. It doesn't come out very well, so I turn and take one in the mirror. Then I quickly edit out the reflection of my phone, because I hate pictures like that.

I send the picture to Chris.

> To Chris:
> Sam thinks I shouldn't have worn this out today.
> What do you think?

I know I am blatantly flirting with him, but I like it when he flirts back. It makes me feel better about myself. I'm a terrible person. I know this is completely inappropriate. Why can't I stop? I don't have to wait long for his response.

> From Chris:
> Will you wear it again when you come to LA?

> To Chris:
> Does that mean you think it is okay for me to be
> seen like this?

My phone rings. It's Chris, of course.

"I think that is the only thing you should ever wear again."

"It might get a little cold in the winter."

"You can add a coat." I laugh. "Speaking of when you come to

78

LA..." he trails off.

"Yes?"

"When might that be?"

"I don't know. I haven't actually looked at it yet."

"Okay, well, when you decide –"

"You'll be the first to know."

"Ug. We *are* rehearsing today, so I have to go."

"No problem. Work hard, and then come see me!"

"Toodles."

"Did you just say –" But he's already gone.

I watch fireworks on TV. Sam is working in the office. "It isn't a holiday anywhere else in the world," he tells me when I start to complain. He always has some sort of stupid quip like that ready. Allison finally calls me back.

"Hey! Sorry I didn't get your text last night. Do you still want to talk about it?"

"Not really. Are you going to go see some fireworks later?"

"Yeah, Tom has some friends that – it's not important. Are you okay?"

"I'm okay. But, you're interrupting the grand finale."

"Fine, fine! Enjoy your fireworks. We'll talk soon!"

"Yup. Love ya."

I shouldn't have even answered. I really didn't feel like talking and now I feel like I was short with my sister because I'm mad at my husband. Oh, well. She'll forgive me.

To Allison:
Sorry. I'm still mad at Sam. Not you.

From Allison:
No worries. I love you.

Chapter 10

Sam doesn't leave Thursday night, as he originally told me he would. He leaves Thursday afternoon – early afternoon at that. And the worst part is that I'm glad. I'm hoping that he doesn't come back next weekend. I feel terrible, but I can't help it. But I would rather spend time with Chris and Short Mark without him. Life is easier with them.

It's a slow week. I go about my normal chores, but the summer is always hard. There is just not enough to fill my time. I sign up as a possible summer school substitute, in case someone could use me. I go to book club. I clean the house and change all the sheets. At least we have a lot of guest rooms, so that takes some time. I talk to Chris every day.

"How is the album coming?"

"Really good! I've been working on a new song. Cannadiak is helping me. I've never written one before."

"Wow! That's great! What is it about? Is that a normal question to ask about a song? I'm unfamiliar with song writing etiquette."

"So am I. This is going to sound stupid, but I don't know if I can talk about it. It's really hard and I don't want to admit to anything, in case it's terrible."

"I'm sure it's not. Hopefully, I'll get to hear it someday!"

"Hopefully you'll know all the words."

"But no pressure, right?"

"Well, at least you won't be able to hide it if you hate it. I will be able to count on you for an honest opinion."

"Crap. That hadn't occurred to me. I can't lie and tell you I love it if it's awful, can I?"

"Well, you could. But if you can't sing it to me, I'll know you're lying."

"Huh. Then make it good. I can't stand the idea of hurting your feelings."

"I wouldn't want to offend you with bad music! But, I have to go. I'll see you at eight, your time, Friday morning."

"I can't wait!"

I can't sleep Thursday night. I know it's stupid, but I'm really excited about seeing the guys. I'm at the airport a good 15 minutes before their flight is due to land. I sit and wait for them between the two security gates. It's as close as I can get and it means I will see them that much sooner. I bounce my leg impatiently as I wait.

Soon enough though, there is a mass of people heading my way and I'm sure they're in there somewhere. Actually they're towards the front of the crowd. I guess first class gives you the benefit of getting off the plane first.

I hop up and run towards them. Chris opens his arms and I jump into them. He swings me around in a big hug. "Sara!"

"Hi! I'm so glad you're here! This week has completely sucked."

Short Mark wraps me in a hug next and kisses me on the cheek. He doesn't have to bend down to do it like Chris does.

People are staring. I made a scene running the way I did, and I'm sure it won't be long before people start to recognize them. "Let's go! Did you check anything?"

"Yeah, we did." Short Mark is smiling. "Lead the way to baggage claim."

Chris holds my hand as we walk towards the escalators to the bottom level. "I missed you," he tells me.

"You've mentioned that."

Short Mark punches him in the arm. "He is very mopey without you around, Shorty."

Chris drops my hand to swing back. "Of course I am. She is a million times more fun to be around than you clowns."

"I highly doubt that," I say.

Chris slings his arm around my shoulders. "Trust me."

While we wait for their luggage, more people are staring. Short Mark nods at me, like he knows I'm wondering if these people realize who they are. "A lot of them were on our plane and they already know who we are."

"I figured." I laugh when I see a young girl heading our way with a pen and a piece of paper. "It begins."

She fumbles a little when she gets close and I can tell she is nervous. Short Mark saves her from her misery.

"Would you like an autograph?" She nods and he holds out his hand. "What's your name?"

"Becky," she whispers.

Short Mark smiles. He signs his name and then hands the paper and pen to Chris, who has to let go of my shoulders to sign it. Chris beams at her as he hands it back and she looks like she is going to faint. "Thanks," she whispers, and she stumbles a little as she walks away.

I watch her jump as the buzzer announces the arrival of the luggage. I look at Chris and Short Mark, who are both holding a carry all suitcase. "What did you check? How long are you planning on staying?"

Chris smiles. "A while." And he steps away to pick up something from the carousel. It's a guitar case. Then he grabs another one that is right behind it, and Short Mark picks up a big rectangular case that is clearly holding an instrument – his keyboard, maybe?

"So, I'll get these, then?" I sigh dramatically as I pick up their suitcases, one in each hand.

"I would never let a lady carry my luggage," Short Mark says as he shifts his keyboard to one hand and extends the handle on his suitcase to pull it behind him.

"Me neither," says Chris as he wraps the strap from one case around his chest and one shoulder, picks up the other case in one hand, and pulls out the handle of his carry all.

I look around behind me. "I thought I wasn't a lady. And I don't see anyone wearing a dress circa 1950, so who are you referring to?"

"Come on, you idiot. These are heavy."

When we get to my car it takes a few minutes to fit everything in the small space afforded by my compact, but we manage.

"You could have warned me that you were bringing so much. I would have brought a bigger vehicle. Are you planning on getting some work done?" I ask as we drive out of the parking deck.

"We were thinking about it," Short Mark says. "I have some songs I want to test out on you."

I manage to push out a laugh, but I can't help making comparisons. Sam travels all the time for work. Chris travels all the time for "work". Sam works at home whenever he is there. Chris brings "work" with him when *he* is there. Hmph.

"What?" Chris asks.

"Nothing," I say as brightly as I can. "I'm ready to help. Bring it on."

When we get to the house, I give Short Mark a quick tour and show him to the room he will sleep in. "You're in the same room you were last time," I tell Chris. We set up their instruments in the formal living room because that room has the most space. Chris brought his bass and his guitar. Short Mark sets up his keyboard on the stand that was also in the case.

I lounge on the couch and offer random bits of opinions as they tool around with the music they are working on. Around lunchtime they quit.

"So, is Sam going to be here this weekend?" Short Mark asks. Chris looks up with sudden interest. They are looking at some pictures of us on the shelves.

"I don't actually know. He never really said one way or the other. But I think he is really going to try. Maybe he is trying to surprise me so that he can check to make sure we aren't having wild three-way sex in his absence." I laugh at the looks on their faces. "He's been giving me some crap."

"Ah, yes," Short Mark adopts a formal tone. "I would have trouble trusting my beautiful wife around good-for-nothing rock stars, personally. Wait – I am a good-for-nothing rock star, so does that mean I have to get an ugly wife or just never trust her around myself?"

"I would go with an ugly wife."

"I don't think he is actually going to get much of a choice where that is concerned. What beautiful woman is going to have you?" Chris asks Short Mark.

"Sara would have me, wouldn't you?" he asks me.

"Well, I'm kind of already spoken for, so I'm not sure I could offer an unbiased opinion on the matter."

"And even if she wasn't," Chris adds, "she would have better taste than you, my friend."

Short Mark smiles. "Even if she wasn't spoken for now, I believe I would not be the next person in line. Besides, she's too short for me."

"Hey!" I say. "I'm still here!"

"Good thing too, sweetheart," Chris says, "because we would be lost without you. Now, what do you want to do for lunch?"

It's still too hot outside to eat much of anything with substance, so we sit around the kitchen with cold cut sandwiches and beer. Well, the guys drink beer, but I have lemonade. Chris tells me about the release of the album. "It's due to come out in late September. Then we'll start our tour at the end of the month."

"Of September?" I ask. Chris nods. "How long will the tour last?" I ask.

"Probably about three months or so," Short Mark tells me. "Then we might take a brief international stint, or so the label tells us. Do you have a passport, Shorty?"

"Actually, I don't."

"Then you better get one, because Eck isn't going to want to do every show without you there."

"Not *every* show," Chris agrees.

"Well, I'll start the paperwork."

But then I jump as Sam's voice says, "Paperwork for what?"

"Sam! What are you doing home?" I stand up and start towards him, but stop short when a woman comes in behind him. She is about my height, blond, thin, and arrogant. She is literally looking down her nose at me. When I notice her shoes I realize that she isn't really my height, she's probably several inches shorter. Chris gets to his feet, which I know he does because he can feel my discomfort and he is using his height as a weapon against the much shorter Sam.

"I told you I'd be home," Sam says in my direction, but he hasn't taken his eyes off of Chris.

"No," I correct him. "You said you *might* be able to come home on *Saturday*."

"Well, I wasn't going to have as much time as I thought, and I wanted to get a chance to meet your new friends so we came a little earlier."

He still hasn't introduced the woman. I'm not going to go first. He actually knows who these guys are, but I have no idea who the blond bombshell behind him is.

Sam hasn't taken his eyes from Chris (neither has Blondie) but I am staring at him, waiting for him to say something. When he looks in my direction, finally, he starts. "What?" I just look at him. "Oh. This is Anna." I keep looking at him. "Anna?" he asks like I should know who she is. "I work with her. She travels with me."

"It's nice to meet you, Anna." I hold out my hand in her direction, but she just looks at it.

"Likewise."

"Um, right. Okay. Well, Sam, this is Chris Eck and Mark Evans. Guys, this is my husband." I hold my hand out in Sam's direction. I feel like a line has been drawn across the kitchen floor and we are on one side with Sam and Anna on the other.

"Hello," says Sam and he holds his hand out in Chris's direction. But Chris did not take Anna's slight well, so he just stares at it with a look of disdain on his face. Short Mark is resolutely sitting in his chair and he doesn't look like he is getting up any time soon.

This is going well.

"How was your flight?" I ask brightly.

"It was fine," Sam says tightly. He looks at me again.

Anna is actually fluttering her eyelashes. "Hello, Chris, Mark. It's *very* nice to meet you." Her smile is practically screaming, "I'll screw you right here if you want!"

But neither Chris nor Short Mark respond.

Anna continues, undeterred. "I told Sam that it was an amazing opportunity to meet such talented musicians. It was really very nice of you to make this trip just to meet us."

Us? I'm pretty sure she wasn't even invited. And what about me?

"I'm sure you're very busy, but it speaks volumes about what kind of people you are that you would take the time to come here, just to meet some fans. I know what it's like to be on the road all the time, so exhausting. Oh! We should get together sometime if we are in the same town." She is talking really fast. "Maybe we'll get lucky and be somewhere when you are in town playing a concert and I could come to the show. You would give me a ticket, wouldn't you?" she simpers.

When no one responds she continues, "I'm very glad to get the chance to get to know you. I'm so looking forward to being friends!"

I'm wondering if I'm the only one who noticed that she is now talking only about herself. She already has decided to that she is a friend of theirs, kind of pretentious if you ask me. I can't believe she flat out asked for tickets. And her body language is over the top. I'm expecting a strip tease right here in the kitchen soon. She clearly thinks a lot of her body and I'm sure she thinks she can use it to convince one or both of them to sleep with her.

Chris looks determined to ignore her, but Short Mark isn't one to stay quiet. He turns to Chris, "Well Christopher, I think we should spend some time with Shorty." I see Anna smirk at Short Mark's nickname for me. "That is why we are here, after all. I don't want to waste any of our time with her. We get so little."

Sam clears his throat and says to me, "Right! Let's do dinner tonight. You can cook something, or we can go out. Anna and I have some work to do this afternoon." He puts his hand on the small of her back as they turn to leave the kitchen, to direct her towards the office, but he yanks it back like he was burned. I hear the office door snap shut.

I turn around slowly and let out a big breath. Chris is still standing there, looking ready for a fight. Short Mark is still lounging in his chair, a look of distaste shadowing his face as well.

"Um," I say quietly.

"He seems very nice," Short Mark says brightly. "And his girlfriend is a gem."

Chris seems to relax. "Yes, she's lovely." He comes over and gives me a hug, resting his chin on the top of my head.

"So, Shorty, are you cooking for the asshole, or should we go out?"

"Um," I say quietly. I blink back tears, and Chris tightens his hold wordlessly.

"Let's go out," he says. "Evans? Call Tom. We need a reservation at a really nice restaurant. I think Sammy-boy needs to be put in his place."

"Yes," Short Mark agrees. "If we play our cards right, we can stick him with the bill."

Two tears spill down my cheeks. I have no idea how he knows, because he cannot see me and I haven't made the slightest noise, but Chris wordlessly moves his head, tips my chin up, and wipes away the tears. "It's okay, Baby Girl. We'll be nice. Mostly." I can still feel waves of anger rolling off of him. "But that bitch better watch her back."

Short Mark spends a lot of time on the phone with Tom while Chris and I mess around in the newly christened "Music Room". "I'm thinking about leaving these here," Chris says as he gestures around the room at the instruments.

"What are you going to play at home?" I ask him.

"Oh, these are just for travel. I would never check my bass. But we have plenty and it would save me a lot of trouble, not having to haul them back and forth." He smiles at me. "I would ask if Sammy-boy would care if they were left here, but I don't think he is here often enough for his opinion to matter." He pauses for a moment, and then looks at me. "Would you mind?"

"Not if it means that you are going to be here a lot. This place is a lot more fun when you are around."

"Okay." He addresses the inanimate instruments. "Well, fellas, I hope you like your new home. Get comfortable. You're going to be here a while." Then he sits down at the keyboard and starts to pick out some songs. He never takes his eyes off of my face and I know he is expecting me to sing the words.

"I'm not in the mood, Christopher Thomas."

"Ouch. The whole name. What did I do?"

"Nothing. I'm just grumpy."

Short Mark comes into the room and he smiles at Chris. "Totally arranged. Darling girl," he says to me, "please tell your husband that we have reservations at 7." He smiles at me.

"Okay, where are we going?"

"Ruth's Chris Steakhouse."

I should have known. Of course we are going to fanciest, most overpriced steakhouse in town. I pull myself off of the couch and head towards the office. I probably should have knocked, but it's my house so I just open the door. Anna is sitting on the desk and Sam is in the chair, leaning back.

"What do you want me to say, Anna?" he is saying as I come in. "You could have been nicer."

"Well, what about her?"

"What about her? She was perfectly friendly. I'm sorry you don't like her, but you need to be nice." He jumps when he sees me standing there. "Sara!"

"We're going to Ruth's Chris at 7," I say morosely.

"Be ready to leave by 6:15," Short Mark calls from the hallway. "That's when the car will be here." And I hear him walk back into the kitchen.

"Okay," I say and I walk back out without shutting the door. I can hear Chris playing in the music room.

Anna gets up and comes to the door, which she slams behind me. "At least have the decency to shut the damn door so we don't have to listen to that garbage when we're trying to work," she says loud enough to be sure I don't miss a word.

I almost turn around and open the door to ask her why she is even here, and to point out that she didn't think it was garbage until they slighted her, but I decide against it. I go back into the music room to listen to Chris. He is playing something I don't recognize. "I don't know the words to this one," I admit.

"I would hope not," he says with a smile. "If you did, it would mean I ripped the tune off of someone else."

I smile for the first time since Sam walked in the door. "Oh! Is this your song?"

Chris nods shyly. "It's what I'm working on, yes. Do you like it?"

"I love it! Will you sing?"

"Nope. The words are a secret." He smiles at me. I instantly feel so much better that I decide to get back to my real life.

"I'm going to clean out Sam's suitcase." I turn back to the door and it sounds like Chris chokes. I turn back around quickly. "What's wrong?"

"Sweetheart, please let me take you away from here."

"You can. In a week or so, I'll come to LA for a bit. I couldn't stand another day alone in this house anyway. Are you going to help, or what?"

He smiles, despite himself. "Okay, but I'm not touching that man's skivvies for anything." Chris carries Sam's suitcase to the laundry room for me. Short Mark comes out of the kitchen and follows us.

"Is that *her* suitcase?" he asks me.

"I suppose."

"What is it doing here?"

"I don't know. I suppose that means she is staying here."

"Lovely," Short Mark says dryly. "House guests." The way he says it, like he isn't a guest, like he belongs here, makes me smile.

In the laundry room, I grab the dry cleaning bag and start to put Sam's suits and shirts in it. As I lift a pair of his pants from the suitcase a pink, lacy thong drops onto the counter. All three of us stare at it in silence.

Short Mark clears his throat. "So, I think I need to step outside to suffocate for a bit. Excuse me."

I've never seen him uncomfortable before. My mind is surprisingly empty.

"Is that yours?" Chris asks me.

"You may have never actually seen my underwear, but you know me well enough to know I wouldn't wear anything like that."

"You didn't even consider lying to me?"

"Why would I lie to you?"

"Because you might want to keep the fact that your husband is cheating on you to yourself."

"I don't know that he's cheating on me. There could be a dozen reasons why that's in his suitcase."

"Name one," he dares me. "Other than the possibility of an affair."

"It got mixed up in there in the hotel laundry."

"You are very good at denial, sweetheart. But I can play that game." He picks up the thong and throws it in the trashcan I keep by the dryer for lint.

"I thought you weren't going to touch his skivvies for anything," I say.

"Those aren't his, at least I hope not. And I certainly wasn't going to make you do it. And I have seen your underwear. I helped with your laundry."

"Oh, yeah. I forgot." I nod towards the offending pink lace. "Thanks." I line up Sam's toiletries on the counter and put his washables in the machine. I step into the trashcan to push the thong under the lint so that I don't have to look at it. Then I zip up the suitcase and put it on the shelf over the door.

I look at Chris. "Please don't say anything. Please just let it go, okay?"

"Okay. After I say this: Just because you can't have a baby doesn't give him the right to screw someone else."

My eyes widen at him. "How do you always seem to know what I'm thinking?"

"I just do. But it doesn't give him a free pass, Sara. You don't owe him anything. You don't have to make it up to him."

"It's fine," I say. "Let's get ready to go to dinner. I hope you brought some nice clothes."

"Oh, sweetheart. I'm always ready for anything." He smiles at me.

Chapter 11

After I shower, I meticulously dry my hair and put on make-up. I get one of the nicest dresses I own out of my closet and slide the folds of brown satin over my head. It's a long, backless halter dress with a slit up the right thigh. I reach behind me to fasten the neck. There are three people in this house that I could ask for help, but I can think of a good reason to avoid at least two of them. When I can't get it in the end, I look at my options. I decide Short Mark is the best way to go. I leave it undone while I finish my hair. I pull half of it up into a messy bun, and clip little bits of bling randomly throughout. I sigh as I look in the mirror. "Well, Sara," I say to my reflection. "That's as good as it's going to get." It doesn't matter what I do, I'm going to feel inferior standing next to the Ice Queen.

I walk down the hall to Short Mark's room and I knock on the door. He pulls it open and his jaw drops. He lets out a low whistle. "Geez, Shorty. If I had known you dressed up this nice I would have taken you to a nicer restaurant in DC." He smiles.

"Thanks. But can you help? I can't –" I gesture uselessly towards my neck and turn around. I lift my hair off of my neck with one hand and hold the top of the dress in place with the other while Short Mark does the buttons. I'm standing in the doorway when the door to Chris's room opens and he steps out.

I swear my heart misses a beat. Chris is unbelievable in a suit, and this one is practically a tuxedo. He isn't wearing a tie, the top button of his shirt is undone and I can see the lines of his neck. His throat is tight, like he is stressed. A tie is hanging from his left hand.

"You all right there?" Short Mark asks me. "You seem a little flushed suddenly." He slides his hand along the top of my shoulder as he finishes the buttons. "Hey, Eck. Where's your tie?"

Chris holds it up. "I was going to ask you if you thought I had to wear it."

Short Mark nods. "I think there is a dress code at this place. But, maybe it's just a jacket, not a tie." He shrugs. "You could risk it." He gives a wry smile. "I hardly think they're going to turn you away. Even if you show up in board shorts and a muscle shirt."

I laugh. "I wouldn't."

Short Mark jabs me in the back. "I'm sure you wouldn't." He peeks over my shoulder. "Doesn't she look awesome, Eck?" Chris nods mutely.

"Why do you always call him Eck?" I turn to ask Short Mark.

"Because they always call me Evans and 'Blond Mark' Cannadiak to make it easier. I don't really let most people refer to me as 'Short Mark' as a general rule of thumb. But, for you Shorty, I can make an exception."

"That's good," I snort. "I didn't have any intention of stopping. Hey, did you guys actually have these in your suitcase?" I gesture towards their clothes.

"No," Short Mark says. "We pulled them out of the closet in here. So thoughtful of you to keep our sizes. Obviously we brought them with us, you idiot."

"Why? Why would you bring a suit for a weekend at my house? How did you fit it all in your suitcase?"

Chris smiles. "I told you, I'm always prepared for anything. And we spend a significant amount of time on the road. I've packed a few suitcases." He turns suddenly and walks back into his room. He quickly comes out again. "The car is here. Where are Sammy-boy and the Ice Queen?"

I burst out laughing.

"What did I say?" Chris asks.

"That's what I call her too."

Chris smiles. "I knew you had some name for her. Someday I'm going to have to sit down with you and figure out what you call everyone behind their backs."

I feign offense. "I don't call *everyone* something behind their backs."

Chris smiles again and grabs my hand. He kisses it before letting it go. "Whatever. Round up the troops, we've got reservations."

Short Mark goes down the stairs in front of us. He is calling out, "The bus is leaving in two minutes! Be on it or be left behind!"

Sam and Anna step out of the office. They have both changed, although I have no idea when. Sam looks like he is ready for a day at the office, and I imagine Anna is dressed how she would for work as well. What other clothes would she have with her? The three of us are definitely more dressed up than the two of them, but they both seem a little overdressed for desk work. I've always thought Sam dressed a little too nicely for work.

Despite herself, she can't hide her reaction to the sight of Chris and Short Mark dressed up. All men look better in suits – they just do. And it definitely makes Short Mark even more wonderful than he already is. But Chris is unbelievable. There has never been, in all of history, a man who makes a suit look better. Anna is frozen in the hallway at the sight of him with her jaw hanging open.

I point to my chin, then hers. "You've got a little drool there, honey."

She looks daggers at me and then turns abruptly to head for the front door. Sam smiles at me. "You look amazing, Sara."

I nod as I step past him towards the door. "We're going to be late, Sam. Let's go."

Anna is standing, struck dumb again, on the front porch looking at our ride to the restaurant. Maybe I just got used to the limos carting us around DC, but I think I would have been surprised if anything else had been waiting for us. "I thought you were kidding about the car," she says quietly.

"Good evening Mr. Evans, Mr. Eck." The driver nods to Chris and Short Mark as he opens the door for us to get in. I step past Anna and climb into the back of the car. Chris is right on my tail and Short Mark is just behind him. Chris nudges me towards the middle of the corner seat – it runs along the back of the driver's seat and then curves to run down the driver's side of the vehicle. There is a bar that runs down the passenger side. I sit in the curve of the seat, right where Chris directs me. He sits on my left, facing the back seat, and Short Mark sits on my right, facing the bar. I'm not sure how they manage to take up so much space, but they've both spread out so that the only place left to sit is the back seat.

Anna gets in and glances around before settling in the back seat. Sam sits next to her, but he is staring at me and the guys. "Nice ride," he says.

"Thanks," Short Mark replies. "I keep one in every town." I know he is just goading Sam, but I keep my mouth clamped shut.

Chris reaches over into the bar and pulls out a hard lemonade. I didn't even see him get a key, but he pops off the top and hands it to me. "Evans?" Short Mark nods and Chris pops the top on a beer and hands it to him. Then he looks pointedly at Sam, who also nods. Chris opens a beer for Sam and then one more. He puts the key down and takes a swig without ever even glancing in the Ice Queen's direction.

She clears her throat, but Chris turns to me and says, "I never did tell you how fantastic you look tonight, Baby Girl." I can see Sam flinch.

"What did you call her?" he asks.

"Her given name. Surely you've heard the story, Sammy." Chris looks at him with mock surprise. "It's really a very cute story. See, Joe and Betty couldn't decide –"

"I know the story," Sam interrupts. "I just didn't realize you did."

"Oh. Well, I do."

"Well, *I* don't," Anna says.

Short Mark looks at her. "Really? Sammy hasn't told you? Hm. That surprises me." He looks back at me. "How far is it to this place, Shorty?"

"I don't know. A half hour, maybe?"

The ride to the restaurant was beginning to look like a disaster, but it actually isn't. Anna sits and sulks in the corner the whole way there. Chris and Short Mark are unexpectedly nice to Sam and they talk about the places they have all traveled to. A couple of beers go down, and the conversation seems to get even easier. Anna is not offered a single drink the whole way. I'm surprised that even Sam seems to be ignoring her.

At the restaurant we are greeted by name as soon as we walk in. I'm almost surprised, but then I remember that two of our party are major rock stars and are easily recognizable. "Good evening, Mr. Evans, Mr. Eck, Mr. Clarke. Right this way, please."

We are shown to a six top in the corner of the restaurant. There are several waiters standing by. "Mrs. Clarke?" one of them says to me as he pulls back a chair at one end of the table. Chris is already standing behind the chair to my right, and Short Mark is at my left. Sam resignedly walks to the seat directly across from me and Anna pulls her own chair out between Sam and Chris. She sits down in a huff. Chris and Short Mark seem to be going to a lot of trouble to exclude her as much as possible.

"You don't mind if we sit next to your wife, do you Sam? It's just we don't get to see her very often and we would really like to make the most of our trip." Short Mark has a look of innocence on his face that I can see straight through. I know he is still trying to make a point to the Ice Queen – that he is here to see me, not meet them.

Sam shakes he head, "Of course not." What he is supposed to say? "I don't ever see her either" would make him sound like an awful husband.

As I sit down, the waiter places my napkin in my lap. Chris and Short Mark both wait until I am seated before sitting down. The waiters hand us menus and then quietly step away. A single waiter immediately steps forward and introduces himself as Carl, our waiter for the evening. He pulls out a bottle of champagne and looks at Short Mark, who nods. Carl looks over his shoulder and two waiters return quickly, placing champagne flutes in front of each of us while Carl pours. He tells us to take a moment to look over the menus before he quietly retreats. They really seem to be tripping over themselves to provide the best service they can. I wonder what Short Mark told them because they are ignoring Anna as much as possible.

"Whatever you want tonight, Shorty," Short Mark says to me. "I feel like celebrating!"

I smile weakly. Sam speaks up from the end of the table, "No, no. We got off to a rough start, I think. I appreciate you making arrangements for dinner and the car. Dinner is on me." He looks at Short Mark, daring him to disagree. "Not that that changes anything, darling." He smiles at me. "You can still order anything you like."

Short Mark smiles at Chris and then looks at Sam. "Fine by me, my good man. Thanks."

Dinner goes surprisingly well, as well as the limo ride. The drink is flowing and the men are discussing everything from cars to the economy to the best website to order hiking boots (don't ask.) Anna is visibly getting more and more angry, but I'm not sure who she is more mad at – me or Sam. She volleys her glares between the two of us equally.

Sam gets me going after a few drinks, comparing the guys in the band. "Who plays the loudest?"

"Definitely Blond Mark."

"Sings the worst?"

"Drew." Chris and Short Mark both laugh loudly at that one.

"Takes the longest to get ready?"

"*Definitely* Blond Mark." They laugh even louder.

"Eats the most?"

"Um, Chris I think." I glance in his direction and he nods sheepishly.

"Funniest?"

"Short Mark."

"Hey!" says Chris at the same time Anna bursts out laughing.

"You let her call you 'Short Mark'?" she scoffs.

"Yes, I do. It's a term of endearment." Short Mark smiles at me.

"I love you too, dear," I tell him.

"I know you do, Shorty."

Anna's voice is way too loud for the relatively quiet restaurant when she squawks out, "Best fuck? Who in the group is the best fuck, Sara? Or have you not had a chance to compare them *all* yet?"

There's a beat of silence as most of the restaurant looks in our direction. Chris puts one hand up in apology and says, "I'm sorry, everyone. She has had too much to drink. Please continue with your dinners."

Our table is still silent, but Short Mark breaks the tension, as only he can. "Oh, me. Definitely."

"Sara?" Sam looks at me. "Do you think we could talk for a second?" He nods his head in the direction of the bar. I nod and get up to follow him. A waiter leaps forward and pulls out my chair for me. He puts his hand out for my napkin. Chris and Short Mark stand up in unison until I step away from the table when they sit back down. I'm a little worried about leaving them alone with Anna. There might be bloodshed.

I make eyes at Chris. He usually seems to know what I'm thinking so I very carefully channel, "Be nice!" in his direction before I leave. I see him nod at me from the corner of my eye. It makes me smile.

Sam puts his hand on the small of my bare back and leads me to the bar. We sit at a high table and immediately a waiter puts napkins in front of both us and asks us if we would like a drink. Sam orders a scotch on the rocks and I ask for a sex on the beach, just to make Sam consider the possibilities.

"You've made your point, Sara," Sam says as the waiter goes to the bar for our drinks. "You can call off your dogs now."

"I don't know what you're talking about."

"Oh, yes you bloody well do."

"First of all, you are not British. Stop pretending. And, I *don't*. I haven't asked them to do anything. They are very protective of me. They did not like the way Anna treated me. Neither did I, actually, but they took it more personally than I did."

"I'm sorry about that. She's very insecure. And she really wanted to meet them, which is why I let her come. It was a mistake. I'm sorry."

The waiter brings our drinks.

"Why are they so protective of you?" Sam asks.

I tell him the story of Walter Anderson at the diner in DC.

"Why didn't you press charges?" Sam is indignant.

"I didn't need to. They arrested him anyway."

Sam looks almost hurt as he quietly asks, "Why didn't you tell me before?"

"When?"

"Okay, fair enough." He sighs and stands up. "Let's go back now.

But seriously, you could back off a bit."

I almost say that *I* haven't done anything and then I remember the drool comment. "I haven't done anything she didn't have coming. And you know it." I consider asking about the thong before I get up. But now is not the time or place. I think I would rather just forget it like I asked Chris to.

I'm not sure what they said to Anna while we were gone, but she looks subdued when we get back. We get through the rest of the meal without a word from her.

In the limo, on the way home, Short Mark starts to test me on songs again. He sings a few lines of a song, then stops and looks at me to finish. I've had enough to drink that I play along. By the time we get home, I feel like we've made it through a hefty chunk of the eighties and nineties. Short Mark is practically crowing. "I can't believe it! That is the most amazing thing I've ever heard!"

Sam looks really proud, and possessive, as he reaches out to put his hand on my back to walk into the house. But his hand hits Chris's because *he* is doing the same thing. Chris had the exact same look on his face until he met Sam's hand.

My husband can be a bit of an angry drunk, and he has definitely had too much to drink. I'm wary the second he opens his mouth. "I think I'll take *my wife* upstairs to *our* room, if that is okay with her bodyguards."

Chris's face is like thunder but he doesn't say anything. Short Mark glances back and forth between them and then ducks inside – to avoid the brewing battle, I imagine.

But Anna speaks up first. "Actually, *Sam*. I would like you to take me to a hotel. I don't think I want to stay here tonight."

I freeze in my tracks and Sam almost trips over me. Short Mark is hovering just inside the door, but Chris seems to have relaxed suddenly. He is the only one with a huge smile on his face.

Sam turns around slowly to look at Anna, who has planted her feet on the sidewalk. She is standing with her hands on her hips and a look of fury on her face. "I *don't* want to stay here tonight," she repeats.

Sam's voice is very cool, "And I've had a few drinks so I can't exactly drive you anywhere. If you don't want to stay here, call a cab."

Anna looks like she has been slapped. I can feel the indignation emanating from her.

"What did you just say?" she asks quietly.

"Anna, you are making a scene, *and only embarrassing yourself.*"

Sam enunciates his words carefully, like he is trying to convey a warning.

Anna suddenly shoves past us into the house. She pushes Short Mark out of her way when she bursts through the door and marches upstairs. I can hear her bedroom door slam before we even get to the threshold.

Short Mark wanders into the music room and sits down at his keyboard. He idly taps on the keys. Chris and I follow him in and sit on the couch. Sam stands in the doorway, looking at us. "I'm going to bed," he says gruffly.

I nod. "Good night."

As soon as he is gone, Chris takes my hand. "Well, that was fun," he says brightly.

"Yes," agrees Short Mark. "I always enjoy watching people embarrass themselves."

"Ah, I finally understand," I say glumly.

"What?" Chris turns to look at me.

"Why you guys like to hang out with me so much."

"Yup, that's it," Chris agrees, teasing me. "We love to see you embarrass yourself."

"I thought so." I put my head back on the couch. Chris squeezes my hand lightly, and then I pull mine free. I fall asleep without remembering anything else.

When I wake up Saturday morning, Sam is standing in the doorway of the music room, in exactly the same position as the last time I saw him. "I'm leaving."

I sit up groggily. Short Mark is asleep on the other couch and Chris is stretched across the middle of the floor. "What? Now?"

"Yeah, we're going to get down to Atlanta for a company outing this afternoon."

"A company outing?"

"Yeah, it's a 'team building' thing."

"Oh. Okay. When will you be back?"

"I don't know, Sara."

"Okay, well, I love you. Travel safe." I give him a weak smile.

"Yes, I will." With that, he leaves. I hear him greet Anna in the kitchen. "Yes, the car is outside. Would you like to say good-bye to –?"

But she cuts him off. "They're assholes, Sam. I just want to leave."

I can see the side of Chris's face rise in a smile. When the door slams I start laughing. Chris rolls over and sits up. "Good morning!"

he says brightly. "I love your new pajamas."

I look down at my dress, and then I reach up to feel the mess on the top of my head. Hm, maybe I should have brushed it before I went to sleep. Yuck. I didn't wash my face either. "I think I'm going to take a shower." I get up and stretch, then walk into the hall.

I freeze and listen when I hear Short Mark's voice. "Did you hear that? We're assholes."

Chris laughs quietly. "I'm sure she feels that way about a lot of people. I'm sure most people revert to some form of asshole-ism when they are forced into her company."

Short Mark laughs. Suddenly he's serious. "Do you think it's her?"

"Oh, there's no doubt in my mind."

"What is Shorty going to do?"

"Continue to ignore it, I'm sure."

I don't want to hear any more. I go upstairs to take my shower.

Chapter 12

The guys have already gotten clean, and found food by the looks of it, by the time I get back downstairs. They're sitting in the music room with a notebook. Short Mark is writing and Chris is saying, "I don't know if I'll finish it. I don't even know if I'll release it if I do."

"Oh you will, and you will. I just think it would be nice to slow it down there and I think six –" He stops suddenly when he sees me.

"Morning, Shorty."

Chris turns around and blinds me with his smile. "Good morning. How was your shower?"

I nod. "Morning, boys. What are we doing today? Working on the album?"

Chris explains that most of the album is "done" already. They still have a couple of songs to record and they are still "tweaking" two of them, but for the most part they are focusing on the tour now.

Short Mark nods. "We have to choreograph the show, well, finish choreographing."

"And then what?" I ask.

"Then we rehearse."

"Until the end of September?" That seems like a long time to me.

"That's really not that long." Can he hear my thoughts? "We have to learn the whole show."

I nod. "Is there dancing involved or something?"

They both howl with laughter. "No," Short Mark wipes tears from his face. "It's just the order of the songs and anything we want to add or do special. But we have to be able to play them perfectly, every time. Memorize the words, practice intros, stuff like that."

"Well, get to work. I'm going to go change some sheets."

I go upstairs and start in my room. I rip the sheets off of my bed. I know it's weird to feel the need to change my sheets because my husband slept on them, but it's the situation I have found myself in. When I go into Anna's room, my mouth drops open.

"Chris!" I yell. I can hear him running up the stairs.

"Where are you?" he calls.

I can't seem to make any more words so I step into the hall. The look on my face must be pretty bad, because both Chris and Short Mark, who is right behind him, jump.

"What? What is it?"

I point into the guest room and they both rush over.

Short Mark lets out a low whistle. "Sweet mother of..." he whispers.

The room is *trashed*. "I can't believe she did this and none of us heard anything," I say stupidly.

Chris looks at Short Mark and nods before turning to go back downstairs. Short Mark takes out his phone and starts taking pictures of the damage.

"What are you doing?"

He winks at me. "Recording this for posterity. You know, before we clean it up."

"Oh. What should I do?"

"You could clean it up, or you could leave it for Sammy-boy to deal with. You're definitely sending him some of these pictures though."

"Why?" I scoff. "Do you think he'll make her pay for damages?"

"I highly doubt it. I would imagine he would send me the bill first."

"You?! Why?"

"Oh, this is our fault, as she sees it, I'm sure. If we weren't so mean to her, if we hadn't hurt her fragile feelings, she wouldn't have felt the need to destroy your house."

Chris is carrying a box of big trash bags when he comes back in. "Definitely our fault," he agrees.

Thankfully the actual damage is kind of limited. Anything fragile that had been in the room, a picture frame, a vase, and the lamp, is now smashed into little bits. The sheets are destroyed, but the bed is okay. She yanked all of the drawers out of the dresser and threw them around, but only one got scratched – although the walls didn't fare *as* well. She pulled the curtains down, ripping the rod out of the wall in the process, but the curtains themselves are not damaged. Chris surprises me by being able to repair the damage to the wall and re-hang the curtains.

"What?" he asks as I watch him.

"I just didn't think pretty boys were so handy around the house."

Short Mark snorts. "Usually they're not, but Eck is a special specimen." The turns away, muttering "Pretty boy!" under his breath and laughing.

After we clean the mess up, we go out to grab some lunch. We go to my favorite pizza place. People stare, but again, it could just be because Chris is so amazingly hot. I'm guessing a few people recognize Short Mark, but they can't quite place him, so we get to eat in peace.

Back home, the boys go back into the music room. Now that it is later in the day, their West Coast counterparts are up, so they can video-conference. I decide to give them some space to work, and I call Matt to see if he's busy.

"I've got a hot date tonight – well, she's okay looking, but I'm free until then."

"Great. I need to get out of the house for a little while, can I come over?"

I peek into the music room. Chris and Short Mark are both huddled around the computer and I can hear Drew's voice. I quietly back out and leave them to work. I turn the radio on in my car on the way to Matt's house, something I almost never do. I really prefer cds or my iPod because I hate commercials. The only song I have time to hear is Evansgate's latest big hit. I'm laughing when I get out of the car.

"What's so funny?" Matt asks from the door.

"Nothing. Really. I'm just looking at the world differently these days."

Matt smiles. "Good. You needed a new outlook on life."

He grabs a couple of beers from the fridge and we sit in his sun room – ironically named because the trees in his yard create so much shadow. I tell him the story of the Ice Queen and everything that happened last night. Then I tell him about the state of the guest room this morning.

"She sounds like a real prize," Matt says.

"Chris and Short Mark think that Sam is sleeping with her."

Matt snorts some of his beer. "Why? Do you?"

"I sure as hell hope not. I mean, even if he was cheating, I would hope he would have better taste than that!"

"Okay, but that's not what I asked. Do you think he is, even if you hope that he isn't?"

"I don't know..." I say slowly. I can't bring myself to tell him about the pink thong. Maybe Chris was right and I do want to keep the idea of my husband cheating on me to myself.

My phone rings. It's Chris. "Oh!"

"What?" asks Matt. "Is it Sam?"

"No! It's Chris."

"Are we upset about this? I thought that we liked him."

"I do! I just didn't tell him I was leaving. I didn't think he would notice."

"Well – answer your phone! Before he assumes you were abducted."

I nod. "Yes?" I say very meekly.

"Sara! Where are you?"

"I, uh, decided to give you some space to work."

"Where are you?"

"I'm at Matt's house. It's, like, two minutes away."

"You nearly gave me a heart attack! I've been looking everywhere for you!"

"I'm sorry! You were working so hard, I didn't want to disturb you."

"Please come home. We'll stop for the day, okay?"

"On my way!" I hang up and Matt puts his hand out for my beer bottle. "Thanks for the beer," I tell him. "And for listening."

"Whatever. You live a very exciting life now. I like to live vicariously."

"You are part of my life dearest; if it's exciting, so are you."

"Hardly. Will I get to hang out with you and your new friends this weekend?"

"I thought you had a hot date."

"I corrected myself; I told you she was only okay looking. But that's tonight. Let's go out tomorrow?"

"I'll see. Maybe you can just come over and hang out or something."

He nods and I take off. Chris is waiting outside. "Geez!" I call as I get out of the car. "I said I would be right back."

"I know. But I flew a long way to see you. And then you take off on me."

"You came a long way to meet Sam, remember?"

He puts his arms around me. "No, sweetheart, I came to see you. You just offered that as a reason to make the trip."

We go into the house and Short Mark looks up from the computer he is working at. "Shorty! Why did you disappear on us?"

"I was just trying to let you work." I add, "Sorry!" quickly when I see Chris's face. "I will stay right here for the rest of the time you are here."

Chris takes my hand. "I will hold on, just to be sure." He smiles at me.

We spend Sunday lying around the house and shooting pool. The guys are impressed with my skill on the pool table until I point out that there is a pool table in my house. "I'm alone and bored all the time. What do you think I do with all that time? I have to fill it somehow."

Matt brings beer in the late afternoon. He had met Chris the last time, but I could tell he was excited to meet Mark Evans. Matt was actually the one who introduced me to Evansgate and long before they had their first number one.

"Matt is a huge fan," I warn them. "He is actually the reason I listen to your music, so be nice."

Chris smiles, "So, without this man, we would never have met?"

"Probably not. Allison wouldn't have bothered to get tickets to that concert if you weren't my favorite band."

Short Mark gasps with mock indignation. "Are you telling me that if this guy hadn't made you love our music, you never would have come to that conclusion on your own?"

"I take all of my musical cues from him."

"Well," Short Mark puts on a haughty voice, "he apparently has good taste, so I guess I can accept that."

Matt wins himself a lot of favor when he shows up with an entire case. Short Mark wants to know how we met. I look at Matt. He starts, "We had a couple of classes together freshman year."

"Ah," Short Mark agrees knowingly, "you couldn't resist her beauty? We all seem to be suckers for it."

"Hardly! He just wanted help on his chem homework."

Chris shakes his head at me. "Sometimes your innocence is so cute. That's what they all say, sweetheart." Then he turns to Matt, "What is it that you do again?"

Matt laughs. "I'm a bio-chemist."

Short Mark snorts his beer. "Yes, I'm sure he needed help with his Intro to Chemistry homework."

"Whatever," I say. "It's never been like that."

"Yes," Matt agrees, deadpan. "Apparently because she has seen me naked."

"I have not! I told you that, Matthew!"

Chris and Short Mark are purple in the face. Chris is laughing so hard, he is fighting tears. He turns to Matt, "She can be so cruel."

"That's what I said!"

"Okay, enough!" I interject. "Be nice to me, or I'm going to kick you all out. This is my house, remember."

Matt wanders around the front of the house and then comes back into the kitchen. He points his thumb in the direction of the formal living room. "I like what you've done with the place."

"They're theirs," I wave my hand towards Chris and Short Mark.

"Yes, I worked that out." Matt laughs at me. He turns to the guys,

"Have you actually been playing? I bet Sam loved that."

Short Mark smiles. "Not as much as his girlfriend did."

Matt looks at me. "The Ice Queen?"

"Sam never offered an opinion on the subject, *actually*," I say.

Chris looks at Matt. "Do you play?"

"Yes!" I jump in. "Yes he does! Very well, no matter what he tells you."

Matt is staring daggers at me. "Not really."

But it doesn't take much to convince Matt to pick up Chris's guitar. We spend the rest of the time in the music room, the guys playing Van Morrison and trying to convince me to sing.

"Isn't that just the craziest thing you've ever seen?" Matt asks the guys about my "ability." I stick my tongue out at him and he winks at me. "It just makes you special, honey."

"Yeah, short bus special," Short Mark says.

Short Mark is playing Van's "Someone Like You" on the keyboard and to distract them all, I start singing. Matt and Chris start playing and I can't help but finish the song. Chris keeps his eyes on me and changes to "Into the Mystic", the song he played the day we first met. I sing it for him, but then I don't sing again until they play "These are the Days" because it's my favorite.

"How do you know how to play all these songs?" I ask.

Short Mark points to his tablet, which has a special spot on his keyboard to sit, like a music stand. "I have the music." He smiles. Oh, exactly like a music stand.

"But what about you guys?" I ask Matt and Chris.

Chris answers first. "It's easier to follow someone, remember? I just play off of what Evans plays."

Matt nods in agreement. "I mean, I've heard the songs plenty, so I know what to expect."

Sometimes Short Mark sings, sometimes they just play. I know that Matt is in heaven, playing with his favorite musicians. I close my eyes and lay back; this is pretty close to my heaven too. Eventually, I drift to sleep. The last song I remember is "Tupelo Honey".

I wake up in Chris's arms. "Shh, go back to sleep. I'm just taking you to bed."

"I can walk," I say sleepily.

"It's okay," he assures me. "I've been really lazy for days. I need the exercise."

"Well, in that case, feel free to walk around a bit." I lean my head against his shoulder and breathe in his smell. "I don't mind."

He laughs softly. "I appreciate that." But he gently lays me in my bed and pulls the blankets over me. He kisses my forehead and then brushes my hair away. "Sleep now."

I wait until he is gone and then whisper, "I love you."

Chapter 13

Chris and Short Mark fly out Monday afternoon. "We really have to get back to the studio," Chris is apologizing.

I can't completely keep the sadness out of my voice, "I know."

"We'll talk every day, I promise."

I'm trying really hard not to sulk. "I know. I'm sorry, I'm being stupid. It's just really lonely around here now when you're gone."

His eyes tighten. "It won't be long. You'll come to LA."

I stand and watch them go through security. Chris waves before they turn the corner and go out of my sight. I stay there for a long time.

On my way home, I call Matt at work. "Did you have a nice time last night?"

I can hear his smile through the phone. "That was the best night of my life."

"Does that mean your hot date Saturday night wasn't?"

"Number one, I told you she is only okay. Number two, that's about the best thing I can say about her."

"Ouch. Not going to be seeing this one again?"

"What? I said she's okay! That's a lot better than the last couple I've had the pleasure of taking out."

"I wish you would find someone and settle down."

"I wish you would leave your asshole husband, lower your standards, and marry me."

"As if. I would make you crazy."

"Indeed. But everyone's crazy, honey." He pauses. "Are they gone?"

"I'm on my way back from the airport now."

"Be careful there. I think you could be in trouble."

"I think you're right. But I'm sure that there's not much I can do about it now."

"Be careful," he repeats. "One night this week? Sine's?"

"Definitely. It's summer, and I'm bored."

"You could come to the lab, you know. I'm sure I could get you a job."

"What? And give up my summers?"

He laughs. "Call me."

I purposely waited until the guys left to call Sam about the guest room and what Anna did. I email him the pictures before I dial.

"Hello, Sara."

"Hi, Sam. I sent you an email."

"Okay."

He isn't even going to ask why? "I'd like to talk to you."

"Yes, that is usually the reason to make a phone call."

Okay, fine. If he won't ask, I'll just tell him. "Sam, Anna trashed our house."

"I know."

"What?!" How could he possibly know? Did Short Mark – no, he couldn't have because he doesn't have Sam's number.

"She told me. She feels really bad."

"Oh, that's great. You know, I was the one who cleaned up. She could have apologized to me."

"Don't make this into something it doesn't have to be, Sara."

"Is she going to pay for the damages?"

"What damages?"

"Oh, I don't know... the broken lamp, the broken vase, the broken picture frame, the scratches in the walls, the sheets that she destroyed, any of that? I don't know what she told you, Sam, but I was serious. She *trashed our house*."

"And she is sorry. Let it go."

"So, that's a no, she's not going to pay for the damages?"

"She was angry, Sara. It wasn't the best way to handle it, but it's don. It can't be undone. Now let it go."

I can't help the bitter laugh that escapes when I remember what Short Mark said about how it was their fault. "That's lovely, Sam. Have a great day. I love you."

"You're really going to make this difficult, aren't you? Christ, Sara, just let it go."

"I'm pretty sure hanging up the phone and ending our conversation about it *is* letting it go."

"Fine." The line cuts off. He must have hung up on me.

I immediately dial my sister.

"Gah!" I squawk when she answers.

"Well, hello, Sara. Are you having a good day?"

"You are not going to believe the weekend I had!" I tell her all about Anna, Ruth's Chris, and the trashed room.

"Wow. That's. Um. Wow."

"Yeah, that's what I said."

"Other than that, did you have a good time with the guys?"

"Of course! Everything is more fun with them. I'm going to LA next week!"

"I would hate for you to go more than a few days without them."

"I know you're being smart, but I really would hate it. I'm alone here, remember? I'm sure it's going to be a lot more fun hanging out with them in LA."

"I'm sure you're right. Have fun. And, Sara?"

"Yeah?"

"Be careful."

I'm really excited about my trip to LA. Chris sent me a ticket and it's first class! I know it's stupid, but I've never flown first class and I've always wanted to. When I tell Chris, he laughs. "I almost want to fly out there, just to fly back with you so I can be with you for your first time."

"Okay," I challenge him, "but, really, that's just wasting money. You shouldn't have even got me a ticket in the first place."

"Oh, yes I should have. Even first class, I probably have a long way to go to make up the dinner tab."

"Good point. You really did kind of bleed me dry there. Okay, I'll even let you fly here to go with me."

He is quiet. "I'm kidding Chris!"

"I'm not. I wouldn't mind having the time just to be with you."

"That's really very wasteful. You'll just have to wait until I get there."

Honestly though, I'm not surprised to find him waiting for me on the other side of security at the airport. "Surprise!" he says. "I really didn't want to miss your first time in first class." He smiles sheepishly. "But I flew coach out here, if that makes you feel better."

"Well, I'm sure you'll appreciate the flight back that much more."

He nods earnestly. "You have no idea. There is really no room back there." I glance at his knees. It hadn't occurred to me that he would have a harder time than most fitting into the nonexistent space of a coach class seat.

"You shouldn't have done that. That was just torturing yourself for no reason."

"It's okay. I'm here now! Just in time to fly back!" He puts out his arm for me to take as we walk towards the gate and he takes my carry all from me. "I'll get that."

I can already feel myself relaxing, just because he is here. I lean my head in and sniff his shoulder. He gives me a funny look. "What? I like the way you smell. And you haven't given me a hug yet, so I didn't get a chance to smell you."

He stops suddenly in the middle of the hall. "You're right. How did I miss that?" He drops my suitcase and grabs me in a big hug. "Hi, sweetheart. I missed you."

I pull my head back. "What?" he asks.

"You smell like an airplane." I wrinkle my nose. "It's not so good on you."

He laughs as he picks my suitcase back up. "Sorry, love. I'll take a shower when we get in."

I notice that people are staring at us, and I point it out to him.

"Do you think they know who I am?" he asks.

"Maybe. Or maybe it's just because you're a million feet tall."

"Could be," he agrees with a wry smile.

But when we get to our gate and sit down to wait, I can tell that the group of girls sitting across from us recognize him. I poke him in the ribs. "Take pity and offer yourself for a picture."

"No way. I'm not that pretentious."

"If they ask, will you?"

"What do you think I should do?"

"What would you have done if I wasn't here to offer an opinion?"

"We'll just wait and see if they work up the nerve."

"What are we going to do in LA?"

"Whatever you want. But I promised the guys we would hang out with them for a while. And Bethany and Angie want to meet you. *And* I have to work in the studio some."

"I'm up for whatever. I've never been to LA, so you can lead the way."

One of the girls chooses that moment to get brave. "Excuse me, but are you Chris Eck?"

He smiles at her and she nearly faints. "As a matter of fact, I am."

She nods, like she is encouraging herself. "Do you think I could get a picture with you?"

Chris glances at me and smiles. "Sure," he tells her and he stands up. The poor girl's eyes look like they are going to fall out of her head. She looks to her friends and waves them over. They take turns posing with him and he gives them each a hug.

"Thanks again!" the girls call out as they head back to their seats.

I laugh at him. "I thought I was special, but you treat all the girls the same."

"Yup," he reaches for my hand as our flight is announced. "I fly back and forth across the country in the same day for every girl I meet."

"I knew it," I feign insult. "I'm not special at all."

He elbows me. "Come on, you idiot. Get on the plane."

"Hey! I bruise easily!"

Chris stops and looks at me. "Oh, I know," he says very seriously.

I follow him down the jetway, but when we get to the end he steps aside to let me go in front. "You want the window seat, don't you?" he says. I nod. I'm not surprised how well he knows me anymore. "Then you go first."

I step in front of him, walk to the sixth row, and step into my seat. Chris hands my suitcase to a flight attendant to put away.

"Wow, they don't even make you lug your own baggage around in first class? A girl could get used to this, you know."

"Go ahead. This is your life, sweetheart."

I sit down and push my shoulder bag under the seat in front of me. Chris gets the attention of the flight attendant and orders me a vodka cranberry. "It'll help," he says. When I look at him, he says, "I know you're a nervous flier."

"Not with you."

Chris smiles and sits down next to me. "Drink it anyway. I like my women loose."

I punch him in the arm and sink back. But I do drink it when she brings it. Chris immediately orders me another one and a beer for himself. "Not loose enough?" I ask as she walks away.

"Not yet." Then he changes tack. "How's Sam? Where's Sam?"

"He's actually still in Atlanta. He's been in a much better mood since Ruth's Chris."

"That's good. When is he coming home next?"

"I don't know. I think he was going to come home this weekend, but I won't be there. He still might, I guess."

The flight attendant brings our drinks. "Do you wish you would have stayed home?"

"Not on your life! I don't care. He's left me to rot alone in that house plenty of times. I'm really looking forward to this!"

"Good. I was hoping you would say that." He smiles at me.

The flight is very pleasant, of course. But, three vodka cranberries will do that to you. I fall asleep for a little while and when I wake up, Chris is staring at me. "What?" I sit up. "Am I drooling?"

"A little." He laughs when I wipe my face and find it dry. "No, stupid. I just like to look at your beautiful face. You are so sweet when you sleep."

I'm falling in love with him. I know I am. I'm trying to stop. I think about Sam. I concentrate on how great he was with my mom. I remember all of the reasons that I fell in love with him in the first place.

The first time we went on a "date", Sam showed up at my house with flowers, chicken soup for my mom, and a movie rental. I told him I couldn't go out because my mom was sick and I had to stay with her. He didn't know what kind of sick, but that was the sweetest thing anyone had ever done. He started to come by all the time, and he would bring me something little and romantic (like a single Hershey's kiss) and something for my mom: crossword puzzles, magazines, and once, orange juice because he said that more vitamin C couldn't hurt anything.

I remember him at my mom's funeral, how he handled everything, but how devastated he was to lose her. He had so many wonderful things to say about her. He just held me while I cried and told me stories about the great things he remembered. He took a lot of time off of work for that, just to be with me. He got me excited about choosing a new place to live – and it helped to take my mind off of everything.

How many times did he schedule a long layover in Richmond so that he could surprise me? It was so romantic, the way he would sweep in with flowers and food. We would make the most of the few hours that he stole for us – I wasn't always the only one in that bed. That was when I started getting suitcases ready for him. I always had one on hand, just so that whenever he came he could get a fresh set of clothes and things.

Sam used to tell me that he loved me all the time. He would say it at the most random times, like when we were eating breakfast or grocery shopping. He would call in the middle of the night, from wherever in the world he was just to say those three little words. When he was home, he would grab my hand and say, "I love you, did you know that?" and I would laugh. I touch my cheek when I think about how he used to brush my hair back and tell me that I was the most beautiful woman on the planet.

When we were looking for our house, he was like a kid: so excited about all of them. He would tell me that I could have anything I wanted; he would make it happen for me. "But make it big, Baby Girl, because we are going to need some rooms to fill!" he said. I remember how excited he was to start a family. He was already talking about changing things so that he wouldn't have to travel anymore, even if it meant finding another job.

I try not to think about my fall from grace, or how fast things fell apart, but it's hard to keep my mind from going there. He started to pull away on the ride home from the doctor's office when they gave us the news. At first, it was hard to see, but the little cracks were there right away. He stopped surprising me, stopped telling me that he loved me, stopped talking, stopped calling, and at some point, stopped loving me. I wasn't good enough for him; I couldn't give him the family he wanted. I loved him so much – there was nothing I wouldn't do to make up for that. I wanted things to go back to the way they were, but we were broken. Is it my fault?

My little exercise is effective. My heart aches for my marriage. I miss Sam and what we used to have. I still love him very much. But it's a hard place to be. I'm stuck between what *was* great with Sam and what *could* be great with Chris. Sam and I can get it back... can't we?

I am quiet for a long time. Chris grabs my chin and pulls it towards him. "What are you thinking?"

"Nothing." I answer too quickly. He raises his eyebrows. "I was thinking about Sam." I see the hurt flash across his face, but he hides it quickly. That was why I didn't want to tell him. I try to distract him – and me. "When do we land?"

Chris looks at his watch. "Soon, I would guess." He reaches up and touches the screen in the headrest of the seat in front of him. "Twenty seven minutes."

Sure enough, the flight attendant comes by to ask us if we want a last drink. I shake my head, but Chris gets another beer. Then the captain comes on telling us to turn off all electronic devices in preparation for landing.

When we get off the plane and into the airport, I see a group of people in suits holding signs with names on them. "I always wanted to have someone standing there with a sign for me. It has to make you feel so special."

"I wouldn't know. My sign always says 'Evans'. But we don't need a sign. I know my driver." We step outside and head towards an area full of limos. Chris looks around for a minute and then smiles and starts towards a car.

"Hello, Mr. Eck," says the driver as he opens the door to a Town Car.

"What?" I say to Chris in mock surprise. "No limo?"

"Just get in and shut up." He gives my suitcase to the driver, who puts it in the trunk. I slide in and put my shoulder bag on the seat between us. Chris climbs in and grabs my bag. He scoots next to me and deposits my bag on his other side. He puts his arm around my shoulder. "I didn't fly across the country to sit on the other side of the car, sweetheart."

I wrinkle my nose at him. "You still smell like an airplane."

"Yeah, well, you don't smell like roses yourself." I laugh and then settle back to watch the scenery go by. "Was it everything you hoped for and more?" he asks me with a smile in his voice.

"Flying first class? I suppose. But I'm not going to lie. We could have been in the cargo hold and that would have been the best flight of my life." I wink at him. "So, I guess you tainted my first first class experience with your awesomeness."

He laughs. "I'd be upset, but that was a compliment, I think?" I nod. "I'll take 'em where I can get 'em."

"Yes, because I'm sure you're really hurting for compliments." He pulls me closer. I lay back into his chest, but keep my eyes out the window. When I'm with Chris it's hard to remember Sam. How can I forget my husband? I spin the rings on my finger. We're quiet for the rest of the drive.

I know nothing about LA, I'm learning. The studio that Evansgate works in most of the time isn't even in Los Angeles. It's in some place called Culver City, which I had never even heard of. Chris said it's because it is so much closer to Santa Monica, where they live. "You mean you don't live in Hollywood?"

Chris finds that amusing. "No, I don't. But it's not far."

"Beverly Hills?"

"Not far, either."

We drive straight to the studio. It's kind of early still, I guess because of the time difference, and the band is recording today. "Do you mind?" Chris asks.

"Not at all."

The inside of the recording studio is not what I expect. I guess I thought it would be bigger, and fancier. It's kind of nondescript and quite cramped, actually.

"Shorty!" Short Mark grabs me in a big hug. I get hugs from Drew and Blond Mark too.

"How was your flight?" Blond Mark asks with a wink.

"It was great, thanks. Oh, and I appreciate you sending Chris to fetch me." They all laugh.

"Okay," Short Mark says. "But he took the whole morning off for that stunt and we need to get to work. He takes me into the booth and shows me where I can sit.

There are already four people in there – and one of them I recognize. "Hi, Tom!"

"Hey, Sara! How was your flight?" He looks at Chris, though, when he asks.

"It was great. I'll be super good, I promise." I climb up to the seat that Short Mark had pointed at. The room is really small and the front wall is a big window facing the sound room. In front of the window there is a long table covered in sound equipment and things. At the back of the room there is a platform covered in carpet with three chairs. After I hoist myself up the front, I realize there are steps cut into the platform on the other side. Oops.

Chris gives me a huge smile (I think he might be laughing at me) and follows the other guys out. They file into the sound room, which already has their instruments in place.

Tom sits in the seat next to me. "They're just working today. This isn't the 'real deal' yet, if you will. If all goes well, though, they will release this song first when the album comes out."

I nod like I know what he is talking about. Then I sit back to listen, absolutely engrossed. The guys are getting settled and they are talking. It is really weird because the sound is coming in over a speaker. Although I can tell they are talking quietly, it sounds really loud in the booth. The guys are arranged in a U around Blond Mark, who sits at his drums. Short Mark stands at a keyboard with a microphone between Blond Mark and Chris. Drew sits with his guitar, but Chris stands with his bass at another microphone. Blond Mark also has a microphone, but Drew doesn't. He is the only one that doesn't ever sing. I remind myself to tease him about that. All of them have music stands in front of them.

They play the song once without any singing. One of the guys in the booth says something through a microphone, and oddly enough I can't hear what he's saying. But the guys are nodding. Drew holds his hand flat and makes a motion to Chris, who nods. I hear Blond Mark say, "But not until the third count." Chris nods again. His face is very serious, much more so than I'm used to seeing it.

The guy in the booth is talking again and I realize that the mics only go one way at a time. Short Mark turns around and is talking to Blond Mark. "Just start in slower, because I'm going to wait through two."

Drew shakes his head. "That's too long."

The guy in the booth says, "Do it longer and cut it later," but Short Mark starts shaking his head adamantly. The guy says something else about cutting and then pushes back from the table. "They're going to have to work this out," he says to us.

I'm engrossed in the conversation Evansgate is having in the sound room. They clearly disagree, but they're so relaxed about it. Tom calls my name twice before I respond. "Oh! Sorry! Yes, Tom?" I turn to face him.

He smiles at me. "I thought I would introduce you to the team while we are waiting for them to decide to try it both ways and then decide." Then he points out the guys in front of me. They are all wearing headphones and sitting in front of complicated sound boards. The one with the mic is Steve. The other two are Ted and Teddy. I'm not sure what they do, but they say, "Hi," and wave at me. "This is Sara, Chris's –" he stops and looks at me. "Friend?" he asks.

I nod. "Something like that." Tom smiles at me and then looks forward again.

I laugh as I hear Short Mark say, "Let's just record it both ways and then decide." Tom winks at me.

They start playing again and this time Short Mark starts singing. He only sings a couple of lines and they stop. Short Mark nods back at Blond Mark who starts a different intro and Short Mark sings the same two lines again. They stop again and Drew says, "Tom?" Tom gets up and walks out of the booth. A moment later he opens the door and steps into the sound room.

"Okay, Steve," he says. Steve nods at Ted or Teddy, I don't know which is which, and he fiddles with something. I can tell the guys are listening to playback that I can't hear.

When it stops though, I can hear Short Mark again. "I just think it fits better."

Drew shakes his head. "I'm telling you, Evans, it's too long. You can use it, just come in a count sooner."

Blond Mark turns to Tom. "What do you think?"

Tom looks through the window to Steve. "Play them both through two more times, one then the other, please." The guys listen quietly at first but they are talking before the playback is finished. When the speaker comes back on Tom is saying, "– just think it might be a good compromise. I know –" he says over Drew when he starts to say something. "But you have to consider the possibility that you both might, in fact, be right. Play it again," he says over his shoulder as he steps back out of the sound room.

A moment later he reappears in the booth. He smiles at me. "Sorry, but this probably isn't going to be very much fun for you. They need to get it done, though."

I nod. "I'm actually enjoying myself."

We both go back to listening as they record the third attempt to start the song. Same two lines, stop, playback. Tom goes over to the mic to talk to the guys. "It will work, at least for now, and you can change it later, if you need to."

Short Mark nods, and Blond Mark counts them off. They start the song for the fourth times, but this time they don't stop. I can't put my finger on it, but it sounds off for some reason, kind of flat. I like it, but it just seems so different. Steve puts it on playback again. And while they listen, Short Mark holds his hand up sometimes. Chris is concentrating on Short Mark, still more serious than I have ever seen him. He is also making notes on the music in front of him. When the song ends, Short Mark turns his back to us. "What do you think?"

Blond Mark says, "That seems fine. Eck?"

"I'll take front."

Blond Mark pretends to be offended. "You always take front."

Chris laughs. "Well, I'm the front man."

Short Mark nods towards the booth and Blond Mark counts them in again. This time through, Chris and Blond Mark sing back up and it sounds better, so much fuller – and more like Evansgate. I smile. But there is still something off. It sounds great, but I'm waiting for them to add something else, because it still seems like something is missing. They don't though. They sing the song exactly like that one more time.

I wish I could say that was the end of our time in the studio, but no. We spend hours there, recording, playing, listening (well, *I* actually couldn't hear anything) and doing it again. I can feel boredom setting in. Chris seems so different when he is in the sound room. Although the difference is intriguing, my bum is starting to get numb.

At one point Tom has food delivered, and the guys take a break to eat. "Are you going to give us trouble about eating our food again this time, Shorty, or can you finally just accept that you are part of this group?" Short Mark puts his arm around me as he asks me.

"I'll eat, thanks," I say dryly. "Tom asked me what I wanted specifically and ordered something for me."

Then they get back to work, and I can feel the numbness setting in again. Finally Short Mark says, "Let's sleep on it and try it again in the morning, okay?" Tom stands up and stretches. I follow suit. The guys carefully replace their instruments and leave the sound room. Drew is the last one out and I watch him lock the door. Tom is walking out of the booth, so I follow him.

Chris, breathtakingly beautiful, is leaning against the wall outside the booth. He smiles but he looks almost nervous when he asks, "What did you think?"

All of Evansgate is quiet, waiting for my answer. "My butt is numb."

Chris laughs and throws his arm over my shoulder. "Does that mean you hated it?"

"No, that means I sat there for a long time. I loved it."

Short Mark grabs my arm and spins me to face him. "Really?" When I nod, he says, "Sing it."

"Now?!"

Blond Mark says, "Yeah! Now! Great idea. Holst, get your guitar. If she can't sing it, she hated it, right?" He looks at Chris.

"Pretty much," Chris says.

Drew goes back into the sound room, but when he comes out, he is empty handed. "Come in here. It's stupid to drag it out there." He turns back around and everyone follows him in. Chris is dragging me, and I'm following most unwillingly.

"Of course," Short Mark is saying, "this would have been a better test if we had asked her to sing it back after she heard it the first time."

"We'll take what we can get," Blond Mark says. He sits down at his drums. "Might as well. Eck?"

Chris picks up his bass, and now I'm really nervous. Short Mark plonks some headphones over my ears and pushes me in front of a microphone in the middle of the U. "Just close your eyes," he whispers, "and pretend we're not here." I nod weakly. Then he walks back to his keyboard.

I close my eyes and listen to the music. Blond Mark counts us in. I'm sure I sound terrible, but I sing the whole song. Blond Mark and Chris even sing back up like they did for Short Mark.

"Well, I'm out of a job," Short Mark says.

"Let's get out of here," Blond Mark says. "She liked it."

Chapter 14

We step out onto the sidewalk and a car is already there waiting. It's a limo again. We all pile in and it takes us around, dropping Drew off first, then Chris and I are the next stop. "Home sweet home," Chris says and he gestures to the building in front of me. "Evans and I live here when we're recording."

"Then why didn't he get out too?"

"Oh, he'll be back later. After every session those two hash it out. They'll make us do something different tomorrow morning." He smiles at me.

"Okay. Lead the way then." Something occurs to me. "Hey! Where's my stuff? We left it in the Town Car!"

Chris shakes his head. "No, I had Jeff bring it here and put it in the condo."

"Oh. It must be nice to have minions."

He laughs and takes my hand again to lead me inside. We ride an elevator to the twelfth floor: the top. "Let me guess, the penthouse?" I ask him.

"Of course. Short Mark has a complex, remember? He has to make up for it by being extravagant in every other area of his life."

I laugh as we go inside. My jaw drops. The place is amazing, of course. The floors are wide plank wood that looks old and new at the same time. The walls are pale gray, and covered with expensive artwork. The furniture is lush, and the living room set alone probably costs more than my whole house.

"Why don't you live here all the time?"

"I don't know. I probably spend most of my time here."

"Not with Andrew and Laura?"

"Ha ha. No. But I am going to be going that way soon. Do you want to go to Portland with me and meet my parents?"

"Meet the parents? Isn't it a little early in the relationship for a step that big?"

"We're way past that point, sweetheart." He shows me to the room where I will sleep. Sure enough, my stuff is already in it. Then I get a tour of the rest of the house. The place is very big, very spacious. And very clean. The kitchen is full of top end appliances that look like they've never been used. There is not a single speck of dust or one thing out of place.

"You must have a housekeeper."

"Is it that obvious?" I nod. "What can I say? We're lazy."

"You're also busy, so it can be forgiven."

"Thanks. Hey, I promised you I would shower when we got home. I'm going to make good on that, okay?"

"Sure, I might do the same. Can we shower at the same time?"

"I thought you'd never ask." He gives me his vaudeville-style eyebrow waggle again. I don't say anything, just look at him. "Yes, dear. There's plenty of hot water."

Every bedroom in this place (all six of them) has its own bathroom, so I head into mine as Chris walks down the hall into his room. The bedroom I'm sleeping in has thick white carpet, dark wood furniture, and a king size bed covered in mounds of white linen. The pure white walls have black and white photographs of city landscapes in dark wood frames hanging on them. Everything in the whole room is dark and white except for an enormous vase of fresh, bright red flowers on the dresser. I walk around and look at the pictures. I don't know all of the cities, but I can pick out New York – which was taken before September 11th – and Seattle.

The bathroom is huge. There is a big shower stall and a separate jacuzzi tub. A door separates the toilet from the rest of the bathroom. There are two sinks and a wide counter in front of a framed mirror that takes up most of one wall. It's all white marble with dark wood cabinets and black accents. The only color in the room is a stack of thick bright red towels that I am tempted to take out and compare to the flowers. I'm sure they are an exact match. I can't believe this place. I have to meet this housekeeper.

I take a quick shower to wash off the airplane stink. I feel a lot better when I get out. I dry off and throw on a sundress. Then I go in search of Chris. His door is still shut, so I go into the living room and sink into the couch. I sit there for a long time before I start to wonder what is keeping him.

I head back down the hall. His door is still shut so I put my ear against it. I don't hear anything. I knock lightly. Nothing. "Chris?" Nothing. I open the door a little, and then a little more. Chris is asleep, stretched out across his bed wearing nothing but a towel. I stand there for a moment and marvel at his perfection. I stand in the door trying to decide what to do. I know I should let him sleep. (I could go for a nap myself.) But I really want to curl up with him. It is so wrong, but I can't help myself. I creep over to his bed and very carefully climb in next to him. I put my head on his shoulder and fit myself into the crook of his arm.

He immediately wraps his arm around me and kisses the top of my head. "I'm sorry I fell asleep." He yawns. "I had an early start today."

"I know. Please, go back to sleep. I didn't really want to wake you up, but I figured if we were both going to take a nap, at least we could be together. I did fly a long way to spend some time with you."

I can feel his smile. "Okay." He kisses the top of my head again. It feels so good to be lying in a man's arms, I fall asleep almost instantly.

When I wake up, it's dark outside. Chris is already awake, but he is lying still so that he won't disturb me. I can hear Short Mark singing through the door that I left open when I came in. "Is he taking a shower?"

"Yes. Sorry. He always does that when we're recording."

"It's not like I find his singing voice offensive."

"I didn't want to wake you up, but I'm going to put on pants now." He smiles at me. "Unless you can give me a good reason to leave them off?"

I shove him off the bed. "Put on some pants." I get up to leave.

"Where are you going?" he sounds surprised.

"Down the hall. You get dressed. We'll go from there."

"Good Lord, woman. You could have just closed your eyes for a second."

"I wouldn't trust myself to keep them that way. It would be way too tempting to take a peek." I wink and shut his door behind me. Let him chew on that for a minute. He is always driving me crazy with all of his little innuendos and invitations.

I sit on the couch again. Short Mark comes out before Chris does. "Hey, Shorty. Did you have a nice nap?" He winks.

"Actually I did." I stick my tongue out at him.

"You should cut that poor boy some slack, you know."

"I cut him plenty. Don't I?"

"Just be careful, please, Shorty. I think he loves you."

"Please don't say that," I beg.

"Why? It's true."

But I don't answer him. Just loud enough for my own ears I whisper, "Because I think I love him. And I can't."

Chris comes down the hall then. "What's the plan?"

I yawn. "I don't know. I'm tired."

Short Mark laughs. "Didn't get enough sleep?" He elbows Chris, who pushes him back.

"Ha ha. It's –" I look at my watch, "– almost 1 am, my time." After all, I didn't sleep last night because I was too excited about my trip and going to sleep at 8 pm isn't *that* bad – considering that's what time it was on the east coast when I fell asleep with Chris. "It's the middle of the night!"

Chris pats me on the head, patronizing me. "True. But I'm starving. I'm ordering a pizza." Chris looks at Short Mark. "Did you and Cannadiak eat?"

"Actually, we didn't. He took Angie out tonight."

"Okay, I'm ordering two."

I don't go back to the studio with the guys the next morning. I decide to just hang out and read. Chris kisses my forehead when he goes. "Have a lovely morning, dear."

"Yes, have a great day at work."

"Have dinner on the table when I get home."

"I'm not sure that I could use anything in that kitchen without breaking something. Besides, I don't even know what time you'll be home."

"Good point. It better be long before dinnertime. Are you sure you don't mind?"

"I'm sure. Have fun."

"Oh, Giada will probably be here soon."

"Giada? Do I finally get to meet your girlfriend?"

"Yes. And she is excellent at keeping this place clean. You should take notes on how to be a good girlfriend."

"Lucky for me, I'm through that phase of my life. I'll be sure to teach her how to be a lazy wife while she's here."

"Seriously though, she doesn't speak much English. How's your Spanish?"

"I'll hide in my room."

I curl back up in my bed to read once they're gone. I'm feeling awfully lazy. I don't know what it is about this place, but I'm definitely catching up on my sleep, because I doze off while I'm reading.

I wake up when I feel Chris climbing into bed with me. "Oh, no, my love," he says. "It's my turn today. Scoot over. We're taking a nap."

I laugh. "What time is it?"

"Nap time." He is pushing me over towards the far side of the bed.

"Nuh-uh. This is my side. Walk your lazy butt around and you can have that side."

"Okay." I'm surprised he gives in without an argument. He pulls back the blankets and slides in behind me. He wraps one long arm around my waist and pulls me into him. *This* might be my idea of heaven. I snuggle in and close my eyes.

"This is what my life has been missing," I tell him.

"I know. That's why you're here."

"Okay, shut up. It's hard to sleep with all your blabbering."

He laughs quietly. "Look who's talking," he mutters.

"Hey! I heard that."

"Good. Then shut up."

I've slept too much to fall asleep again. But I'm so comfortable and happy, I could stay here forever. I know I'm in big trouble, that I'm playing with fire. But it feels so right that today, I don't care. I can't help the fantasies that play out in my mind as I lie there. It would be so easy to make them happen, and no one would have to know – Chris shut the door on his way in. I know Chris wouldn't ever tell anyone. He doesn't want to sleep with a married woman anymore than I want to cheat on my husband.

When I can't stand it anymore, I drag myself out of his arms and get out of bed. "Come on, lazy bones. Let's do something."

We go out to dinner that night with everyone. I meet Drew's Bethany and Blond Mark's Angie. I like them both a lot, but Bethany is very quiet. Angie and I hit it off and I can tell we're going to be good friends some day.

"How long have you been with Blond Mark?" I ask her.

She laughs. "They warned me that was what you called him, but I forgot. I've actually known him most of my life. We went to high school together."

"High school sweethearts." I smile. "Always makes a good story to tell the grandkids."

"Oh, no. We didn't date in high school. Actually, I kind of hated him. I thought he was a pretentious jerk."

I laugh.

"No, I'm serious. He was very full of himself."

"He still is," I point out.

"He's not as bad. I promise he was worse."

"So when did you stop hating him?"

"I ran into him when we were both home from college one winter break. He asked me to hang out. And the rest, as they say, is history."

Blond Mark slings his arm across her shoulders. "She couldn't resist my charms any longer." He smiles.

Angie and I look at each other. "Still full of himself," we say at the same time. Everyone at the table laughs.

"What do you do?" I ask her.

"I'm in marketing. I work at a PR firm."

"Do you live in LA?"

"Nope, San Diego. I'm just visiting. But I'm thinking about getting a job here if I can find one. It would be easier." I nod. "I hear you're a teacher?"

"Yeah, chemistry."

"I hated chemistry. Sorry." She smiles sheepishly.

"Hate the science, not the teacher."

"I'm pretty sure I hated my teacher too."

I sigh. "Everyone does."

"Sorry. It's just too much of an association with difficult subject matter."

Chris leans over. "Her students don't hate her anymore. They're all going to be really nice and kiss up because they're hoping that she will get them tickets to an Evansgate concert."

"Yes, my students love me now because of Chris. Speaking of full of himself..."

I acquire a new nickname later in the night when Bethany tells everyone that when she was a kid, she named her teddy bear Sara.

Blond Mark claps me on the back. "What do you think about that Sare-Bear? You must have a good name!"

"Yes, well, it beats 'Baby Girl' at least."

Short Mark jumps suddenly. "That's right! I hear there is a story about that. Apparently the Ice Queen and I are the only ones who haven't heard it."

Blond Mark scoffs. "Even I've heard it, Evans. Where have you been?"

I look at Blond Mark, "When did *you* hear it?"

"Eck told me, of course."

"Of course," I agree. Chris looks at me with a question in his eyes. "No, you're not in trouble, and yes, you can tell the story to everyone else." Chris smiles at me and then tells the story of my birth certificate.

We all end up drinking way too much. Well, everyone except Bethany. "See why I love her?" Drew asks me. "She keeps us on the straight and narrow."

"Yes, very straight," I agree as I watch him stumble.

"You don't seem very straight yourself," he retorts when I trip on the smooth sidewalk.

"I never claimed to be." He concedes with a smile and throws his arms around Bethany's neck. I turn away as he whispers sweet nothings in her ear. I don't really want to know what he's saying.

I look at Chris instead and he is watching Drew and Bethany with a sad look on his face. I stumble up to him and take his hand. "Why the long face?"

He shakes his head and smiles. "No long face. I'm just tired."

"Tired?! You had a nap this afternoon, remember?"

"Yes and the contents of a keg since then. That can really take it out of a man." He wraps his arm around my shoulders, crushing me to his side. "Let's go home, Baby Girl, and sleep it off."

My bed seems empty without Chris in it when I climb in that night. I don't know why I assumed I wouldn't be sleeping alone. Chris and I have taken plenty of naps together, but we have never actually slept a night in the same bed. It's probably for the best, I remind myself. I am married. It's easier to fall asleep than I expect after my morning nap. But I guess half of a bottle of vodka really takes it out of a woman.

The next morning I find Chris and Short Mark in their music room. It's one of the bedrooms that they "fixed up". The walls look really thick because they have hung heavy panels to help with noise. Several instruments fill the place, as well as a really nice stereo. The walls are covered with awards and pictures of big events. It's my favorite room in the place. After they go to the studio, I stay in there, just looking around. And that is where Chris finds me, asleep, when he gets back.

"There are plenty of beds here," he says when he picks me up. "You really don't have to sleep on the floor."

"It's good carpet."

"True. Do you ever do anything other than sleep?"

I swat at him and he nearly drops me. "Yes, I do, thank you very much. But, you are so boring that when I'm around you, I can't help but nod off."

He dumps me out of his arms, but he is laughing. "I'm sorry that I'm such a bore, sweetheart. I'll try to liven things up for you."

Chapter 15

I spend almost a week in LA. Chris has to go into the studio everyday for at least a few hours. Angie stays in town through the weekend, and we go out to see the sights while the guys are recording. Mostly, we see the inside of stores because Angie is on a mission to find specific boots for an outfit she recently acquired, but in between I get to see the stars on the sidewalk, the Hollywood sign, and Rodeo Drive. Well, I get to see a good bit of Rodeo, actually.

I cook dinner twice. Chris ran his mouth and Short Mark heard that I had taken a cooking class, so he begged. I'm really not a very good cook, but no one complains. Chris is very good about helping, which is necessary because I wasn't kidding about their kitchen. I don't even know what half of the appliances do, let alone how to use them.

The penthouse is not far from the beach, so we walk over to the ocean every night. On my last night in town, we go over before dark. "Before this week, I had only come over here once since I moved in," Chris tells me.

"Why?" I can't hide my surprise. "It's beautiful."

Chris looks at me for a long moment. "It is now."

I shove him, and at first I think he wasn't expecting it because he goes down. But he grabs my hand and pulls me down on top of him. "Get comfortable, sweetheart. Let's watch the sunset."

"I've never seen the sunset over the ocean before."

"Really? What do you do at the beach?"

"Watch the sun *rise*. I'm from the east, you idiot."

"You've never been to the West Coast?"

"Nope. I hear they eat avocado over here."

He laughs. "You are dissing an entire section of the United States over a fruit?"

"It's slimy and gross."

"You're an idiot."

"Well, I will admit, it's nicer to be able to watch the sunset than to have to get up before sunrise."

Chris sits up and pulls me between his legs. I lean back into his chest and we look out to the horizon. Chris starts singing softly.

"Lumineers?" I ask with a smile.

Chris smiles at me, but he doesn't stop singing. I almost start to laugh, because it seems like "Ho Hey" could have been written about us, but then I realize that I'm almost sad listening to the words. "I find myself listening to that song a lot now," he tells me. "I feel like it's about us."

I laugh, and a tear falls at the same time. "I was thinking the exact same thing."

"Star-crossed lovers have a lot of songs written about them." Then we sit back and wait for the sun to go down in silence.

It seems like as soon as it clears the horizon, the wind picks up. I wrap my hair around my hands, but Chris reaches into his pocket and pulls out a pony tail holder.

"Where did you get that?" I ask, as I gladly take it and tie back my hair.

"Your stuff. I knew you would want it."

"Why don't you have a girlfriend? Wait, it's because you're a serial player and you knew I would need this because you have brought *so many* girls down here that you began to detect a pattern, isn't it? Is this even mine – or did you dig it out of your sofa cushions?"

"If it was in my sofa, it's because you lost it there earlier."

"Or it could be from one of Short Mark's women."

Chris looks at me with a serious expression. "Evans is really careful. I can't remember the last time he had a girlfriend."

"Uh, just because a pony tail holder ended up in the couch, doesn't mean it came from a 'girlfriend'."

"It would in his case."

"Seriously, why don't you two have girlfriends?"

"It's really hard, Sara. I had a girlfriend for a while, but things got weird when people started to take notice of us. She was enjoying the limelight that came from dating a member of a major group more than she was enjoying me. After that, I was guarded. It seemed like every girl I came across was more interested in my fame than anything else. I don't want someone who wants me only because of that." He tweaks my nose. "That's why I asked you to the club, you know. You were so different. When you didn't tell that guy who I was... I knew."

"Knew what?"

"That you wouldn't ever want to be with me just so that you could say you were."

"But, you don't ever just want to take what you can get? I mean, most guys would jump at the chance to sleep with any girl they could."

"Most guys don't have to worry about girls sleeping with them just because they're famous."

"I'm beginning to sense that you guys aren't the typical rock star kind of guys."

"No, I don't think we are. I tried to tell you that."

"What's the story? I mean, you guys are so down to earth, so normal. How did you hook up? What happened?"

He laughs at all of my questions. "Evans and Cannadiak have known each other since they were in diapers, I think. But, Evans moved when he was in high school – to *my* high school. We started playing in his garage in tenth grade. By the time we were seniors, we had formed a band and we thought we were pretty hot stuff. We won a couple of local Battles of the Bands and were pretty much ready to give up on the idea of college to go hit it big." He laughs at his memories. "Ah, so young and stupid. But, obviously, that little group didn't last. Evans and I both ended up getting into Colburn so we roomed together and we stayed close. After we graduated, Evans and Cannadiak hooked up again and started a new band with a few other guys from school. I moved to Seattle, and did what every other upstanding citizen with a degree in music does there: got a job at Starbucks."

I can't help it, I laugh. He gives me a look down his nose. "Sorry, please continue."

"Cannadiak dropped out to move to San Diego with Angie, but Evans didn't want to give up on the idea of a band. He wrote a lot of music and waited tables in LA. He was playing at an open mic night and the right person heard him. They offered him a shot, solo, but he didn't want to do it alone. He called Cannadiak first – I try to not let that hurt my feelings," he winks, "but he has known him longer. Cannadiak wasn't interested and I was second on the list. I think the one thing that helped me was that Evans knew I could go in a lot of different directions, as need dictated. But the two of us weren't going to be enough. The label actually offered Holst up as an option. He had been on their back burner for a while and they thought that he would be a good match for Evans – personality wise. We still needed a drummer though and Evans wasn't interested in anyone other than Cannadiak.

"I'm surprised the label had so much faith in us. I know enough now to know that Evans is lucky that they didn't just kick him to the curb while he was messing around trying to get a group together. He drove to San Diego one night and came back the next morning with Cannadiak and his drums in the back. I think there was a large amount of alcohol responsible for the agreement, but whatever. I'm glad that Evans persisted, because honestly, those two *together* are what make us who we are."

I'm quiet for so long, Chris asks, "Did you fall asleep?"

"No! I'm just thinking about what you said. I guess I still don't understand how you all managed to keep your heads."

"We didn't exactly become a huge success over night. It was one lucky break, one song that somebody liked and played a lot. Our first number one was on our third album."

"I know. I've been listening to you for a long time."

"Oh." He sounds surprised.

"Matt had your first album. His grandmother gave it to him. She's famous for that, but it's really worked out in our favor. We've been introduced to a lot of great bands no one has ever heard of." He gives me a questioning look. "She gives him totally random cds for Christmas and things. Usually they're complete crap, but we took a liking to you."

"Remind me to thank Matt's grandmother."

"So how did you get Tom?"

"He came with Holst."

"Oh, well, he seems like a really good fit."

"He is. We all are, really. They're like my brothers, Sara. We do everything together – things people do with their families, I do with the band. We live together, travel, spend holidays. I can't imagine my life without them."

I smile. "I'm glad. You guys are great."

He holds me tighter. "So are you. And, you're in like Flynn. Angie and Bethany like you a lot. I'm sorry to say, we can only admit people to this crowd on a unanimous basis."

"I appreciate the support. So what's the deal with Angie and Blond Mark? How come they're not married?"

"It's tough. Angie doesn't want to give up her life, and she doesn't want to be married to someone who isn't there." He eyes me meaningfully.

"But she stays with him?"

"Yes, some people are hopeless and can't leave, even when there's no future."

Flying home is really hard. Not only do I have to leave Chris (and everyone else) behind, I have to go home to an empty house. I'm dreading it.

I sigh heavily one more time as we walk through the airport. Chris looks at me. "Ten days, it's only ten days."

"Says the guy with his three closest friends to keep him company night and day."

"I would come with you if I could."

"I know. At least I have my conference."

Chris and I have made plans to meet in Portland to see his parents for the second weekend in August. I have a teaching conference Monday through Thursday of that week to occupy some of my time.

"Call Matt. He'll come keep you company."

"I know. I'll miss you." I stand on my tip toes, but I'm still too short, so I step up on the chair behind me and kiss his nose. "Go rehearse."

I turn and go. Chris holds my hand until our arms are completely outstretched and then he has to let go.

The flight home is long, and it seems even longer when I get home and have lost three hours. Matt meets me at the airport and drives me home.

"I'm so glad I have you," I tell him as I climb in the car.

"You should be."

Chapter 16

The recording is done, but Evansgate is busier now. Chris told me that everything just has to be edited and cleaned up. Short Mark is getting more and more excited about the release, and it's getting harder and harder to talk to Chris. They have to work on cover art, go to photo shoots, design posters and things. They are recording another video, but this time they're working in a studio in LA.

The time at home goes by faster than I would have expected. It's only ten days and I know the four days spent in my conference helped, but I still expected it to drag more. Now that I'm packing, I'm starting to get nervous. I'm meeting his parents!

Sam isn't very happy to hear that I was taking another trip with Chris.

"If you're going to Portland, are you at least going to stop in and see my parents?" he asks me sulkily during our one phone conversation in the ten days I spend at home.

"Sam, they're in Paris." Thank God.

"Oh, right. I just don't know why you are going to *his* parents."

"Because I am. It's something to do."

"You have your conference."

"It's over."

"You're spending an awful lot on plane tickets. I don't think you should."

"Nice try, but Chris is paying."

"You're practically his hooker, Sara."

"*What?!*"

He knows that he went too far. "It's just he's spending all this money on you."

"Yes, but the definition of a hooker would mean that he would be getting sex in return for that money. And he's not."

Sam isn't really conceding, but at least he lets it go. "Have fun."

"Oh, I will. Love you." I jab at the END button on my phone, but I wish that we still had the satisfaction of being able to slam a phone into its handset. As angry as I am, I can't ever hang up without saying "I love you" because I'm always afraid something will happen and I'll regret not saying it one last time or something.

Matt picks me up to take me to the airport, again. "I'm starting to feel like a taxi," he complains when I get in.

"I offered to pay you."

"I couldn't take your money. In return, you have to listen to me complain."

"Okay, that's fine. Do you want to hear about my latest fight with Sam?"

"Of course."

"He called me a hooker."

Matt is actually shocked for a second. "He did not."

"I swear. He said I was practically Chris's hooker."

"You're starting to look better to him now that someone else is making a move. I bet he's starting to regret treating you like crap for months. He's just lashing out. What do they call it? Projecting his anger?"

"I don't know. I have no idea what you're talking about."

"Well, I'm a chemist, not a psychologist."

"Keep your day job, Lucy. I'll spend my nickels somewhere else."

"Lucy pretends to be a psychiatrist. That's very different."

"Yes, of course it is. No one in their right mind would give you license to dispense drugs."

"The key is to catch someone *not* in their right mind."

"Thanks for the ride. See you on Monday?"

"Unless my not-so-hot date Saturday night goes *very* well."

"Well, text me if things are looking up and I'll find another ride."

"Be careful this weekend."

"I will!"

I call Allison while I sit there. "I just thought I'd chat with you while I wait for my plane."

"Your plane? Where are you going now?"

"Uh, Portland. Didn't I tell you?"

"Going to visit the in-laws?"

"Um, no. I'm actually going to see Andrew and Laura – they're, uh, Chris's parents."

"What?! Sara!"

"I know. But it's not like I've never gone to Matt's parents for a weekend."

"You really need to be careful."

"You have no idea. I've been thinking about how hard it is to live on the opposite coast from him. It's not easy maintaining a relationship – friendship! I meant friendship! It's not easy maintaining a *friendship* with 3000 miles between us."

"Those are dangerous thoughts."

"I know."

"Well, have fun! Just don't do anything stupid."

"Have you ever known me to do something stupid?"

"Really? Do you actually want me to answer that? How about the time you broke the window when –"

"We don't really need to remember that. I've matured a lot since then."

"I'm sure. A year is a really long time."

"Shut up."

"I love you, Baby Girl!"

Chris is waiting for me at my gate. "Hi!" I squeal when I see him. "No one gets met at their gate anymore!"

He smiles and rubs his ear. "A little high pitched there, sweetheart. Yes, it's the benefit of meeting someone who is also flying in and therefore already on this side of security." He grabs me into a hug and then picks my bag up when he sets me down. He only has a duffel for the weekend, which is flung over his shoulder. That's a really small bag for – two days. Ug, that's all we get. Two days. I sigh.

"What?"

"I was just thinking about having to go home."

"You just got here!"

"I know, but I have to leave in just a couple of days."

"Will you come to LA for Labor Day? Bethany is having a cookout or something."

"I can't."

"Why not?"

"Because school starts on the fourth."

"Oh, well, maybe she'll have it on Sunday."

"I have to work the week before school starts."

"So fly out Friday afternoon and fly back Monday night. You don't need a good night's sleep the night before the first day of school, right?"

"I wasn't planning on getting one; you know, all that residual anxiety from the first time through high school."

He laughs. "Great, then it's settled."

Chris's mom meets us at the airport. Laura is very sweet and I can see where Chris gets his sense of humor right away. The ride to their house takes about 45 minutes, but it goes quickly. Time always speeds by with Chris, though.

The house is really big. "Is this where you grew up?" I ask Chris as we get out of the car.

"Yeah, it's the only place I've ever lived." I smile. "What?" he asks.

"I just think it's great to have someplace like that to call home."

"Your mom? She... she..."

"Yes, she died in the house that I was born in. Well actually, she died in the hospital that I was born in, but we lived at that house for both occasions. Dad sold it after she was gone."

Chris's mom looks at me. "You are a special girl." I look at her with surprise. "I mean it," she continues. "You aren't looking for pity, are you?"

"Why would I?"

"A lot of people do, after they lose someone they loved."

"And I might have, if my mom hadn't been happy and content. I wish that she had lived longer, I really do. But she was okay with God calling her home when He did. Who am I to argue with that?"

She smiles at me. Then she gives Chris a significant look and herds us in the house. Chris gives me a tour of the main floor and second story while his mom goes to cook dinner. "I have to warn you before I take you downstairs. I... Well, they *are* my parents."

I smile. "And they're proud of their only son?"

"Something like that." We start down the stairs to the basement. "Technically, this is where I live."

"Technically?"

"Well, I don't ever sleep down here anymore. It creeps me out."

"I can't wait to see it."

It's like the music room in the penthouse, only magnified. I think *every* mention of Chris ever made is on the walls. Newspapers, magazines, pictures of TV interviews. Pictures of them receiving awards, pictures of them on the red carpet, pictures of them on stage. But it's so much better than that. There are pictures of him in the garage with Short Mark from when they were kids, his diploma from Colburn, old awards from Battles of the Bands, his Starbucks name tag (I'm not kidding), pictures of him playing the piano on stage as a child, pictures of him playing the guitar as a teenager. If it relates to Chris and music in any way, it's down here. There's a baby grand piano in the corner, two guitars – one acoustic and one electric, and a bass. I start there.

"Are these what you learned to play on?"

"They were my first, so yes, I suppose."

"Wow. How many people know this is down here?"

"Including you?" He counts for a second. "Five."

"Seriously?"

"Yeah, mom and dad, me, Evans, and now you."

"You know, this stuff would go for a fortune on eBay."

Chris's mom comes down the stairs. "And that's why no one knows it's here."

I look at the pride in her eyes. "This place is amazing," I tell her honestly. "I think I could live down here."

"You do? Because it's his place, and he won't even sleep here."

"It's not *my* face on the wall. Maybe I would like it less if it were."

Laura nods. "Maybe. Dinner is ready, if you are."

"I'm always ready to eat, Mom." We start back up the stairs behind her. I look wistfully over my shoulder. Chris laughs at me. "You can come back down."

"Okay, I will."

Chris's dad is home now and I meet him in the dining room. He puts his hand out, "Andrew Eck. It's very nice to meet you, Sara."

I shake his hand. "Thank you for having me."

Laura is bringing in food. "Of course, dear. We're very glad you're here."

Chris looks a lot like his dad. I imagine the two of them together turn quite a few heads. Andrew is even taller than Chris, which I find surprising. He has the exact same shade of hair, but his eyes are dark. Chris has his mom's eyes.

"Sara likes the basement," Laura tells her husband.

"Oh! You let her see that, did you?" he asks Chris.

"Don't listen to him. He actually has a very big head and is always looking for new ways to show off. That was a perfect opportunity," I say before I realize that these are his parents. Not only might they not appreciate me insulting their son, I just presumed to know more about him than they do. I look up apologetically, but no need.

Andrew roars with laughter. "That's right," he tells me. "Don't let him get too self-important. You keep him in his place, okay?"

I nod. "I'll do my best."

After dinner, I try to help Laura with the dishes, but she swats me away. "No, no, I've got it. You can sit in here and talk to me though."

"Only if you'll let me dry."

She smiles. "I typically just let them dry in the dishwasher."

"Ah, yes, that's a good plan too." I end up sitting on the counter, talking, while she loads the dishwasher.

She asks me about teaching, about my sister, about Virginia. Then she asks me about my mom. "I hope you don't mind. But she sounds like someone I would have liked to have met."

"You would have. She was amazing. She was so strong. The

cancer never broke her, if that makes sense... considering that it killed her. But she was whole, even at the end." I realize that there is a tear on my cheek and I brush it away.

"I'm sorry," Laura hands me a tissue.

"No, really, it's fine. Most people don't ever want to talk about her. It's kind of nice. Has Chris told you about my weird little talent?"

"From what I understand, it's not 'little'. But, yes, I have heard about it."

"My mom could do it too, only she could play it on the piano."

"Anything?"

"Anything. She could hear it once and then play it. It makes just knowing the words seem kind of lame."

"Did you ever learn to play?"

"No. That was my mom's thing. But she used to have me sing sometimes while she played."

"I hear you have a lovely voice."

"Then someone lied to you."

She laughs. "Really, I've heard good things. Have you ever sung?"

"Do you mean in front of other people on purpose?"

"I was just wondering. Chris told me you sing like a bird."

I almost choke as I try to swallow that. "No, I don't sing. My voice isn't that great. But even if it was, I would never have the nerve."

She nods and then swats at me with the dishtowel she is holding. "Now, go find the boys. I'm just going to wipe up and sweep."

I hop off the counter and go looking for Chris and his dad. I can hear them talking in the living room, and they're talking about me. I know I shouldn't, but I stop to listen.

"She's married, Son," Andrew is saying.

"I know she is. I'm not going to... do anything."

"You better not. A marriage is important."

"Don't worry, she won't either. Even though he is awful. I mean, *awful*, Dad."

"He doesn't hit her, does he?"

"I know marriage is sacred, and all that, but do you think I would let him still be walking if that was the case?"

"Good point."

"No, it's not that. He's just an asshole. He is sleeping with this pretentious bitch that he works with, and you should hear him talk to Sara. It took every ounce of my will power to not deck him." I'm surprised to hear the anger in his voice.

"I'm glad you didn't."

"You would have, if you had been there."

"Probably, but you're a better man than I am."

"I wish I had hit him. Just thinking about it makes me angry."

"Just think about Sara, Son. I'm sure she appreciates that you didn't."

"She doesn't know what's good for her."

Andrew laughs. "Don't let her hear you say that."

"No kidding. But..." Chris is quiet. "I love her, Dad."

"That sucks, kid."

Chris laughs bitterly. "Thanks."

I hear them moving around, and I'm afraid to get caught standing in the hallway. I bang my hand into the wall on purpose and call out, "Ouch!" Then I walk around the corner into the living room.

Chris is looking at me with concern. "Did you hurt yourself?"

"Uh, it's nothing. I'm sure it will bruise, but..."

"But, you bruise easily, I know."

"Can we go back downstairs now? Please?"

"I thought we agreed that you would keep him in his place. Don't let him think that you're too impressed with all that," Andrew teases.

"Okay, I won't." I smile.

When we get downstairs, I ask Chris to play for me.

He looks around. "Play what?"

I point to the piano. "Play something without words, please."

He smiles. "Okay." He sits down on the bench and starts to play "Flight of the Bumblebee". I crawl under the piano and lay on my back, like I did when I was a child. Chris stops and peers under at me. "What are you doing?"

I can feel the tears running down my face. "I'm remembering. Now, play, please."

He looks at me for another second and then sits back up and starts again.

We stay like that for a long time. I cry so much that I start to get thirsty. I climb out and he stops. "No! Please don't stop! I'm thirsty. I'm going to go up and get a drink, but I'll be able to hear you. Please don't stop," I say again. He smiles and keeps playing.

I walk up the stairs backwards (which is actually really hard) so that I can watch him. When I lose sight of him, I turn around and head to the kitchen. I don't get very far before I hear Andrew again, only this time he is talking to Laura.

"I'm worried about him."

Laura sighs. "I'm not worried so much as just sad."

"Why?"

"Because I love her! She would be perfect for him! She's everything he said she was."

"And she's already married to someone else. Not you too, Laura."

"No! I said *would*, but you have to admit, he doesn't sound like a real prize."

"I'm sorry, that is for sure. But I won't have our son breaking up someone's marriage."

"Someone should."

"Don't encourage him to do something stupid."

"I'm not saying anything. But I really love her."

"I know. So do I."

My heart breaks a little. I could be a part of this, if I let myself. But then I remember what Andrew said and I hurry into the kitchen.

Chris is still playing when I get back downstairs. I bring the glass of water I got for him to the piano. "Can I stop playing to drink it, or are you going to hold it for me? It would have been better if you had brought a straw."

"I couldn't find one."

His hands stop moving. "Will you talk to me now?"

"I thought I was."

"I'm serious."

"My mom played the piano."

"I know."

"Then what do you want to talk about?"

He reaches out and takes the glass from me. "You."

"What about me?" I look around. "I think we should talk about you. Clearly, there is a lot more subject material."

He pulls me down next to him on the piano bench. "You never learned anything?"

"I can play my scales."

"Okay."

"What? Play them?"

"Yeah. I want to see what I have to work with."

"What is it that you are trying to accomplish?"

"We'll see."

I play the scales for him. He nods. "Okay. Now this."

We go back and forth for an hour as he tries to teach me "Heart and Soul".

"Gah! I'm terrible! I give up!" The man must have the patience of Job, because he is still smiling.

"Okay, we'll try again tomorrow."

We go upstairs to the living room, where Chris's parents are reading magazines. Laura smiles when she sees us. "I haven't heard him play the piano in ages. Thank you."

Chris ducks his head, almost like he's embarrassed. "Anyone want to play Trivial Pursuit?"

"I'm terrible at that game," I tell him.

"Good," he says. "So am I. Maybe I won't lose today." He smiles at his parents.

He doesn't come in last. I do. But, I'm so tired that I don't even care. I'm starting to droop pretty hard by midnight.

Laura jumps up and waves her hands at the guys. "Move! It's almost three in the morning, her time! Take her to bed!"

Chris looks at me in surprise. "I'm sorry! I forgot we are on different times."

He walks me upstairs to a guest room. He is sleeping in the other one, even though there is a perfectly nice bed for him in the basement. Something occurs to me. "If you aren't going to sleep in the room of your glory, can I?"

"What? You want to sleep in the basement?"

I nod. "I love it down there."

"Okay." He grabs my stuff and we go back down the stairs. "Mom?" he calls out. "Can this crazy lady sleep in the basement?"

Laura comes around the corner. "What? Why would you put her in the basement?"

"I'm not putting her there. She wants to sleep there."

Andrew comes down the hall. "Now, Sara, you really are going to make him think that there is something special down there." He laughs.

Laura pats my arm. "Of course you can sleep down there, honey."

Chris hauls my stuff downstairs and I step into the bedroom to change. "Don't leave!" I call out. I drag the comforter off of the bed and go out into the main room. Chris looks at me. "Please play some more." I lie down on the floor and give him puppy dog eyes.

"You don't have to go to any effort, woman. I would do anything you ask, without the eyes." He sits back down at the piano. He plays very softly and I fall asleep.

Chapter 17

When I wake up, I'm in the bed. Chris must have carried me in. I stretch and roll over. Then I brush my teeth and go upstairs. I've slept very late, East Coast time, but it's still kind of early here.

The Ecks are all in the kitchen having coffee. "Good morning, dear," Laura says when I come in. "Would you like some breakfast?"

"Some coffee would be wonderful." But Chris is already getting me a cup. He makes it exactly the way I like it – huge cup, half filled (so it's still a whole cup of coffee) and then milk to the top and some sugar, without even asking.

"You know," I say when he hands it to me, "I don't think Sam could tell me how I take my coffee if his life depended on it."

"I'm not Sam," Chris says.

"No, you're not," I agree as Andrew and Laura exchange a look.

There's a tense silence that lasts a few seconds. Andrew claps and rubs his hands together, "So! What should we do today? Are you still up for a round of golf with your old man?" he asks Chris.

Chris looks at me. "Please! Please go golf with your dad! You're here to visit with them." I glance at Laura. "Would I be in your way?"

"Absolutely not, dear. We can find something to do with ourselves, I'm sure."

Chris smiles at me. "Are you sure?"

"Definitely. I don't mind spending some time with your mom."

Andrew claps Chris on the back. "We'll just do nine, okay?"

The guys change into clothes for golf and load their clubs into the trunk. Chris kisses my forehead before he leaves. I can feel his dad's eyes on me. I smile, "Have fun!"

Laura is still straightening the kitchen after breakfast when I come back in. "Well," she says, "what would you like to do?"

I shrug. "I have no idea. I always have trouble coming up with something to do."

"Chris told me that you spend a lot of time alone." I nod. "Does it bother you?"

"It didn't used to. But I'll tell you the truth, your son has started to change that. I've never really had the opportunity to spend so much time with someone that I notice when he's gone. I really do miss Chris and the other guys when they're not there."

"Not even your husband?"

"We have spent most of our time apart. Even when we were

dating. He was getting his MBA when I was an undergrad, but I was taking care of my mom most of the time. We graduated at the same time, but then I stayed to get my Masters and he went to New York to get a job. He asked me to marry him before he went to Atlanta, but I stayed with my parents until the wedding – we got married right after I graduated and I moved to Atlanta. He didn't travel *as much* then, but he was still on the road a lot of the time. I got a job in a lab and I worked funny hours, so I was working most of the time that we would have had together, a lot of weekends and stuff. Then my mom got sick again and he was gone three to three and half weeks a month so I decided it was best to just go be with her. While I was there he came to New York as often as he stayed in Atlanta so his boss agreed that we could move wherever we wanted when my mom died, because I didn't want to go back to Atlanta.

"My best friend from college, Matt, had moved to the Richmond area, and he told me that it was a great place for families. My sister, Allison, was still in DC then, so I thought it would be good to be close to her and to have Matt around since Sam was still going to be on the road all the time. But Allison moved to Dallas almost right away and Sam got to the point where he was only home a day here and there. I guess it happened gradually enough that I got used to it, but I'm pretty much alone all the time.

"Or I was before Chris and the rest of Evansgate came into my life. I have spent more time with them since I met them less than two months ago than I have spent with my husband in the last two years."

"When did your mom die?"

"Last January. It's been a year and a half."

I have decided that one of my favorite things about Chris's mom is that she doesn't look at me with pity when I talk about my mom. She nods, and almost looks a little sad, but I can tell that she doesn't feel sorry for me.

"You've been dealt a tough hand, dear, but I think you're playing well."

"Thanks. I'm doing the best I can."

"Are you close to your dad?"

"Not as close as I'd like to be. But we have a better relationship than a lot of people I know have with their dads."

"How is he doing with everything?"

"You mean losing my mom?" She nods. "It was really hard on him, but all of us could see the blessing in her death. She was so sick, Laura. She fought so hard for so long. I think my dad was relieved that she didn't have to anymore, that she was finally at peace. He is doing really well, I think."

"That's good."

"So, your turn."

"My turn?"

"Yes, I've been doing all the talking. It's your turn."

"I don't have much to talk about."

"What do you do?"

"I'm in sales and customer service for a little company that does software support."

"Do you like it?"

"Well enough, I suppose."

"Do you get to see a lot of Chris?"

"Not as much as I would like, but he is really busy."

"Do you get to see a lot of his shows?"

"We don't go to many, not now that they have gotten so big. Maybe once a tour, sometimes not at all. This time we'll probably try to see one because I think they'll be playing on Thanksgiving and we might try to be there. But, maybe not."

"Is it weird having a super famous son?"

"Not really. He is still the same kid to me. He really hasn't changed at all, even with all of the fame. I'm very proud of him."

"I think about that all the time actually, how normal the guys are even though they're so crazy famous."

She nods. "I was worried, because a lot of people get into trouble when that many opportunities open up for bad decisions. But he has done well remembering who he is."

"And for that you should be proud of yourself. You obviously did something right when you raised him."

She laughs at that assessment. "I don't know how much I did, but thanks for the vote of confidence in my parenting."

I'm quiet when I think about the fact that if by some strange twist of fate I were to end up with Chris, Laura and Andrew would never have any grandchildren. Add that to the ever-growing list of reasons that it would never work, which I have actually started to write down to help me keep some proper perspective. I keep thinking that the longer that list gets, the easier it will be to put some distance between us, but that doesn't seem to be the case.

"What's on your mind?" Laura asks.

I shake the thoughts from my head and smile as brightly as I can. "Nothing. What would you normally do on a Saturday?"

"I suppose that depends on the Saturday. We could go to the weekend Farmers' Market. That's always an adventure."

"That sounds great!"

I go downstairs to shower and get dressed for the day. I put my hair in a pony tail and go upstairs to find Laura. She is already waiting for me, so we hop in her car and head to the market.

The place is amazing. They have so many different things for sale. I was expecting vegetables, but it is so much bigger than that. There are vegetables and fruits – fresh and canned, but there is also milk, eggs, meat from a variety of animals, butter, jams and jellies, honey, bread, pies, ice cream, nuts – all fresh from local farms. There are other things too, like sweaters and scarves made from wool that someone sheared from her own sheep, spun, dyed, and knitted into something beautiful. There are flowers, cut and in pots. There are things built from wood that someone cut into planks himself, little toys to big pieces of furniture.

"I could spend all day here," I tell Laura.

"Yes," she agrees, "and not see it all." She is smiling at my reaction. "Should I call the men and tell them they have time for 18 holes?"

"They could probably fit in 36 before I got bored with this place."

Laura does call them to tell them that we are well entertained and they don't have to hurry back, but Chris wants to meet us at the market so they stick with their original plan. Laura and I wander from stall to stall, talking to the farmers and their families, learning about the things they have brought to sell and how they came to be. It's wonderful.

I'm surprised when Chris and his dad get there. "That was really fast!" I say to Chris.

"I'm glad you are enjoying yourself. Sara, we've been hours."

"We've been here for hours?"

Laura looks at her watch and nods. "More than two." She smiles. "I'm really glad you like it here."

"I love it."

"You should visit Seattle sometime and go to the Pike Place Market," Chris says.

"How do you know I haven't been?"

"Because Seattle is on the west coast."

"Oh. Good point."

We split up for a little bit. Chris's parents wander one way and Chris and I head another. "Let's buy stuff for dinner tonight, okay?"

Chris smiles. "Sure, I'm sure we can make quite a meal here."

We do. We start with the easy stuff and buy beautiful vegetables to make a salad, corn on the cob and asparagus to grill. Chris picks really big thick steaks and we find a marinade for them. We buy fresh bread and butter. Then I find a strawberry-rhubarb pie for dessert.

When we meet up with Andrew and Laura again, they laugh at our armfuls of food. "Did you find something you liked?" Andrew asks.

"Yes, we're cooking dinner tonight."

Laura takes a picture of us with her phone, then goes to get a basket from her car, which I happily unload my arms into. Chris hauls it around as I hunt for flowers for Laura's table.

We climb back into the cars – I ride back with Laura, and Chris with his dad, though I'm not sure why. "You really didn't need to do that," she tells me.

"I wanted to. I felt like a kid in a candy store! I had to buy *something* and making dinner for you seems like a good way to thank you for having me."

She shakes her head. "Part of having you to stay is keeping you fed."

"And you've done an excellent job thus far, but I can take care of *one* meal while I'm here."

We unload our spoils and Chris and I set to work in the kitchen. I realize this is what a marriage should be like. Doing things like this together. I think back over all of the things that Chris and I have done and I realize we do the regular, everyday, must-get-done kind of things like cleaning, cooking, laundry, a lot. We always have. He just slipped into my life, like there was a Chris sized hole waiting for him. Did Sam and I ever do this stuff together? I don't think so. Chris is so much more like my husband than Sam is. I swallow back the thought. Chris is just my friend.

In no time, we're ready to eat. It turned out quite well, if I do say so myself.

"That was excellent," Andrew says, sliding back from the table after his pie.

"Yes," Laura agrees. "You can definitely taste the difference when it's fresh from the grower's hands."

Chris and I clean the kitchen together, but we didn't make much mess so it doesn't take long. Then we sit down and play cards with his parents.

Laura clears her throat, and I can tell that she is hesitant to say something. "Sara?"

"Yes?" I wish there was some way to put her at ease, even though

I have no idea what she is going to say.

"We normally go to church on Sunday mornings."

"Okay! I'm glad I brought something appropriate to wear."

She smiles. "I just wanted to be sure you were okay with that."

"Of course. I'm not very good about going myself, mostly Christmas and Easter, but I wish I went more."

She smiles again and then looks at Chris. He puts his hands up. "You know I wish I went more. I don't have a good excuse, Mom. I just don't."

"I know." She clears her throat. "Well, I'm going to go to bed. We'll leave around 9:30, Sara."

"I'll be ready."

Andrew and Laura say good night, and then Chris and I go back to the basement.

"I could spend all my time down here, you know."

"Why?"

"I just like being surrounded by all of this stuff. It's what makes you *you*."

He laughs. "You could just hang around me."

"I could. But then I have to listen to you talk."

He gives me a playful shove. "What is it exactly that you like about me if you would rather I didn't talk?"

"I'm just using you as eye candy. I thought you knew that."

He sighs dramatically. "I'm so sick of being used for my body."

A jolt rushes through me, even through my unmentionable parts. I'd like to use that body. Gah! I'm married! He's my friend. There is a list of reasons that we would never work. *You can't have him, Sara. Let it go.*

I manage a weak laugh. "It must be so hard to be beautiful."

"Don't you find it tiresome sometimes?" He winks.

"My beauty isn't in such excess that I have to worry about it."

"We could have this back and forth about how you really are beautiful, you don't think so, you really are, you don't think so, but I don't want to. You are. Leave it."

"Why do you get the last word?"

"Because I'm bigger than you."

"Fine then. Will you play?"

"Will you sing?"

"No. Won't you?"

"I suppose. What should I play tonight?"

I point to his acoustic guitar and he picks it up. He sits on the couch and plucks at it while he adjusts the strings. "Any requests?"

"Whatever you're in the mood for."

He plays Eric Clapton, Rolling Stones, and even Dave Matthews Band. He sings quietly sometimes, sometimes he just plays. I fall asleep laid out on the carpet again.

I wake up in the bed; Chris must have moved me again. I look at my watch and at first I freak out and jump out of bed because Laura told me we were leaving at 9:30 and it says 10:15. But then I remember that my watch is on east coast time. It's really only 7:15. I stretch and climb into the shower.

I'm ready for church by the time I get to the kitchen where Andrew and Chris are drinking coffee. "Good morning!" I greet them.

"Good morning, my dear," Andrew says.

Chris is already getting my coffee. "Good morning," he says as he hands it to me. "You look nice this morning."

"Thanks. I slept very well."

The church service is very nice and afterward we go to brunch. "Do you do this every Sunday?" I ask Laura.

"No, we only go to brunch sometimes. But every time Chris is in town we do."

I smile. "Same restaurant?"

Andrew smiles at me. "Trying to figure out what to expect the next time you come?"

"I like to be prepared," I say. But inside I'm smiling. They are expecting me to come back! I love it here; I love it with them. I really feel like this is how life is supposed to be. But, I'm married. *To someone else.* I need to remember that.

We spend Sunday afternoon sitting on the back deck, drinking iced tea, and talking. Mid-afternoon, Andrew tells us that he has a client coming by the house later that evening. "Don't look at me like that, Laura. I don't like working on a Sunday anymore than you like me to. But he's been out of town for a few weeks and he is going to have to leave again tomorrow for something. He really needs to see me for a couple of things. It won't take long."

"It's Sunday, yes, but we also have company, Andrew."

I'm trying to decide if I should step in and say that I don't mind in the slightest, but I don't want to get in the middle.

Chris does it for me. "We're hardly *company*, Mother. It's no big deal."

Laura concedes and the rest of the afternoon goes by really quickly. I'm surprised when the sun is starting to set. Laura jumps up.

"Dinner! I haven't even thought about dinner!"

Andrew puts his hand on his wife's arm. "We'll order pizza." He looks at us to see if we agree.

"Sounds good to me," Chris says and I nod.

Laura opens a bottle of wine; Andrew gets a couple of beers for himself and Chris. We stay on the darkening deck and wait for the pizza delivery guy to get there. "This is what it's all about," Andrew says leaning back. I couldn't agree more. I feel like I fit into Chris's life as well as he fits into mine.

I'm inside when the doorbell rings. I call out the window, "Pizza's here!" and go to answer the door. But it's not pizza.

Chapter 18

Standing on the doorstep is my father-in-law.

"Sara?"

"Um, hello... Dad." The word sticks in my throat. I've never been very close to my in-laws. "What are you doing here? I thought you were in Paris."

Chris comes down the hall at that moment and slides his hand around my back in a completely natural motion. He's done it a hundred times. Chris has his arm around me as often as he doesn't. "Oh, not the pizza guy," he says, smiling.

Sam's dad looks like he is going to explode.

"Sara! What is this?"

Chris's smile vanishes and he looks back and forth between us. "Do you know each other?"

"Chris, this is my father-in-law, Peter Clarke." Chris looks back and forth one more time and then quickly drops his arm and steps across the hall from me. The situation is officially worse now, because that means Chris was doing something that he would *not* do in front of my in-laws.

"Where is Sam?"

"Um, I'm not sure. Germany, maybe?"

"What are you doing here?" he repeats.

"I'm visiting my friend." I gesture in Chris's direction.

"I can't – you – does Sam know?!" Peter splutters.

"That I'm here? Yes."

"Does he know what you're doing here?" Peter's voice is nearing a yell.

Chris has always been protective. "He knows she's visiting me, if that's what you mean."

"I can't believe this!" Yup, definitely a yell now.

Andrew comes hurrying down that hall, to investigate the commotion I'm sure. "Peter! I didn't think you would be here until later. Come in, come in!"

But Peter is rooted to the doorstep. Andrew's face falls. "What's wrong?"

My father-in-law explodes. "What's wrong?! What's wrong?! My daughter-in-law is cheating on my son! In your house!"

Andrew looks at me. "Sara Clarke. I didn't realize. I'm sorry."

Peter is still screaming. "You didn't realize what? That you were setting them up to get caught? That you were going to let me walk into this? This is ridiculous!"

Laura has joined us in the hall.

"Peter!" I have to yell over him. "I am *not* cheating on Sam! Chris is my friend. Sam knows that I'm here *with Chris*, visiting his parents."

"Even if that is true, and believe me, missy, I'm going to check, I'll bet he doesn't know how it is between you."

"How do you think it is between us?" I ask, but there's no way he heard me because Chris is nearly yelling now.

"Did you just call her '*missy*'?" Chris makes it sound like a threat somehow.

Chris might be angry, but Peter looks like he is going to spit. "You stay out of this, asshole!"

"Now wait! There's no need for that!" Andrew interjects. "I think we need to calm down. Clearly, there has been a misunderstanding –" but he doesn't get to finish.

"I'm not sure how *this*" Peter waves his hands at us, "could be considered a 'misunderstanding!' It is clear to any idiot what's going on!"

"Nothing is going on!" I say, but no one is listening to me.

Chris isn't yelling anymore, but he is still loud enough to drown me out, "And clearly you're an idiot!"

Peter looks at Andrew and then he *does* spit, right on the floor inside the door. "I no longer require your services." Then he turns on his heel and marches back down the path. He almost knocks the pizza guy over, who looks very confused.

Chris pays the pizza guy and hands the food to his mom. I'm frozen in my spot next to the door, dumbstruck. Andrew puts his hand on my shoulder, but Chris shakes his head. He turns and follows his wife.

Chris looks at me and smiles. "Well, that could have been worse."

I thaw out and look at him. "What? He could have hit you?" I drop to my knees and use my shirt to wipe the spit from the floor.

"Sara! That's disgusting! Why did you do that?"

"I'm so sorry." I run down the hall and then down the basement stairs, Chris right behind me. I very carefully pull my shirt over my head, because he's right; that was disgusting. I put on a clean shirt, toss the one I was wearing in the trash can and go back upstairs, Chris still trailing in my wake.

I find Andrew and Laura in the kitchen. "I'm so sorry. I am so, so sorry. I'll –"

Laura grabs my arm to stop me. Andrew still looks angry when he practically shouts, "For what? What do you have to be sorry for?"

"Andrew!" Laura admonishes her husband. "Calm down now."

He inhales a couple of deep breaths. "Sorry. But you have *nothing* to be sorry for."

"I do!" I can feel tears running down my face. I look at Andrew, "You lost a client!" Then I look at Laura, "He spit on your floor!" I fling around to look at Chris. "He called you an asshole!"

Chris laughs. "I've been called worse."

Andrew laughs too. "*He's* an asshole, Sara. I'm glad to be rid of him, frankly."

Laura hands me a tissue. "I'm sorry, Sara. I'm sorry that happened. But, I *am* going to go clean that spit off of my floor." She starts to grab a towel, but Chris stops her.

"Sara wiped it up with her shirt."

Laura looks shocked. She looks at my shirt. "I threw it away, don't worry," I tell her.

"Sara, that was disgusting, you did *not* have to do that. Now forget it, and come eat pizza." I take a deep breath and we all sit around the table.

After a few minutes, we start to relax and return to normal. We are talking again, and laughing. Then everyone jumps a mile, "Sara!" It's my phone.

Sam put a special ring tone on it for himself. He recorded himself yelling my name. He said that would be more like him being at home, like a normal marriage. When he needed me, he would yell for me. And he's yelling. "Sara!"

I gulp. "Um, I'll be right back." I grab my phone out of my purse on the counter and run to the living room. I would have gone downstairs to the basement, but there is no cell reception down there. "Hello?" I practically whisper.

"Sara! What the hell is going on?"

I glance at the clock. It's about eight. If he is in Germany, it's about five am. This is not going to be good, but maybe he was already awake.

"I ran into your dad."

"Yes, I heard."

"I can't believe he called you."

"What did you expect him to do?"

"Wait until you were back in the States."

"I can't believe this!"

"What? You know where I am."

"My dad thinks my wife is cheating on me!"

"And you know I'm not."

"Do I?"

"Sam, don't be ridiculous. I've never hidden my friendship with Chris from you."

"That doesn't mean that it's not more than a friendship."

"Well, it's not. I don't know what else to tell you."

"Sara, my dad thinks my wife is cheating on me. Do you know how bad that is?"

"Didn't you tell him I'm not?"

"Well..."

"You didn't?!" I yell into the phone. Then I remember where I am and quickly lower my voice. "What did you say to him?"

"Not much. He wasn't in the mood to listen."

"Sam, what did you tell him?"

"I was half asleep, Sara!"

I don't like where this is going. "What did you tell him?"

"That no, I didn't know where you were."

"Sam!" I yell again before I can control myself. "You lied? You lied! And your dad thinks I'm cheating on you!"

"Whose fault is that?"

"Oh, don't even. This conversation is over."

"I don't think it is."

"Sam, I'm not cheating on you. I love you. There's nothing else to say." And I hang up.

I'm standing in the middle of the living room, shaking, when Chris comes in to find me. "He told his dad that he didn't know where I was. My father-in-law thinks that I'm cheating."

"You never care what anyone thinks."

"This is different and you know it."

"It will be okay. It will blow over, he'll calm down, and he'll realize that he was wrong. How often do you see them?"

"Often enough that the rest of my life should be uncomfortable."

Laura comes in with a big glass of wine. "Well, there's nothing that can be done now, unfortunately. You might as well get comfortable for as long as you can." She reminds me of a mother chicken, clucking over her chicks as she settles me into the couch. I suddenly really miss my mom. The tears spill over quickly. Laura leans in and whispers in my ear, "She's with you, wherever you go. I'm just helping her for a moment." And now I'm bawling. What is it with these Ecks? Why do they always seem to know what I'm thinking?

Chris sits down next to me and pulls me into his chest, and his shirt gets very wet, very quickly. Andrew strides into the room carrying a guitar, which I'm expecting him to give to Chris. But he sits down and starts playing.

I don't recognize all of the songs that he plays, but it's really comforting. I start to calm down. "I'm sorry," I say as I try to sit up. But Chris keeps me tucked into his side.

He kisses the top of my head. "It's okay, Baby Girl."

We spend the rest of the night watching home movies of Chris when he was younger. We watch piano recitals and band concerts. But the best is watching him and Short Mark in their first band. "Seriously," I ask between laughs, "you guys won Battles of the Bands? I don't believe it!" He shoves me off of the couch and I roll on the floor laughing for a little while.

Laura and Andrew both have to be at work in the morning, so Chris has a car come to take us to the airport. The flight home is awful, of course. I'm already lonely. The idea of going back to the big house by myself depresses me. But at least I have the ride home with Matt. He always cheers me up.

"Hello, Sunshine. How was the west coast?"

"It was great, Matt. Really great. Too great."

"I'm not sure something can be 'too great', honey. It's kind of like the ludicrous idea of being 'too rich'; it just can't happen."

"It can when you have to leave it behind you."

"Oh, I see. What made it so great?"

"I could almost imagine being married to him and that could have been a regular weekend with my in-laws. Only, I *like* them, unlike my current set of in-laws."

"Almost imagine?"

"Right. I totally spent the weekend fantasizing that this is actually my life. That's what I meant."

"And that's exactly what I heard."

"I actually had to deal with my real in-laws."

"What? Why? How?"

"Sam's dad works with Chris's dad. Well, he used to."

"No more?"

"He thinks I'm cheating on Sam. He spit on their floor."

"Oh, that's lovely. It's nice to know he left a good impression of his self restraint."

"Seriously though, it was horrible."

"I thought you said you had a great weekend."

"I did, except for that little bit. But, back to the real world."

"Yes, now you just have to suffer through having me as your only friend to hang out with." He gives me a pout. "Aren't I enough anymore?"

"*You* are."

"But, Sam's not?"

"No, everything is fine. Let's just forget I said anything."

"Okay. Sam is wonderful, you are happy, and I am hungry. Dinner?"

"Sure."

Matt and I go to a Mexican dive for dinner and then he drops me at home. I unpack and start some laundry and settle back into my regular routine. But I'm so much more lonely now than I used to be. I miss Chris so much. I know I need to distract myself.

I get through the rest of the week and then I spend the weekend at Matt's. I even sleep on a couch so that I don't have to go home – ah, distractions. But we don't do anything. I mostly just read and Matt plays Xbox. At least I'm reading a funny book – it lightens my mood.

"You're laughing a lot," Matt comments. "What are you reading?"

"Oh, it's just some chick lit. But it *is* really funny. You should read it."

"Do I look like a fourteen year old girl to you?"

"Is that your way of telling me you would rather not?"

"That's right. You read your drivel. I'm going to rot my brain with video games."

I end up staying until Monday morning when Matt leaves for work, just to put off going home as long as I can.

"Thanks for letting me hang out here all weekend."

"Of course, honey. You can stay here whenever you want."

"Unless, of course, you bring home a hot date."

"Well, that's completely up to you. I mean, if you don't mind..." He laughs. "Just remember that I'm used to being able to use the whole house any way I chose."

"Okay, thank you for that mental picture. Go to work now."

"Sara!" It's either very late, or very early. I'm half asleep and my phone is going off.

I grab it and sleepily answer. "Sam?"

"Sara – what the hell is this?"

"I don't know. I can't see you. What the hell is what?"

"Don't play stupid with me! First that thing with my dad and now you are in OK! magazine with that male slut you insist on hanging out with all the damn time. There's a whole article about those assholes. And *you* are listed as Chris Eck's *fiancée*. What the hell, Sara? Are you divorcing me for him? Because some notice from the horse's mouth would have been nice. I'm glad I got to find out with the rest of the world at the grocery store check out."

"Sam, I have no idea what you are talking about. It's –" I look at the clock "– four in the morning –"

Sam cuts me off. "I bloody well know what bloody time it is! What I don't know is why *my wife* is listed as someone else's fiancée in a national magazine. International! Because Anna got it here, I think!"

I'm waking up more and more. "What are you talking about? I'm not anyone's fiancée. Wait! Chris? It says Chris and I are getting married? What magazine is this?"

"Don't treat me like an idiot, Sara. *It* doesn't say anything. *Chris* is quoted – he says, 'Sara no "H" Clarke with an "E", that's how you spell her name.'"

"Sam! That's a joke. It's a joke we have. I don't know how it would have ended up in a magazine, and I can't imagine how you got that into me being his fiancée, but seriously. It's a tabloid."

"I got that because that's what it says. They interviewed the band and when they asked those assholes if there was anyone special in their lives, Chris named you. At the end you are mentioned again. It says, 'Chris and his fiancée, Sara Clarke, are going to be breaking hearts all over town.'"

"Seriously, Sam, you can't believe that crap. It's tabloid trash. I'm sorry." What exactly am I even apologizing for? "I'm not sure what happened, but I'm positive things were taken out of context and contorted until they didn't resemble anything the guys actually said. I don't even know why they did an interview with that stupid magazine."

"That's what you're worried about? That they did an interview? Not that you are named as someone else's fiancée?! People are going to read this, Sara! What are they going to think?"

"Is that what this is about? You're worried about what the neighbors are going to think?"

"Aren't you?"

"No! Why would I be? Anyone that matters knows the truth."

"No, Sara. My boss matters. My co-workers matter."

"Then tell them it's not true. Besides, it's not like my name is unique. I'm sure that people are not going to immediately think that it's your wife. The most that might happen to connect me to it is that people might think, 'Hey! I know a Sara Clarke!' That's it."

"You're not taking this seriously enough." But he is running out of steam now.

"No, Sam, you're taking this way too seriously. It's garbage."

"I'm sorry that I woke you up."

"It's not like I have anything to do today."

"Yes, well. I'm sorry. It's just very hard to read something like that and not get upset."

"How *did* you even read that? Just out of curiosity. It doesn't really seem like a magazine that you would pick up in the first place."

"Oh, Anna was reading it. She showed it to me."

"Of course."

"What's that supposed to mean?"

"Okay Sam, I'm not fighting with you at 4 am. Have a lovely afternoon."

"We haven't talked in a week, and that's how you're going to hang up?"

"You're right; we haven't talked in a week. But this is not really the best time. It's pretty much the middle of the night for me. I'm tired. You probably need to be working. We'll talk next week."

"What's wrong with you Sara? You're different."

"Yes. I am. Good-bye Sam." And with that, I hang up. Later I realize that I didn't tell him that I love him. I don't think I have ever hung up the phone with him without telling him that I love him. I really am different.

Later in the day, I call Chris. "So, I'm your fiancée, huh?"

"Oh, sh–. Sorry. I should have warned you. I told them not to print it, but they don't really care. They'll just print a retraction next month, that no one will read, and act like it's fine. I'm sorry. Evans was being an idiot and they took him at his word."

"What was he saying?"

"That I was going to marry you someday."

"Sam said you were quoted spelling my name."

"Sam told you?"

"Yes, I got a phone call at 4 am. He was very upset that his wife is marrying someone else."

"I can understand that," Chris allows.

"All the same. What did you say?"

154

"Evans was calling you 'Shorty' and they really wanted to know who you were. Holst told them your name, but yes, I did spell it when they asked, immediately followed by 'But she's not my fiancée.' I'm sorry Sara."

"I don't really care. It's my 15 minutes of fame! But, if Sam ever asks, I'm going on record as having given you crap about it."

"Yes, ma'am."

"Why did you even do an interview with them?"

"The label makes us do a certain number of interviews. It will get worse when the new album is actually released."

"Well, please leave me out of them in the future."

"Done and done."

"So, what's going on?"

"Just finishing up the album and rehearsing."

"You've been 'finishing up' for a while."

"Yeah, but I always feel like after the actual recording it is all just gravy."

"But there's a lot of gravy?"

"Yeah, there is." He laughs. "Any chance you'll let me come visit?"

"I could probably allow it. When are you thinking?"

"This weekend?" It's Monday; I've been home from Portland for exactly one week.

"Um, teacher work week starts Monday."

"I can leave Sunday. I'll come on Thursday."

"You really don't have anything you should be doing?"

"I'm sure there are a ton of things I *should* be doing. But I'd rather come visit."

"Okay, I'll contribute to your indolence. Am I still coming to LA the next weekend?"

"Of course. I'll see you Thursday."

"Okay. Tell Short Mark it was your idea."

He laughs. "Keep it between the lines!"

I know he's expecting me to ask what he means. "And dirty side down!"

Chris is completely silent. Then, "Are you sure you won't marry me?"

"Why?"

"Because you know trucker talk."

"I don't think that's a good reason to marry someone."

"I do. But, I'm actually going to hang up now. Ten-ten." Ten-ten is signing off.

"Eighty-eights!" It means "Love and Kisses".

I can hear him laughing as I hit "END". I'm sure we'll be having a conversation about this in the near future.

Chapter 19

I pick him up at the airport Thursday afternoon. He had to have left LA in the dark. Flying east is the harder direction because it seems to take so much longer, and he gets in so much later than I do when I go to him. I feel like we get more time when I go west – I get in earlier and I don't care how late I get home.

I meet him between the security gates, like I always do. I can see his smile as soon as I can see him, and he starts walking faster. I'm already as close to the security line as they're going to let me get, so I just have to settle for bouncing on my toes. He scoops me into a big hug.

"I don't know how to say 'hello' in trucker," are the first words out of his mouth.

"Hm. Actually, neither do I. Got your ears on? 10-8?"

He looks at me, incredulously. "How do you know all of that?"

"My grandpa drove a truck. I grew up hearing it. How do you?"

"Tour buses are a lot like trucks, I guess. Our drivers spend a lot of time on the radio. I have to tell you though, I didn't know what 'eighty-eights' meant. I had to look it up."

I laugh. "Your drivers don't use that one much?"

"I actually can't think of a situation where I would be comfortable with a trucker using that over the airways."

"Sometimes they talk to their families."

"Oh. So, what are we going to do this weekend?"

"It's my last weekend of the summer. Traditionally, I'd use it to go to the beach."

"By yourself?"

"Matt went with me last year."

"Wait. Traditionally?"

"Well, if I did it this year it would have officially become a tradition."

"As in, you did it more than once?"

I shove him. "As in, I'd have done it every year since I started teaching."

He is laughing. "So, twice. Well, I would hate to break tradition. Let's go to the beach."

It seems silly to drive back to my house first since to go to the beach we will have to turn around and drive right back past the airport, but unfortunately, it's necessary.

At home, I pack up some stuff while Chris tries to get us a hotel room. "I'm really not sure you'll be able to get one so last minute!" I call to him.

"Have some faith in me, sweetheart."

Of course he manages to find one. It's only a couple of hours to Virginia Beach so we should be able to get there in time for a late dinner.

"How did you decide to start teaching?" he asks as we drive.

"When we moved to Virginia, I didn't want to go back to a lab. I didn't know what to do with myself and Matt told me I should teach chemistry. He was joking, but I thought it might actually be a good idea. So I applied. I had to get a license, but they gave me something called a 'provisional' so that I could start right away. I actually don't have a full teaching license yet. But I have, like, five years before I have to."

"By then, you may decide to move on to something else."

"Yeah, like touring with a rock band."

"Yeah, that could be an interesting career choice."

"Are you hiring any roadies?"

"Probably not. Maybe you would just have to hang out with us all the time."

"Wow, you would really pay me to sit on my butt and watch other people work?"

"I'm sure 'Eye Candy' is an actual occupation choice on a tax return."

"Yes, but it probably means 'Really, I'm a prostitute, and also an honest citizen so I still file taxes.'"

He laughs. "Maybe you could be our maid."

"Sure, I would like nothing more than to wash your dirty socks and dishes."

"I'll start wearing my socks only once and then throwing them away for a new pair. And I'll only eat on paper products."

"That is terrible for our environment. Besides, you are used to Giada, and there is no way I could live up to those standards."

"Ah, yes. She does set the bar kind of high, doesn't she?"

I nod. "Does she tour with you?"

"Alas, no. But I lament it greatly."

"I'm sure you do. Who keeps your tour bus clean?"

"Actually, we do have a maid type person. She's crew."

"A life of excess in the extreme. I could totally get used to that."

"Please do. *Mi vida es su vida*, sweetheart."

"I think that phrase is typically about a house."

"Typically, but I don't know 'tour bus' in Spanish. Besides, we were talking about an entire lifestyle."

"We were. Teacher by day, superstar by night!" I say in the most announcer-type voice I can manage.

"It does have a nice ring to it," he says.

"Wait!" I blurt out. "Short Mark already offered me a job!"

"He did?"

"Yeah, on the first day I met him. He wanted to hire me to be his prompter, remember?"

"And we already established that is a real job, so you're hired."

"Ah, if only it were that easy." But I'm laughing.

Our hotel isn't so much a hotel as a five star resort. I raise my eyebrows at Chris when we check in. "It's a lifestyle, remember?" He waggles his eyebrows in his vaudeville way.

"I have a feeling this is going to hurt the tradition slightly."

"Why?"

"Because next year, when I stay in some piddly, po-dunk hotel it won't feel the same. The point of a tradition is sameness."

"Would you like me to try to get a room for you at your piddly hotel from last year?"

"Um, no. I'll take it when I can get it."

"I'll just be sure we stay here every year."

I spin in a slow circle as I check out the posh lobby. "Okay. I think I could handle that."

Our room is amazing as well. He only got one room though, something I am quick to point out. "Ah, yes," he says, "but two beds, see? And come on! It was a last minute reservation in summer! What do you want from me?"

"I think you could have made it happen if you wanted to. I'm starting to think no doors are closed to the great Chris Eck." The bell hop helping us with our luggage turns in surprise and looks closely at Chris. I pretend that I don't notice. "I don't really mind. I'm just teasing. This place is a palace. Two of them would have been quite excessive."

He laughs as he gives the bell hop a tip, who has been dragging his feet considering how little luggage we actually have.

"Do I even want to know what my half of this room is going to cost?" I ask him.

"You can take care of meals."

"This is an all-inclusive place, isn't it?" I'm guessing he wouldn't really let me pay for anything. He never does.

He nods and laughs.

"So," I start, "beach or food first?" He just looks at me. "Right, of course. Let's go get something to eat."

The dinner rush is over so we practically have the restaurant to ourselves.

"I'm getting way too used to spending time with you," I tell him.

"Why do you say that?"

"Because pretty soon, I won't be able to. I'll be working and you'll be touring."

"Yeah, that's going to suck."

"At least you'll have your band-mates."

"True. You'll have your students."

"Uh-huh. That's totally the same thing."

"You could always give it all up and go with us as eye candy." Chris puts his hands up in a half shrug, like it's my fault my life isn't awesome.

"I'm sure Sam would love that."

"Fine, go as our 'prompter'."

"I don't think he would like that either."

"I don't think we would actually *have* to tell him."

"Right. Because that's healthy for a marriage."

"Where is he right now?"

"Asia? Hong Kong? I'm not sure." Is Hong Kong *in* Asia? Geography has never been my strong suit.

He laughs at me. "Hong Kong is in Asia, you idiot."

"Well, I think he's over there somewhere. What's your point?"

"You don't know where he is right now. That's my point."

"Yes, but he's not living a double life."

"He's not?"

"No!" I would never admit that it's something I worry about sometimes.

"How do you know that? The whole point of a double life is that it's secret."

"Thanks. Now I'll be worried that he *is*."

"Ah, seeds of doubt. My job is done."

"Are you trying to break up my marriage?"

"Not exactly. I'm trying to convince you to tour with us."

"Well, I can't. I have a lot of students to torture with chemistry."

"It's more torturous if the teacher sucks. If that's really your goal, you should quit."

"How do you know that I don't suck?"

"I'm going with my gut on this one."

We take a walk on the beach after we eat. We started dinner so late and spent so long eating that it is completely dark. I dump my shoes and walk in the shallows of the waves. Chris isn't wearing his shoes either, but he is walking on dry land.

"The best part of coming at the end of summer is that the water is really warm."

"Yeah, and at night it's full of sharks."

I laugh at him. "Are you afraid of sharks?"

"I live on the west coast. I have good reason to be."

"Well, I'm pretty sure I'm safe here in my two inches of water."

"You never know. Didn't Jaws come up on land?"

"I'll be sure to keep my eye out for any mechanical sharks on the loose."

"When something grabs you, I'm not coming in to drag your sorry ass back out. You're on your own, sweetheart."

"You would let me be eaten?"

"No point in both of us going." I kick water at him. "Hey!" he yells. It was a good shot. He jumps in front of me and kicks water back in my direction. He's better at it, and suddenly I'm soaked.

We're in a full out water battle now. We're both laughing and running up and down the beach in the shallows. We're also both completely soaked. Even my hair is dripping. Chris is running backwards in front of me and I'm trying to chase him. Suddenly he changes direction and charges at me. He tackles me to the ground, but he catches me even as we fall so I don't get hurt as we collapse in the wet sand.

He's lying on top of me, our faces are inches apart. Water dripping from a man definitely makes him sexier, and I was unaware that it was possible for Chris to be any sexier. He is staring in my eyes and his breath is coming out in short bursts. The water is lapping at my side. My whole body is tingling with desire, so I do the only thing I can. I shove him off. I try to laugh to break the sexual tension that is so thick it's almost visible.

"I win," he says.

"And now I need a shower."

"Let's head back then."

As I stand up I realize that I'm completely covered in sand, my hair is an absolute mess, and my dress is suddenly sticking to me and see through. I start there and try to pull it off of my skin. Then I run my fingers through my hair a bunch of times, trying to comb it out a little.

Chris reaches up and grabs my hand. "If it is even possible, you are more gorgeous now then when we walked out here. You can stop."

"Whatever. But I'm still not thrilled to walk through the lobby in a see through dress."

He takes a step back and looks me up and down. A little more closely than necessary, probably. Then he pulls his shirt off and stuffs it over my head.

"What about you?" I ask.

"I'd rather be naked that let anyone else see *you* naked."

"I'm hardly *naked*!"

"Um, seriously sweetheart, you might as well have been." He laughs and throws his arm around my shoulders as we start back up the beach.

He is dripping wet and half naked. And touching me. I feel like something inside of me is going to explode. I take a deep breath. We are just friends, I remind myself. I'm married to Sam. *So what? He's cheating on you!* a little voice in my head is yelling. But I don't know that for *sure* and even if he is, *I'm* not a cheater. Right. Get a grip.

We turn more than a few heads as we cross the lobby for the elevator. I'm not sure if it is because I look so horrible, or because Chris is so hot. It's probably some of both. He still has his arm around my shoulders and I'm guessing everyone in there is wondering what someone like him is doing with someone like me.

We get in the elevator with a couple of men who look like they might be here for work or something, because they are both wearing suits. Their eyes pop a little when we step in behind them. Chris pushes me to the corner and then stands between me and the men. I appreciate his chivalry.

He lets me shower first, which I also appreciate. The sand is caked in my hair and I feel disgusting. When I get out I find him on the floor, with his back against the wall, watching TV. "Couch uncomfortable?" I ask.

"I didn't want to get anything wet. That was the longest shower you have ever taken."

"Sorry. It took a while to get all of the sand out of my hair. You have only yourself to blame."

"Fair enough," he allows.

I'm standing there in a towel, but for some reason I'm not at all self conscious. Maybe because he told me a minute ago that I was practically naked? Everything is just so easy around him, so *right*. He gets up and hops in the shower while I put on my pjs, then brush out my hair. I bought new pajamas a little while ago. I tried to convince myself that it really was just time to get new ones and that I wasn't doing it because Chris sees me in them so much. I'm still not completely convinced.

Once Chris is clean, dried, and dressed in his pajama pants and white t-shirt, we flop down on one of the beds. "I bought these pants just for you, you know."

"You did? Why?"

"Because I used to just sleep in my underwear and I didn't think you would appreciate that."

I laugh. "I bought these," I pluck my pajamas, "just for you. As much as I try to convince myself that I didn't."

"I'm glad you got something so sexy."

I look down. I'm wearing pajama pants and a matching tank top. Not really sexy. "I'm kidding," he says. "Usually when a woman tells a man that she bought pajamas for him, they're more of a lingerie variety."

"Well, I bought them for the exact opposite reason. I couldn't be running around in skimpy pjs around my friend, you know."

"I appreciate it. That would have been cruel."

We look through the selection of movies on our TV and settle on an old eighties movie. "Ah, the classics of my childhood," I tease.

"Yes," he agrees. "Gotta love the Coreys. You had a major crush on them, didn't you?"

"Didn't everyone?"

"Oh yes, I used to pine for them every night. I had posters of them all over my walls."

"I knew it."

I fall asleep watching the movie and I wake up tucked into the other bed. Either I was half asleep and don't remember moving, or Chris moved me again.

After breakfast, we spend the whole day on the beach. Chris even has the hotel bring lunch out to us. We sit on lounge chairs provided by the hotel and after a while, we get an umbrella from them too. Smearing sunscreen on his back once was hard enough, and I enjoyed it way too much when he did mine.

"I'm sure you have more photo shoots coming up and I don't want you sunburned in them," I tell him as they set up the umbrella for us.

"I'm sure Evans appreciates your consideration."

"Be sure to tell him so that I get credit."

"I will. You know, he's going to be mad that we came to the beach without him."

"So, don't tell him that part."

"Hey, Evans, I just wanted to let you know that Sara was conscientious enough to be sure that after a few hours I got under an umbrella so that I didn't get sunburned. But, we weren't at the beach or anything. We were just in the backyard. It probably would have been better to go inside, but she just brought out a sun umbrella."

"Right. Why wouldn't he believe that?"

He laughs and jumps when his phone goes off. He picks it up and looks at the display. He laughs again. "Speak of the devil..." He answers, "Hey, man. What's up?"

"Do you get calls from anyone other than the guys and me?"

"My mother. Nothing, I'm talking to Sara. She's making me sound pathetic." I smirk at him. "Yeah, I can't right now; I don't have easy access." Then to me, "Sara, you didn't bring your laptop did you?" I shake my head. "Sorry, dude. It'll have to wait. I'm, uh... We took a little road trip." He winks at me. "Sara told me I'm not allowed to tell you." Chris hands me the phone.

"Hello, Short Mark."

"Hey, Shorty! Where are you?"

"We took a little trip. It's a tradition."

"What kind of tradition?"

"The kind that involves a trip."

"A trip to where?"

"Here."

He sighs dramatically. "Are you being difficult on purpose?"

"As a matter of fact, I am." Should I just tell him? "We're at the beach."

"What?! You went to the beach without me?"

"You're a butthead, do you know that?"

"Yup. Let me talk to Eck."

I hand the phone back to Chris. "Yeah? Well, I can talk to you now." He looks at me with raised eyebrows. I nod. "I know I can't, but we'll see how far we can get." I settle back in my seat and pull out the book I stuck in my bag. He's quiet for a long time.

"Why don't you all just take out all of the ones that you are dead set against?" It makes me jump to hear his voice suddenly. I forgot he was even on the phone. He smiles at me. Chris talks to the guys for several more minutes, but his end of the conversation doesn't make any sense to me, so I try to tune it out.

Chris seems frustrated as he hangs up the phone. "Sorry. We have to pick some artwork for a couple of things."

"And it would be easier if you were there and could see it, I imagine."

"Or at least be able to video-conference with them."

"Sorry. Do you want to go back?"

"To your house or the hotel?"

"Either. I'm sure the hotel has computers you could use."

"Yeah, but this isn't really something that I could do in a public place."

"Maybe they'll let you take a laptop to our room."

He's quiet for a moment while he considers it. "It's worth asking, I guess. Do you mind?"

"Not at all. I'll just read." I hold up my book.

He smiles. "Okay, I'll probably be back very soon."

"They'll let you borrow one. You're the amazing Chris Eck."

He laughs and walks away. Apparently they do let him, because he is gone for a long time. I read several chapters and then decide I'm hot, so I walk down to the water.

I wade out until the water is a little over my knees. The thing about Virginia Beach is that the beach is really steep and it drops off suddenly if you don't pay attention. I splash some water on myself and look out to the horizon as the waves wash over my thighs. A guy holding a Frisbee comes over to me.

"Hey, there."

"Hi."

"A couple of my friends and I are playing Frisbee – want to join the game?"

I glance down at my left hand. I left my rings at home because I didn't want to lose them on the beach. "Um, no thanks." Even if I was interested in being picked up, playing Frisbee in a string bikini isn't a great idea. "I'm not exactly dressed right."

"We could do something else."

"I – Um, really, thanks but I'm good."

"Are you sure? I hate to leave you to enjoy the beach by yourself."

"I –" But before I can say anything, Chris comes crashing through the water.

He grabs me around the waist and smiles at the guy when he says,

"God! I can't leave you alone for a second, can I?"

The guy looks down at the water, slightly dejected. "Oh, well, have a good day," he mumbles as he walks away.

"Thanks."

"Beating them off with sticks," Chris mutters half under his breath. Then aloud he says, "I don't understand how Sam leaves you to your own devices all the time."

"Why?"

"Never mind. Enjoying the water?"

"Sure. I was getting hot. Did you decide on the artwork?"

"Yes, as a matter of fact we did. Thanks, your idea was genius."

I look at him pointedly. "Of course it was; I'm a genius."

He picks me up and dumps me in the water. I come up spluttering and jump on him, my sad attempt at a tackle. But he just stands there laughing and holding me. I glance down to make sure my bathing suit survived.

"Nice try, sweetheart." He throws me over his shoulder and starts back towards the shore.

"Ahh! Please put me down! Please! I don't appreciate you showing my big bum to the world!"

He smacks said rear end, but he puts me down. "*You* do not have a big butt."

"I actually agree with you, but when you put it up there like that, of course it *looks* big."

"Right. And, as a friend, I'm supposed to be on the lookout for that. Sorry."

"You're right, you are."

As we reach the water's edge Chris flips his head up the beach. "*That* is a big butt."

I turn and see an *enormous* woman walking down the beach with a tiny little dog on a leash. "Whoa. That is a big butt. Would you still love me if I looked like that?"

"Probably, but I'd stop asking you to tour with us."

"Why? Would you be embarrassed to be seen with me?"

"No. That butt wouldn't fit through the door to get on the bus." I laugh. "No, I'm serious, I really don't think it would."

We settle back into our chairs under the umbrella. We're quiet for a while, just sitting and looking out to the ocean. But it's a comfortable silence. Everything with Chris is comfortable.

When the sun drops behind the high rises behind us and bathes the beach in shadows, we decide to go in. He lets me shower first again, and I try to be quick this time. As soon as I get out, he gets in. I spend the time trying to get ready for dinner, since I know he will be ready to eat almost as soon as he's out of the shower.

Sure enough, the first words out of his mouth are, "Do you want to go somewhere for dinner tonight, or just eat in one of the hotel's restaurants?"

"We can just eat here. For some reason, being in the sun really drains me and I'm tired. We can at least eat in a different one."

"Okay, sounds good to me."

We wander around downstairs for a little while. Each restaurant has its menu posted near its door, so we walk around reading them all before we decide where we want to eat. I can feel people watching us. Finally we decide and the lucky hostess working that restaurant looks at Chris with eyes like saucers. I swear, she's practically drooling. When he smiles at her, I think she's going to faint. But then, he has that effect on women.

She shows us to a table right away, even though there are people ahead of us waiting. I think the sight of Chris was too much for her and she forgot how things like this work. I wonder what those people are thinking. I hope they assume that we had a reservation or something.

The food is excellent and I eat way too much. It doesn't help that I drink almost a whole bottle of wine by myself. Chris is lining up his dead soldiers on the table. Our waiter keeps trying to take them away, but Chris won't let him. "I've got to keep track of how many I've had," he tells him. As a comparison, I flip each wine glass I finish over and line them up next to his beer bottles. By the time we are done, we are running out of room on the table. He has out drank me more than two to one.

"I think it might be time to quit," I tell him.

"Okay. What should we do now?"

"Go pass out. I was already tired. Now I've eaten too much and drank *way* too much."

"Good. I like my women loose."

"I remember."

Chris leaves a huge tip on the table. He looks at me, "We were really kind of a pain in his ass."

"I am sure you have more than made up for it." I wobble a little as I get up.

Chris grabs my arm and laughs at me. "All right, bedtime – before you break something."

I teeter up to our room and fall onto my bed. "Aren't you even going to put on your pjs?" Chris asks me.

"I'm not sure I'm capable."

"Would you let Matt help you?"

"Probably, why? Is he here?"

"No, but if you'd let Matt, then you can let me, right? We're both just your friends."

"That was diabolical."

I push myself up and go to the vanity to brush my teeth and wash the makeup off my face. "I hate wearing makeup," I mutter.

"Then don't."

"I think it's a requirement for women."

"It's really not. I think you should quit."

"It's not like I wear it that often. Only when you take me out. Maybe you should just quit taking me out."

"Fine. It would save me a fortune."

I throw my hairbrush at him. He catches it on the fly. I stick my tongue out. "I'm going to bed now," I tell him.

"Do you still want help with your jammies?"

"I didn't ask for help in the first place. And, no, I'm fine."

Chris stares at me with a smile on his face as I pull my pants up under my dress and then slip my arms through my dress and slide them into my shirt. I put my shirt on as I take my dress off in one movement. And then I pull my bra off from under my shirt.

"That was amazing. Can all girls do that?"

"What? Change clothes without letting anything be seen? Yes, they teach us how in high school."

"They don't teach guys any useful life lessons like that."

"Sorry."

He pulls down the blankets on my bed. I climb in and he tucks them back up around my chin. I giggle. "I feel like a little kid."

"You're not, I promise. You just look like you could use some TLC tonight."

"Thanks." My eyes are already closing. Chris kisses my forehead and I drift off.

That night I have a dream about Chris. I've only had, like, two sex dreams in my entire life. I'm not thrilled that I had to have one while sharing a room with the lead character in it. I mean, I guess that would be great if it was someone that I could actually do something with, but instead I have to lie there frustrated. I'm hoping that Chris is asleep and didn't realize I was dreaming. But, even thinking about him in bed, less than three feet away, is making me crazy. This is getting ridiculous. I think of my list, but it doesn't help. I might have to stop being his friend.

I roll away from that side of the room and curl into a little ball on my side. Would it hurt to just kiss him? Ha! Like I would be able to stop there. If I want to be with Chris, I have to leave Sam *first*. I just have to decide if I'm willing to do that.

When Sam and I got engaged my mom asked me if I was sure. She asked me again when I was getting ready to walk down the aisle. Maybe she knew something? But I told her, "I better be, because I don't believe in divorce." My mom died, confident in the knowledge that I was never going to get divorced.

Chapter 20

I roll over to my back. Then I sit up, fluff my pillow, and lay back. Then I flip over to my stomach and push my pillow out of the way so my head is flat on the bed. Then I turn my head the other way.

Chris's eyes are open and he's looking at me. "Can't sleep?"

I glance at the clock: 4:42. "Sorry, did I wake you?"

"No, I always get up before five am."

I want to climb in bed with him. I want him to wrap his arms around me and go back to sleep. I've done it dozens of times, but I know it's a terrible idea with the lust raging inside of me. "I'm sorry," I tell him again.

He sits up. "Whatever. You went to sleep really early, so I did too. Does this mean you're ready to get up?"

"No. But I might as well, because I'm not going back to sleep."

"We could go watch the sunrise."

I laugh as I remember telling him that was one advantage of the west coast: watching the sunset instead of having to get up before sunrise. I sit up. "Okay."

I throw on a pair of shorts and a t-shirt and put my hair in a pony tail. Chris, very politely, steps around a wall in our palace to change.

The beach is completely deserted, of course – it's still nighttime really. "I thought watching the sunrise was what you people did on the east coast." He nudges me with his shoulder.

"I said that was our only choice. Not very many people do it. And even if they do, I imagine they wait until a little closer to the actual event to come out on the beach."

"I see. That's a good point." He takes my hand and we walk. It is still completely dark, there isn't even gray on the horizon yet. The sun doesn't come up for a *long* time.

"It's summer," I whine. "I thought the sun came up super early."

"Sara, it is earlier than super early. And, it's almost fall." He pulls out his phone and messes around for a second. Then he holds it out to show me. "Sunrise," he says, "6:31 am. And it's only 5:40, sweetheart. We've got some time."

We had been walking up and down the beach in front of our hotel and I pull him back in that general direction. Once we are squarely in front of the hotel, I sit down in the sand and pull him with me. Then I lie back, parallel to the water. He lies back next to me.

"No," I say. "Put your feet the other way and put your head right here." I indicate the space between my head and shoulder. He moves and then lies down so we are ear to ear.

"Better?" he asks.

"Yup."

"Now what?"

"Um, we look at the space where stars should be?" Virginia Beach is really bright anyway, but we are starting to get closer to dawn and the horizon is lightening.

"It's great. So... blank."

"Well, then it's a canvas. And we can put anything up there we want."

"You have a wonderful imagination, did you know that?"

"That's what my kindergarten teacher told me."

"Well, you haven't changed much."

We fall silent and draw our own pictures in the sky. Eventually I drift back off to sleep, because I wake up when I get wet. "Hey!" I sit straight up. The tide is coming in and it has reached us.

"It's a good thing the tide came in now." He points to the horizon. "We almost missed sunrise."

We sit back and watch the sun come up. "Okay, I'm wet and sandy. Do I have to shower before they will feed us?"

Chris smiles. "Come on. We'll order room service."

We spend all day Saturday on the beach, just like Friday. This time we use more sunscreen and no umbrella, but I bought spray so there isn't any rubbing involved. I wear a different bathing suit, one with a little more staying power and we play in the sand: Frisbee, paddle ball, bocce, and catch with a football. The hotel has a great stash of toys.

They also have a lot of girls around, and all of them are interested in Chris – but who can blame them? He is half naked, wet, and perfect. I'm only a little bit jealous. The best part of my day is when we are playing Frisbee and a girl walks by not paying attention. She catches sight of Chris, presumably on his own and turns to talk to him. I've already let go of the Frisbee and she is standing directly in its path. I am sure that the sight of it hitting the back of her head will bring laughter to my lips for years to come. Even Chris can't keep from smiling.

"Sorry!" I yell, but I'm sure she can tell I'm not.

Around lunchtime someone recognizes Chris and comes to ask for an autograph. I have never seen him turn anyone away, but he does.

"I'm sorry, but not today. I'm on vacation and I would appreciate some privacy. Thank you." His smile does little to console the girl.

"She thinks you're a huge jerk, you know that, right?"

"Yeah, she probably does. But I'm not in the mood today."

"Are you ever actually in the mood?"

"Good point." He rummages in my bag and pulls out my book and a pen. I can feel my jaw drop when he tears a page out and signs it. Then he runs off after the girl. I can see him talking to her for a minute before he comes back.

"That was my book," I tell him.

"I'll buy you a new one. You were the one who told me I was being a jerk."

"What did you tell her?"

"That my girlfriend is a shrew and she doesn't like me to talk to other girls."

"Were you referring to me?"

"I couldn't leave her with the impression that Evansgate is full of jerks, could I? I had to have someone to blame it on."

"How did you explain being able to get away to give her the autograph?"

He winks. "Don't worry. I just did."

"I don't want to actually know, do I?"

"Probably not."

"Fine. At least Evansgate's stellar reputation is intact."

"Even if their eye candy is a bitch."

"I thought I was your prompter."

"Her too."

I see the guy from yesterday and he gives me a smile and a wave. Today, he is playing beach volleyball with his friends, and they invite us over to their game. Chris and I are on opposite teams and we are competitive for the first time all day. I'm the only girl, although not the shortest player, who is also on my team, and Chris is so much taller than everyone that his side definitely has the advantage. We lose, of course. Chris offers to buy a round of beers, but the guy that had tried to pick me up in the first place won't let him. "The losers have to buy the beer, dude."

By dinner, I'm beat. I don't know how Chris has so much energy.

"I haven't been going for my morning run, so I have to make up for it by doing a lot of other things."

"You've never gone for a run."

"Not in Virginia. Good Lord, woman, I would suffocate."

"Oh. Do you in LA?"

"Every day. I get up early to run."

"I thought you were teasing when you said you get up before five every day."

"I was. 6:30 is still early."

"How long?"

"I don't know. About an hour, or a little more, maybe." The look on Chris's face makes me think he might be serious.

"How far do you go?"

He shrugs. "Uh, somewhere between eight and ten miles."

"Please tell me you're kidding."

"Nope. I don't really do a lot of other exercise, so I run."

"I hate running."

"Then you would really hate it with me. I run with weights."

"You do *what*? I was unaware that you could make running any worse."

"Yup. It's the best way to stay in shape. At least, it is for me."

I really want to say that it's working because his body is so smoking hot, but I decide against it.

We order room service because I'm too tired to make myself presentable. "It's okay," Chris says. "I have to go home tomorrow, so I'd rather not share my time with you."

"Share with who?"

"The general public."

We watch another movie, and I fall asleep again.

I wake up in my bed, and it's really early again. I try to go to sleep, but I can't. And in the process, I wake Chris up again.

"In DC, I don't think you were up earlier than noon most days. In LA, you did almost nothing *but* sleep. I'm not bringing you back to the Atlantic ocean if it means you get up before five every day."

"Sorry. What can I say? It's being so close to your awesomeness; it wakes me up."

He fans himself with his hands. "You should try being in the same bed. You have no idea how hard it is to sleep with so much awesomeness."

"I can imagine." I'm laughing. "Do you want to go back to sleep? Or try to see the sunrise again? Or breakfast?"

"You have a lot of options for so early in the morning."

"That's not really that many. If you really want options though..." I trail off.

"What? We could streak through the lobby? Go deep sea fishing?

Prank call the front desk?"

"Why do my options seem so much more feasible than yours?"

"You just don't have the same sense of adventure."

"You guys get in a lot of trouble when you're on tour, don't you?"

"Not really. I save it for when I can take you down with me."

"Thanks," I say dryly. "I appreciate it."

"I'm always thinking of you, sweetheart."

"Well, let's get up and do *something*. We're running out of time."

"Only you could make getting out of bed before five sound like a good idea."

"I try."

We get room service for breakfast, if for no other reason than the restaurants don't open until six. Then we decide to go back out to the beach and try to see the sunrise again.

Chris takes my hand as we walk and brings it to his lips. He smiles. "I'm really starting to see the positive side of getting on the beach so early."

"Yeah?"

"Yeah. I don't have to worry about all of the guys ogling you."

"Yes, because that happens so much. More like you don't have to worry about running from all the girls."

"I don't get hit on that much."

"Really? What about yesterday? I'm not sure I could count the number of girls who fell over themselves."

"But how many of them actually talked to me?"

"Enough."

"Sara! Are you jealous?"

"Not even a little bit. I got to sleep in your room."

He laughs. "I guess it would have been awkward if I had brought one of them back with me, wouldn't it?"

"I think we would have had to have a serious discussion about our friendship."

"I love you."

"You know I love you too, don't you?"

"Yes, I do, even if *you* don't."

We pack up our things and leave after we eat an early lunch. Chris needs to be at the airport before three, and I'm afraid beach traffic will be bad. It's much easier to say good-bye at the airport than it normally is, because I know I am going to see him again in five days.

"Have a good week at work!" he tells me.

"Ug. Why did you have to remind me?"

He laughs. "I didn't want you to forget to go."
"Fly safe! I'll see you on Friday!"
I sigh as I watch him walk away.

Chapter 21

Monday morning my alarm goes off early, but I'm already awake. I fell asleep really early after being up so early Sunday morning. I'm really mixed up. I better get this straight before I go to LA, because if I wake up at five am *my* time when I'm out there, everyone else will just be going to bed. I promise to make myself stay up really late tonight.

I'm surprised when my phone rings. Who would call this early? It's probably Chris, but then, it's *really* early in LA. I look at the display before answering.

"Hey, big sister. It's awfully early in Dallas. What are you doing up?"

"I'm not in Dallas. But, it's really early in St. Louis, too."

"St. Louis, huh? So why *are* you up?"

"I'm on a layover. I'm flying to Portugal actually. And, I thought I would take advantage and call to tell you to get this year off to a good start."

"Thanks," I answer dryly. "I'll be sure *now* to do my best."

Allison laughs. "I knew you needed my reminder! But, I've got a flight to catch. Love you!"

"I love you, too, you nut. Fly safe."

The day goes exactly as would be expected. A lot of meetings – school wide, department wide, teachers of seniors, and whatever other areas they could dream up. We get our schedules and twiddle our thumbs as we hear the same things they told us last year. Last year I actually needed to hear this stuff, as I had no idea what I was doing. It didn't occur to me at the time that I would have to listen to the same stuff every year or that everyone else in the room was hearing it for the umpteenth time.

At lunch, a bunch of the teachers that I'm friendly with sit together to eat. We exchange questions about our summers, and Gwen Turley, an English teacher, turns to me. "I hear you spent some time with Chris Eck of Evansgate."

"How did you hear that?" I ask.

"I saw a couple of students at the mall, and they were talking about it."

"What did they say?"

"They asked if I thought you could get them to play prom."

I frown. "Probably not, but I guess I could ask."

Her eyes bug out a little. "So you do know them?"

I hadn't actually thought about the fact that people might ask. "Um, yeah, I do. We met this summer." I officially have the attention of everyone in hearing range.

"They're releasing an album, aren't they?" another science teacher asks.

"Did you actually meet Chris Eck? He is so hot!" the French teacher is practically drooling.

"Where did you meet them?"

"*How* did you meet them?!"

Questions are coming from all around. "I met them in DC when I was visiting my sister and I went to a show. Yes, they are releasing an album; it should be out by the end of the month. Yes, I'm actually really good friends with Chris, well, with all of them I guess."

"How well do you know them?!" I don't even know who asked that one.

"Pretty well. I saw them a lot."

My fellow teachers have officially dissolved into teenage girls. Even the men look slightly awed. "I can't believe that!"

"Can you get me an autograph?"

"Do you think they *would* play prom?"

"Can you get tickets to a concert for me?"

I look around, kind of stupidly. I don't know what to say. Sometimes I forget they are so famous. "I, uh, I don't know." I feel like that answers all of them.

"What are they like?!"

I'm really struggling for words and I can feel my phone buzz in my pocket. "Um, hang on... I just... have to check this." I pull my phone out and put my nose down.

From Chris:
How is your first day at work going?

Speak of the devil...

To Chris:
It's going. Word got around that I know Evansgate and the great Chris Eck and I'm currently being mauled.

"Who is it, Sara?" I'm still the center of attention. I glance up and realize the whole room is silent and all eyes are on me.

"Um, it's... um," I stutter. My phone buzzes again.

"It's *him*, isn't it?!"

177

From Chris:
Now you know how I feel. Evans wants to know if you
need security detail now.

But I get a text from Short Mark before I'm even finished reading
the one from Chris.

From Mark E:
If you need security, I need to know now. I'm working
on the budget. :)

People are still staring at me. "Um, if you could just excuse me for
a minute." I jump out and run into the hall, dialing on my way.

"What's happenin' hot stuff?" Chris answers.

"Tell Short Mark that I do not need security. His budget is safe."

"I'm not sure. I like to keep my people protected, maybe I should
let him send someone your way."

"Don't be stupid."

"Don't worry, the budget is actually done in June."

Does that mean I would have to wait until June to be assigned
security if I said I wanted it? It's probably best not to ask, because I'm
sure he would actually send someone. "What am I supposed to tell
people?"

"About what?"

"About you."

"Whatever you want."

"It's not that easy."

"Sara, you were named in a magazine because of me. You can tell
people whatever you want."

"But I don't know!"

"What you want?"

"What's appropriate."

"Now you're being stupid. Tell people whatever."

"It's just weird." I can see my principal coming. "Oh, I gotta go!"

"Okay, be good. I'll call you – oh, call me. You call me later."

"Okay. Tell Short Mark I said he can keep his goons on the west
coast."

"All right. Ten-ten."

"Eighty-eights." I slip my phone in my pocket and turn to my
principal. "Hi, Karen! How was your summer?"

"It was fine, Sara. How was yours?"

"Oh, lovely, just lovely. Do we have another meeting now?"

"Yeah, we have to talk about the new tardy procedures."

"Joy." These are the parts of teaching I hate.

"Yeah, you know, the fun stuff."

Somehow I get through the next few days, but I have become a legend in the building. I suddenly have more friends at school than I ever did before. I find it rather disconcerting.

Chris sends me a geek stick with the new album. It comes on Wednesday in a box with messages from all of the guys. And pictures of them screwing around in the studio. I take my laptop up to my room and close the door, pull the shades, and turn off the lights. I send Chris a text:

> To Chris:
> I'm listening!

I plug it in, lay down, and close my eyes. I want to fully appreciate this. Also, I know I have to listen, and I *have* to like it because they will ask me for the words. I'm suddenly afraid. What if I don't like it?

But, no worries. The music is excellent, of course. I have a huge smile on my face – I love listening to them. I miss them all so much and this is like being in the same room with them again. The third song is the one I heard them record when I was in LA. I can't quite figure out what's different. Then I realize – it's me. They must have recorded me when they made me sing and they've turned the song into a sort of duet.

I jump up and grab my phone. But I stop before I finish dialing. I'm sure they did it just to be funny – just on this one that they sent to me. I'll call once I listen to the whole album and give them crap for it.

I wonder which song is the video they were taping in DC. I laugh when I realize that I watched the making of the video, but I never actually heard it.

And then I get to the last song. I immediately recognize the music. It's Chris's song. He never told me if it actually was going to be on the album or not. But here it is. I reach over and start it again before the words start. When they do, I'm surprised that Short Mark is singing. I just assumed Chris would sing it since it's his song, but I guess that's part of being in a group.

I don't care if someone else can you call you his
'Cause, baby girl, he don't love you
He don't treat you right
I don't care if you want to fight it
When you wake up tomorrow, I'll still be here
You told me that you're crazy
You said "Six kinds!"
But, baby girl,
Six kinds is the right amount for me
I'm not jealous of him
I won't lose sleep, no
I'm not jealous of him
You can be my friend
One day he will realize just how much you're worth
But it will be too late for that
You will be all mine
He can try to say that he loves you
But where was he when you went to sleep last night
I warned them that you're crazy
But they don't care
And, baby girl,
Six kinds is the right amount for me
I'm not jealous of him
I won't lose sleep, no
I'm not jealous of him
You can be my friend
You can be my best friend
I love you and your crazy
I love you and all six kinds
You can be my best friend

By the end, tears are streaming down my face. I grab the box and rifle through it. On the bottom is a song list. Short Mark knows that I like to know song titles. This one is called "Six Kinds of Crazy". And it's about me. I know it is. I can't even believe he remembers it, but I told him that the first day we met. The first time when he asked me to marry him, I told him I couldn't because I didn't know his name and then I warned him that I am six kinds of crazy. Those were my words!

I'm stunned into silence. I wonder if it's the last song on purpose. Because I wouldn't hear anything else, even if there was a marching band on the bed with me, I wouldn't hear it. He wrote a song about me. He just told the whole world that he loves me. Well, not yet, because technically the album hasn't been released. But he's planning on it. In his own way.

Oh, God! What if Sam hears it? What will he say? He flipped out over that article in that stupid tabloid, surely this is worse? I feel like I should call someone, but I don't know who to call. I don't even know what I would say. There are no words for the way I feel right now.

A very small part of me is celebrating. He loves me! I may have already known that, but he is openly declaring it now – he must really mean it! But the rest of me feels sick. That shouldn't make me happy. Sam is my husband.

There is really only one person to call. And I was going to have to anyway. Chris answers on the first ring, "Sara?"

"I don't know what to say."

"Did you like it?"

"The song or the album?"

"Yes."

"Yes. But I have a bone to pick with you – all of you. You scared me for a minute! I almost thought that you were going to release a song with my voice in it."

"Well, we're hoping to."

"What?"

"Evans will talk to you about it. But, I don't care about that right now. Can I release it, Sara?"

"I can't tell you that you can't."

"Yes, you can. I won't if you don't want me to."

"I can't tell you that you can't," I repeat stubbornly.

"You don't want me to."

"It's not that. I'm just afraid. Sam went crazy when that article came out, remember? What would he think if he heard that?"

"He wouldn't know that it's about you."

"Chris, you used my name."

"Oh. Good point."

We're both silent for a minute. "It's a good song."

"Thanks. I'm really glad you like it." He's quiet again for a minute. "Unless you specifically tell me not to, I'm going to release it, Sara."

"It's going to change things."

"It doesn't have to. It's not like you didn't know."

He's not saying it, he never would, but I can hear his thoughts through the phone line. *Choose me.*

"I can't."

"No, you won't. I know. But at least I put all my cards on the table."

When we hang up, I lie in bed and cry for hours. Eventually, I fall asleep and I wake up when my alarm goes off for school. Ug. I feel like crap. My head hurts from all of the tears last night. My throat is dry and scratchy. I feel yucky from sleeping in my clothes and not brushing my teeth or washing my face. But worst of all, I feel a great emptiness. I feel like Chris and I broke up or something. I have this awful feeling that I'm never going to see him again, that I signed my own death sentence with my words last night and he is out of my life forever. I hit snooze and lay there staring at the ceiling.

If Sam called me today and told me that he never wanted to see me again, would it hurt this bad? I know that I want to be faithful, honor my wedding vows and all that, but is it really fair if I truly love someone else more? My thoughts slip back to the pink thong again. It's impossible not to think about it. Does he even still love me? When was the last time we had sex? What the hell am I doing? I literally have a list of reasons to stay away from Chris, I remind myself, *again*.

But Chris has become important to me. He's probably my best friend. Does this mean that we can't be friends anymore? I mean, I basically just told him that I know he wants more but I don't. A very small voice in the back of my mind asks if that's true. Do I want something more? Gah! Maybe it's for the best, because being friends has become really hard.

Who am I kidding? I need him in my life.

I'm sorely tempted to throw my alarm clock at the wall when it goes off again. The last thing I feel like doing today is going to work, but I drag myself out of bed anyway. I feel a little better after my shower. I take some Tylenol to keep the edges of the headache away. I mentally mark off my calendar for the night: MOPING (busy).

I drag myself through the day. I avoid people as much as possible. I sit in the back of all of my meetings and keep my head down. I work on my lesson plans and syllabus in an empty classroom instead of in the department office. I know that my face is showing some of my turmoil because today, even with my new celebrity status, everyone leaves me alone.

I don't know what to do about this weekend. I haven't heard from Chris all day. I don't think I've gone this long without a text, phone call, email, *something* from him since we met. I drive home slowly, trying to see through my tears. I hurt him really bad. He probably doesn't want me around. I won't go this weekend unless I hear from him.

I'm so grateful when I pull onto my street. I make a deal with myself: I can have this night to cry and mourn, but then I have to get up and move on. I can't spend the rest of my life regretting him. I pull into my driveway and almost crash into the garage door because I don't put it up when I see Short Mark sitting on my front porch.

I punch the button for the garage, but I don't bother to wait for the door to go up so I can drive in. I turn the car off and get out. The sight of Short Mark – alone – makes it official. He would have come too if there was any way for us to still be *us*. I can't help it. I start to cry again.

Short Mark stands up slowly and walks towards me. "Hey, Shorty, what's wrong?"

"You don't know?"

"Eck?"

"Of course. I know it's hard to understand, but I need him, Short Mark. I need him and now he's gone." I sink down to the driveway and start to cry in earnest. It's not my best moment, but I'm sure Short Mark has seen me in worse situations, usually with alcohol involved.

"Get up. What are you talking about? Where did he go?"

"It was awful. We talked last night, and it was awful."

"I know you talked. I was there, standing next to him. He told you I was going to talk to you about the single."

"I know. But that was the least important part of the conversation. We can't be friends anymore."

"When did that happen?"

"It's complicated."

"Shorty, get up," he repeats. "I don't know what you think happened last night, but nothing has changed. He still loves you, I think he always will, but he knows how things stand. He is still your friend, and he will be until you tell him to go away."

"Then why didn't he come with you?"

Short Mark actually laughs. "Because he is in a very similar state back home, thinking that you don't want him here."

"I don't know if we can be friends anymore, Short Mark. I'm married and I love him."

"Him? Eck?"

I nod miserably. "If you tell him that, I will kill you. As a matter of fact, if you tell another living soul that, I will be sure no one ever finds your body. Don't forget that I'm well versed in chemistry. I could dissolve you."

"That might be the scariest threat I have ever received. Of course, there is also Allison to consider. Yes, I think I will try very hard to remain on your good side."

Despite myself, I smile.

"Can we go inside?" he asks. "I really have to pee."

I pull myself up. "Lead the way."

We sit in the music room to talk about *the single*, as he keeps referring to it. Short Mark mindlessly picks out a tune on the keyboard as we talk. "You were there. You know that song was missing something. None of us could agree on how to fix it."

"I never thought there was anything wrong with it."

"Yes you did, even if you won't admit it. But, it doesn't matter because I did – we did. When you sang it, everything fell into place. It was your voice that was missing."

"But, Short Mark, I can't actually sing."

"Yes, you can."

"Not very well, not well enough."

"The song sounds amazing, you can't deny it."

"I don't know. But does it really make any difference to the world at large? Release it, I don't care. But please don't give me credit for it or anything."

"I have to. I have to put your name on the box if your voice is in the song."

"Okay, fine. But, still, what difference does it make?"

"Would you consider going on stage at some of our bigger shows to sing it with me?"

"No."

"Feel free to take a moment to think it over."

"No."

"What would it take to convince you?"

"You can't. I'm not an idiot, Short Mark. I can't sing. I certainly can't sing in front of a huge crowd of your fans."

"Shorty, the song needs you. It doesn't sound right without you. And if I'm ever going to play it live, I'll need you there with me."

"No."

"I won't sing it in every show. But, I'd like to sing it at the launch, and in the biggest venues: Vegas, New York, you know."

"No."

"I won't give up."

"Neither will I."

"We haven't even started to talk about money. You'll get a percentage of the royalties, and you would get paid for every performance."

"No."

"Let me release it, please."

"Release it. But don't expect me to ever sing it again."

"Shorty, please. I need you to do this." He holds up his hand to stop my protest. "Please think about it. Please. I don't think it would be as bad as you think."

"I'm sure it would be worse."

He blows out a long breath. "You're so stubborn."

"It's not like you're backing down either," I point out.

"Except I'm being reasonable. You're just being stubborn."

"There would be more to it, and you know it. There would be contracts to sign, commitments that I can't actually make."

Before he goes, Short Mark gives me a piece of paper full of dates. It's their tour schedule.

"You're playing in Dallas on my birthday!" I say brightly.

"I know," he says quietly.

After Short Mark leaves, I go back up to my room and pull out the box to see the song titles again. I laugh when I see it: #3 "the Single".

Chapter 22

I get through my first week of work this school year and then Matt drives me to the airport in a mad dash to get to my plane on time.

When I get off of the plane in LA, Chris is standing there in a suit with a sign that says "CLARKE" in bold, black letters. My heart swells at the sight of him, and clenches when I notice the look on his face. I haven't talked to him since the horrible phone call, only texted a couple of times. Can I pretend everything is fine? They say to put a smile on your face even if you're unhappy because pretending you are happy can *make* you happy. "God, I've missed you!" I tell him. I throw my arms around him and drink in his smell.

"Do you feel special?" he asks me. Even his voice is strained. Oh, how bad is this going to be? Can we still be friends?

Okay – going to pretend like everything is fine for now. I smile at him. "Of course."

"Great." But he doesn't sound like he means it. He throws the sign in a nearby trash can and puts his arm around my shoulder as he leads me out of the airport. I can feel the tension in his muscles.

Jeff is waiting for us with the Town Car in the limo lot. He smiles at me as I climb through the door he is holding open. Chris climbs in behind me. "I feel like we should be making out like teenagers back here," he says.

Oddly enough, I understand what he means. It almost feels weird to *not* be kissing him. "Hm. You're right." I put my hand up. "But, alas, we cannot."

He nods, resigned. "I know."

This might be the time. "Should we talk about...?" I trail off. I don't know how to start this conversation.

"Nope. We're fine, sweetheart." I laugh to hear "sweetheart" in his goofy way. I know we're not fine. Of course we aren't – he told me that he loves me and I said *thanks, but no thanks.* I wish I could tell him that I do love him; I would love him if things were different. But playing the what-if game isn't going to get us anywhere and it's not a can of worms I want to open. I *shouldn't* love him.

It's after nine by the time we get to the penthouse. "Where's Short Mark?" I ask as we walk in.

"I don't know," Chris admits as he walks down the hall to put my suitcase in my room. "I expected him to be here."

"He's mad at me, isn't he?"

"I don't think I would say mad. More like disappointed."

"What is it about that song?"

"He's been working on *that song*, his 'Single' as he has always called it, for years. He thought he had finally worked it out, but he still wasn't happy – until he heard you sing it."

"Why doesn't he just ask some female artist to do it, if it's a woman's voice that's missing?"

"That's not the way Evans works. You know that. It wasn't missing a female voice. It was missing yours."

"You don't believe that."

"It was missing something."

We sit on opposite ends of the couch in the living room and watch a bad movie. Things are so uncomfortable. Before the movie is even over, Chris stands up and stretches. "I've had kind of a long day, sweetheart. I think I'm going to hit it."

I swallow back the words that want to burst out. *What? Why would you go to bed now?! Do you hate me now? Can you ever forgive me? Can't we just go back to the way it was?* I settle for, "Um, okay. Good night."

When I wake up in the morning, I find Short Mark in the music room, pacing around. "Are you bored?" I ask him.

He looks up and smiles. "Hey, Shorty. No, not bored. Just ready to go."

I nod sagely. "How are you going to make it until the launch?"

"Very carefully. And possibly with large quantities of alcohol."

He stops pacing and comes over to me. "How are you doing?" he asks.

"I'm okay. But I'm much more likely to cry now than I was before. Don't push me."

He steps back. "Fair enough. How was your flight?"

"Fine. Not as nice as my first flight out to LA."

"Of course not. The fulgurant Eck was here with me."

"That is a big word. I'm afraid I'm unfamiliar."

"I don't actually know what it means. Something like 'amazing'."

Chris calls from the living room, "It means 'flashing like lightning'!"

Short Mark and I look at each other. "How did you know that?" I call back.

"Dictionary.com." Short Mark and I both start laughing.

"I'm glad you're here, Shorty."

"I'm glad to be here, Short Mark."

"Go be with our boy. He missed you."

But when I go out to the living room, Chris is gone. I walk back to his room and find him sitting on his bed. "Hey, what's up?"

"Not much. How've ya been?"

"Okay."

"How was teacher work week?"

"Stupid. But I have become a celebrity at school."

He smiles. "Why's that?"

"Because everyone heard that I know Evansgate. That makes me special."

"You were special before you met me, sweetheart."

"Ah, but in only my dad's eyes."

He laughs. "What do you want to do today?"

"I don't know. Do you have to go to the studio?" I wink.

"Actually, I don't." He smiles. "I'm all yours."

"Well, I have no idea. The last time I was here we spent all of our time taking naps." I smile at the memory.

"Are you tired?"

"Nope. You?"

"Come on."

Over the course of the day, I feel like we fall back into our old groove. I guess the pretending thing worked because the tension dissolves. We spend the day at the beach, just because it's easy. Short Mark goes with us this time and we play sand sports all day.

"Am I going to get to see the other guys this trip?" I ask mid-afternoon.

"Yeah, Bethany's cookout is tomorrow." Chris tells me.

"Who's going to be there? Is Angie in town?"

Chris smiles. "Yes, she is. And it's just going to be us."

I turn to Short Mark. "We really need to get you someone."

He shakes his head. "Nah. I'm no good, Shorty."

I'm shocked, because he seems completely serious, which is so unlike Short Mark that it's worth taking notice of by itself, but how could he think that? "Short Mark, you are one of the best people I know."

"Um, duh. I know *that*. You don't know that many people, really, but I know I'm better than all of them put together." He pushes me. "Seriously though, I'm married to my music."

"You just haven't found the right girl yet."

"Who said I was interested in girls?" I can't tell if he's serious or not. But he starts to laugh. "You should see your face right now, Shorty. I like girls."

"It wouldn't really have mattered one way or the other." I can tell by the look on his face that he doesn't think I meant that, even though I did. "Really, I wouldn't have cared at all. I just was trying to decide if you were serious. But you're not allowed to bust on my friends."

"Would you forgive me if I apologized?"

"Probably."

"Thanks, Shorty. Now, let's do dinner. I'm hungry."

"You didn't apologize!"

"Oh, I know. I'm not sorry – I always speak the truth and I won't apologize for that. But, I wanted to be sure that you *would* have forgiven me if I had been sorry."

I can't come up with a good response, so I stick my tongue out at him.

"That's mature," he says, and he rubs my head. "Really – time for food. Let's go."

It's early, but by the time we get back to the penthouse and get showered it is definitely time to eat. We go to a restaurant that is extremely popular and most people would wait hours for a table, but Short Mark and Chris are enough to get us seated right away.

The next day we go over to Drew and Bethany's place in the early afternoon. I've never seen the inside of their house, so Bethany gives me a quick tour. It's so different from the penthouse. I'm sure Drew makes quite a bit of money, but there are few traces of that in their house. It's kind of small, I will call it "cozy", but it's nice.

We all hang out in the backyard all afternoon.

"Ah, don't get used to it boys, the time is coming," Short Mark says.

I assume that he is talking about being on tour. Bethany's face has gone tight. "But, make the best of it while you can," she says. She goes back in the house and comes out with a tray of fruit and cheese.

"Yeah, it's going to suck to not have you around to baby us, Beth," Blond Mark says with a wink.

The afternoon passes away lazily. The guys are horsing around and having a great time. I look around and realize that it's a family, and somehow I became a part of it. Well, kind of. I guess I'm standing on the other side of the fence, but at least I get to watch. I have a husband (and a list of reasons) that will keep me from ever being a full-fledged member of this group. I wonder if it would feel different if I were married to Chris? Or even if I were his girlfriend. Probably.

Almost as if she can hear my thoughts, Angie asks me about Sam. "I don't know anything about him!" she laughs.

"Oh, well. There really isn't a lot to tell." What in the world am I supposed to say about him to these people? That's a totally separate part of my life and I don't think I really want them to overlap anymore.

"He travels a lot?"

I can see Chris's jaw tighten and his eyes narrow. "Yeah, that's kind of his most distinguishing feature. He travels a lot." I'm anxious to change the subject, but I don't know how.

"Do you have a picture? I'd love to see what he looks like."

"Yes," puts in Blond Mark. "We wouldn't want you to be married to an ugly man. It would definitely drop my opinion of you."

They can't be serious? But Angie reaches out. "On your phone? Don't you have a picture of him on your phone?"

"Uh, yeah, I do." I fumble with my phone and bring up a picture of Sam and I at Sine's with Matt.

"He's definitely cute! I didn't really picture him as a blond, though."

"He's not." I can't help but laugh. "That's Matt, my friend. Sam is the one with the dark hair."

Chris stands up so suddenly that his chair flips backwards. He doesn't even stop to pick it back up, he just marches into the house. Everyone is silent. I look to Short Mark because I don't know what I should do. "I'll go, Shorty. Just... stay here." He picks up Chris's chair before he follows him.

We stay until very late. Bethany, I assume, hung strings of big light bulbs around the yard and it would have been wonderful to just sit out and enjoy it. But the thunder hasn't left Chris's face. It took Short Mark a long time to convince him to come back out and when he did, he took a seat on the outside edge of the group. He hasn't spoken to me all night and I haven't spoken to anyone.

My flight the next day is earlier than I would have liked, but it's Labor Day, so I'm trying to be prepared for delays and things. I have to get back for school. It's hard to leave because I don't know exactly where we stand or when I'll see Chris again.

"It's pathetic how much I miss you when you're not around," I tell him.

"And yet, still so good for my self esteem." He smiles.

I elbow him in the stomach. I would have gone for the ribs, but they're a little high. "I'm glad that my misery brings you so much joy."

Chris is suddenly very serious. "Sara Elizabeth Harris Clarke, do not ever think that I am happy when you are sad. My whole world revolves around your happiness."

I have to lighten the mood. "Well, that and Short Mark's demands."

"Yes, and those." He pauses. "I hope you had a good time." So much for a lighter mood.

"Of course I did." Not really. I was miserable for most of last night, but I don't want to tell him that.

"I know you didn't. I'm sorry that I was such a jerk."

I don't want to talk about this! "It's okay – really. I'm... I'm sorry." I'm not sure what I'm apologizing for – hurting him? being married? talking to Angie about Sam?

"No, I'm sorry. I'm not going to say that I'm fine with this, because I wish it were different. But, I promise I've gotten over myself. I'll be better behaved from now on."

"I don't want to lose your friendship."

"And you won't. We really are fine. I promise." He smiles. "I'm really glad you came. I'll see you soon – I promise. Chris pulls me into a tight hug. "I'll miss you. I do already. I wish I hadn't wasted our time together pouting like a little brat." He kisses my forehead as he pulls away. "Fly safe!"

Matt meets me at the airport, as always. "How was your trip?"

"It was..."

"Not fun?"

"No, it was like going home. There were some tough moments, but I just felt like I was where I belonged."

"You're not allowed to move to LA for some glamorous life and leave me to suffer here on the East Coast."

"Okay, well, if moving ever becomes a possibility, you'll have to come with me."

He touches my nose. "It's a possibility."

"I'm married."

"For now."

"Don't. Please don't. This is hard enough. I need one person in my life to support my decision to stay married to my husband. It's the right thing to do."

"You know how I really feel about the situation?" he asks. I nod. "Okay, well then I'll at least pretend to support you."

"Thanks," I say dryly. "I appreciate it."

I'm so tired at the end of the first week of school. It's been hard to get back into the swing of things this year. I know that's because of Chris. I'm looking forward to a weekend of nothing, but my heart sinks when I go in the house and see Sam's suitcase in the hall.

"Hey!" I call out. "What are you doing home?"

"I live here," comes a very grouchy reply from the office.

I stick my head in the door. "I just didn't know you were coming."

"Do I always have to tell you when I'm coming?"

I wonder what is wrong with him. "Um, no. But you always have."

"Yeah, well I wasn't really planning on it. But I'm here. Is that okay with you?"

"It's fine. Do you want to do dinner or something?" I'm trying really hard to act like everything is fine, but inside I'm dying. I do not want to have to deal with Sam right now, even if he would have been in a good mood which he clearly is not.

"I ate on the plane."

"Okay. Well, Matt and I were going to go out to celebrate the end of my first week. Do you want to come?"

"You and *Matt*?"

"Um, yes?"

"What happened to *Chris*?"

"I'm pretty sure he is in LA. Why?" I can play stupid just as well as the next girl.

"I just didn't think you had any other friends."

"Well, I do." I fight the urge to name the other members of Evansgate. "And we're going out. Do you want to come?"

"No, actually I don't. Most of us work all the time and there is no reason to celebrate the end of a week."

I could almost burn myself for this, but I'm going to do it anyway. "You could celebrate that you're home."

He's silent for a beat and I can hear him thinking that it's no reason to celebrate. "I'm tired. It's been a long day," he says kind of lamely. "But have fun with Matt."

"Okay." I go upstairs and change into the most un-teacherish thing I can find. That's the whole point of this exercise, after all. Plus, I know it will really piss Sam off.

But when I go downstairs to wait for Matt, Sam is gone. Oh well, so much the better, I guess. Matt and I go out for dinner and then to Sine's. Our favorite bartender is working, so we don't pay for nearly as many drinks as we actually consume. At least we had the foresight to take a cab out, so we don't have a car to worry about.

I sleep really late on Saturday, trying to avoid a hangover. My phone wakes me up around noon. It's Chris, of course.

"You were still sleeping, weren't you?"

"Um, yeah."

"Is it only when you have the power to wake me at an ungodly hour that you get up earlier than noon?"

"Um, yeah."

"Seriously, sweetheart. Why are you still in bed? Big night?"

"I told you I was going out with Matt."

"Right. Are you ready to get up yet?"

"No, actually, I'm not."

"Well, then, call me when you are."

"It's too late now! I'm awake! And, if I have a hangover, I blame you!"

"Sorry. Do you have a hangover?"

"I don't know yet."

"Oh. Well, then let's hope the answer is no. Did you have a good first week?"

"Chris, I talked to you every day. You know how my week went."

"It's still polite to ask."

"Yes, I had a lovely week. And you?"

"It was slow. I miss you."

"Yeah, me too."

"But you get to see you every day," he teases.

"I know. And it's not often enough," I shoot back.

"And that's why I love you. So what's on tap for this weekend?"

"I don't know. Sam is home."

"He is?"

"Yeah... that's exactly what I said."

"Did he go out with you last night?"

"Nope. He was tired." I try to hide my relief.

"Where is he now?"

"I don't know. I haven't seen him since I got home from school yesterday."

"Oh. Well, have a great afternoon."

"There was no reason for this call, was there?"

"Only to wake you up and give you a hangover."

"That's what I thought."

"Ten-ten, sweetheart."

"Eighty-eights."

I roll over very slowly, trying it out to see if I do have a hangover. I seem to be okay, so I get up. I take a deep breath and I still seem fine so I go downstairs.

Chapter 23

I don't see Sam anywhere, but when I peek in the office I find him asleep on the couch. I put on some coffee and wonder what I'm going to do today. Is Sam being here going to change my plans? Do I have any plans? I fix myself a cup of coffee and turn to go back upstairs.

"Thanks." Sam's voice is cold.

"For what?"

"Exactly." I must have missed a piece of this conversation, and apparently that shows on my face because he continues. "I would love a cup of coffee, thanks for offering." It's nice to see that his mood has improved.

"Um, Sam. You were asleep. But I made plenty." I gesture towards the still full pot.

"You could have made me a cup."

"Yes, but *you were asleep* and I didn't really see the point of making a cup just so it could sit on the counter and get cold."

Sam opens the fridge and then turns back around with an angry look on his face. "We don't have any of my creamer."

"You didn't tell me you were coming, or I would have bought some."

"You don't think *my house* should just be stocked with my creamer?"

"It seems a little silly to let it go bad. I'd really rather only buy it when you're in town."

"I'm in town. Go buy it."

My jaw is hanging open. "Look, I don't know who peed in your Wheaties, but you can stop taking it out on me."

"You could have gotten some when you were out last night – oh, I'm sorry. You were too busy with your man friend of the moment to think about your husband."

I'm itching to slap him, so I turn and march out of the kitchen. I grab my keys and go out through the garage without even slowing down. I know I'm wearing my pajamas, no shoes, carrying a cup of coffee, and I don't have my wallet or my phone, but I'm not staying in that house for another second. I drive to Matt's and quietly knock on his front door. I don't want to wake him, but if he's up I want him to let me in. I have a key to his house, but it's hanging on the hook in my laundry room at the moment.

Matt doesn't answer so I settle myself on his front porch with my coffee and try to enjoy the early afternoon. The problem is that it is still really hot by early afternoon in September. I try knocking again, this time a little louder. Still no answer. I walk around the back to look in his garage. At least his car is here.

When I get back to the front porch the door is open. I step inside and tentatively call out, "Matt?"

"Who did you think it would be? This is my house," Matt says as he comes back into the entry way. "What the hell are you doing here?"

"Um, hiding."

"Where are your shoes?"

"I imagine they are at my house."

"Did you bring any for me?" He points to my coffee.

"Sorry. There really wasn't time."

Matt sighs dramatically. "What happened?"

I tell him the story and when I get to the part where I leave with nothing but my pjs and coffee, he pulls out his phone. "What are you doing?"

"I'm texting Chris. You don't want him calling now. I assume your phone is locked?" I shake my head. "Sara! I've taught you better than that. Well, then we really don't want it to ring and draw Sam's attention to it, do we?"

"I'm so glad I surround myself with people who think of these things."

"I know. Come in. I'm making myself some coffee."

As Matt puts on a pot, his phone rings. He glances at it and then tosses it to me. "I assume that it's for you."

I look at the display. It's Chris.

"Well, hello."

"Sara? What the hell is going on? Why am I not allowed to call you?"

"Because I don't have my phone and Matt didn't want you to call and have Sam answer."

"I feel as though there might be a story behind this."

"Maybe. I'll let Matt tell you sometime."

"Sara."

"Fine. Sam was being an asshole so I left in a bit of a hurry."

"Define 'asshole'."

I tell Chris the story. "You should buy some and then pour it down the drain in front of him."

"Why would I do that?"

"You could tell him you thought it was as effective as having it in the house all the time. Of course, if it were me, I would pour it on him."

"No you wouldn't, you would hit him."

"I'm still considering it. It's not that much to fly there; certainly it would cost less than the satisfaction I would gain from it."

"That's not even funny."

"I'm not laughing."

Matt interrupts loudly, "Chris, you're not allowed to hit him."

I say, "How did you know that's what he said?" at the exact same time that Chris says, "How did he know that's what I said?"

Matt smiles. "Because that's what I want to do too, but we can't. This is your fight, Sara."

"I don't know if I like that sentiment or not."

"Well," Chris says, "call me when you get your phone back. Or if you decide I can fly in to hit him. Either way."

"Yes, I will."

I stay at Matt's until close to dinnertime and then I go home. I've cooled down considerably, but I'm still really hoping that he won't be home. Unfortunately, his car is still there. When I go inside, I find him asleep in the office again, so I quietly creep upstairs to take a shower. I check my phone first and find that I didn't really miss much: just a text from my dad and a call from Allison. Turns out, my life is kind of sad.

When I get out of the shower, I hunker down in my bed with a book. I'm avoiding Sam and I know it, but I'm still not going downstairs. My phone buzzes. "Hi, Matt."

"Have you seen him yet?"

"Kind of."

"Did you hit him?"

"No."

"Oh." He sounds kind of disappointed. "There's always next time."

"Matt!"

"What? He totally deserves it."

"Whatever. What are you doing tonight?"

"I'm going into the lab."

"What? Why? You haven't had to work on a Saturday in years."

"It's actually only been about nine months, thank you, but this is important. I can't trust a lab assistant for important things."

"Or, you *won't*."

"That too. If you want something done right," he starts.

"You should let me do it," I finish.

"I'm more than happy to let you. Would you like to come in?"

"Probably not. What is it?"

"I'm actually not allowed to tell you."

"So I'm actually not allowed to do it for you."

"No, unfortunately not."

"Well, go to work then."

"Okay. Don't hit him without videoing it or something."

"I'm not going to hit him!"

"Oh, well, if you change your mind..."

"What happened to pretending to support me?"

"Uh, it's really hard. Sorry. I forgot."

"Good-bye, Matt."

"Bye, Sara."

I hang up and notice Sam standing in my door. "I probably deserve that, I suppose?" he asks.

"What do you think?"

"I'm sorry. It's been –"

But I cut him off. "I don't really want to hear any excuse. Go away. You're not forgiven. Now get out of my room."

"This is –"

I cut him off again. "Don't even say this is *our* room. This is *my* room and I want you to get out."

He leaves, but he slams his door on the way. I can hear him grumbling on the other side, "*Every* damn bitch in my life..."

I'm going to pretend like I didn't hear that. And also, that I don't know what he meant by it, even though now I know why he's in such a bad mood – and probably why he is home this weekend.

I pick my book up again, but I can't concentrate so I call Allison back. I still haven't said anything to her about my suspicions about Sam and Anna, but maybe it's time to confide in my sister. She is surprisingly supportive.

"I know the evidence is damning, but you don't know for sure. You either have to confront him about it or really be okay with it and let it go."

"Neither of those sound very appealing."

"You don't have to do it right now."

"What would you do?"

"If it was Tom? I honestly don't know. I think I would probably bury my head and try to pretend like it was fine."

"I think I might do that for a little longer, at least."

"I'm here if you need to talk again."

I fall asleep reading and wake up early Sunday morning. The first thing I do is text Chris to let him know that it is possible for me to wake up at an ungodly hour without him. Then I decide to take a bath for a while.

When I go downstairs, there is a pot of coffee waiting, as well as a big bouquet of roses and a note from Sam.

You don't have to hear my excuses.

I was a jerk — sorry

I make myself a cup of coffee and then slip back up to my room, hopefully unnoticed. Sam and I tiptoe around each other all day and I don't really see him until I'm in bed for the night. He taps on the door, which I have closed. "Yes?"

He sticks his head in. "I'm leaving tomorrow."

"Good."

"Sara."

"What?"

"I said 'I'm sorry'."

"Sam."

"Yes?" He has a smile on his face now.

"Go away."

His smile fades. "I just wanted to say good-bye."

"Bye. Now, go."

I could have probably been nicer, but I guess I'm still really mad.

After my miserable weekend with Sam, I'm glad to get back to work on Monday. I'm more glad that *Sam* gets back to work too and he will be gone by the time I get home from school. I drag my feet through the week though. With the release getting closer, Chris is really busy and I don't get to talk to him as much. By the time I get out of school, he is usually already on a set somewhere, doing an interview or something.

I can't believe it's only the second week of school and I'm already thinking about dashing out early on Friday. By the end of the year, half the teachers are gone with the final bell on Friday, but through the first semester we usually try to stay as late as we are contracted to. I stay at my desk and grade the first quizzes of the year until 3:30 on the dot, and then I'm out the door.

I must have left the garage door up when I went to school this morning, because it's open when I get home. Well, I hope no one is inside, because I don't lock the door from the garage to the house or set the alarm when I'm only going to be gone for the day. I grab the mail and go in. I turn on some music in the kitchen and start dancing around while I unload the dishwasher. I love Of Monsters and Men, so of course I'm singing along. "Little Talks" is one of my favorites and I belt out Nanna's first line.

I drop the plate I'm holding when a man's voice sings Raggi's line back to me. I whirl around and find Chris standing in my kitchen.

"What are you doing here?" I yell in surprise.

But he doesn't answer me; he just sings Raggi's next line. I play along and we sing the entire duet. Actually, the song seems kind of relevant. Chris sweeps me into a big hug and we dance around the kitchen, carefully avoiding the shattered plate.

"Sorry about that." He nods in the direction of the ceramic shards.

"What are you doing here?" I repeat.

"I'm taking a tour of major Civil War battlefields and I thought I would stop in for a little on my way through."

"How do you come up with this stuff so quickly?"

"I don't know." He pauses, then he almost looks guilty when he says, "Okay, Matt gave me that one."

I laugh. "Okay, so what are you really doing here?"

"What do you think, woman? I'm visiting you."

"Did Matt pick you up?"

"Yeah."

"Good, does that mean he let you in?"

"Yeah, why?"

"I thought I had left my house unlocked and open to the world all day."

"I told him that we would go out with him tomorrow night."

"Okay. Sounds like fun."

Chris and I chat about unimportant things for a while. He tells me that the album is ready for release, but we don't really talk about it. He invites me to the launch, but seeing as how it's on a Tuesday, I can't make it. "I can only take off so much time from school, Chris. Unfortunately that means that I'm going to have to miss a lot of stuff that happens any time outside of summer."

"This one's kind of important."

"Yeah, and it's still the first month of school. I can't. I'm really sorry, but I can't."

"Will you come to the opener?"

"In San Francisco?"

He nods. "You could go with Angie and Bethany."

It's on a Saturday. "I can probably do that."

"What about Thanksgiving? Will you come to New York for Thanksgiving?"

"Um, Chris. I have family to consider. Sam might actually be around for the holiday and it's his year."

"His year?"

"Yeah, this Thanksgiving, we're supposed to be with his family."

"Oh. Ouch."

"Yeah, well, it's not a holiday anywhere else in the world, which he always points out to me when it's convenient, so maybe I'll get lucky and he'll have to work."

We order Chinese for dinner and watch bad reality TV that I have on the DVR. "This stuff is awful," Chris complains.

"I know. But it makes me feel better about my life."

"That's really quite sad, sweetheart."

"One of these days I'm going to be watching one of these about Evansgate. A fly-on-the-wall documentary about life on the road or something."

"Unlikely. Evans would never go for it."

"Would you?"

"No, I guess none of us would. But even if we did, you wouldn't be watching it, you'd be in it, remember? This is your life too."

"I imagine they would edit me out. Who would want to watch me?"

"Are you kidding? The drama and intrigue of your life keeps me up at night."

"I'm sorry. I'll try to tone it down a little so you can get some rest."

"I can handle it."

We fall asleep on the couches in front of the TV. I wake up stiff and very uncomfortable in the middle of the night. I nudge Chris and tell him I'm going to a bed and then drag myself upstairs. Chris only grunts at me and rolls over, so I assume he is just going to stay put.

In the morning, Chris has coffee waiting for me downstairs. "Are you trying to make a point?" I ask him as I walk into the kitchen.

"Not really. I just like you better after you've had your morning coffee."

"Hey! I'm not that bad."

"No, you're not," he admits. "I'm just trying to make a point."

I let it go and enjoy my coffee. Allison was right; it is nice to have a cup waiting for you.

"So what should we do with ourselves today?" I ask brightly, before I get a chance to over examine my life and its problems.

"Tour some major Civil War battlefields?"

"I think I would rather not, but I hear there are plenty to see around here if you'd like to try to take a few in. You can use my car."

We end up doing nothing, like we usually do. Chris plays for a little while in the music room, and I end up singing because sometimes I can't help it. He doesn't play any of Evansgate's music though, just Van Morrison which has kind of become our thing, I guess.

I call Matt and ask him if he wants to do dinner too, so we decide to go out earlier than usual to get something to eat first. Chris asks if I want him to get a car, but I'm not planning on drinking, so I just drive. We eat at a nice restaurant downtown, just around the corner from Sine's, and then walk to the bar.

Saturday night is live music and tonight is a really good local band with Irish undertones. They're pretty popular in the Richmond scene so the place is packed. We stay pretty late, but leave before last call.

We drop Matt off and Chris falls asleep almost as soon as we get in the house. At least I get him up to a bed this night. I lie in mine for a while after Chris is asleep thinking about how much I miss him when he's gone, how much things are better when he's around. I try really hard to focus on other things, but my mind keeps drifting back to him. I get up and get my list out to read.

It doesn't help as much as I was hoping it would. I can't stop the thought before it's in my head: I could flip this paper over and make a list that would be so much longer than this one of reasons that Chris and I are right together. Eventually, I drift off.

Surprisingly, I wake up early, considering how long it took me to fall asleep. I hurry down to the kitchen and make Chris a cup of coffee. He is just coming in when I finish and I hand it to him happily. He smiles.

"It was my turn," I say as I grab my coffee mug and make my own.

"So the launch is Tuesday. And by this time next week, we'll have the first show of the tour under our belts."

"Are you nervous?"

"Only because I wrote one of the songs this time. What if the world hates it?"

"Who cares what they think? It's a good song."

Chris smiles, but his eyes look sad. "That's why I love you.

Thanks."

We shoot pool until it's time to go to the airport. It's always sad to say good-bye, but we don't have long. "I'll see you in less than a week," he promises as he leaves.

Chapter 24

Short Mark is as good as his word. When the album is released, "the Single" is noticeably absent. Well, I notice. Chris's song is still there, bringing up the rear. I've decided to take an ostrich approach to the situation and act like everything is fine until it's not.

I'm getting ready to fly to LA so that I can drive up to San Francisco with Angie and Bethany. But I'm having the hardest time packing because I'm not sure what to wear to these things. I end up calling Angie for advice. With her help, I get everything together and feel like I'm ready for anything.

After school on Friday, Matt drives me in another mad dash to the airport. I kiss him on the cheek as I hop out. "I'll see you on Sunday!"

He smiles. "Be safe, Baby Girl."

Chris is waiting for me at the airport in LA. I'm surprised to see him. "I thought you had to go to San Francisco!"

"We're leaving very soon. I'm just going to take you to the penthouse."

"I thought I was going to stay with Angie."

"She's going to stay with you there."

"Okay." He smiles and takes my hand and my suitcase. "How was the launch?" I ask him.

"Great! I'm glad it's over though. Now we just play."

"And here that's what I thought you were doing all along."

"Oh, no. That was way too much like work."

"I'm glad it's behind you."

"How's school going?"

"It's way too much like work."

He laughs. "Someone has to do it."

"And I'm so glad it's me."

He pokes me in the arm. "We've offered. You could be touring with us, but you've given it all up to teach. Lucky little SOBs probably don't even know what they're getting."

"Are you referring to my students?"

"Yes, them."

"Well, you were right about one thing."

"Only one?"

"Yes, *only* one. My students are much better this year because they all heard how cool I am because I hang out with Evansgate."

"I did make you cooler!"

"Yeah," I say grudgingly, "you did."

The ride to the penthouse feels really short, and when we get there, the car doesn't even leave. Chris walks me upstairs and kisses my cheek at the door. "Angie is in there. I'll see you after the show."

"We never ride with them to their first show of the tour," Bethany explains to me. "This is just their time to get their heads ready."

I nod. That makes perfectly good sense to me. We leave LA early Saturday morning. We are going to take a scenic trip up the historic 101, and it will take us all day, at least.

"When we get there," Angie warns, "we won't see them. Not before the first show. I'm almost sorry that your first time is an opener. It's a lot more fun when we can hang out with them back stage first."

Bethany nods. "We really don't want to get in the way. We'll take you back after the show, okay?"

"Sounds great. I'm at your mercy, ladies. I have no idea what I'm doing."

Angie smiles. "For now? Just enjoy the West Coast. I have been told that you have not learned how to appreciate it yet."

"Ah, what did Chris tell you?"

"That you don't like avocados."

"Will stunning Pacific views change that?"

"It can't hurt."

I lie back in the seat. We take 405 north for a little while and then get on 101. We drive through trees and hills for a little while, then, suddenly, the ocean is to our left. Angie puts the top of her convertible down and turns up the music. I tug my hair into a pony tail and breathe in the salty air.

Bethany taps me on the shoulder from the back seat. "Do you like avocados yet?"

Angie and I both laugh. "Not yet," I admit," but I'm willing to give them another chance."

We left Santa Monica before eight, but it is still after six by the time we get to our hotel in San Francisco. If we had stuck with Angie's original plan, we would have made better time, but I was reluctant to lose sight of the ocean when the 101 went in-land. Angie agreed to stay on Route 1 and it added hours to our trip.

We're stiff when we finally get out of the car. We did not stop much because Bethany was worried that our detour would cost us too much time. She had a good point, because the guys are due on stage in about two hours and we still have to get ready.

I get into my room and rush through my normal routine. Chris told me they would send a car for us, and it was already here and waiting when we came in. I have not talked to Chris since yesterday. After what Angie and Bethany had said, I decided it was best to lay low.

I'm wearing the same skirt that I wore to the concert in DC, the one that Chris complimented. But I bought a new shirt to go with it – on Angie's advice. I don't look much like a teacher. But then, I don't want to feel like a teacher tonight, so that's good. I smile at my reflection and head out.

Bethany is already downstairs in the lobby when I get there, so we wait for Angie together. "I'm sorry that I made us late," I apologize.

Bethany smiles. "I don't mind. It gives us a good excuse to miss the opening act. I really don't like Kiro! I don't normally see it, because I'm usually back stage with Drew for as long as possible." She gives me a forced smile. "I'm not going to lie, Sara, this really isn't my idea of a good time. I don't really love anything about this."

I wonder how she can be married to a major musician and not like going to concerts, but I just smile sympathetically.

Angie comes rushing into the lobby in a cloud of perfume and hair spray. She is wearing her new outfit with the boots that we were never able to find together. "Totally worth the hunt, right?" She winks at me. "All right *chicas*, let's go!"

In the limo, Angie pulls out her cell phone. "They're in the red room tonight." Bethany nods, but I have no idea what she is talking about. Angie turns to me. "The guys never advertise which room they are in back stage. Some groups will have a sign on the door that says, 'BAND'S ROOM' or something, but our guys aren't like that. They don't give out backstage passes really, but if somehow someone ends up with one, they can't find the group without already knowing where they are."

"How would someone end up with one?"

"Oh, sometimes someone at the venue will give one out or something. A couple of times I think someone with the label got roped into giving one as a favor or something. It makes me laugh, though, because some poor schmuck gets a purple pass and thinks he's going to get to meet Evansgate, but then he just ends up wandering around back stage for a while."

Bethany laughs.

"Aren't there usually tons of people running around? Couldn't someone just follow someone to the guys?" I ask.

Angie shakes her head. "It's actually really quiet and calm back stage usually. Evans is all about the music and he keeps it close to himself."

"I see. So how will we find them?"

Angie holds up her phone. "Mark told me 'red room' so we just have to figure out what that means when we get there." She pauses. "Or Tom will help us."

As we pull into the venue, a huge coliseum/arena, we find that Tom is actually waiting to meet us. "Hi, girls!" He gives us each a hug. "Here are your passes." He hands us laminated purple cards hanging from lanyards. Angie and Bethany drop theirs over their heads and I do the same. After tucking it under her own shirt, Bethany comes to help me get mine under my (*much* tighter) top.

"Trust me," she says. Angie is struggling to get hers under her shirt as well. It is long enough that the card is right on the smooth part of my tummy, and it actually fits under my shirt just fine. I lift the front of my shirt and study the card. It says "San Francisco – 9/22/12" in bold print. On the back is the band's logo and "San Francisco" in smaller print than on the front.

Tom smiles at Angie. "You're late, my dear."

"It's my fault!" I jump in to defend her. "I wanted to take the scenic route."

"I thought you were planning on taking the 101?" Tom asks Angie.

"We were," she tells him. "We just took 1 for a while too."

"Oh, no wonder you're late." He smiles at me. "Do you like avocados yet?"

"I am forced to wonder what you people talk about when I am not around."

Tom laughs. "You, obviously. Come on, we'll go through the back or you'll never get to the club."

The other girls follow him without a word, but I wonder what he meant. Angie is pulling out more cards on lanyards. She gives one to me and one to Bethany before putting one around her own neck. I don't even have to ask. "Club tickets. It's the space in between the 'seats' and the stage. You have to have a pass to be there. It makes it easier for security to keep things straight."

"So this is my ticket?" I ask as I drop it over my head.

Angie nods. "Yeah, that's as good as it gets."

We follow Tom around the edge of the building to a solid, nondescript door with a security guard standing in front of it. Tom nods at him and then pulls out a key to let us in. "Three," he says to the guard, glancing over his shoulder.

I look at Angie again. "He was telling him how many people are with him."

I nod. This is starting to get kind of intimidating.

Through the door, there is a narrow hallway with no doors or passages off it. The floor slopes down for as far as I can see. At the bottom, the passage Ts and we go left. I'm hoping that I don't have to find my way out of here. We wander through turn after turn, passing doors, and other hallways. Eventually we start going up again. We pass by several doors marked "PRIVATE" with different colored backgrounds. Angie nudges me and points to one that is red. I smile at her. The red room. Is Chris behind that door right now?

But we walk right by. Tom seems to be hurrying now. Finally, we turn a corner and are greeted by a big, heavy curtain. "Have fun, girls," Tom says as he waves us off. There is a lot of noise on the other side of the curtain. Bethany's face is stony.

Angie touches her arm. "It's okay, Beth. Just look for Drew." She nods, and then Angie turns to me. "We always stand stage left, but you might want to go right. If we get separated, we will meet right here after the show. You can't get back right when the show is over, because Mike can't just let you through. He has to wait until there are other people to help him. You can either come back before the last song, or wait." I nod. "Let me introduce you to Mike, okay?" I nod again.

When Angie pulls back the curtain the noise hits us like a blast. There is a narrow hallway that ends in a chest high gate, blocked by a large man. Angie starts down the hall first. Bethany pales, but squares her shoulders and walks through. I follow behind them. It would be hard to walk side by side the hall is so narrow. Angie reaches up and taps the security guard on the shoulder. He glances back, smiles, and then turns away again.

I can see another guard moving in as the man comes through the gate towards us. Bethany turns and gives me a little shove past her. "Hi, Mike!" Angie has to practically yell.

The man looks at me. He is the same guy that took my ticket at the coffee shop. He smiles. "Shorty?"

"That's what some people call me."

He smiles broadly. "I'm Mike. You can't get through without getting through me, okay? Don't ever *ever* let anyone else tell you they can get you back to see the band." I'm shocked at the serious warning in his voice.

Angie nods. "I'll explain later. Sorry, I should have remembered to say something." Then to Mike she says, "Sara is going to go stage right, okay?" He nods, and then we push through the gate. Mike immediately plants himself in front of it again, and the other guard helps ford a path between the crowd towards the stage for Angie and Bethany. I can see at least four other guards spaced out around the stage.

As I watch the girls disappear into the crowd I start to feel a little sick. I feel a firm hand on my shoulder and I turn back to see Mike smiling at me. It's a little reassuring and I take a steadying breath. Mike points to another guard and says, "He'll help you get to the stage, Sara."

"Put your hands on me and stay as close as you can, okay?" he tells me.

As we push through the crowd, I look around the "club area" and see that it is a fairly small space between the stage and a chain link barrier in front of the front row of seats. I can see one gate to get into the club, guarded by two more men. As small as the space is, there are more people crammed in than I could easily count. On my right, the stage is looming about shoulder high and for the moment, it is empty.

The guard digs a way through the fans with me hanging on his back. We stop right at the stage. He doesn't walk away, like I expected him to. He just turns to face the crowd, so his back is against the stage and he is right next to me. Is he my own personal body guard?

"I'm Paul!" he is almost yelling to be heard over the roar of the waiting fans. If it's this loud now, I am nervous about the noise level when the band is actually on stage.

"I'm Sara!" I yell back.

He smiles and nods at me. "I'll be right here, but I'm going to keep my eyes this way, okay?" He is using his head to indicate the direction to my right and behind me. The crowd is so tight, I'm not sure he could have used his hands.

The arena is enormous. I wonder how many people are at this concert tonight and I warily look over my shoulder. Ten thousand? More? I wonder where Angie and Bethany are. I can usually handle myself pretty well, but I'm starting to feel kind of claustrophobic.

Suddenly everything goes completely dark, and people scream. I can feel the music in my chest before I can hear it. In a brilliant flash of light, Evansgate is on stage and the concert has started. Chris is right in front of me and he smiles when he sees me.

It's impossible to not get caught up in the energy of the crowd. Everyone is dancing and jumping around, so I do too. Then I start singing, but no one can hear me. Short Mark is *alive* like I have never seen him. This entire experience is so different from the little gig in DC, it could be a different group. I remember what Chris said about Short Mark and Blond Mark making the group, but watching Short Mark and *Chris* is the most entertaining part of the show. They play off of each other really well.

From my spot in the audience, I am struck with how different they seem on stage. They seem like a real rock group now, not my friends. Their personalities are shadowed by their stage presence. Evansgate is a great group to watch live. Their shows are fun and energetic. But they don't feel like Short Mark, Blond Mark, Drew, and Chris from down here. I thought I would feel different from the other people in the crowd – special because my friends are on the stage. But they seem like strangers, entertainers, *stars*. I'm just another fan, watching my favorite group.

It's great.

When they start "Six Kinds of Crazy" I freeze. People are still jumping and moving all around me, but I can't seem to unlock my joints. It suddenly occurs to me that Bethany and Angie have probably heard this song by now. What do they think? Do they know it's about me? I manage to not cry, and I am really grateful when it's over.

They're on stage for almost two hours. I don't know how they're still standing. I'm exhausted and I've just been in the audience. But my last view of Chris's face tells me he has more energy now than when he got up this morning.

Even with the band gone, the crowd in the club area isn't dissipating much. Probably partly because there is nowhere for them to go, and partly because they don't want to go anywhere. Paul helps me fight through the people towards Mike. The gate to backstage is probably only 15 feet away now, and I can see Mike defending his territory. I assume most of these people have been to a lot of concerts, because before tonight, I would never have known where to go to try to get backstage, and this crowd knows. They are begging Mike to let them through, and he is just standing, stony faced, with his arms crossed against his large chest, shaking his head. Even with Paul, we can't get far.

I see more guards coming onto the stage. They are spacing themselves between the guys spread out around the front. How many security guards does one concert need?

It occurs to me that maybe Chris would be in danger without all of these men between him and his fans. The thought makes me shiver.

It's getting harder to get anywhere and I wish we could just stop to wait until they get bored, realize Mike is never going to let them through, and give up. But Paul is determined.

We catch up with Angie, Paul is obviously doing a good job because she was much closer to backstage than I was. "Hey, Sara!" She's still yelling at top volume, even though it is probably not necessary anymore. "Did you like the show?" When did she get alcohol? I can tell she has had quite a bit since the last time I saw her.

"It was great! Did you?" She nods. "What happened to Bethany?"

"She decided halfway through to go wait backstage for Drew." We are only about five feet from the gate now. Angie pushes herself up to her toes. "MIKE!" she yells. "MIKE!"

He looks at us and waves us towards him. But I can tell he's upset.

It takes about one second for me to figure out why.

"Mike!"

"Mike!"

"MIKE!"

People are yelling his name from everywhere. And they are getting crazier by the second. It's like knowing Mike's name added fuel to their fire. Paul pushes me in front of him and then reaches around me to ford a path through the crowd. I'm surprised to find myself at the gate.

Mike lets me squeeze through the smallest possible opening in the gate and immediately turns back to fending off everyone else. "Please, Mike! Let me through!" I can hear people yelling.

Paul didn't follow me. I wish I had gotten a chance to thank him. Angie is still struggling to reach the gate, so I lean against the wall to wait for her. Eventually she gets through too, and we walk up the hallway. At the curtain, there is another security guard. Angie pulls her shirt up to show him her pass, so I do the same.

I knock softly on the red room door. I can hear a lot of commotion on the other side. Blond Mark opens it, I'm sure he is looking for Angie, and greets us with a huge smile. I see Bethany in the corner with a bottle of water; Drew is standing in front of her. Short Mark is with a group of people I don't know, and I see Tom and another guy talking. Everyone is drinking champagne (everyone except Bethany) and laughing. I scan the room again. The man is taller than anyone here, surely he shouldn't be that hard to find?

Chris steps out from behind the door and grabs me in a hug. He is sweaty and kind of gross, but I don't mind. "Sara! What did you think?"

I laugh as he whirls me around and plonks me in the corner. "It was... Amazing. I... I wasn't expecting it to be like that."

"What? Were you expecting us to suck?"

"No! I was expecting something more like DC."

"Oh! Was that the only concert of ours you have been to?"

I nod sheepishly. "Yeah. I don't really do a lot of concerts. What was the deal with that one in DC anyway? Why was it so different from your normal ones?"

"We were in DC for the video and we were asked to do it... as a favor to a friend of a friend."

"Oh." I try to look like that makes any sense to me. "That's quite a favor."

"He's a good friend."

"Oh. Do I know him?"

Chris touches my nose. "I don't know. Do you know Tom?"

"We've met. So, it was a friend of Tom's?"

But, before Chris can answer, Short Mark grabs me, "Shorty! Did you like it?" I nod. "You could have been up there with us, you know."

"Yeah, thanks, but no thanks."

He shrugs. "I'm not giving up on you yet."

"Good luck with that."

The guys duck out for a little bit to grab showers. Angie tells me more about concert life while they're gone. "There are a lot of people at the shows who are bad news, and you have to watch out for them. Mike always says that he'll do his best, but we have to meet him halfway."

"His best?"

"To keep us safe."

"Does Mike go with the group?"

"Yeah, he's crew. He's the head of security."

"So no matter where we go...?"

"Mike will be the only gatekeeper for backstage. There are guys who prey on stupid girls trying to find a way to sneak back to see the band – I mean at all concerts, not just ours, and they'll lure them into dark corners and do all kinds of awful things." She raises her eyebrows at me, but I don't really need her to lay it out. I'm sure my face registers my feelings though, because she nods at me.

"And you have to be careful, Sara, that you don't talk to people. If someone realizes that you're with the band, you become a target. And don't ever mention anything about where to find the guys backstage, just in case."

The look on Angie's face makes me think that this might be something that she has firsthand experience with, but I can't quite work out whether she was in trouble because she was someone's prey or because she said something she shouldn't have. Maybe both. I decide it's a good idea to heed her words.

"How many concerts do you go to?"

"Oh, not many, really. I'll probably make it to four or five, *maybe*, the whole tour. I always try to make it to the opener, and I'll go to a couple of the bigger venues, Vegas and stuff. I'll definitely be in New York for Thanksgiving."

Her words make me sad. She clearly loves Blond Mark, and he is definitely head over heels for her, but they have to be apart for so long. On the other hand, I'm almost jealous of how confident she gets to be about spending the holiday with them.

I can smell Chris before I feel his arm snake around my waist as he comes up behind me. I close my eyes as he pulls me against his chest. Yum. He kisses the top of my head and then laughs. Hm, he has had a lot to drink; now all I smell is alcohol.

We celebrate in the red room for what seems like a long time. There are a bunch of people from the label, Tom, a handful of crew and roadies, and us, which may not be a lot of people, but the liquor is flowing and it feels like a party. I'm just starting to get buzzed when Chris tells me it's time to go.

We go out the way we came in, and there are several cars waiting by the door. The closest is a very long limo, bigger than any I've ridden in yet. Evansgate, Angie, and I get in. Bethany kisses Drew and then gets into a regular taxi. Drew looks a little sad when he climbs in alone. I want to ask why she isn't going in our car, but I don't think I should.

Chris is drunker than I have ever seen him and he pulls me into his lap. I rest my head on his shoulder. "Aren't you tired?" I ask him. I watch in amazement as he leans in, because for one instant I'm sure he's going to kiss me. There is a serious fire burning in his eyes. But he stops suddenly and looks at Short Mark, who is sitting next to us shaking his head. Chris pushes me out of his lap and I land in a heap next to him.

Before I can decide if I'm offended, Short Mark moves around and squeezes himself between Chris and I. "I'm sorry, Shorty." He looks like he means it. "Give Eck some space for a few minutes, okay?" I nod mutely and move to sit next to Drew. Angie and Blond Mark need their own space for a minute, it would appear.

Drew looks up, surprised when I sit down in the seat next to him. "Hey, Sare-Bear."

"Hi, Drew."

"You okay?"

"I'm not sure. You?"

Drew smiles. "Not sure."

"I'm sorry."

Even though we both know he knows I'm talking about Bethany he asks, "About what?"

I put my hand on his arm. "You're a good man, Charlie Brown."

"Ah, but I've got nothing on her."

I smile. "I agree." I look over at Short Mark and Chris. Short Mark is talking, and Chris is looking thunderous. "I'm not sure what I did," I tell Drew.

"Nothing," Drew looks surprised. "You didn't do anything. He's just pumped up after the first show, had too much to drink and he forgot who he is for a second. Evans will straighten him out."

"Oh. Okay. Hey, Drew?"

"Yeah?"

"Where are we going?"

"You'll see, Baby Girl."

Chapter 25

We spend the night going from club to club, but this isn't like clubbing as I remember it from college, or even like our little outing in DC. These places are packed, lines around the block, jammed full of people – all of whom are very excited to see our crew roll up. At the first club, Blond Mark climbs out first, with Angie right behind him. I look to Drew for my cue, because I'm not sure what I'm supposed to do. He takes my hand and pulls me out right behind him, then on sidewalk, he stands mostly in front of me. Chris gets out next and the crowd goes *crazy*. He smiles and waves. I can't believe how cool he is handling the screaming mass. Then Short Mark gets out waving and smiling at everyone.

If the people were screaming for Chris, they are hysterical for Short Mark. I'm surprised to see Mike suddenly step in front of a couple of girls who look like they might be willing to do some damage for a chance to be with Mark Evans or Chris Eck. "Where did he come from?" I ask Drew.

"We travel with our own security, kiddo. We have to." He gestures to the car in front of the limo. Apparently Mike and three other guys from the crew, including Paul, got to the club ahead of us. The bouncers at the club suddenly have their hands very full, but they were waiting for us, so it seems to be under control. There are velvet ropes lining an entrance to the club (I know, *really*) and we are whisked right in. Drew has his arm around my waist like an iron band. He has one hand up in front of us as we walk in. I duck my head into his shoulder and follow his lead. How could Bethany stand this? No wonder she didn't come.

It is unreal. I can't believe that the guys are still normal, if this is a "normal" night out. I can't imagine the caliber of character necessary to keep this from going to your head. Well, I guess I don't have to imagine it, because there are four guys in front of me overflowing with it.

There are people everywhere screaming and reaching for the guys. Cameras are flashing all around us and I wonder how many are just cell phones, and how many are actual paparazzi. We get to go upstairs, to an area roped off for VIPs. The entire second and third floors only wrap around the outside and are open to the dance floor in the middle, below. The second floor is restricted access, so we have to be escorted up and then things calm down a little because there are a lot less people, and most of them are used to rubbing elbows with superstars, I guess.

I really appreciate Drew taking care of me, but I miss Chris. I'm not completely sure why he is so angry when he looks at me, but I have an idea. And as much as I want it to be *his* arm around my waist, I'm guessing that is exactly why it *can't* be.

The guys stand at the balcony for a while, watching the people on the dance floor below. I know they are just making themselves visible because that's why we're here. The dance floor is actually raised off of the ground floor, so we are not that far above it. There's even more alcohol to be had here, and people are doing some serious drinking. It's hard to limit yourself when the supply is endless, because the bar on the second floor is open.

One of Evansgate's old songs comes on and the guys start to do some quasi-dance routine on the balcony. It's clearly been rehearsed, but it could almost pass as impromptu. Then I realize what it is. They're playing "Yesterday's News" and this is the dance they do in the video. Angie and I are around the corner from them, we can see them across the empty space between us. She is dancing like crazy, but I'm just watching. Their dance doesn't last very long, it was only through one verse or something, but the crowd down below is going nuts. Nearly everyone is swarming over to that side of the club, reaching up and screaming.

As I watch Chris lean down to grab some random, screaming girl's hand I feel an overwhelming pang of jealousy. Crap, I'm in trouble. I have a husband, the man is completely off limits, but I want him so bad. I want him for myself and I'm bitterly resenting a perfect stranger who has less of a chance with him than I do. I walk away from the balcony. I don't want to watch any more. I find a table in the corner, out of the reach of lights. I grab my second drink, a vodka martini, from the bartender on my way.

I pout in the corner, drowning my own sorrows in vodka. I can't believe I'm feeling sorry for myself right now. There are hundreds of people downstairs who only want to be up here where I am. I get another drink. The difference, of course, is that most of those people wouldn't care if they are married or not and would sleep with Chris Eck in an instant – or less if there aren't buttons or zippers involved. This time I get a shot. I remind myself that Chris would never sleep with any of them, but that includes me. Despite how many I've already had, that thought makes me feel like I actually need the next shot I get.

Suddenly I'm not alone though. "I think maybe you have had

enough, Shorty," Short Mark says as he takes the glass from my hand.

I scowl at him. "I'm a grown up. I can make that decision myself, thank you." And I grab it back.

"Well, finish it up. We've got to go, because we're just getting started."

We go to three more clubs before we head back to the hotel, and I'm pretty sure the sun is close to coming up. Chris hasn't even looked in my direction the entire night. It's probably for the best, but I'm still pouting. Drew has kept me tucked into his side all night. I love Drew, I really do, but I'm starting to resent the hell out of him. Or that could be the gallons of vodka talking.

We drag ourselves into the elevator at the hotel. Short Mark immediately slides down the wall and sits on the floor, his head resting against the mirrored back of the small space. His eyes close and a small smile plays across his lips. I have quickly learned that when Angie and Blond Mark have been drinking excessively it's best to avert your eyes, so I'm carefully avoiding that corner. Drew is playing an air guitar and mouthing the words to some song; his eyes are closed too. My options are either to close my own eyes, avoid everyone, or glance in Chris's direction.

I can't help it. The sight of his face is like a breath after being under water too long. I inhale deeply, and then exhale quietly. He is staring at my face. "I'm sorry," he mouths. I want to jump over Short Mark's prone form and into his arms, but I restrain myself.

I settle for staring back. "Me too," I mouth. I won't look away first, I tell myself. He doesn't look away either, and when the elevator stops we're still staring. The doors open, ding, and start to close again.

Drew comes to first and leaps forward, shoving his arm between the closing doors. "Let's go people, there are beds waiting." He nudges Short Mark's foot with his toe. Blond Mark and Angie fall out of the elevator, still entangled. Short Mark rolls over and crawls out. Drew looks between me and Chris. "Are you two coming, or riding this thing all night?" When neither of us even blink, Drew shrugs and steps out. The doors slide shut and Chris and I are alone, still staring at each other.

Suddenly, he launches himself across the small space and presses me against the wall, his hands planted on either side of my head. We still haven't looked away and I feel my whole body tingling with desire. He leans towards me, and I'm about to go up on my toes to meet him halfway, when the doors ding and open again. Short Mark grabs Chris's shoulder and tries to yank him back. Chris still doesn't look away from my face and appears to have no intention of moving. He has almost an entire foot on Short Mark, so I'm putting my money on Chris winning this struggle.

Chris takes one hand from the wall and reaches up to push Short Mark's hand from his shoulder, but completely undaunted, Short Mark ducks under Chris's arm and plants himself between us, facing Chris. He puts his hand in Chris's face instead. "I mean it, Chris. You'll never forgive yourself."

Chris blinks twice, and then looks at Short Mark. He nods and turns on his heel and stomps out of the elevator, stopping the doors just before they close again.

Short Mark takes a step and then turns back to face me. "You too, Shorty. Go to bed before you do something stupid." I can feel a tear run down my cheek and his expression softens. Very gently, Short Mark wipes my cheek with his thumb. "You don't want it like this," he whispers. Then he wraps his arm around my waist, sticks his other arm between the closing doors to force them open again, and half drags me to my door. "Good night, Shorty. It will be better in the morning." He doesn't walk away before I shut the door.

I turn my back against the door and slide down to the floor, like Short Mark had done in the elevator. I fall asleep crying, right there.

I wake up to a quiet commotion in the hallway. "It's fine, Mike. I'm fine. Go to an actual bed."

There are muffled words that I can't understand.

"Then stand right there, but knock on the damn door."

I roll over and scoot back. I reach up and open the door, then slump against it, still sitting on the floor. "Chris?" Chris and Mike are standing outside my door. "What time is it?"

Mike doesn't look at me. "Go back to your room, Eck."

"What? What's going on? What time is it?" I repeat.

Chris glances at me. "It's a little after eight. And I want to talk to you." But he says the second part while he is looking at Mike.

"Then can I go to bed?" I can't figure out why he needs to talk to Mike outside my door, but if I'm not needed I'd rather not be here.

Chris looks back at me. "You don't look very good, Baby Girl. Are you —?"

I turn and crawl as quickly as possible to puke before he can finish. Thankfully, the bathroom isn't far. As I vomit up the vodka that is poisoning my system, I can hear a scuffle still going on. Very loudly I hear Chris, "Do you really think something is going to happen while she's throwing up? MOVE, Mike!"

I really don't want Chris in here while I'm being sick, but I'm too far gone to fight him off when he comes in anyway. He grabs my hair from my grasp and settles himself down next to me. "I'm so sorry, Sara. I'm so sorry." He keeps up a quiet mantra of an apology.

When I'm pretty sure there is nothing left to come up, I roll over to the cool tile of the bathroom floor and groan. "Oh, God, please take me now," I mutter.

Chris gets me a cold, wet washcloth. "Are you going to be okay?" he asks quietly.

"I will be," I whisper. "But I'm not yet."

"If it's any consolation," he says, "I wish I were dead."

"Why would that be consolation?"

"I don't actually know, but that's what people always say."

I try to nod, but it brings on another wave of nausea and I have to bring my head over the toilet again. Chris rubs my back with the hand not holding my hair and sings Van Morrison's "Crazy Love" which seems like an odd choice as a soundtrack for the situation, but I'll take it. After several dry heaves, I'm pretty sure I'm done so I lay down on the tile again. I'm actually feeling much better.

"Please go away," I say.

"Okay. I just wanted to tell you that I'm sorry, Sara." He starts to stand up.

I grab the leg of his jeans. "Where are you going?"

"You told me to leave."

"Yes, of course I did. That's the way these things work. Didn't you know that? I'm embarrassed to be seen throwing up, so I ask you to go. You say it's okay and stay anyway. I wouldn't have to explain this to a man with a girlfriend."

"You want me to leave because you're embarrassed to throw up in front of me?"

"Yes. Why else would I want you to go?"

"Because you're mad at me for last night."

"You mean this morning?"

"That too." He takes a deep breath. "I'm so sorry."

"It's okay. What I want to know is why you seem fine. You drank way more than I did."

"Two reasons. One, I have a lot more practice. Two, I already threw it all up."

I laugh weakly. "That makes me feel better I guess."

"You're seriously going to let it go at that?"

"Let what go? At what?"

"Sara, I was awful."

"No you weren't. It's fine. Chris, there is an excellent chance that something happened that you remember that I don't. But, I don't remember you doing anything bad."

"I —"

"Although that tired dance routine for "Yesterday's News" was pretty bad."

"I —"

"If there is something else, please don't tell me."

"You remember."

"Of course I do, but I still don't know what you're apologizing for."

"I deserve to get slapped, and she says there's nothing wrong."

"Are you talking to me?"

"No, sweetheart. Go to sleep."

I wake up on the bed, back to back with Chris who is completely passed out. Short Mark is sitting on the end of the bed, looking at me. "Good Morning, Shorty."

"Hey. What time is it?"

"Time to consider going to the airport."

"Dammit."

"Are you okay now?"

"I'm better. Still miserable and I'm sure I'll spend some time swearing that I'll never drink again. But I'll make a full recovery."

"Yes, I'm sure we'll have you drinking again in no time." He looks at Chris. "You two make up?"

"Were we fighting?"

"I think so."

"Oh, well, then yes, we made up."

"Good. Go take a shower."

"Yes, sir." I groan as I roll out of the bed. I give up and crawl to the bathroom. Short Mark swats my butt and lies back in my spot in the bed.

"You don't have all day!" he reminds me.

"Why are you so damn chipper?"

"Because I didn't drink a swimming pool of vodka."

"Right, of course. If you hear a loud thump you might want to come check."

"I'll send one of my minions."

I feel a lot better after a shower. I have to hurry to pack up my crap because I really do have to get to the airport. Chris is still asleep on my bed, and Short Mark is watching me. "When do you guys leave?"

"Oh, they'll let us sleep off last night all day in a nice bed. We'll leave after dark, I'm sure."

"You're playing tomorrow?"

"Yup. LA. I hate that."

"What going up and then right back?"

"Yup. But whatever." I nod. "When are we going to see you again, Shorty?"

"I don't know. I'm really glad I made it for this one, but I have to work now. Real world and stuff, you know how it is." Then it occurs to me that Short Mark has never worked a regular nine to five. "Oh, maybe you don't."

He throws a pillow at me. "Ah, you could give it all up and tour with us, you know."

"I think I'll stick with chemistry."

"Say good-bye to Eck. I'm going to take you to the airport."

"What? Why? Surely one of your minions can do it."

"Oh, that's what I meant. Whenever I say *I* am going to do something, I really mean that I'm going to have someone else do it for me."

"Then I will just do it," Chris says. He rolls over. "Hey, is it really time to go?"

"For me at least."

"Okay, well, say good-bye to Evans. Someone is going to take you to the airport."

I kiss Short Mark on the cheek. "Tell the guys I said 'good-bye' for me."

"Okay. *Try* to stay out of trouble, Shorty."

"I'll do my best."

Chapter 26

Now that the tour is underway, I imagine Chris will be too busy for me. I'm glad that school is back in session to keep my mind on something. But there really isn't that much of a change. Chris calls a lot from the road, when there's nothing else to do. He still sends me text messages a hundred times a day. And now there is one great addition to our communication. He sends me post cards. He sends one every day, from wherever they are at the moment.

> Greetings from the Evansgate tour bus!
> Official tour day number 3
> Days since I've seen you: 1
> We're back in LA tonight. It's like we never
> left. Love, Chris

The next one has a picture of LA on the front, too.

> Tour Day 4, Days since I've seen you: 2
> So, 4 guys walk into a bar. Uh, I can't
> remember the rest. Love, Chris

They don't come every day. Sometimes I get two in the same day. But I know he is writing them every day and my trip to the mailbox becomes the highlight of my day. I already know that I'm going to dread Sundays.

> Day 5, Days since I've seen you: 3
> How did we live before Google? Everyone says
> hi. Love, Chris

> Day 6, Days since I've seen you: 4
> I'm sure the inside of this bus will get boring
> very soon, but so far, so good. (It would be
> better if you were in it though.)
> Love, Chris

I put them in a box under my bed. I wonder how big of a box I'm going to need by the time the tour is over. I carefully file them in order and read them all every night before I go to bed.

Day 7, Days since I've seen you: 5
It's all fun and games until someone loses an eye. Then it's freaking hilarious.
Love, Chris

Day 8, Days since I've seen you: 6
I'm thinking that I want to take up chess. Want to play? Love, Chris

Day 9, Days since I've seen you: 7
Stupidity seems to be on the rise. Do you think there is a ceiling for this or are we all doomed? Love, Chris

Day 10, Days since I've seen you: 8
Turns out, I am not very good at chess. Maybe I will attempt to master checkers instead. Love, Chris

Day 11, Days since I've seen you: 9
It was a hard ride to Calgary and I don't feel like playing tonight. "There'll be days like this" Love, Chris

I smile as I read the last one again. It's a reference to the first day we met when I was singing the Van Morrison songs, I know it is. I miss him so much. I pull out my phone to text Chris before I go to sleep. They're playing in Omaha tonight, so I'm sure he can't talk.

To Chris:
I hope the show goes well. Thanks for my postcards.

It's the first time I've mentioned them, even though I've gotten so many. I touch them one last time and slide the box under my bed.

The next day is Saturday, and Chris calls me in the early afternoon. It's mid-morning his time, so I know he just got up.

"Good morning sweetheart!" I feel better just hearing his goofy "sweetheart."

"How was the show last night?"

"It was fine. Evans is still lamenting the loss of his 'Single'."

"Are you trying to make me feel guilty?"

"Yes. When he asks, please tell him that I did my best."

I laugh. "All right. What are you doing today?"

"Driving somewhere. What else?" Chris sounds bored.

"I thought you loved touring."

"I used to. I still would..." he trails off.

I already know what he's going to say, but I ask anyway, "If?"

"If you were here too."

"I'm sure I would not add very much."

"Do you really like the post cards?"

"Are you kidding? I love them!"

"I find them slightly depressing."

I'm surprised. "Why?"

"Because the numbers just keep going up. When are you going to come to another show? I'd rather be looking forward to the next time I see you than looking back at how long it's been. How about Vegas?"

I pick up a copy of the tour dates. I made several copies of the page Short Mark had left with me and I keep them all over the house. "How about Phoenix?"

"That's still two weeks!"

"Well, that's what I can do. Take it or leave it."

"You're so cruel, woman."

"I'll see you in Phoenix?"

"Maybe. I'll think about it."

I laugh. "Well, let me know when you decide."

I know he really wants me to come to Vegas while they are there. They have two shows a day for three days before they move on, and I think they even get a day off. I wish that I could, but Sam is going to be home that week for a couple of days and I can't just take off. Plus, I do have a job.

I collect my daily postcard a little later.

Day 12, Days since I've seen you: 10
It's all fun and games until it starts
to itch. Love, Chris

I spend the rest of the day moping around the house, but I decide to go out with Matt for the night. We go downtown, back to Sine's, like it's the only place in town. It's crowded again tonight because they have another really good band playing.

Matt and I take up residence in a corner booth. "Do you miss him?"

"Him Sam or him Chris?"

"Chris, of course. I know you're too used to Sam being gone to miss him much."

"I used to."

"You don't anymore?"

"No, now I miss Chris."

He laughs. "That's who I thought we were talking about."

"Oh, no. I meant: I used to miss Sam. But now that I've spent more time with Chris in the house than I've ever spent there with Sam, I can actually feel his absence."

Matt nods. "That makes sense."

"It's terrible. I'm a terrible person. I feel like I'm cheating on Sam every time I think about Chris."

"Cut yourself some slack. That right there is proof that you're not. Sleep easy – you're good to Sam. Too good, if you ask me."

"What happened to your support?"

He shrugs. "What can I say?" Matt looks at me carefully before he speaks again. "How is the Ice Queen doing these days?"

"What? Oh! Anna? I don't know. I haven't heard or seen anything about her since that super fun night out."

We stay until last call and then end up having to get a cab home. "I promise I will take you back to get your car first thing tomorrow," I practically slur. I'm drunker than I thought.

Matt nods sleepily. "I'll call you when I wake up."

He has the cab take me to my house first. I roll out and fumble with my keys. When I get the door open, I turn and wave. Matt always waits until I get inside before he drives away. I guess that applies to cabs, too.

I really want to talk to Chris, probably because I'm drunk. I don't even remember what time zone he is in though, and I think he has a show tomorrow night so he's probably asleep. I settle for a text. There are several from Chris waiting for me.

From Chris:
Do you think I can beat Holst in an arm wrestling contest?
3 hours ago

From Chris:
I'm really thinking about trying it, but I thought I would get your opinion first. Are you around?
3 hours ago

From Chris:
I lost. I wish you had been around to tell me not to try.
3 hours ago

From Chris:
I'm wondering where you are tonight. Text me?
2 hours ago

From Chris:
Are you mad at me?
1 hour ago

I don't like to text with people when I am with someone else. I think it is extremely rude when other people do it, so I make a point of *not* doing it. Chris knows that about me. But I guess he assumed that with my wonderfully lame life, I would be at home doing nothing all night as usual.

To Chris:
Sorry! I went out with Matt tonight.

To Chris:
Just got in.

To Chris:
Missing you.

To Chris:
Show tomorrow?

Hm, maybe I should have sent all of those as one. I'm surprised when my phone rings. It's Chris.

"What are you doing awake?" I demand as a greeting.

"What are you doing texting me a million times in the middle of the night?" he returns sleepily. "I thought it might have been important, so I got up to check after the third or fourth one."

"I only sent four."

"That was enough."

"Sorry," I say sheepishly.

"It's okay. Did you have fun with Matt tonight?"

"Yeah, I did."

"What did you – ah, never mind. Sine's?"

"Is there anywhere else?"

"I hear Ruth's Chris is nice."

"I'm really sorry I woke you up. Go back to sleep."

"Are you drunk?" he sounds almost angry.

"Um, yeah, I think so."

"I thought we cured that in San Francisco."

"I'm a slow learner."

"Clearly. I miss you."

"I miss you too." That might have been a little serious.

But Chris changes his tone right away to match mine. "Come to Vegas. Please?"

"I can't. You already know that. Stop asking! You just keep making me feel worse."

"Okay, fine," he sulks. "I'm going back to sleep now."

"Okay. Do you have a show tomorrow?"

"You really are drunk."

"Why do you say that?"

"Because you are the only person who knows the tour schedule better than Evans. Or at least, when you're sober. No, sweetheart, we don't have a show tomorrow. Call me from the grocery store."

I smile. He knows me so well. "Okay. Eighty-eights."

I can hear his smile. "Ten-ten."

I pull my cards out to look at them before I turn off the light. I read through all 10, and then go to sleep.

Day 13, Days since I've seen you: 11
It's a long road to Omaha. You probably aren't
familiar with college baseball references
though. Love, Chris

Day 14, Days since I've seen you: 12
Evans thinks he's funnier than he actually is.
That's all I'm going to say. Love, Chris

Sam comes home for a few days. I feel like I'm seeing a lot more of him suddenly and I think about different reasons for that. Matt said that I look better to him now that Chris is in my life and sniffing around. Or maybe he's just fighting with his girlfriend – but I bite that one back as soon as it jumps into my mind. Maybe things are just changing with his company and it's all just a coincidence.

He gets in by dinnertime on the same day I get my Day 14 postcard. I'm trying really hard to be cordial after our last time together, so we go out to eat. Then he works in the office for a couple of hours.

I'm in the middle of my nightly ritual of reading my postcards when Sam comes up to our room. I'm startled to see him there. "Sam!" I feel guilty, like I've been caught doing something I shouldn't be doing.

"I just wanted to say good night. What are you doing?"

"Oh, I'm just looking at some postcards." I drop them in the box and push it under the bed.

Sam gives me a funny look. "Okay, well get a good night's sleep. I've got a couple more hours tonight and then I'll probably just crash on the office couch."

I nod. "Good night."

When he leaves, I scramble to get the box back out. I start at the beginning and read them all again. Then I meticulously put them in order and slide the box back under my bed. I lie down to go to sleep, but suddenly I don't want to leave the box where Sam saw me put it. I get up and move it to my hope chest at the foot of the bed. I'll put it back when he's gone.

I don't get a postcard the next day. At least, there isn't one in the mailbox when I get home from school. The mailman has come though, and I'm afraid that Sam went through and took it out before I got home.

That night, Sam goes to bed at the same time I do. I honestly can't remember the last time he did that. I'm uncomfortable changing in front of him. He is my husband! This is ridiculous! I can't pull my cards out to read them in front of Sam and I hate it. The paranoid part of me starts to wonder if that is why he came to bed now.

I feel like I'm climbing into bed with a stranger. I'm hoping that he doesn't want to have sex or anything, because I don't know if I could do it. The whole situation is giving me a creepy feeling up my spine.

"Good night, Sara," Sam says as he pulls the covers over himself. "I usually sleep on that side of the bed, you know." He nods in my direction.

"This has always been my side of the bed, Sam. See my nightstand over here and yours over there?

"Well, I sleep on that side every night." He is smiling, but I feel like he is accusing me of something.

"I sleep on this side of *this* bed every night," I point out.

"Whatever. Sleep well." He rolls over and puts his head on his pillow. I don't think he could be any further away without actually getting out of the bed and sleeping on the floor. The sad thing is that I wish he was on the floor. Was he actually trying to be friendly? Maybe he was trying to point out how we're similar. I can't tell if I overreacted or decide if I feel bad.

I can't sleep at all. I don't know if it's the creepy feeling of sleeping with a stranger or because I didn't get to read my postcards. Either way, I lay rigid and tense for hours. At some point I must drift off, because my alarm wakes me up. Sam grunts at me, so I turn if off quickly. It's so weird to have him here. Usually when he's home we sleep in opposite shifts, or he just catnaps on the couch in the office.

I get ready for work as quietly as I can. Getting out of the house feels like I've been liberated. I don't know when Sam is leaving again, but it's either the red-eye tonight or early tomorrow morning. Please let it be the red-eye.

I'm very glad to be at school today. Usually I wish I were somewhere else, preferably a couple thousand miles west, but somewhere I could text and talk to Chris all day. But today, I'm grateful to have my own place to go. I stay after to help some students with their homework, looking for any excuse to delay going back to the house, to Sam. I know there is something seriously wrong with my marriage, but I don't want to think about it right now.

On the drive home I think about Chris and the rest of Evansgate. Tonight they have their first show in Vegas. I know this is one of the biggest events of the tour. If I had agreed to Short Mark's ludicrous proposal I probably would have had to have been there too. The thought makes me wistful. I almost wish that I had agreed *then* so that I would be with them *now*. When I pull in my driveway, I get out my phone to text Chris before I go inside.

To Chris:
Good luck tonight! (Or break a leg?) Please pass on
whichever sentiment is more appropriate to the rest of
the crew.

There's a flutter of anticipation in my chest as I head to the mailbox. I can feel my phone buzz as I pull out the mail, but instead of answering it I dig through the stack looking for my post card. I want to see it and tuck it away safely before I see Sam. My heart leaps when I find it.

Day 16, Days until we meet: 12
Thanks for drunk texting me last night.
That just doesn't roll off your tongue as
nicely as drunk dialing, does it? Love, Chris

Day 16? What happened to day 15? I was right! Sam found it yesterday and took it! I'm so angry with him I'm shaking. I stifle the urge to march into the house and slap him, and force myself to calm down. I look through the rest of the mail in an attempt to distract myself for a moment. There is an envelope from Chris; that should do it. I rip it open and find a post card and a folded piece of paper. I read the post card first.

Day 15, Days until we meet: 13
It still seems like a long time, but at least I
have a date to look forward to. Love, Chris

The paper is flight information. He booked a ticket for me to fly to Phoenix the day before the show. A handwritten message at the bottom of the page gives me my hotel information. Then he wrote:

I'll be waiting at the airport. Love, Chris

I let out a shaky breath. I wobble a little as I finally head towards the house. I'm so glad I did not rush in and accuse Sam of stealing my mail. That could have been ugly. I tuck my stuff from Chris into my bag before I go into the kitchen and drop the rest of the mail on the counter. I check my phone and find a text from Chris and one from Short Mark.

From Chris:
Thanks for the well wishes and ominous command. I would rather not break my leg if it's all the same to you.

From Mark E:
Wishing you were here with us getting ready to go on stage. Reconsider?

I dial Chris.

"Hey!" he answers on the first ring.

"Hi. Could you please pass a message to Short Mark for me?"

"Sure."

"Tell him I would rather not break my leg either."

"Evans!" I hear him say. "She doesn't want to go on stage." Then to me, "One and done."

"Thanks." I notice Sam's suitcase in the hall. Red-eye it is. I let out a relieved breath.

"What just went well?"

"I, uh, can't really say right now."

"Sam leaving soon?"

"Are you asking that as an actual question or guessing that's what made me smile?"

"Both."

"You know me so well. But we'll talk about it later. Are you ready?"

"It's just another show, sweetheart."

"Does Short Mark feel the same way?"

"No."

"I didn't think so. Is he ready?"

"He never thinks he's ready for these. But, yes, he is."

"I got my flight information today. Thanks."

"You're welcome."

"You didn't have to do that, you know. I would have flown myself out."

"I know. Don't worry, I'm going to make you buy your ticket."

"They're not sold out yet?"

"Hm, good point. Well, I hope you're ready to pay a lot to get one off of a scalper."

"To sit in the nose bleed section?"

"Probably."

"Then it's probably not worth it. I'll just pass on this one and try to get a good seat through Ticketmaster for the next one."

"Okay, fine. I'll let you in, too. Geez, I have to do everything."

"Hey! I *just* told you that you didn't."

"Yeah, yeah. You say that after I already did all the work."

"Chris?"

"Yeah?"

"Shut up." He doesn't respond. I love it when he listens. "I can't wait to see you."

"Can I talk now?" he asks.

"I suppose."

"I can't wait to see you either. But, hey – I gotta go."

"Bye!"

"Bye..."

That night I retrieve my box from the hope chest. I add days 15 and 16, then re-read through them all before I slide it back under the bed. I fall asleep quickly.

Chapter 27

All of the next day I push away thoughts about Sam. Can I really do this for the rest of my life? Think about something else. Would things really change if I ended up with Chris or would it turn out exactly the same? Something else – think about something else! If I don't think about it, then I don't have to make a decision. Maybe Sam will just divorce me. Something else!

I skip to the mailbox after school, but there isn't a postcard today. I try to remind myself that I got two yesterday, but then I remember that was to make up for the fact that I didn't get one the day before that. Grrrr, stupid postal service.

I'm glad it's Friday, and I'm glad that Sam is gone. (Think about something else.) I brought home papers to grade, so I sit down to work on that. I can't concentrate on it for very long. This time next week, I'll be getting on a plane bound for Phoenix. My phone buzzes and interrupts my daydream.

"Hi, Chris!"

"How do you always know it's me?"

"Oh, it's this thing called 'Caller ID'. They invented it a while ago. You should consider getting it for yourself."

"I'll look into it. This time next week, you'll be getting on a plane for Phoenix."

"I know! I was just thinking the same thing!"

"I can't wait."

"Unfortunately, you have to. How were the shows last night?"

"They were great! Evans really feeds off of the energy at these big venues. It's really fun to be on stage with him."

"I'm smiling, you just can't see it."

"But I wish I could. I can hear it though."

"Someday, I'll get a new phone and we'll be able to make video calls."

"How do you know I don't need to get a new phone too?"

"Because I know you don't."

"Oh. Okay."

"I know you have to go."

"Later tater." He hangs up before I can even respond.

The weekend drags by and eases back into the work week. I call Allison and make arrangements to go to Dallas for my birthday.

"Hey, big sister."

"Hey! How are you doing? I feel like it's been a long time since we've talked."

"It kind of has been, I guess. How was Portugal?"

"Exhausting. But I'm home now for a good long while. I don't have another trip planned for almost two months!"

"That's great! Are you going to be home for my birthday?"

"Home home or home in Dallas?"

"Dallas."

"I think so, why?"

"I'm coming for a visit."

"Oh, well please don't hesitate to invite yourself."

"I won't."

"What brought this on?"

"We're going to a concert that night."

"Ah. I should have known. Let me know when you've got your flight booked."

"Will do. Go save the world."

"Bye, Baby Girl."

I *live* for my post cards. Day 17 still hasn't shown up. I wonder if he didn't send one that day.

> Day 18, Days until we meet: 10
> It's all fun and games until your mom sees the pictures. Love, Chris

> Day 19, Days until we meet: 9
> Hit single digits today! Turns out, trying to find new uses for Tang only results in dying things orange. Love, Chris

> Day 20, Days until we meet: 8
> Why is it that the biggest person in the room is always wearing the least amount of clothing? Love, Chris

I get two cards on Wednesday. Those are the best days!

Day 21, Days until we meet: 7
I think I've finally lost it. Fortunately, I can't
remember what it is. Love, Chris

Day 22, Days until we meet: 6
When you are especially sleep deprived it's a
short hop to crazy town. Love, Chris

No post cards on Thursday, but I can almost stand it because I'll be on my way tomorrow. I pack before I go to sleep because I'll be rushing to the airport after school. I read through my cards and tuck the box under my bed. I have trouble falling asleep because I'm so excited. "Get a grip," I tell myself. "You're an adult."

The school day seems to go on forever. I cannot wait to get out of here. As soon as the bell rings, I take off. I'm almost pushing students out of my way to get to my car. I rush to my house to get my things together before Matt comes to get me. I check the mailbox just to see, and I'm well rewarded for my efforts.

Day 23, Days until we meet: 5
It's all fun and games until you wake up with
a hangover. Love, Chris

Day 24, Days until we meet: 4
Sometimes I think it would be funny to walk
through the airport wearing a parachute.
Love, Chris

The flight seems never ending, of course, but I'm tired because I didn't sleep much last night. Gratefully, I nod off for a considerable portion of the time. When it's time to get off of the plane, I'm glad that Chris sprung for first class so that I don't have to wait for many people to disembark ahead of me. Although, maybe that's why he did it.

I'm excited about the concert because I know a little bit more about what to expect. But I'm also nervous because I know it will be different from San Francisco and Angie won't be here to tell me what to do.

I push my way through Sky Harbor Airport, desperate to see Chris's face. It's been almost a month, and it's weird that that's weird. We live on opposite coasts, but I was used to seeing him every ten days or so and for a long time each visit. Now, a couple of days a month – that's it! I freeze suddenly and two people bounce off of my back.

"Hey!"

"Watch it!"

"Sorry," I mutter as they push past me. I only see my husband a couple of days a month usually. Why doesn't it bother me as much as not seeing Chris more often than that? Think about something else! Right. It doesn't matter and I'm going to see Chris now. I start moving again.

As soon as I pass security, I start looking. I'm disappointed that he isn't right there, waiting for me. I'm being horribly selfish, I know. The man *is* on tour, it's not like he doesn't have anything else to worry about. I wonder if he sent a minion for me. I drag my feet and sulk as I continue towards baggage claim, because I can't think of anywhere else to go.

"Sara!"

At the sound of Chris's voice, I look up. "Chris!" But I don't see him.

"Sara," he's laughing. I push up to my tip toes and flip my head in every direction.

"Sara, I'm right here." He is still laughing. I'm standing in front of him, and he is sitting in a chair.

"You're supposed to be tall! Why would I be looking down?"

He stands up and grabs me in a hug. I close my eyes and breath in his smell. I'm vaguely aware that he is talking, but I'm not listening.

"And then I was afraid that I missed you. Sara? Are you listening to me?"

I shake my head and press my face into his chest.

"I missed you, woman."

"I missed you, too," I mumble against his shirt.

"Come on, I've got things to do, which you would know if you had been listening."

"Okay," I mumble.

He puts his hands under my arms and picks me up, like one would lift a child. He is *really* strong! "Sara," he says when my face is level with his.

"Yes?"

"I need you to stop smelling me so we can walk, okay?"

"No, it's not, but I will anyway."

He laughs and puts me down. He grabs my suitcase with one hand and puts his other arm around my shoulders. "Let's go, crazy lady."

There's a Town Car waiting for us, and we ride to a hotel not far from the airport. Chris thanks the driver and gets my suitcase from the back. We don't even slow down in the lobby, he just breezes straight towards the elevators.

We ride up to the 11th floor, and Mike greets us when we step off of the elevator. "Do they make you work 24/7?" I ask him.

"Pretty much. How are you doing, Sara?"

"Much better than the last time you saw me." I cringe as I remember. "Sorry about that."

He pats my arm. "It's fine, honey. I've seen a lot worse."

"I'm sure you have."

Chris pulls a card from his pocket and unlocks a room. "This is you."

"Why is Mike in the hallway?"

"To make sure that no one gets off of the elevator that shouldn't."

"Do you have the whole floor?"

"Yeah. We always do."

"Right. Because who doesn't get an entire floor at every hotel they stay at? Stupid me."

"Sweetheart, there are, like, 30 people in our crew. And, it helps with security to just know that the whole floor is off limits."

"When does Mike get to sleep?"

"Whenever he wants, he's the boss. If he didn't want to be standing there right now, he would have someone else do it."

"Oh, right."

He pushes me into the room and his voice softens, "How was your flight?"

"It was great. Thanks for the first class." I smile at him.

"Hey, baby, only the best." The door swings shut behind him. He puts my stuff on the table and throws himself on my bed.

"I thought you had things to do."

"I'm doing them."

"Lying on my bed was on your list of things to do?"

He rolls over and gives me his vaudeville eyebrows. "Your bed is always on my to-do list. But, really, I could have had important things to do, which you wouldn't have known because you weren't listening."

"So, it was all a clever ploy to make me feel bad for ignoring you when you talk?"

"Yes." He laughs. "But I did tell you that this is all we're going to get. Tomorrow we have some stuff to do before sound check and dress."

"Dress?"

He gives me a look that says I should know what he is talking about. "Dress rehearsal."

"You still have to have dress rehearsals? How many of these have you done in the last month?"

"In Phoenix?"

"Oh. Good point."

Chris opens his arms to me. "Come on. I know you're tired, it's after midnight at home."

"I don't want to go to sleep. I don't have much time with you."

"We can talk any time, but I can only hug you for a little while. Come on."

I am tired. I curl up against his chest and he sings to me until I fall asleep. It doesn't take very long.

"Hey! Shorty! It's not even 11! Wake up!"

"No," I mumble. "I'm sleeping."

"I see that. Now get up."

"Why?"

"Because I said so."

"You can't tell me what to do. I'm not one of your minions."

"Oh, I thought Eck had finally hired you as eye candy or something like that. Well, get up, *please*."

I laugh and roll over. "Where did Chris go?"

"I'm right here!" he yells from the bathroom.

"Good! I was going to get angry that you tricked me into bed and then left!"

Short Mark scoffs. "He tricked you into bed? Do you know how bad that sounds?"

"I know. He's evil."

"I'm not *that* bad," Chris disagrees as he comes back into the room.

I yawn. "How long did I get to sleep?"

"Oh, a long time." Chris looks at his watch. "Almost 20 minutes, I think."

Someone starts pounding on the door. "Well, now I know why the hotel is so willing to give you an entire floor," I say.

"Why?" Chris asks as Short Mark goes to open the door.

"Because you people make so much noise, the other guests would complain. Which reminds me... How come I didn't notice we had our own floor in San Francisco?"

"Because you are amazingly unobservant when you are drunk," Blond Mark tells me as he comes in. "Thanks for saying good-bye before you left that floor, by the way." He jumps on the bed. "I am glad to know I mean so much to you that you can leave without a word."

"Hey! I left word. But I was not about to deliver it in person."

"Is this going to be some kind of ugly, mind-in-the-gutter reference to me and Angie?"

"It could be. But I'll leave it alone. Where's Drew?"

Blond Mark shrugs. "I actually thought he was in here."

Chris shakes his head. "No, he went down to the gym."

Blond Mark looks at me. "He's in the gym, Sare-Bear."

"Thanks," I say dryly.

Chris shoves Blond Mark off the bed and lies back down next to me. "He's probably back in his room by now."

"What are we doing tonight?" Blond Mark looks around. "Did Sara bring any vodka? I heard from a little birdie that is what she likes to drink. Oh, wait, I heard that from half of San Francisco."

"Ha ha. I couldn't say what your drink of choice is, but only because you consumed quite a bit of *everything*."

"That's right, baby. I'm an equal opportunity drinker, myself."

Short Mark is digging through my suitcase. "Is this really what you brought to wear to our show?"

"Hey! What are you doing?"

"Being a good friend. What happened to that brown dress? Let's go shopping."

"Short Mark, it's after 11. Nowhere is open, except the internet and that wouldn't help me with something to wear tomorrow."

"Fair point. But I'm bored. What are we going to do?"

"I don't know," I look around at all of them. "You people are rock stars; surely you have something fun we could do?"

Chris smirks. "I have something fun to do." He looks at the Marks. "Go away."

Short Mark shakes his head. "Oh, no. I'm not leaving you alone in her room. After the last trip, you two need a chaperone at all times."

"Yes," I say, "because that is so much fun for everyone."

"Hey, what do I care?" Short Mark laughs. "I'll just have a minion do it. No skin off of my back."

In the end, we get a pay-per-view movie and we all fall asleep on my bed. I wake up between Chris and Short Mark. Blond Mark moved to the couch at some point, and Drew is on the floor. "Well, you guys are the most boring rock stars I've ever had the pleasure of knowing," I say loudly.

"Ug," Short Mark waves his hand at me. "Brush your teeth."

Chris reaches over me and hits him. "Thanks," I say.

"No problem, sweetheart."

"I'm so glad that you paid for an entire floor. You really made good use of those rooms."

"Shut up, Shorty. We're still sleeping."

I roll back over and close my eyes. Short Mark throws his arm around me and pulls me towards him. "Stay away from Eck. He's the only person I've ever met with worse morning breath than you."

This time I hit him and Chris says, "Thanks."

"No problem."

I have trouble going back to sleep. It's two hours later at home, so I feel like I've really slept in. I try to stay still – I know that the guys really do need sleep, but my eyes pop open. Chris is staring at me. "Hi," I mouth.

He smiles. "Hi," he mouths back. He slides out of the bed and pulls me with him.

"Sleeping here, Shorty," Short Mark says.

"So sleep," Chris retorts. "Sara and I are going to get some breakfast."

Blond Mark sits up. "I could do breakfast."

Drew doesn't open his eyes, but from the floor he says, "I could too."

Short Mark sits up. "Fine. What are we eating?"

We order room service for breakfast and then everyone goes their own way to shower and get ready. After I shower, Chris comes back to my room before we leave.

"We have to go to the venue first, to check on set-up. Then we are being interviewed by a local radio station, and we have this meet and greet thing. Then we come back to the venue for sound and dress."

"Wow, it's already after nine. How do you have time for all of that?"

"It doesn't take that long." He glances at his watch. "Come on, the car is leaving in a few minutes."

Mike isn't in the hallway anymore. Chris introduces me to the current guy on watch. "Sara, this is Pete, he's on security too. Pete, this is my friend, Sara."

Pete sticks his hand out and smiles. "Shorty?" he asks.

"That's me." I shake his hand. Pete is a lot smaller than Mike, but he still isn't someone I would mess with in a dark alley.

In the lobby we meet up with Short Mark and Drew. "We're still waiting for the pretty boy," Drew says. "Even the *girl* gets ready faster than he does."

Short Mark laughs. "Shorty is a unique girl."

"Cannadiak is a unique dude," Drew is saying as Blond Mark steps out of the elevator.

"And don't you forget it," he says. "What are we waiting for? Let's go."

Drew mutters, "You," as we walk out, but he's laughing.

In the limo I have time to ask some questions.

"So you don't give out *any* backstage passes?"

Short Mark shakes his head. "Why? Was there someone you were hoping to impress with one?"

"Who? Most of my friends are in this car, and I'm pretty sure you all are allowed back there."

Blond Mark shakes his head. "You live a sad life, little one."

"Okay, maybe, but that's not the point. Chris said that you have an interview with a radio station. Don't they normally like to give away backstage passes and things as prizes?"

Short Mark nods. "Yeah, we do different things, like we'll give them club tickets, but I don't like a lot of strangers running around backstage."

"But surely, sometimes you have to give in?"

Short Mark gasps with mock indignation. "Now you're calling me Shirley?" I just look at him. "Yes, occasionally the label makes us. There was a four pack of club tickets, backstage passes, and 'a chance to meet Evansgate' at the Saturday show in New York that we had to sign off on. I think they also threw in a limo ride or something."

"Is it possible to *buy* club tickets, or do you have to have some way to *get* them?"

"I think that might depend on the venue. The label keeps a certain amount of them for every show, but if the venue is big enough, they can sell what's left."

"Do you get as many tickets as you want?"

"Actually, no, we don't," Blond Mark laughs. "I have to clear it with the suits if I want my mom to be able to come to a show!"

Chris looks at me. "They would never tell us that we couldn't have any tickets that we asked for. Unless, of course, I want enough for your entire graduating class or something."

Short Mark shoves Chris. "Yes, I imagine even Evelyn wouldn't agree to that."

I look at Chris. "Who's Evelyn?"

But Blond Mark answers me. "She's with the suits, and she has a major crush on Mr. Eck. She gives him a lot of things that she would deny – say – me, for instance."

Chris laughs at him. "What is it that you have asked for that has been denied? I'll see what I can do."

"I don't want your cast offs."

"Hey, if that's the best you can get..."

The guys start shoving and horsing around. "Someone is going to get hurt, and then won't you look stupid on stage with a black eye?"

The guys all freeze and look at me. "Yes, Mom," they chorus. Everyone is laughing.

Drew nudges my shoulder. "You've definitely been spending some time with Bethany, haven't you? I think she is starting to rub off on you."

Chapter 28

The venue is an arena, similar to San Francisco. We go through another solid gray, nondescript door that leads into another maze of passages and tunnels. "How do you know where to go?!" I cry out in frustration. How does everyone know how to navigate these places?

Short Mark points to the wall, where a sign is hanging with directional cues. "We read the signs, Shorty." I can tell that they are all laughing at me on the inside.

"Oh. I see. That makes sense." As if those could help me. I don't even know what our final destination is, but I guess if you do, those signs would tell you how to get there.

Tom is waiting for us. "Hi, Sara!"

"Hey, Tom. How are you doing?"

"I'm great. You?"

"I can't complain." I look at the guys. "Go! Go work! I'll lose myself down here for a while." Both Marks and Drew go with Tom, but Chris hangs back.

"There really isn't much that needs to be done right now. Let's go look around. Evans won't be too long."

Chris leads me towards the stage area. As we pass one of the doors marked "PRIVATE" he points at it with his thumb. "The red room?" I ask.

"The red room?"

"In San Francisco you were in the red room."

He smiles. "Yes, the red room."

"How do you know this time? All of the signs are white."

"Yes, this time you just have to know."

"Oh, well, then I'm screwed." He looks at me with a question in his eyes. "I'll never remember which one!"

He takes my hand. "Then you better just stay with me."

"I'm sure Short Mark would love that." I drop my voice lower and pretend to be Short Mark. "'Hey, Eck, why is Shorty standing on stage with us?'" Then I turn my head to face the other way, pretending to be Chris. "'Oh, because she's an idiot and I couldn't trust her to find her way back.'" I flip the back the other way. "'Haven't you ever heard of bread crumbs?'"

Chris is roaring with laughter. "Evans would love it if you were on stage, but you could stay just behind the curtain if you would prefer."

When we get to the stage area, there are people everywhere,

moving things around, setting things up. "How many of these people came with you and how many of them were already here?"

"We have our stage manager, Terri – I'll introduce you to her in a second, three sound monkeys, two guys on lights, Mike and he has five guys with him," Chris is ticking them off on his fingers, "a guitar, bass, keyboard, and drum tech, three hands, and a couple of other general lackeys. Then there's Tom, of course, and his assistant."

"Wow. What do they all do?"

"That could take some time to explain. Basically? Whatever Evans tells them to."

"Yes, his minions."

Chris laughs. "Evans is a really great guy to work with – as long as you don't screw up."

"Oh, so no pressure."

"I mean, he takes the time to get to know everyone we tour with. A lot of roadies can't say they know the band as well as ours do."

"But I've never met any of them."

"They're good at their jobs. They stay out of the way."

"What's a sound monkey?"

"You're full of questions today."

"I'm curious. It's a whole lifestyle and I'm learning."

"A sound monkey is in charge of mics and speakers."

"What about the instruments? Doesn't someone have to...?" I trail off because I'm not even sure what I'm asking, but I know they have to be set up to make sound, too.

"The techs have to do that. They're in charge of setting up the instruments and making sure they're ready to play." I nod. Chris reaches out and grabs somebody walking by carrying a box. "Beth! This is Sara."

The girl turns around and smiles. "Hi, Sara."

I stick my hand out to shake hers and Chris continues. "She is in charge of Evans's keyboard."

Part of me really wants to say, "That's it?" but I hold it back.

She nods. "It's nice to meet you. I've got to –" and she rushes off.

"They're busy," Chris tells me.

"Who is in charge of your bass?"

"Alex. But I don't know where he is."

"Does he play it?"

"*The* bass or *my* bass?"

"Yes."

Chris laughs. "Yes. He has to tune it before the show, he has to know how."

Drew comes over. "We gotta go! We have about 20 minutes to get to the station!" Short Mark rushes by, talking to a girl with her hair in a pony tail. Blond Mark is in step with them.

"Let's go!" Tom pushes us from behind.

"That's Terri," Chris points to the girl with Short Mark as we walk.

Short Mark is nodding at her. "We'll be back by three for sound. Just tape it down and I'll try to remember that it's there, okay?"

She nods and hurries off in the direction we came from.

The interview at the radio station only takes about 20 minutes, once everyone is seated and settled. Tom is with us now, so I sit with him in the booth and we watch the guys talk to the DJs. They talk about the tour, where they've been, where they're going. They talk about the new album, which songs are their favorites, that kind of thing. Then the girl DJ turns to Chris. "So I heard that you are engaged. There are plenty of broken hearted girls running around out there. When is the wedding?" Chris glances in my direction before he answers and the DJ quickly follows his line of sight.

"No fiancée, no wedding. I don't even have a girlfriend." Chris forces a laugh.

But even as he is answering, the DJ smiles and asks, "Is *that* her? Sara?"

I look at Tom in horror. Tom is shaking his head in her direction; the frown on his face would be hard to miss.

"I don't have a girlfriend, Trixie, I promise," Chris is trying to convince the DJ.

She looks at me with doubt in her eyes. "Well, that's good news for the rest of us girls! You heard it here on XS 101, ladies, Chris Eck is still on the market!"

Chris's smile is brittle, but he stays quiet.

When we leave, Chris doesn't come anywhere near me. Blond Mark puts his arm around my shoulders instead. "You're Angie, if anyone asks," he mutters at me.

I wrap both of my arms around his waist, look at him and plaster my face with love. "Did you have fun, honey?" I ask him and reach up to kiss his cheek.

"Yes, dear. Loads."

Short Mark slides his arm around my waist as he walks next to us. "You were very well behaved. I think we can let you come with us again sometime."

"I didn't realize that I was being tested."

"Lucky for you, you passed anyway."

The "meet and greet", as Chris called it, is actually a much bigger deal than he made it out to be. Or, at least it is for the people that get to meet Evansgate. Short Mark said that they had to give away a chance to meet the group for New York, but apparently the same sort of thing happened in Phoenix. "It's not exactly the same thing," Chris tells me. "The radio station had a contest that ran for a week and everyday a couple of people won a chance to bring a friend and meet Evansgate.

"The station is just having a party, and all of those people are coming. We'll be there too, and I guess we'll meet some people. But, I need you to pretend to be Angie because that stupid DJ is going to be there and I really don't want anything to get around. Okay?"

I nod, because I totally understand. I still wish I could be with Chris though. I wouldn't really mind if the world thought I was his girlfriend. Uh, except for Sam. It would be bad if Sam thought I was Chris's girlfriend.

The radio station rented a ballroom type place in a local hotel for their party. Mike and two of his guys meet us at the door. Trixie, the DJ, is still eying me meaningfully, so I wrap my arms around Blond Mark and kiss him. "This should be fun!" I trill.

Blond Mark grabs my butt and laughs. "Behave."

I fall back to walk with Tom when he grabs my hand. He smiles at me, "Thanks. You handled that very well."

"Are you kidding? Everyone in this place thinks I'm dating a member of Evansgate."

He laughs. "Thanks anyway."

The party is, of course, quite lame. Most everyone there is really nervous about meeting super stars, so they're huddling in the corners. There are more people there than I expect though. I guess I was taking Chris literally and thought there would be about 20 "guests", but there are probably more than a hundred people in the ballroom. The music is way too loud for the space and it all has a weird middle school feeling, but maybe because it's the middle of the day. Since it's over lunch time there is food set up, but it looks kind of gross.

The people wake up a little when we come in. There is a lot of cheering and screaming. I lean into Blond Mark, "I wonder why that never happens when I walk into a room without you guys." He laughs, but Short Mark overheard me and looks over his shoulder to answer me.

"Don't blame the world, Shorty. They're nothing but haters." He steps into the room with both of his arms up in a pseudo wave.

I drink flat ginger ale and stand in a corner with Tom while the guys circulate. They have their pictures taken over and over, sign everything that is shoved in front of them, hug and smile, wave, and basically just exude coolness over the whole place.

"Who are all of these people?" I ask Tom. "I thought Chris said they only gave away a few tickets to this shindig thing."

"I'm sure they sold this thing as much as possible for the whole week. I'm sure the ninth caller, or whatever, got an invite every hour or so. Plus, anyone that is connected with the station is not going to miss this chance."

"So how long do we have to be here?"

"We agreed on two hours."

I sigh and look around for a chair.

When we are finally finished with our contracted two hours, the guys wave good-bye and we all head out, Blond Mark's arm around my waist for good measure. In the limo the guys lay back and relax.

"Well, that was fun!" I say brightly.

"Yes," agrees Chris sarcastically, "there is nothing better than being grabbed at for hours."

"Whatever, you love it," I tell him. "It's just another chance for you to measure how wonderful the world thinks you are."

"Right, I forgot. I live for the attention of my screaming fans." He smirks. "I'm starving, guys. Let's get something to eat."

We have a couple of hours until they have to be back at the venue, so we actually go through a drive through (which I have never done in a limo before) and then go to the hotel to chill out for a little while. Like the exciting rock stars they are, everyone falls asleep and we nap until it's time to go back for sound check.

At the venue, I sit in a back room, catch up on email and read while they do what they need to on the stage. The show starts at seven, and Chris told me that they go on stage between 8:30 and 9:00. They're finished practicing, or whatever, by five. Food, much better than what they had at the "party" earlier, is brought in and we eat.

"So, what happens backstage I wonder...?" I say to no one in particular. "Do you have any idea how many people would pay good money to be where I am right now?"

Short Mark looks at me and says, very seriously, "Do you know how many people would pay good money to be where *I* am? You're with Evansgate, Shorty. Not much happens back here. We basically just relax until it's time to go on stage."

We're in the "red room" sitting on couches and drinking water. There is a phone on the table that rings occasionally. Blond Mark is playing a set of imaginary drums with his eyes closed. Drew seems to be napping, but he talks to Bethany on the phone for a little bit. Short Mark paces, sits, lies down, paces, makes notes, and then does it again. Chris is just holding me against his chest. I can't see him, but I know his eyes are closed.

"Is he always like this?" I ask, referring to Short Mark.

"Yeah, pretty much. He has a lot going on in his head and he is trying to keep up with it."

"They make pills for that," I mutter, but not quietly enough because Short Mark hears and throws a wadded up napkin at me.

Around 8:30, the phone rings again. Someone had called to say that Kiro was on stage, and then again when they went off. I'm guessing this call is telling the guys it's time for them to go on stage. I don't know what to do. "Should I go out to the audience now?" I ask Chris as quietly as I can.

He nods and gives me a kiss – right on the lips, and then turns to the guys. My whole body has locked in place and I can't seem to move. It could have passed as completely platonic, but it didn't feel that way to me. I'm barely aware of the guys standing in the center of the room.

Suddenly Short Mark stands up straight and looks at me. "What did you do to her, Eck? I think she's broken. Fix her!"

I can't make my mouth smile because I can't seem to make my muscles do anything, but I'm smiling on the inside. The guys are all laughing now. "That didn't happen when I kissed her this afternoon!" Blond Mark points out, and suddenly I return to reality.

"That's because *I* kissed *you*," I tell him. "Have fun guys." When I turn towards the door I see them huddle back up again.

The show is exactly the same as the one in San Francisco, but different at the same time. It's another great show. I don't wait until the very end to try to go backstage this time. When Short Mark starts the last song, I push away from the crowd and muscle my way to Mike. He smiles and lets me through.

I'm waiting in the "red room" when the guys come in. "Hey, Shorty!" Short Mark says when he sees me. "Did you even see the show?"

I shrug. "Meh. I felt like if I saw one, that was enough. It is, isn't it?" I laugh at the look on his face. "Of course I saw it, you idiot. I just snuck out during the last song so I didn't have to wade through the masses to see you."

Chris has already downed an entire bottle of water and he is starting on his second. "Did you have fun, sweetheart?" he asks. He is a little out of breath.

I nod. "You're gross."

"It's hot on that stage, thank you."

"Yeah, geez, Eck. Didn't you know that it's possible to be cool and clean at the same time? Go take a shower!" Short Mark is teasing me, and I know it.

"Well, look who's talking," I tell him. "You aren't exactly a bowl of roses yourself. Go shower – all of you – and stop making me smell you."

They are laughing when they file out, but I can hear Short Mark, "Where did you find her, Eck? Are we sure we want to keep her? She's awfully pushy." He blows me a kiss over his shoulder.

It's much more low key after the show than it was in San Francisco. Instead of going to a club, we go to the bar in the hotel. We don't even stay very long before we pack it in and call it a night.

They have a few days until they have to be in Indianapolis. Sunday morning we go sightseeing around Phoenix until I have to go to the airport to catch my plane home. Arizona is really quite beautiful, and I really enjoy having the time to just hang out with the guys. I hate not knowing when I'm going to see them again; it makes saying good-bye so much harder.

My flight out is in the late afternoon, which means evening at home. I don't get home until really late. Matt picks me up from the airport, as has become our custom. "How was the concert?"

"It was great, I guess."

"That's the best you've got? Maybe these tickets aren't as terrific as I was hoping." He is holding an envelope, and I can see lanyard cord poking out of the end.

"What tickets?"

"Oh, your boyfriends mailed me tickets for the concert at Hampton Roads."

"They did? Are they club?"

"Yeah. There are two. Am I supposed to take you?"

"Why, is there someone else you would rather?"

"Not yet, but I'd like to keep my options open."

"I can probably wrangle my own way in if you find a better choice."

"Thank God. I hate having needy friends."

"Yeah, me too. You know what's worse? People who shamelessly abuse connections afforded to them by their friends."

"Ah, yes. Those people suck. I'm glad you don't actually know any."

"Me too."

There is a post card in the box when I collect the mail.

> Day 25, Days until we meet: 3
> Today I invented 4 new karate moves while trying to get an automatic paper towel dispenser to work. Love, Chris

I miss him so much. It's like an itch that can't be scratched, I can't think of anything else. Saying good-bye to him in Phoenix was physically painful because I don't know when I'll see him again. I can't keep going like this.

> Day 26, Days until we meet: 2
> It's all fun and games until someone gets arrested. (It wasn't me.) Love, Chris

> Day 27, Days until we meet: 1
> I like deadlines. They make fun noises when they go by. Love, Chris

> Day 28, Hours until I pick you up: 9
> Do you ever get the feeling that the TSA people are actually the terrorists? They do their best to make Americans suffer.
> Love, Chris

> Day 29, We're together!
> Hope it wasn't Evans that I was spooning last night. Love, Chris

Day 30, Days since I've seen you: 0
If you're flammable and have legs, you are never blocking a fire exit. In the event of a fire, I just call that being at the front of the line. Love, Chris

Day 31, Days since I've seen you: 1
Too many suburban white boys like Lil' Bow Wow. I don't even know who that is.
Love, Chris

Day 32, Days since I've seen you: 2
I'm thinking of going as something clever for Halloween this year. Love, Chris

Day 33, Days since I've seen you: 3
It's all fun and games until someone get herpes. I have hundreds of these, but I'll stop now. Love, Chris

Sam is coming home again for a couple of days. It's time to think about things for real. I remember how uncomfortable it was when he was home the last time. I have to completely eliminate Chris from this equation and look at it as objectively as possible. Things are terrible between me and Sam. He is never home, we hardly ever talk anymore, and there's always that pink thong to consider.

I can't completely discount Chris though. How much of this is *because* of Chris? I mean, obviously he has nothing to do with the pink thong. Or Sam's traveling. But I feel differently about the situation now. Is that just because of Chris?

Although, this marriage stinks. I can't stay in it forever just because I'm afraid that another man is a factor in my decision. Or because my mother died thinking I would. She might be dead, but she would want me happy. My husband feels like a stranger. He gives me the creeps. I can't stay married to him. Even if those things are because of the way I potentially feel about someone else, my mom wouldn't want me to stay like this forever.

It really isn't fair to anyone to stay in this marriage when I very clearly love someone else. (Try as hard as I might, I know that I do.) The thought of Chris walking out of my life forever brings prickles of tears to my eyes. That would be unimaginably painful. Wait. I'm trying to leave Chris out of this decision.

I do still love Sam. I know the whole thing with the babies is hard on him. Maybe that's what we need to talk about. Maybe things could get better. Is that really what I want? I can't really know until things are better, because it's too hard to judge when things are hard. But I'm starting to feel like a doormat. I know I tried really hard to make up for my failures, but Sam is really taking advantage of me.

If nothing else, I have the pink thong. That is something that I absolutely did not affect. It's a concrete thing, no feelings or anything. It was there; it can't be denied. I think it's time to talk to Sam about it. That's the only decision I will make for now. I will talk to him about the thong and we will go from there.

But when he gets in on Sunday I'm afraid to bring it up. I don't know how to start. It was months ago now. How do I explain why I tried to ignore it for so long? How do I explain why I'm not ignoring it anymore?

Things are uncomfortable, for both of us it seems. We tiptoe around each other when we're both in the house. He sleeps in the office Sunday night. It's a relief to be at school on Monday, and Sam is out when I get home. I get the mail and look for my post card. I'm hoping to get some courage.

> Day 34, Days since I've seen you: 4
> Apparently I need a chaperone at all times.
> I should never be left to my own devices.
> Love, Chris

I tuck it into its place in the box before Sam gets back. It's pretty late when he finally does. "Where have you been all night?" I ask him.

I wasn't trying to accuse him of anything, but he is defensive. "I went for a drive."

"You could have called."

"You could have too," he counters.

"I think we need to talk, Sam."

He nods. "You're probably right. But maybe not tonight, okay?"

I've been procrastinating on this for so long, what's one more day? "How about dinner tomorrow night?"

"That sounds great. I have a couple of errands to run tomorrow morning. I'll get something for dinner while I'm out."

"Okay."

"I'll be downstairs in the office. Good night."

"Good night, Sam."

When he goes downstairs I get my box from the hope chest. I still don't want Sam to find it, so I put it in there before he got home. I read through all of my cards and put it back. I get into bed and text Chris just before I go to sleep.

> To Chris:
> Sam and I are going to talk tomorrow. Send me some encouraging thoughts!

Before he can respond, I turn my phone off and go to sleep. In the morning, when I turn my phone back on, there are a bunch of texts from Chris waiting for me.

From Chris:
I send you encouraging thoughts all day, every day, but I'll include some extras tomorrow.

From Chris:
What are you going to talk about?

From Chris:
I'm nervous, and I don't know why.

From Chris:
I know you've turned your phone off and gone to sleep.

From Chris:
Call me tomorrow?

I decide not to text him back since he asked me to call. It's way too early to so I'll just wait until later. Sam is already gone by the time I come downstairs. I wonder where he was going today. I'm throwing some things together for lunch when I'm surprised to hear a knock at the door.

Chapter 29

There are several times in your life when you know something very bad has just happened. When your dad calls at two in the morning. When every channel on TV is showing the same news footage. But worst of all is when two uniformed policemen show up on your doorstep before 7 am. It doesn't really matter what the news is; they can't possibly be there for a happy reason.

"Mrs. Clarke?"

I gulp. "Yes?"

"Can we come in, please?"

I gulp again. "Yes?" I step back and hold the door open. I was worried, but I realize how bad it really is the moment they both take off their hats. "What? What is it?!" I'm already getting hysterical.

"Ma'am, we are here because there has been an accident."

Suddenly I feel about two inches tall. I sit down very quickly on the tiles under my feet. "Is it Sam? Where is my husband?" I can already feel the tears coming.

"He died very quickly."

"Oh." Then suddenly I'm angry. I yell, "Does that somehow make it better?!"

One of the officers reaches out and puts his hand on my shoulder. "He didn't suffer."

My voice lashes out, "You don't know that. Were you with him? What happened?" I break off for a second and the tears are pouring down my cheeks. "What happened?" I ask in a very small voice.

"It's hard to say for certain. But his car was in a collision with a dump truck."

"Oh." I am at a complete loss. Things have been tough, and I'm sure that I love someone else, but I still loved Sam. He was with me through a lot; we weren't always at odds. He was there for me when my mom died. And he's gone – just like that. Oh, God! I didn't tell him that I love him last night. Did he die thinking that I hate him? "Oh, Sam!" I think. "I love you! Despite everything, I really do!" Tears are streaming down my face, and I don't even really feel like I'm crying. How could he be dead? We were going to have dinner. My head is a jumbled mess.

"What happens now?" This is different from when my mom died. Mom died in the hospital. She was sick. We knew it was coming. She helped plan her own funeral. What am I supposed to do?

"We're going to need you to come to the hospital to ID the body."

"Do I have to?"

"I'm afraid so, ma'am."

"Do I have to do it alone? Do I have to go *right* now?"

"No and no. But as soon as possible. Who would you like to go with you? How quickly can they get here?"

I start crying harder. "I don't know. Does it have to be a family member?" My thoughts immediately go to Chris. I want him here with me. He's my best friend. But that seems so wrong. I'm pretty sure that I was going to leave Sam. I'm pretty sure I was going to leave him *for Chris*. And that makes me feel so guilty. He's dead. And I almost have a reason to be grateful.

I call Allison, of course. She's in Dallas, but she says she will be at my house in less than 6 hours. She will go with me to the hospital. Then she asks the big question, "Have you called Chris?"

I immediately burst into fresh tears. "NO! I can't, Ally. I just can't. It seems wrong. Like I'm being unfaithful. And I would never be unfaithful. It's terrible. Because I want him here so badly. He's my best friend, Al. No matter what, he *is* my best friend. But it doesn't even matter because they're on tour. He can't... I can't... Just get here!" I hang up and go upstairs to cry in my bed. The police have given me as much information as they can. I know what hospital to go to. I know vaguely where to go when I get there. I know that I have to call the tow company that they gave me a card for to see about the remains of his vehicle and anything that was in it. But Allison will do all of that. I know she will.

I feel like this is all my fault. Somehow I tipped the scales of the universe and I made him die. I wanted to be with Chris, I wanted to not be married anymore, and God made it happen. I feel like Tom Hanks in *Big* – I suddenly have what I want, but at what cost? I can't ever be honest with Sam now. I can't ever move on because I never got the chance to actually tell him that although things were bad and I didn't want to be married anymore, I still loved him – just not like I used to. I'll always be married because I never got a chance to tell him I didn't want to be anymore.

I lay in my bed and cry – and try very hard not to think – for the next 7 ½ hours. She's late, but when Allison gets there she comes right up and starts to make everything better. She brushes my hair and helps me find my shoes. She gets me my coat and helps me get outside. As we're walking down the sidewalk, I realize someone else is there.

I look *up*. It's Chris. I look at Allison and she shrugs. "I knew you wanted him here. He had every right to know, Sara. He wants to be here."

Chris grabs me and pulls me up into a big hug. "I'm so sorry, Baby Girl," he whispers into my hair. "I'm so sorry."

I don't really remember much about going to the hospital. Chris walks with us, but he stays outside when they take me and Allison to ID Sam's body. It's awful, but somehow I get through it.

I pretty much just lie in bed and cry for the next three days. Tom flies in to help Allison because she is taking care of everything. Chris has stayed by my side the whole time. He just rubs my back while I cry. A couple of times when I've looked at him, he's crying too. I wonder about that. Why is Chris sad? Isn't this what he wanted? But I can't really think about that. I'm so sick about the whole thing. I feel like a cheater. I just want Sam back. I want to tell him that I love him – and mean it. I want him to be enough.

That thought brings me up short. He wasn't enough. He wasn't ever around. He didn't stay with me, or listen to me, or talk to me. We didn't have much of a marriage. And now I feel worse. This is the circle my thoughts take. Over and over – I try to numb myself by pointing out his shortcomings and why I won't miss him. And then I feel super guilty because a man is dead and I am trying to point out his shortcomings.

Every once in a while Chris goes to talk to Allison. When they are in the hall outside my door, I try very hard not to listen, but it's hard to miss it all.

"Have you heard any more about what happened?" Chris is asking Allison.

"Apparently, the dump truck ran a red light. The driver said that it was early, the roads were pretty much deserted, and he wasn't paying that much attention."

"Right, because red lights only apply when traffic is heavy. Any idea why he was out that early?"

"No, and I don't think we will ever know for sure. But he had a huge bouquet of roses in the front seat."

I put my pillow over my head and try to drown them out. Were the roses for me? Was he trying to smooth things over between us? Was he going to apologize and try to make things better? It's awful! I'll never know!

Sam's mother and father fly in from Oregon. I don't think they were expecting to encounter Chris at my house. It's one of the few times that Allison has coaxed me out of my bed and I'm downstairs drinking coffee in the kitchen. Sam has been dead for two days, and I still don't think I'm completely aware of that. It's not like I'm used to him being in the house or anything. Allison, Chris and I are sitting at the bar when Tom opens the door for my in-laws. Maybe they were willing to forgive and forget when they first got there, but I'll never know because the first person they see is Chris.

"What the hell are you doing here?" Peter says quietly. I appreciate the switch from the yelling that dominated our last conversation.

"I'm here for Sara," Chris says calmly, but I can hear the ice in his voice.

"I can't *believe* you would show your face here! This is such... This is – *disrespect* for a dead man!" At his words, Eryn, my mother-in-law, dissolves into hysterical tears. Now Peter is roaring. "And! You've upset my wife! This is hard enough without having to look in the face of the person making a fool of my son!"

Chris is still really calm. I know he's keeping his cool for me, because I am already shaking. "You are only making a fool of yourself. Everyone in this room knows that there is nothing between me and Sara, and there never has been."

He doesn't get his entire sentence out before Peter is screaming again. "Now listen here, *asshole*! I want you to get out of my son's house!"

"It's Sara's house. I'm only leaving when she makes me."

Peter launches himself across the kitchen and takes a tremendous swing at Chris. I know it hurts when he connects with Chris's face, but Chris doesn't even flinch. He is still eerily calm. He glances at me and then hauls off and decks my father-in-law in the face. Chris didn't flinch, but Peter drops like a rock.

Eryn is beside herself. She is screaming hysterically while Peter keeps up a string of profanity from the floor. I feel like I'm watching someone else's life. This can't be *me*. I look at Allison, desperately.

She clears her throat. "I think it might be best if you stay in a hotel." Chris and Tom haul Peter up off the floor and drag him towards the front door. Allison puts her arm around Eryn, with a fair amount of compassion really, and leads her after them. I can hear another scuffle at the door, and more profanity from Peter. "I'll call you with the final details for the funeral," I hear Allison say.

My dad comes in from New York. He helps Allison take care of the last details. A couple of times she comes into my room to ask me questions about how I want this thing or other handled. "Whatever you think is best," I tell her. I'm so grateful that she is here.

I still wonder about Chris. I'm sure he is supposed to be on stage somewhere, but I can't work up enough courage to ask. I don't talk to him at all. I feel too guilty that he is here to actually acknowledge him, and also I'm afraid he will leave if I mention it. But he doesn't go anywhere. His eye blackens over the course of the next day.

Chapter 30

The funeral is on a Saturday. I have to sit in the front pew with my dad on one side and Allison on the other. I have no idea where Chris is, but just knowing he is in the room makes me feel a little better – and then more guilty. I don't pay attention to a single thing that is said. I just sit there in complete agony. Sam's mother is hysterical, his father is ramrod straight, grim, and both of his eyes are black. I can't even look at them. I'm sure they can see something on my face that says, "I'm guilty of something, even if I'm not sure what it is."

We had Sam cremated so there is nothing else to do when the service ends, but we stand around as people take turns offering their condolences. Allison is standing so close we are touching. I nod at anyone who talks to me, but I don't know what to say. My dad walks over to talk to Sam's parents, and Allison tells me that she needs to use the bathroom. "Tom will stay with you, honey."

As soon as Allison dashes off, a woman I only vaguely recognize marches up towards me. There are waves of anger rolling off of her. Anna! It's Anna!

"I don't know why you are so upset." She spits the words at me. "How do you think *I* feel?"

I can't answer her because I'm not sure what she means. I feel Tom step closer.

"Here you are! Crying! Everyone feeling sorry for *you*! No one cares about what *I* lost! No one feels sorry for me! I don't get to sit at the front where I belong! I have to sit and skulk in the back! He loved *me*!" She whirls around to the room at large. "Do you hear me? He loved *me*!" She turns back to me. I wonder if she has been drinking. "Do you understand what that means? He didn't love you. I don't even know why he didn't just leave you. He loved *me*."

Suddenly, Chris is there, next to me, trying to step between us, trying to shield me from her words. I don't know where he came from.

But for some reason, I feel up to this challenge. "A man is dead here, Anna –" My voice breaks for a second, but I recover quickly. "And I really don't think the best way to honor him is to accuse him of cheating on his wife. At his funeral. In front of everyone he knows – knew. But then, maybe you knew him better than I did? Maybe he would have appreciated this? I think it's distasteful, but that's just me."

Anna's face has turned an interesting color. "I couldn't care two licks about you. This isn't about *you*, Sara. This is about justice.

People need to know that *I* suffered a loss. I deserve this as much as you do – more so. He actually loved *me*."

Chris puts his hands up. "I really think it's time for you to leave." He nods at someone over my shoulder. The entire room is silent and I can feel everyone's eyes on me.

But Anna's not done yet. "Of course! Of course you would defend her! Because she was so honorable! It's not like she wasn't sleeping with you! Everyone knew it! It made Sam feel better because he said at least he wasn't the only one who didn't care about that joke of a marriage."

She is yelling over her shoulder because she is being half led, half dragged from the room. Chris is still standing in front of me, blocking most of my view, but I can see that it's Drew and Blond Mark that are hauling her out. Chris glances back at me as he starts to walk away and Short Mark lightly squeezes my arm as he falls in step behind him.

I don't know what to say. She just accused me of cheating on a dead man – in front of everyone. Should I defend myself? I step after them all and speak, but just loud enough to be sure that she can hear me. The room is still silent, so that's not very loud. I'm careful to keep my voice steady and ice cold, "If you are trying to hurt me, you can keep trying. He is dead. My husband is dead. And *nothing* you say can hurt more than that."

I turn back, desperate to hide the tears that are freely flowing down my face now. I grab onto Allison like a life line, so grateful that she is back and standing there behind me. I bury my face in her shoulder. "That's not true," I whisper. "That hurt. So much more. He was, Allison. He didn't care about me. He was cheating on me." I'm almost choking now. Allison's arms are wrapped around me and I can hear a lot of commotion as people begin to digest that little scene.

"It's okay. It really is. Don't worry about her. Don't worry about what she said. Maybe she was mad at Sam because he loved you and this is her way of getting revenge."

I pull back to look at her. My tears suddenly stop. "Do you really think that? But what if he was –" and I break again, tears flowing, "and they broke up and that's why she's mad? Allison! If he was, it was *her*? *That* was who he chose? *That* was the person he loved in my place?"

Allison pulls me back in again. I can hear her muffled voice; she is talking to people around us. She rubs my back as she talks to them. My thoughts are a jumbled mess again. I knew it, of course I knew it. But to have it thrown in my face, by *her*, at his funeral is more than I think I can take. How much of a failure do I have to be to have been replaced by that? But, maybe Allison was right and she was mad at me and trying to hurt me – but not about Sam, about Evansgate. That actually seems really feasible.

My dad is whispering in my ear, "Sara? Come away for a moment." I look up to see his face, looking very concerned. My dad is very tall, not tall like Chris, but taller than most people he comes across. He has Allison's eyes and my nose – or we have his, I guess. His brown hair is slowly receding further and further up his forehead, but he is wearing it longer in the front, so you can hardly tell. He's still a really good looking man, actually. "Come with me, honey." He puts his arm around my shoulder and eases me out from under Allison's hug. I hulk down under his arm as he leads us from the room.

When I raise my head again we are in a little room, barely bigger than a closet, with a small sofa and a table with a lamp. There is some generic, dull artwork hanging on the walls and a mirror.

Dad gives me a weak smile. "I learned about these little rooms during your mom's funeral." For a second his eyes are very bright, but he blinks and takes a deep breath. "Handy little places to hide for a moment when things get to be too much." I nod mutely. "I'm sorry, honey, but I'm proud of you. You handled that very well. Unfortunately, I have to ask you to push it down and wait to deal with it until you have space. They say funerals are not for the dead, 'they're for the family' but that's a load a crap."

I start and look up at him in surprise. He's not done. "Funerals are not designed to make *you* feel better. It's just a creative way of torturing someone who is already hurting beyond words. And you have gotten that in spades. But it is really there to make *other people* feel better about themselves because they got to come out and tell you how sorry they are. You have to put on a brave face. You have to pretend like that didn't happen and hold your head up high. You have to go back out there and let people tell you they're sorry. You have to look like you're listening, even if you're not. Don't let them beat you. He was an asshole, Sara. He never treated you well." For a moment his voice is hard and angry, "I'm glad he's dead."

I'm starting to wonder if I knew my dad at all before this moment. "But if everyone out there gets to see you broken because of what she said, then they won. Don't let them beat you now. You are stronger than that. Better than that. Better than *them*. He was an asshole and you are better off without him."

My dad has a fierce look on his face. He nods at me and turns to open the door. But he turns back. "Sara – let Chris love you." Then he just walks out, leaving me speechless. I take a deep breath or two, thinking about what my dad said. Clearly he doesn't think that there is any chance she was lying; he is convinced that Sam was cheating. But, he's right. I have to get back out there. I can do this. I *will* do this. I wipe my eyes, brush my hair back from my face, take another steadying breath, and walk out with my head high.

When I first step out of the closet, I'm lost for a moment. I hadn't been paying any attention and now I'm not even sure where to go. But there is a man who obviously works at the funeral home standing there, almost like he was waiting for me. He doesn't say anything, just holds his hand out in the direction I should take. I nod and head back into the funeral.

I look around the room – really – for the first time. There are *a lot* of people there. I guess no one wanted to run out very quickly after my confrontation with Anna. Everyone loves a little drama, and I'm sure it will be a story that gets passed around a lot. But I can't think about that now. Chris and the guys are standing in the corner by themselves. I shouldn't notice, but oh my! does Chris look amazing in his suit. I shake the thought from my head and decide to start there.

"Oh, you guys aren't conspicuous at all."

Weak smiles, all around. "Hey, Shorty. We're really sorry," Short Mark says.

"Thanks for being here. And, thanks. For. You know." I nod.

Drew responds first. "Of course. I'm so sorry; I really am. About everything."

I nod again. And then something occurs to me. "What are you doing here?!"

Short Mark looks surprised. "Condoling. Do you not want us here?"

"Of course I do! But, aren't you on tour? Shouldn't you be on stage somewhere?"

Short Mark shakes his head and smiles. "We're on a break. You picked a good –" He breaks off. "Sorry. Oh, God, I'm sorry." He looks down.

I reach out to touch his arm. "It's okay. I'm really glad you're here. But I'm sorry this is how you are spending your weekend off."

Short Mark smiles again and wraps me in a hug. "It's a whole week. No worries."

I smile feebly. "Thanks anyway." Short Mark kisses my cheek as he pulls back.

Drew grabs me next. "Bethany wanted me to tell you how sorry she is. She would have been here, but..." He trails off.

I nod. "It's okay."

Blond Mark leans over and kisses me on the cheek. "I'm sorry, Sara. I really am."

Before I can answer, Angie steps in front of him and hugs me. "Me too, Sara."

"Angie! I didn't even know you were here."

She nods. "I wanted to be." She kisses me on the cheek and then steps back quietly behind Blond Mark. He squeezes her hand and then turns to me. "Angie and I are getting married, Sare-Bear." He has a huge smile on his face.

Good news! I cling to it. "That's fantastic! Congratulations!" I reach out to Angie in an age-old gesture of "Show Me the Ring." She is smiling big time now as she holds out her left hand. The ring is *huge* and unbelievably gorgeous. "Wow! When's the big day?"

Angie opens her mouth to reply, but she stops before she starts and looks over my shoulder. I turn to see, and find myself face to face with Sam's boss.

"Oh, hello, Eric. Thank you for coming."

"Sara. I'm very sorry for your loss. I'm also very sorry for Anna's behavior. I assure you that I had no idea, but it will be dealt with." He nods curtly. "I'm sorry to bring up business, but unfortunately I have to go. I'll need you to come by the office to get his things and fill out some paperwork for the insurance and things." When I nod he continues, "Please call Renee to set something up." He nods again and shakes my hand with both of his before turning to go.

I turn back to my Evansgate friends, but I don't get a chance to say anything before someone else comes up. Eric has apparently restarted the line of condolences and my next door neighbors are looking at me expectantly. "Give me just one second, please," I say and turn back to Evansgate. "Thanks for being here. Really. It means a lot."

Then I turn and walk back over to my spot with my family while I listen (or don't listen) to my neighbors, who walk with me. Allison takes my hand and squeezes it. She gives me an encouraging smile. My dad puts his hand across my shoulders. "That's my girl," he whispers. I nod.

The line continues to move through. I shake hands, nod, say thank you a lot. I don't really listen to what people are saying, but I appreciate it nonetheless. People are trying. My dad is wrong. I am starting to feel better.

Suddenly, I'm looking at Laura and Andrew. "What are you doing here?" I ask.

Laura looks at Andrew. "We're here for you," he says.

She wraps me in a hug. "I'm sorry, honey. I know you don't deserve this."

Andrew claps a hand on my shoulder. "I'm really sorry. Do you need us to do anything?" I shake my head mutely. I don't know what to say.

Laura leans in again, "Just remember that you are strong, and you can get through this. If anyone can, it's you. We're here if you need us." I nod again. "Remember that we love you," she says as she pulls away.

It feels like years before we are finished. Sam's parents disappeared when I was in the closet; they didn't even say good-bye. I guess having their golden child publicly disgraced at his own funeral was more than they could take. I don't blame them.

Matt is the last person to come to me. "I just don't know what to say," he says. The sight of him there, in his suit, gives me a flashback to my mom's funeral. I think he is wearing the same tie. "I'm here, if you need me." He gives me a hug before he leaves.

In the end, only Allison, Tom, my dad, and Chris are left in the room with me. After a few meaningful looks, my family quietly leaves me and Chris alone. He won't even look at me when he says, "I'm sorry, Sara."

"I can't, Chris. I just can't."

He nods. "I'll drive you home though, okay?"

"Okay. Thanks."

We climb into my car and I realize I've never actually seen him drive. "Where's your driver?"

"I imagine he is taking everyone else back to their hotel and then the airport. They're flying back to LA today."

"Oh." I don't really know what else to say. I feel like I don't belong with them anymore, but I don't know why. I think they feel it too. It's funny, the one thing holding me back from completely being a part of that life is what drives a wedge between us when it's gone. It's like Sam was a safety net that kept me at a distance and now that it's gone they're afraid that I'll get too close. Maybe I am too?

We're quiet for the entire ride back to my house. My mind is churning, but I can't think of what to say to Chris. *I don't want you to go. I need you. Please pretend like everything is fine.* It all sounds stupid, and none of it seems to actually convey what I am feeling.

Chris's silence worries me.

Allison's rental car is in the driveway when we get there. I can see her in the window. Chris turns off the ignition and we sit in the silent car for a minute. "I'll get my stuff and go," he says quietly.

I can actually feel my heart break at his words. He is leaving. He doesn't want to be with me. "Okay," I whisper. Will I ever see any of them again?

We climb out of the car and the clunk of the doors shutting sounds ominous to me. Allison is waiting in the door when we go inside. "I'm just going to get my stuff," Chris says to her. Allison looks surprised at his words.

She nods. "Okay."

Allison stays one more day before she has to head back. She needs to be back at work on Monday. "I'm worried about you, Baby Girl. Are you going to be okay?"

I honestly think about it before I answer. "I don't know, Ally. But I'll keep you posted."

She gives me one last hug before her and Tom get into their rental and head to the airport. My dad has been gone since last night. Allison was the last one to leave. I'm alone again. I slump down onto the floor in my entry. I suddenly hate this house. It's too big for one person. It always has been. Why did we stay here?

I don't go back to work on Monday. "I'm not ready yet," I tell my principal. "Maybe next week." She tells me to take as much time as I need.

I call Eric's secretary, Renee, to set up a time to go into Sam's office to get his things and take care of paperwork. The company has offered to fly me to Atlanta, which I think is rather nice of them. We settle on Wednesday. Renee says that she will email me my flight information. I thank her and hang up the phone. I don't know what to do with myself.

I've always been alone in this house. Now I don't know if I can take it. I stomp up the stairs and lay down in the bed that Chris always slept in when he came. The bed he was sleeping in three nights ago. It still smells like him. I curl up under the blankets and go to sleep.

I pretty much stay in bed until Wednesday morning. I don't answer my phone. The only email I look at is the one from Renee with my flight information. I ignore text messages. I only get up to pee and occasionally get a drink of water. But Wednesday, I drag myself out from under Chris's sheets and take a shower. I pack my shoulder bag and drive to the airport.

My flight is on time, and when I get to Atlanta I find myself greeted by a man holding a sign that says "CLARKE" in bold, black letters. "I'm Sara Clarke," I tell him. I'm fighting tears. This time I don't feel special.

The driver looks at me warily. "This way, ma'am." He drives me straight to Sam's office. I haven't been there since we lived in Atlanta, but I still remember it. I go upstairs and into the lobby for his company's office suite, where I tell the receptionist that I'm there to see Renee and I sit down to wait.

She doesn't make me wait long. "I hope you had a good flight, Sara?"

"Yes, thank you."

"I don't think this will take very long. I hope you can get out of here in less than an hour." I nod. We walk down the hall to Eric's office. "There are just some papers that we need you to sign."

I fade out while she is talking about benefits packages and things. I sign what she puts in front of me.

"Well, that should be that," she says as she taps the papers into a neat stack. "You should get the insurance check in six to eight weeks."

"What insurance check?"

Renee looks at me with pity. "His life insurance. Sara, that's why you're here. Sam had life insurance through the company."

"Oh. I guess I knew that. I just never really thought about it."

"No one ever does. But at least Sam saw fit to take care of you."

I nod. "Wait. What do you mean?"

"He took out extra coverage. You'll be getting a check for about $1.4 million."

"What? That can't be right."

"Yes, honey. It's all here. Didn't you even look at what you were signing?" At least she is still pitying me.

"I'm sorry, Renee. I'm not paying that much attention."

"Sara, I need you to focus for a second. This is important."

"Okay." I sit up a little straighter and look her in the eye.

"The insurance company is suing the trucking company, the truck that hit Sam, for the money. You cannot talk to anyone from the trucking company who might try to call you. They will offer to settle with you, but you cannot talk to them at all, do you understand?"

"Yes. I won't. I haven't even been answering my phone, so that shouldn't be hard."

"Okay. Let's go to Sam's office and you can collect any personal belongings you would like to keep." She calls maintenance from the phone on her desk to come and meet us at Sam's office to unlock the door. I take a deep breath to steady myself before we go in.

There are little traces of Sam all over this place. They remind me of our past, happier times in our marriage. I can't stop the tears as they flow down my cheeks. Renee wordlessly hands me a tissue. I sit down behind his desk and before I know it, I slump over and start to cry in earnest. Renee hands me the whole box of tissues and quietly tells me that she will be down the hall if I need her. She, very politely, closes the door behind her.

I sit there for a while and just cry. Then I lift my head and look around. There are no pictures of us anywhere. He has a few little odds and ends on his desk that I have given him over the years, but no pictures. I distinctly remember giving him more than one framed picture of us for his office. I open the top drawer of his desk. Just pens and things. The second drawer is a lot of files. On the other side, in the top drawer, right on top, is a framed picture of Sam and Anna in bathing suits. They are on a beach, holding drinks and hanging on each other. I pick it up carefully. Underneath it is another picture of them, this time they're on skis and they're kissing.

I don't even think about it. I grab it up and hurl it at the wall opposite. The glass shatters when it hits. Then I throw the first one from the beach. It shatters too. Renee comes racing into the room. "Sara! Are you all right?" She looks down at the broken glass around her feet and sees the pictures which have landed face up in the pile. "Oh my," she whispers.

"Burn it all," I tell her, as I get up and walk out.

Chapter 31

I march back out into the lobby and downstairs. My driver from before is sitting on a sofa by the door reading a magazine. He stands up when he sees me. "Ready to go back Mrs. Clarke?"

"Please call me Sara."

"Yes, ma'am. Are you ready?"

I nod and we go out to the car. My hands are shaking I'm so angry. I pick up my phone and call Allison. She answers on the first ring. "Sara! Are you all right? Why haven't you been answering any of my calls or texts?"

"I didn't want to. I was throwing myself a pity party."

"What's wrong?"

"I'm in Atlanta, Allison. I came down here to take care of some stuff at his office. And do you want to know what I found? Well, let's start with what I *didn't* find first. Not a single picture of me – nothing." I take a deep breath then practically scream, "But I did find pictures of him with Anna. He had them framed, Allison. There was one of them kissing."

Allison is silent. "Are you still there?" I demand.

"Yes. I – I don't know what to say. What did you do?"

"I smashed them and then told Renee to burn everything."

"Good for you."

"I'm proud of you, big sister."

"What for?"

"You haven't once said 'I told you so.'"

"I'm not exactly going to gloat over the fact that your husband was a sleazy asshole. Besides, I told you that he might not be, if I recall correctly."

I start to cry again. "Oh, Allison. I'm such a fool. I threw away my life for him."

"It's not too late," she whispers.

"Yes, it is. I have to go."

"Be careful, Baby Girl."

"I love you, Allison. Thank you for everything. I couldn't have gotten through this without you."

"Don't mention it. That's what I'm here for."

When I get back to the airport I still have almost three hours until I'm supposed to board my flight home. I get through security and then find a bar. I keep my bag over my shoulder and spin my phone on the counter as I down my second vodka cranberry. I turned it off after I hung up with Allison, but it's comforting, just having it.

The bar is pretty empty, so the bartender stops to talk when he brings me my third drink. "You okay?" he asks.

"Honestly? Not even a little bit."

"What's wrong, beautiful?"

"You really want to know?" When he nods, I take a deep breath. "My husband died last week. And then at his funeral, a woman made a huge scene when she told me that she had been sleeping with him. Even if I could have ignored that – and the pink thong I found in his suitcase over the summer – the framed pictures of them kissing in his office are kind of hard to deny."

The bartender's eyes are huge. He grabs two shot glasses and a bottle of tequila. He puts a salt shaker and a couple of lemon slices in front of me and pours two shots. "I think you might need something stronger than that," he nods at my drink.

"I agree." I do both shots without blinking an eye.

"Nicely done." He smiles at me. "Now, a beautiful little thing like you, you just need to go out and find some nice fella. There are plenty who would fall all over themselves to treat you well."

"Oh, I must have left that part of the story out. I found him. A wonderful man. A genuinely rich and famous, tall, dark, the whole bit. And he loved me. But I pushed him away because I was married. He was my best friend, the bright spot in my dark days of that horrendous marriage. But just to be sure his torture was complete, my asshole husband destroyed that too."

The bartender nods again with pity in his eyes. He gets me another shot of tequila. "Honey, you should call him. I'm sure he would come running the second the phone rings."

I glance at the TV above the bar when I roll my eyes. There is a commercial for a late-night talk show on, and Chris and the rest of Evansgate are sitting on the stage. I can tell Chris's eye is still a little black, even under the TV make-up. "There he is," I point to the TV. The bartender turns to look and catches sight of the band just before the commercial goes off.

"Evansgate?" he asks.

"Yup. Chris Eck. He was my best friend until very recently. And he loved me."

The bartender looks like he is struggling for a response to that. "They're a great group. They just released a new album."

"Uh-huh. 'Six Kinds of Crazy', have you heard it?"

"Yeah, it's pretty good."

"It's about me." The bartender's eyes tell me that I have officially had too much to drink and he no longer believes the garbage I'm spouting. "I'm serious. Chris wrote it for me. My birth certificate says 'Baby Girl Harris'. That's my given name." I'm really starting to feel the alcohol. It doesn't help that I haven't eaten in days. I seem to have diarrhea of the mouth too, and I can't stop talking. "I met him and he fell in love with me and then wrote a song about it for the whole world to hear. But I told him 'no'. No!"

The more I say, the angrier I get. I start gesturing with my glass, which is sloshing cranberry juice over the bar. "I was faithful to that son of a bitch, even though I had Chris Eck offering himself up on a plate. You find me a sane woman who would turn that down! I really am six kinds of crazy! I was only joking when I told him that, but it's come full circle now, hasn't it?!" I'm pretty much yelling now and probably only making sense to myself. "So that he could what? Screw the Ice Queen and take her on vacations while he left me to rot in that big house by myself! I didn't deserve that! I deserved Chris! I deserved that life! What the hell am I supposed to do with the money? I don't want it! It was bought with my own blood and tears!" I stop. "I guess I should keep it. It's a poor consolation prize, but at least it's something I suppose."

The bartender looks pleased that I have stopped yelling. "That's right, honey. You take his money and run. What time is your flight?"

I shrug. "I don't remember." I take out my boarding pass. "Huh." I look at my watch. "Huh. I should probably go." I reach into my bag for my wallet, but the bartender puts his hand on mine.

"This one is on the house, honey."

"Thanks." He nods, and I know he's glad to see the back of me.

I pick up my phone and put it in my bag as I get off of the bar stool. I avoid the eyes of the staring crowd as I leave the bar, meander to my gate, and get on the plane during the final boarding call. I'm starting to feel a little queasy. I sit in my seat and buckle up. I lean my head back and then I wake up when a flight attendant is nudging my arm. "It's time to get off the plane, dear."

I look around at the emptying plane. "Yes, thank you."

As I walk towards the exit, I wonder if I am sober enough to drive yet. Probably not. It hadn't occurred to me that I would have to drive home. I take out my phone and call Matt.

"Hello," I say glumly. "I'm at the airport and I've had too much to drink. I need a ride home, and also someone to drive my car home. Do you think you can help?"

Matt promises to be there to get me soon – with someone else to drive my car. I sit down on a bench to wait and look at my phone. It's going crazy with notifications. I have 72 unread text messages, 17 voicemail messages (and my mailbox is full), and 209 unread emails.

I start by sifting through the text messages. Most of them are from Allison, of course. There are two from Short Mark and one each from Drew and Blond Mark. Drew and Blond Mark both just say something along the lines of "Thinking of you!" and so does the first one of Short Mark's. But his second just says,

From Mark E.:
Call me. It's important.
3 hours ago

I get a sick feeling in the pit of my stomach. My fingers shake as I dial his number.

"Shorty?" he answers on the first ring.

"What's wrong?"

"Who said anything was wrong?"

"You did. You said..."

"I said it was important. That doesn't mean there is something wrong."

"Is there?"

"Not really. Where are you?"

"I'm at the airport."

"Where are you going?"

"I actually just got back from Atlanta and I've had a really horrible day, Short Mark. What do you need?"

"Nothing."

"Please don't play games with my head today. What is so important?"

"You are. We miss you, Shorty."

"I miss you too. But..."

"I know. We – he – still loves you."

"But what good does that do me now?" I ask gloomily. I see Matt coming in the sliding doors. "Short Mark, my ride is here. I have to go. Tell everyone I said hello and that I miss them."

"Will do, Shorty. Take care."

We hang up and I wave to get Matt's attention. "Thanks for this. I owe you big time."

"It's okay." Matt looks at me closely. "You look like hell."

"I feel like hell, thanks."

"Well, let's get you home then."

I sleep the whole way back to my house, and when I get home I wearily climb the stairs to Chris's bed and climb in. Part of me feels bad for having Matt figure out my car situation and then practically ignoring him, but my brain hurts too much to really think about it. I go right back to sleep and plan on staying that way for a long time.

At one point on Thursday I call my principal and ask her if we can meet the next day. As much as I don't want to get out of bed, there is something that I have to take care of. Other than that, I spend the day smelling Chris and worrying that his scent is disappearing from the bed.

On Friday morning I get showered and dressed, then head into school. I've given it some thought, and if I really have a million dollars coming from Sam, then I can afford to do this.

"I don't want to quit," I start. "But, I'm taking this so much harder than I would have expected." The matronly woman in front of me nods sympathetically. "I think I need a leave of absence."

She clears her throat. "How long are you thinking, Sara? The rest of the semester?"

I shift my feet. "Uh, no. I was thinking the rest of this year."

"Sara." I look up. There is nothing but compassion showing on her face. "This will get easier. I know it doesn't seem like it now, but it will." She pauses for a moment. "I will grant your request, of course I will, but I would like to recommend against it. I don't think it will be good for you to shut yourself away from the world."

I nod. "Thank you, but I just don't have what I need to stand in front of a classroom right now."

"I understand, and I appreciate the fact that you recognize it. But you will again." She pauses. "Once I grant a leave of absence, I can't take it back. Are you sure you want the rest of the year?"

I nod. "I'm sure."

She reaches across the desk and takes my hand. "Are you going to be all right?"

"Yes, I am. I'm probably going to go stay with my sister in Dallas for a while."

I can see the relief spread across her face. "I think that is an excellent idea."

"Is there something I need to sign?"

"Yes, there will be. I will have Wren get the papers together, but it will take a day or two."

"I'm going to leave tomorrow, I think. Can we fax this stuff?"

"No, but we can mail it. Leave your sister's address with Wren before you go, okay?"

"Okay. Thanks, Karen."

She nods as she stands up. "Of course." She wraps me in a hug before she lets me leave her office. "I'm here if you want to talk about it."

"Thanks," I repeat.

I stop at the secretary's desk to give her my sister's address before I leave. I can feel pity oozing from every corner of the office. A lot of these people were at the funeral, and I know even those that weren't have heard the story by now. I'm sure I should say something, but I don't. I'm glad that Wren doesn't know why she is taking an address for me yet. Let them all know that I'm running away when I'm not there to see their faces.

When I get home I start packing. I take Chris's pillowcase, the one his beautiful head slept on, the one I have been sleeping *next* to, and carefully seal it in a bag to take with me. I put it in my post card box. As I pack, I call my dad.

"Hey, kiddo."

"Hi, Dad."

"How are you holding up?"

"Not very well, I must confess. Did you talk to Allison?"

"Yes," he admits. "Do you want to talk about it?"

"Not really."

I can hear the relief in his voice. "What are you going to do now?"

"I just took a leave of absence from school. I'm thinking of going to Allison's for a little bit, but if she won't have me, can I come home?"

"Of course you can, Baby Girl. But Allison has been hoping that you would come, so I'm pretty sure that she'll have you."

"She has?"

"Yeah. She was considering coming back and physically forcing you to go with her. She's really worried." He pauses. "We all are."

But then his voice brightens, "I think this will be good for you."

"Me too. Well, if you need me, I guess I'll be at Allison's."

"Maybe, if I need you, I'll actually be able to get a hold of you while you're there."

"I'm sorry, Dad."

"Don't be. You go to Allison's. Do what you need to do to get through this. Remember that you have a lot of people that love you.

And, you are better off without him."

I laugh weakly. "You've mentioned your opinion on the matter before."

"That's not my opinion, Sara. That is verifiable fact."

"Yes, sir. Whatever you say."

"Be safe. And take care of yourself. When was the last time you had anything to eat?"

"I consumed a fair amount of tequila at the airport the other day. Does that count?"

"No. Get something to eat."

"I will. I love you, Dad."

"I love you, too."

Before I call Allison, which for some reason I am putting off, I go downstairs. Dad has made me consider something. I get a big trash bag and open my fridge. I don't know how long I'll be gone, but a good bit of this stuff needs to get thrown out already. I systematically dump the contents of my fridge into the bag, re-usable containers and all, shelf by shelf, until the only thing left is a box of baking soda. I consider doing the freezer too, but I'm out of energy and it won't stink when I get back.

Instead of calling her, I send Allison an email.

> Allison
> I'm thinking about coming to Dallas for a while, if you'll have me. I took a leave of absence from school. Talk to Tom and let me know if there is a time this weekend that you would be able to pick me up at DFW. I'm going to sleep now, so just email me back.
> Love, Sara

Before I go back upstairs I notice a couple of piles of mail on the counter. I walk over to investigate. One of the stacks is post cards from Chris.

> Day 35, Days since I've seen you: 5
> The communists are at the heart of every problem, aren't they? Love, Chris

Day 36, Days since I've seen you: 6
I'm trying to convince Evans to change the name of the band to LOST DOG. I figure that way there would already be plenty of posters up everywhere advertising for us. Love, Chris

Day 37, Days since I've seen you: 7
Possibly the most pointless structure in America: see front. Love, Chris

Day 38, Days since I've seen you: 8
There are 219 stripes on the blanket I sleep under. Love, Chris

Day 39, Hours until I see you: 6
I'm on my way. Love, Chris

I'm careful that the tears don't land on the cards. I take them upstairs and add them to my box, replacing the sealed pillow case on top. I feel the need to punish myself. Instead of sleeping in Chris's bed, I get into the bed I used to share with Sam – not much lately, but the sentiment is still there. I have trouble sleeping, but I force myself to stay in the bed.

Chapter 32

When I wake up, it's dark. I sit bolt upright, because someone is there. "Who is it?" I call out. I can feel panic clawing at me, but I'm still too numb for it to really take hold.

"It's your sister."

I throw back my blankets and jump up to find her in the dark. "What are you doing here?"

"I came to help you pack. You do remember that you were supposed to be in Dallas next week anyway, right?"

"My birthday!" I hit my forehead with my hand.

"Yes, your birthday. You haven't booked a flight for this weekend yet, have you?"

"No, I was waiting to hear from you first."

"Well, I'm glad, even though you have heard from me at least a dozen times. You just don't listen. But, that's not the point. You should change the flight you already have, instead of booking a new one. There will be a change fee, but that will be cheaper than getting a new ticket, and then you won't have one that you have nothing to do with."

"Okay. How?"

Allison laughs at me, but she takes out her iPad and we sit on the bed. She helps me change my ticket to the flight that she has booked herself home on, and then we change my return flight to an open-ended ticket.

"I'm not sure that was cheaper," I say.

"I just booked a flight out here and back. Trust me, it was cheaper. Sara? Are you going to be okay – financially?"

"Yeah, apparently, I'll be fine. Sam took out quite a bit of life insurance. In about a month, I will be a millionaire."

"Don't seem so happy about it."

"Allison, think about why I am getting that money. Is there really any reason to be happy about it?"

"Yes, there are a lot. Not only do you get rid of that albatross, you get a million dollars for doing it." She starts to laugh. "I know I'm not being very sensitive, Baby Girl. I'm sorry."

"It's okay. I'm sure someday I will be able to see the upside."

"Well, let's get you packed. Our flight is early."

"I am packed."

"Oh, then why am I here?"

"Because you love me."

Allison and I turn on a movie and fall asleep in front of the TV. The next morning, she sets to work locking down my house, making sure all of the trash has been taken out, and setting timers on my lights. Before we leave, she goes next door to talk to my neighbors. She is holding a flat rate Priority Mail box.

She returns a few minutes later, empty handed. "What was that about?" I ask her.

"I don't know how long you'll be with me. I'm going to have you forward your mail, but that can take a couple of days before it starts to work. So I asked them to collect your mail in that box and send it at the end of the week."

"Let me guess, it was already addressed and postage paid?"

"Well, I couldn't very well ask them to pay to send it, could I?"

I shake my head. "You thought of everything. God, I hope nothing ever happens to Tom. I would never be this well organized and prepared."

"I know. You're hopeless."

"Speaking of mail..."

Allison gives me a grimace. "You haven't actually checked your mail since I left, have you?"

I meekly shake my head and go to the mailbox. It is *stuffed*. "Oops."

She laughs and collects all of the mail from the box. I watch her efficiency as she quickly sorts through it and dumps the junk into my recycling bin in the garage. She makes two stacks, hands me one, shoves the other in her bag, then she locks my car into the garage, takes the keys and gets into her rental.

"Let's go, little sister. We have a flight to catch."

I climb in, clutching my mail stack. "Which pile did you keep?"

"I kept the bills and things that need to be taken care of. I don't think you can be trusted to handle any of that yet."

"What did you give me?"

"Cards and letters, stuff like that. I imagine a lot of it is sympathy cards, so be careful if you don't feel like reading that sort of thing." I nod, and she continues. "There is some other stuff in there you might want to see, though."

I flip through the stack as we drive to the airport. She is right. A lot of it bears the look of sympathy cards. I make a stack. There are only two things I keep out to look at: an old postcard from Chris – it's in an envelope that says US Postal Service with a clear front and it looks like it's been chewed on, and a more recent letter. I can feel Allison's eyes on me.

The postcard is the same as all the others. There's a picture of Salt Lake City, Utah on the front. I check my countdown in the corner. It's old.

> Day 17, Days until we meet. 11
> I assume there is a very salty lake here.
> Love, Chris

I take the letter and stuff it in my bag. Allison clears her throat. "Are we still going to a concert Thursday night?"

"I don't know. I never actually got tickets.'

"Oh, well, I did. If you still want to go, we definitely can. Chris sent me two a while ago."

"I don't know. I'll decide later."

Allison nods and drives us to the airport.

I wake up Thursday morning in the guest bed in Allison's apartment and stare at the ceiling. It's a big day. I'm 29 today. Chris and I are in the same town for the first time since the funeral. I can't decide if I should call him or not. I miss him so much and I know the sound of his voice would be like a balm to the wounds that I'm nursing. What if I could see his smile? I think about getting out my box and reading my post cards, but I remember the letter. I still haven't opened it.

I grab my shoulder bag, which, mercifully, is within reach of the bed, and dig through it until I find the envelope. It's kind of battered, but it will still read fine. I close my eyes for a moment to psyche myself up then rip it open.

> Sara,
> I know you feel guilty, and I know why. I'm sorry for everything I did to add to that. You know that I love you. I always will. I know you need space right now and I'm going to give it to you. But I'm not walking away. I will be here, waiting. I'll wait as long as you need.

When you are ready, please come back to me. I'm not asking for more than your friendship. You mean too much to me, I just want you in my life. I'm here. Love, Chris

Suddenly, I'm wide awake. I jump out of bed and rush down the hall to the kitchen. Allison is dressed for work and drinking coffee at the counter.

"Happy Birthday, Baby Girl!" she says as soon as she sees me.

"Yeah, we're going to a concert," I tell her.

She smiles at me. "I'm so glad to hear it. Sorry to leave you to your own devices all day on your birthday, but I *have* to work."

"I know. It's okay. You've babied me more than enough. I don't mind being totally lazy all day in honor of the occasion."

"How is that different from any other day?"

"Hm. Good point. Oh, well. Get to work, save the world, hurry home, okay?"

"Of course. Happy Birthday!" She kisses my forehead as she passes me on her way to the door.

My day is really boring. I have come out of the fog that had been getting me through the monotony of nothingness all day, every day. I hope the tickets are good and I'll be able to see his face clearly. I'm sure that he would have sent her club tickets, but I'm worried all the same. It will be hard to be so close to him and not actually talk or hug him or anything, but I don't care. It will be so good to lay my eyes on him.

Allison and Tom take me out to dinner. I'm grateful that they don't ask the waiters to sing or anything. I don't really eat much; I still haven't gone back on food. Tom is going to drop us off at the concert and then pick us up later so that we don't have to worry about parking. As we climb out of the car Tom says, "Just let me know when you need me to come back." Allison nods. "Have fun. Happy Birthday, Sara!" She kisses his cheek and we climb out of the car.

On the sidewalk, I can feel the tension in my body mounting. I'm going to see Chris! My brain is dancing. "Come on, come on!" I urge impatiently.

"Are you excited about the show, kiddo?"

"Kind of."

We make our way towards the crowded arena. I still haven't asked her where we are sitting. Suddenly she stops, shoves her hand in her bag and pulls out two laminated, purple backstage passes. They're on lanyards, just like the ones I wore in San Francisco and Phoenix. "I promised," she says. "I promised Short Mark that I would not tell Chris that you were here, but that I would bring you back to see him before the show."

"What are you doing? You don't just throw those things around!" I push the passes back into her bag and shove her into a corner made by decorative walls on the outside of the building. "Allison, you have to be careful with those."

She loops one of the passes around my neck. "Come on, he's waiting."

"Wait!" She still hasn't put hers on, she's just carrying it. I push mine under my shirt and then help her. "Seriously, Al. These things are dangerous. You can't just walk around with them hanging out."

She gives me a weird look. "Why?"

"Because someone will steal them. Put your ticket around your neck. You can leave it on the outside of your shirt."

We get through the front gate and follow the rest of the crowd looking for their seats. I follow in Allison's wake as she purposely walks towards the stage. We show our tickets to the guard at the first gate blocking entrance to the club. He studies them and then nods us through. She doesn't even slow down as she crosses to the second gate.

Mike is standing there with his arms across his chest, looking as scary as ever. But when he sees me, his face breaks into a smile. "Sara!" He immediately steps aside to let us through, but he grabs me in a hug before I can get by. "How have you been stranger?"

"I've... I've... Fine. Just fine, Mike. How are you?"

"I'm great, Sare-Bear. Go, go. Evans told me you were coming. He's looking for you."

We slide through the small space Mike allows us and duck around a heavy, black velvet curtain. Allison is staring at me, her mouth hanging open. "What?" I ask her.

"You – just – I don't know. Belong here, don't you?" I shrug. Allison has lost her frenzied pace. She looks at me. "Well, I don't know where to go anymore. This is really more of your area of expertise."

I laugh bitterly. "Hardly an expert. Every place is different, Ally. I don't know where to go either." Then I see Tom turning down a hallway ahead of us. I grab Allison's hand. "Come on!" I turn down the same hall and call out, "Tom!"

He stops and turns around. A huge smile spreads over his face.

"Sara! I heard a rumor that you might show your face tonight!"

"I don't think you've met my sister, Allison. Ally, this is Tom, Evansgate's manager." Allison and Tom shake hands. "I'm looking for Short Mark, can you help?"

"Of course. Come on." Tom turns back and re-traces our steps. We follow him to a door with a sign that says, "PRIVATE", like all of the others.

Tom knocks and nudges me off to the side so that I won't be in the line of sight of whoever opens the door. I hear Drew's voice, "Hey, Tom! What do you need?"

"Evans," Tom replies. "I have something for him."

Short Mark comes out into the hallway, already looking around. He grins when he sees me and grabs my hand. I hear the door shut as Short Mark pulls me further down the hall. Allison is behind me. We step into an empty room. "Hi," he says with a goofy smile.

Kind of an anti-climatic opening, I think, but okay, if that's the way we're going to do it. "Hi."

He grins and turns to Allison. "Thank you. Really, thank you."

Allison smiles. "No problem. I, uh, have some calls to make for work. Is there somewhere I could go for a bit?"

"That's subtle," I tell her.

"You need to talk. Find me later. I really *could* stand to make some calls."

"Go save the world." I wave my hand towards the door. Short Mark steps back into the hallway and returns a moment later, without Allison.

He turns to face me. He looks very serious. "Sit," he commands and points at a couch. I sit and he sits across from me. "I'm glad you're here," he starts. "We've really missed you."

"Me too."

"Eck is in a bad way. I wanted to warn you before you saw him."

"Okay. What kind of bad way?"

"He misses you. A lot. And he's really worried about you. Are you – are you just here tonight, or are you, like, *back* back?"

"I hope I'm back."

"Good, because I wouldn't let you see him if it was any other way. I don't think he could handle it."

"I miss you all like crazy. And I mean that in the most literal way possible. I think I might *actually* be six kinds of crazy."

"I could have told you that before. If I had known that you were unaware, I definitely would have pointed it out for you."

"Thanks."

"Don't mention it." He pauses. "Are you ready to do this?"

"I think so."

We stand up and start towards the door. Short Mark turns back. "Oh, and happy birthday." My stomach is jumping around so much I can only manage a weak smile.

I start to sweat outside the "red room" door. I take a deep breath to calm myself. Short Mark is watching me, waiting until I say it's okay to open the door. This is Chris, I remind myself. It's going to be like putting on my favorite jeans for the first time when the weather turns cool. Familiar and comfortable. I take another deep breath and nod at Short Mark. He opens the door.

"I have a surprise for you," he says as he walks in the room.

Chapter 33

I take a mental deep breath to prepare myself before I walk around the door frame. "Hi."

Everyone is completely silent for a beat and then Chris closes the distance between us in a couple of steps and crushes me a tight hug. "You came!" He doesn't look to be in a bad way to me.

I can't help but smile; I can feel relief settling over me. "Yup. I was in town touring the Texas School Book Depository, so I thought I would stop in on my way through." Chris is still holding me up in his hug. He's laughing, and my feet are dangling inches off the ground. "Uh, Chris? You can put me down now."

"Promise you won't leave?"

"I'm not leaving."

He sets me down and I turn around to give Drew and Blond Mark hugs. "Where are Bethany and Angie?"

"Bethany is visiting her mom," Drew says.

"Angie is at work. I hope she'll give it up and tour with us after the wedding."

"I don't see that happening."

Blond Mark's face slides into a pout. "Me neither."

Drew reaches out and puts his hand on my arm. "How are you doing Sare-Bear? Really?"

"I'm..." I take a deep breath and close my eyes. I put my hand out and touch Chris. I want it to be true before I say it. "I'm fine." I open my eyes and smile.

Blond Mark looks around. "Where's Allison? Didn't you bring her?"

"Yeah, she's 'making some phone calls for work.'" I make finger quotes in the air. I look around the room. It's pretty big, but similar to the others. There are three couches, a TV, a fridge, and a phone on the wall. "What were you guys doing before I interrupted?"

Short Mark smiles. "Just hanging out. You know the drill. Relax, relax, relax until showtime."

I gesture towards the couches. "Well, get on with it."

He points towards the door. "I gotta go see a man about a mic."

Blond Mark slides his sticks out of his back pocket and sits on the edge of the closest couch. He closes his eyes and starts playing the air.

The phone rings and Drew picks it up. "Yeah? Thanks." He hangs up. "Kiro is on stage." Blond Mark doesn't even look up. Short

Mark nods and walks out.

Chris tugs on my hand. "Do you mind missing the opening act?"

"I've never seen the opening act."

"Does that mean you want to, or nothing's changed and you still don't mind skipping it?"

"I'm fine skipping it."

Chris glances around the room. Blond Mark is still playing, and I know he will be for a while. Drew is lying on another couch with his eyes closed. "Come on, we'll leave these guys in peace." We go back to the room I sat in with Short Mark. Chris sits on the couch, kind of sideways, and pulls me down in front of him. I throw my legs up on the rest of couch and lean back into his chest. Yup, just like my favorite jeans.

I can hear his smile. "Happy Birthday! I'm so glad you're here. Are you okay?"

"I am now. I kind of had a rough couple of weeks."

"That's understandable. Did you –" his voice breaks and he clears his throat. "Did you talk to Sam...? before...?"

I squeeze my eyes closed and shake my head.

"I didn't think so." I'm not ready to think about that, and as always, he knows what I'm thinking and changes tack slightly. "Tell me what you've been doing."

"I took a leave of absence from school."

"You did?" I can hear the surprise in his voice.

"You usually already know what I've done, without me having to tell you. Why are you surprised?"

"I just didn't think you would."

"Well, I did. I went down to Atlanta and it almost destroyed me. I need some time."

"I can give you time."

"Not from you, you idiot. From the rest of the world." He squeezes me tighter.

"So, you'll tell me about Atlanta later?" How does he always know what I need?

"I don't want to talk about it right now."

He nods. "I know."

I turn my head to the side and press my face into his bicep. I take a couple of deep breaths and relish his smell.

Chris lifts my hair off of my neck with one hand and lays it over my shoulder. I can feel his breath on my neck and I get a tingle that runs down my spine and makes me shiver. It seems like the most intimate gesture we've ever shared. I can feel my heart squeeze. I want to turn around and kiss him so badly it makes my breath catch.

I don't have to tell him that it's too soon. He already knows. He drops my hair back and wraps both arms around me. "Today is the first day of the rest of your life."

I twist around to look at his face. "What does that even mean?"

"I don't know. That things are going to be different from now on. Better."

"Oh, okay."

"Will you come with us?"

"You mean on the tour?"

"Yeah. It won't be any fun for you, I know, but I want you there."

"Can I think about it?"

"Of course." He smiles. "But the bus leaves at 6:30 tomorrow morning." He winks. "No pressure or anything."

"I'll think about it. You should probably get back to the red room."

He smiles at the memory. "Probably."

I start to stand up, but he pulls me in tighter. I can feel him bury his face in my hair and take a deep breath. Then he lets me go and gives me a little push to help me stand up.

Allison and Short Mark have joined the crew in the band's room. Allison gives me a long look and then smiles. I guess she likes the change she can see in my eyes. I feel like an enormous weight has been lifted off of me and I might float up to the ceiling. I smile back, suddenly very sorry for the worry I've given her in the last few weeks.

Short Mark looks down at Chris and I holding hands. He smiles at me. "Welcome back, Shorty."

We lounge around for a while and then the phone rings again. I stand up and Allison looks up at me. "Is that our cue to leave?" I nod as Short Mark answers the phone.

"All right, boys," he says. Blond Mark spins his sticks and slides them back into his back pocket. As I leave the room I can see them standing together. It makes me smile.

Allison brushes my arm as we walk back down the hallway. "You look great, Baby Girl."

"I feel great. He just makes everything all right."

"I don't know why you shut him out in the first place."

"Yes you do." She allows that. "He asked me to go with them."

"I knew he was going to."

"I did too."

"Are you going to?"

"I told him I'd think about it. What do you think? Should I?"

"I think only you can make that decision. But I know that without him you aren't yourself anymore." She laughs. "'He completes you.'"

It sounds stupid, but then again, I've gotten a lot of good information from movies. And, if I'm honest, she's right.

We push out from behind the curtain and the noise level goes up significantly. I tap Mike on the shoulder so that he can let us back out. The crowd is pretty thick, so he can't actually pay us any attention. Mike takes his job very seriously.

Allison and I elbow and shove our way closer to the stage. No one really wants to let us through, of course, but we make a little headway at least. My biggest goal is to put a little distance between my head and the giant speaker sitting stage left.

When the lights go out there is an explosion of noise from the crowd. I can feel the people I managed to get in front of push forward.

The music is great (of course) and I find myself jumping around in a half dance with the rest of the crowd. I'm singing along, but it's so loud no one can hear me or anything. When they sing "Six Kinds" I can feel Allison freeze next to me, just like I did. She pulls on my arm and gives me a look that says, "Is this about you?" I nod. She smiles and nods back. I wonder if she hadn't heard it before now.

They're about three quarters of the way through the show when Short Mark stops. I look up in surprise. "Hello, Dallas!" he yells. The crowd goes crazy. "There is a very special person in the audience tonight, and she is celebrating a birthday." Ten feet or so to my left a group of girls start screaming. Short Mark gives them a funny look. "I wasn't talking about you." I can see the girls wilt from here. "Uh, sorry. But happy birthday to you, too," Short Mark smiles at her.

He clears his throat. "So, it's her birthday, but I'm hoping that she will give me a gift. And all of you can share it."

Uh-oh. I know where this is going.

"Shorty?" Short Mark scans the people in front of him. "Please come up, Shorty. We'll sing our little song and I'll let you go."

The crowd is screaming. Today is the first day of the rest of my life, he said. I give Allison a quick look and she nods. I start to push my way forward. The crowd doesn't want to let me move. "Here I am! Let me through!"

A security guard starts to clear a path as he comes towards me. It's Paul. When I get to him, he puts his arm around my back and helps me push towards the stage. Two other security guards come to the edge of the stage and squat down to pick me up. Well, at least I went all out to look my best tonight.

A sound monkey comes out with a mic. I look at Short Mark. "You had to see a man about a mic, huh?"

I turn to look at Chris and he makes a motion with his hand. He's telling the sound crew to kill the feed from the mic attached to his head. He reaches out and pulls me towards him. "You can do this, Baby Girl. Just sing to me, okay?"

Short Mark touches my back. "Do I even have to ask if you remember which parts are yours?"

I give him a withering look. "I remember." Chris helps me with the mic, because Short Mark got me one to wear like theirs, instead of one to hold, then he nods at someone offstage to get his mic back on. Short Mark slides an arm around my back and pulls me out to center stage. The lights are so bright I can't really see anything. But I can *hear* all the people that are looking at me.

"You are very lucky, Dallas," Short Mark says and the screaming starts again. "You are the only people that get to hear this song." He looks in my eyes with question in his. I nod. Then I look back at Blond Mark and nod to him. He counts us in. Short Mark holds my hand, and I have no intention of letting go as I close my eyes and pretend that I'm just standing in the studio with the guys.

After the show, I barrel towards the backstage gate. I didn't want to skip out early so that Allison could see the whole show, but I'm starting to regret that decision. I elbow my way through the crowd with Allison hanging on to me so that we don't get separated. Everyone recognizes me and some of them start to let me pass. A lot of them call out, "Happy Birthday!"

When I reach Mike he looks at me apologetically. He has his hands out fending off a couple of very persistent girls. I think they might be promising Mike all kinds of unmentionable things if he'll let them by. "See her pass?" He gestures towards me and I hold up my purple tag. "You need one of those to get through here."

One of the girls throws herself at me. "How much? I'll give you anything if you let me have it!" Thankfully, the other guards are starting to make their way through to the gate to help. It takes a couple more minutes before we are able to disengage ourselves from the throng and get through.

I head straight for the band's room. Allison is just behind me. I throw open the door, half expecting the room to be empty, but they're all there. Chris comes towards me with his arms open and a smile on his face. But the words die on his lips when he sees me. I hold up one hand in his direction.

"Uh-oh," Short Mark at least has the decency to look sorry.

"We're getting divorced," I spit the words at him.

"I am pretty sure you don't believe in divorce."

"How could you do that to me?" I wail.

"Shorty – you were amazing! Don't be upset, be proud!"

"I'm so embarrassed."

"What for? Listen to me: You. Were. Amazing. Honestly though, I didn't expect you to do it. I thought you would just leave me hanging on stage like an idiot."

"You are an idiot. But unlike *some* people, I'm not that cruel."

Blond Mark throws his arm around my shoulder. "Sare-Bear, seriously, you were awesome. I think you should join the band."

"Let's not get crazy," Drew laughs.

I take a deep breath and look at Short Mark. "How could you do that to me?"

"I didn't. I did it for you. I wanted you to see that you *could*. I wanted you to have something else to fret about for a while." He is actually serious, but he is fighting laughter.

"It's really not funny," but I'm starting to feel a smile. "Was I really okay?"

Chris grabs me and spins me around to face him. "You were better than okay, sweetheart. You were spectacular."

"Really, I didn't know you had it in you," Allison chimes in. "But I'm extremely proud to be able to say you're my sister right now."

"You weren't before?"

"You couldn't even get your own mail."

I turn back to look at Short Mark. "This doesn't mean I'm giving in. I'm not agreeing to anything. This isn't going to happen again, got me?"

"Whatever you say, Shorty."

Chris looks at me when he says, "I'm going back to Allison's with Sara tonight." His eyes are asking if that is true.

"Don't miss the bus," Drew says.

The guys rush through their usual showers and Chris grabs a bag of his stuff. We leave through an underground tunnel. There's a limo waiting, but the guys don't get into it. There are two much more regular cars sitting behind it. We don't have to call Allison's Tom for a ride. Short Mark, Blond Mark, and Drew take one car back to their hotel and Allison, Chris, and I take the other to her place. I guess the limo is just a decoy to throw off the fans because it leaves first, still empty. We sit there for a few minutes before we follow. Allison is sitting in the front seat. Chris is holding my hand across the middle of the back seat. We ride all the way to Allison's in silence.

Chapter 34

Chris is lying on my bed in Allison's guest room. My box of post cards is on my pillow and I have to move it to sit next to him. In a spastic moment, I knock the box into his leg and the cards spill out onto the bed. I scramble to pick them up before they get messed up.

"I'm sorry!"

Chris is staring at the cards. "What are those?"

"Uh, it's all the post cards you sent me."

"What's *that*?"

"Uh, that's the pillowcase you slept on at my house."

He smiles. "You saved all the cards?"

"Every one."

"They're well worn."

I look closer at my collection. He's right. The corners have gotten soft and kind of dog-eared. I hadn't noticed. The earlier cards are much worse than the ones at the back. I look down at the bed. "I read them every night."

"All of them?"

"Yeah. It's the only way I can sleep."

Chris is very quiet, but I can't bring myself to look up at him. Suddenly he gets off the bed and walks out of the room. I wouldn't have thought that appreciating the cards so much would have upset him, but apparently I'm wrong. I sit perfectly still as I try to decide what to do.

But, he comes right back in, carrying his bag that he had left in the hallway. He sits on the bed, reaches into it, and rummages through his stuff. He pulls out a rubber-banded stack of post cards. "Here. These are for you."

The stack is really quite thick. I reach out to take it and my hand shakes a little. "Can I read them?"

"No, you can only look at the fronts. Yes, you can read them, they're yours."

I pull off the rubber band and read through each card.

Day 44, Days since I've seen you: 1
I might not send it, but I have to know that
I'm still talking to you. I'm going to be on TV!
Love, Chris

Day 45, Days since I've seen you: 2
We're going to be taping a show today that's
going to air on Friday night. And they call it
"live TV". I've agreed to be in Cannadiak and
Angie's wedding. Love, Chris

Day 46, Days since I've seen you: 3
Evans is singing in the shower. I'm starting
to find his voice offensive, if only because he
is keeping me awake. Love, Chris

Day 47, Days since I've seen you: 4
I watched someone swerve to miss a banana
peel in the road today. I blame Mario Kart.
Love, Chris

Day 48, Days since I've seen you: 5
Sometimes I'm too wrapped up in the
possibilities to be able to see the finished
product. Love, Chris

Day 49, Days since I've seen you: 6
I'm going to be on TV tonight! I wonder if you'll
be watching... Love, Chris

Day 50, Days since I've seen you: 7
There are 2 kinds of people in this world:
people who put nuts in cookies and people I
like. Love, Chris

Day 51, Days since I've seen you: 8
I really am terrible at checkers. How is
that even possible? Love, Chris

Day 52, Days since I've seen you: 9
I'm in Virginia... I wish I were at your house.
Love, Chris

Day 53, Days since I've seen you: 10
I'm hoping permanent marker comes off in
less than 48 hours. Otherwise the people in
Houston might wonder about the new tattoos
covering my arms. Love, Chris

Day 54, Days since I've seen you: 11
Damn them! Marker still there, even if it's
fading. Long sleeves tonight? Love, Chris

Day 55, Days since I've seen you: 12
Happy Birthday! I wish I was celebrating
with you. Wondering if there is any way you
will be at the show tonight.
Love, (marker-free) Chris

I smile at him. "I feel like there is probably a story behind the marker that I might want to hear."

"What can I say? We were in Virginia. I had a few too many beers and I fell asleep. The guys must have been really bored. I'm just glad that they didn't touch my face!"

"You could have always just worn a ski mask."

"I'm not sure which would have been worse."

"When is the wedding?"

"At the beginning of July. We'll be getting ready to go to Europe and stuff after that. I think Angie is going to take a couple of months from work and go with us."

"Blond Mark is hoping that will be enough to convince her to quit, isn't he?"

Chris points at me and touches his nose with one finger. "So," he says quietly. "Are you going to come with me?"

It's the first time he doesn't say "us" and it brings me up short. I wonder if he knows that he has always asked me to go with *them*, but it's totally different if I consider going with *him*. "I'm kind of afraid to now."

"Because of 'the Single'?" I nod. "I won't ever let him do that again." He pauses for a second and then smiles. "I'm a lot bigger than he is. He has to listen to me."

That reminds me that I want to know how involved *Chris* was in my public humiliation. "Did you know that he was planning to do that tonight?"

"On my honor, ma'am, I promise I did not. I didn't even know there was a chance you would be there." Hm, that's a fair point. "But, you're avoiding the question."

"Allison thinks I should. She says I'm a better person when I'm with you."

"I can't judge. I only see you when you're with me." I laugh. "What do you think?" he asks.

"That I'm happier when I'm with you. No, that I'm *happy* when I'm with you, and not when I'm not. If that makes me a better person, then I'm going to have to agree with her."

"I'd say, typically, that's true." He grabs my hand. "So come with me. The guys hate me when you're not around."

"I know. Short Mark said you're mopey."

"He's right. Nothing is as much fun without you."

"Let me sleep on it. But help me pack my crap, just in case."

"Okay, but first, I have a present for you." He smiles out of the corner of his mouth. "You didn't think I would forget your birthday, did you?"

"If I had thought about it..." I trail off. I take the proffered gift with a little apprehension, but as soon as I have the paper off, I start to laugh. It's a copy of the book he tore a page out of at the beach. It's just a stupid paperback of chick lit drivel, and I can't believe he even remembered what book it was. It's oddly heavy for a paperback. "Did you sign it for me?" I ask as I flip it open.

"Would you like me to?"

"Hey! You defiled this one too!" The centers of the pages have been cut out and a box is snugly tucked inside.

"If you are really going to insist that you need a new copy of that crappy book, I would be happy to replace it. But, why don't you open your birthday present for now?"

I lift the lid off of the box to find a delicate necklace nestled in tissue. A tiny hourglass set in a circle of silver hangs from a silver chain.

"I couldn't come up with anything to give you, except time. But the sand in there is a mix from the East and West Coasts."

"How?" I think I am holding the most thoughtful gift I have ever received. "Did you have it made?"

"I know a good jeweler."

In the morning, I go with him. I knew I would. He knew I would. Hell, everyone knew I would. I don't know why I struggled with the decision for so long. I would have been heartbroken to stay behind when the bus left. I sound corny, even to myself, but Chris would have taken a big piece of me with him.

When we get to the hotel, the other guys are bleary-eyed and scruffy. They're already on the bus, waiting for us. Chris is carrying my suitcase and his bag, which he drags up a set of stairs that is almost a ladder.

"Shorty! I knew you'd be here."

"Yeah, yeah. I hope this doesn't mean that you people expect me to go to every show."

Blond Mark yawns. "Wouldn't dream of it."

Drew yawns too. "Get comfortable, girlfriend. We've got some driving ahead of us. We have to be in DC to play tomorrow night."

I feel the bus start. "Here goes nothing," I say under my breath.

A guy steps through a door that leads to the "cockpit" area of the bus. He smiles at me. "Oh, hello," he says to me. Then he looks at Short Mark. "Mr. Evans, we're going. ETA in DC is 8 am Saturday."

Short Mark nods. "Thanks." Then to me, "Grab a seat, Shorty. You don't want to be standing when we start."

Chris comes down the "stairs" and grabs me around the waist. He pulls me down next to him on a couch. "No, you don't." I lean back into him, and rest my head on his shoulder. I'm really tired still and with the motion of the bus I fall asleep quickly. I only sleep for about half an hour and then Chris gives me a tour of the bus.

There are four buses total in our caravan, plus Kiro's bus. We're towards the front, with the equipment in front of us and the crew buses behind. The thing is huge (relatively speaking) and everyone has space to do their own thing. We have to stop every 6 hours for the drivers to rotate. There are three drivers for each bus and only one of them sleeps at a time. No one gets out at these stops usually, but once Short Mark had a quick meeting on a crew bus at a rest area.

On our bus, the "band bus," there are three "rooms" on the main level, plus a bathroom. Just behind the driver is the biggest space. It's kind of like the inside of a regular RV, except *much* nicer. There's a table, a little kitchen area, two plush, very long couches and a couple of giant flat screen TVs. Half of it has a really high ceiling compared to everywhere else, and a chandelier – which somehow doesn't look out of place, even though we're on a *bus*.

In the middle of the bus is a room with seats around the sides and a table in front of a couple of them. A keyboard is mounted to one wall. A couple of cabinets have instruments in them. Chris told me that they sometimes play while they're on the road, but mostly Short Mark uses the space to work on music. The door we use to get on and off the bus is in this room. Next is what the guys call the study. It's a fairly small space with two desks with chairs and some cabinets. At the back of the bus is the bathroom with a ceiling that is about six inches higher and Chris can stand up.

Pseudo-stairs, more like ladders, are in the big room, the back of the music room, and at the back of the bus. The stairs in the back only go into the last room upstairs, but the other two sets go up to a "hallway" that runs along the side of the bus. "Upstairs" is really just four sleeping areas, each with a bed and cabinets for their clothes and things, and there is a door to each off of the mini-hall. The last room, at the back of the bus, is shorter than the others because it is over the bathroom and it has a higher ceiling, but it's bigger because the hall stops there instead of running down the side. Short Mark has that one. He says it's because he's the shortest, but I know it's because it's the biggest.

Chris has the first room, because it's door is right at the top of the first set of stairs so he doesn't have to go far. Chris can only stand up completely straight in the bathroom and the big room, but upstairs he just scoots around on his knees. No one can stand upstairs, not even Short Mark. The ceiling is only about 4 ½ feet, but since they really only sleep up there, it's not a big deal.

"Only four rooms, huh?" I tease Chris during my grand tour. "Four beds. How convenient. You failed to mention that I would have to share a bed for the whole trip."

"I'll sleep on the couch, if that would make you feel better."

"Yeah, I'm going to make you sleep on the couch. Because you don't need sleep at all when you are on tour."

"Are you going to take the couch?" he asks.

"Do you want me to? Or would it be okay if I bunked with you?" I hurry on before he can answer. "I could always sleep in Short Mark's room. It is the biggest."

"Shut up," he says as he pushes me into his room. "That's not even funny."

"Yes it is, and you know it." We've reached the end of our tour and Chris lies on his bed. Truth be told, he really doesn't have a lot of options. I don't think he could sit on his bed even though it's less than a foot off of the ground. I lie next to him and pluck at the blanket. "I hear there are 219 stripes on this thing." The bed is surprisingly comfortable, and really big.

"Do you want to count them?"

"Not particularly. But I am wondering what it is that drove you to."

"Boredom, of course."

I look around his room. The bed fills most of the space, of course. His storage locker is a really nice wooden cabinet with pictures and things taped on it. Across from his bed, there is a flat screen TV mounted to the wall. There are a lot of pictures taped to the walls. When I lay back and look up, I see that there are three taped to the ceiling right above his head. One of them is the two of us that his mom took when we were in Portland, laden down with things at the Farmers' Market. The other two are just me – the one that I had taken July 4th with my cell phone and sent him, the other a shot on the beach by the penthouse. The sight of them makes me cry. The memory of the pictures in Sam's office floods my mind and the image of the kissing picture in the pile of broken glass seems to be burned into my skull.

Chris turns towards me in alarm. "What? What's wrong? It's not *that* boring! Especially since you are here now. Besides, if you hate it, I promise to fly you back to Dallas."

I'm crying so hard that I can't even speak, so I just shake my head. Chris reaches for my chin and tries to pull my face up to his, but I stubbornly tuck it down. He pulls me into his chest and lets me cry for a long time.

When I've cried myself out, I look up at him. "Sorry."

"What's wrong?"

I sniff, but manage to keep the tears at bay. "I have a little story to tell you. Are you ready to hear about Atlanta now?"

"If you're ready to talk about it."

"I had to go sign some papers for Sam's life insurance. As an aside, your girlfriend is now a millionaire." I stop cold. "I'm sorry, that just sort of popped out."

But Chris has an enormous smile on his face. "You can be my girlfriend, if you want to." I pull a face. His smile droops. "Or not."

"Let's focus on the story at hand and then we'll get back to the girlfriend thing, okay?"

"Okay, I can be patient. So you're a millionaire, huh?"

"Yeah. I didn't see that coming. So, anyway, I'm down there to sign the papers and they take me into Sam's office to collect any of his personal belongings that I might want to keep." I take a breath to collect myself and proceed to tell him the story of finding the pictures.

"What did you do?"

"I went to a bar at the airport and proceeded to get completely wasted on three measly shots of tequila and a couple of vodka cranberries because I hadn't eaten anything in, like, a week. And I spill the story all over the bar. Then I see a commercial on TV for your show, and I go through the window."

"Literally?"

"Uh, no. The window between I'm happily buzzed and totally flat out drunk. I go from sharing my story with the bartender to yelling it at a significant portion of Hartsfield-Jackson."

"Okay, you crammed a lot of information in there. One, I thought you had lost weight. Are you back on food or should I be worried about you?"

"I don't have much of an appetite, no. But that's okay; you've always eaten enough for both of us."

"We'll work on that later. Two, 'through the window'? I like it. Where did you get it?"

"From my friend, Nate. Isn't it great?"

He nods. "Three, did you get to see the show? I've been meaning to ask for ages."

"Um, no, I didn't. I was kind of in a major fog at the time. Plus, after the Atlanta trip, I was kind of fragile and seeing you on TV probably would have been the final nail in my coffin."

"Oh. Well, then I'm glad you missed it." He pauses and puts his hand on the side of my face. "So you're crying because your asshole husband cheated? Or because I have pictures of you on my ceiling and you find that creepy?"

I burst out laughing. "I was crying because you have pictures of me, of us, and he didn't. But now that you mention it, it is kind of creepy."

He reaches up to pull them down. I grab his hand. "You don't have to. You *are* talking to the girl who had your pillowcase in a Ziploc bag."

"I don't have to leave them up either. I've got the real deal in bed with me now." He smiles and pulls the pictures of just me down, but he leaves the picture of both of us. Then he reaches over me to stick them to the side of his locker.

I have a moment of screaming, uncontrollable lust when I find myself centimeters from his chest. He is so perfect, so wonderful, so everything I ever wanted. I try to take a couple of steadying breaths, but then I'm drowning in his smell. I have to get myself under control. My husband just died, for Pete's sake. The devil on my shoulder is reminding me that I haven't had sex in, like, a year (okay, maybe not, but a really long time – too long to even know for sure) and that is because my husband was doing it with someone else instead.

Chris settles himself back down in front of me. I take a deep breath. "I knew he didn't love me anymore. I knew he was sleeping with someone else. Before I even met you, if I'm honest with myself. I don't know why I stayed."

"You were punishing yourself for something you have no control over," he says matter of factly. I know he's talking about the babies that I'll never have.

"I don't know. But it doesn't really change anything."

Chris looks into my eyes and for what seems like an eternity we stare at each other. Finally Chris breaks the silence. "Do you love me?"

"Yes," I whisper. What's the point of denying it any longer?

Very slowly, without taking his eyes from mine, he leans in closer. I can feel my heart stutter in my chest. I want him so very badly, but the one sane part of my brain is screaming that it's too soon. When he closes the last bit of distance and our lips touch, I comfort myself with the idea that there's a possibility that it's the only *crazy* part of my brain.

It's a very soft, very sweet kiss, but there is a fire growing in my belly. I throw my arms around his neck and he starts to pull me closer. But I launch myself at him and the momentum pushes him to his back. He clamps his hands, gently but no joke, on either side of my face and brings me with him, never breaking apart. I remember the moment in the Town Car in LA when it felt weird to not be kissing him. If I had known then that it would have felt like this, I would have acted on that, I'm sure.

There are fireworks going off in my brain, each thought exploding in a rush of happiness. I love him. I've loved him since the day I met him. He loves me. We are going to be together. Sam has completely lost his hold on me.

Suddenly I'm wondering if we shut the door. I don't think we did. Would it be totally inappropriate to have sex on the tour bus? Probably. Would the other guys be able to hear us? Probably. But, I'm still considering it. My breath is coming in rapid little bursts and I can feel heat rolling off of Chris. He pushes me back over, and suddenly he is on top of me and I know that he is considering sex too.

He breaks the kiss and reaches up to shut the door. (Seriously, can he hear my thoughts?) He brushes my lips one more time and then moves down my jaw line to my neck. He plants kisses along my collar bone and slips the strap of my tank top over my shoulder. His hand lingers on my bare skin. I can feel his hot breath, and it's all I can do to not rip his clothes off. "Not here," he murmurs. "Not now, not like this."

Not like what? The hottest sex I've ever had?

"I need room to move, sweetheart." Ah! He can read my thoughts! He pulls his face up to mine, and we're nose to nose. "I love you. You are perfect to me, perfect for me, and I am not about to miss anything. It will be perfect."

He exhales and rolls on to his back. I groan with desire and he laughs. "So, we were going to get back to the topic of whether or not you're my girlfriend."

"If I rip off your clothes and ravage your body, would that provide helpful information?"

He laughs again. "It might. But I'm not going to let you."

"Is this because you feel like I was stringing you along for months and now you are trying to get back at me?"

He pushes himself over me and into my line of vision again. "No. I know you weren't stringing me along. You have not done a single thing that would merit revenge." He drops his serious face and a playful smile dances on his face. "Really, this is about location. I told you, I will settle for nothing less than perfection. I promise you, it will be worth waiting for."

I groan again. "I don't doubt it, but I'd still rather not. I'm more of an instant gratification kind of girl."

"Okay, and I'll admit, it feels great to have you throw yourself at me."

"Got to bolster up that self esteem." I groan again. "I might sleep on the couch after all."

"Why?"

"Because there is no way I'm going to *sleep* in this bed."

"You've never had any trouble sleeping with me."

"I've never considered allowing myself to have sex with you."

"And now it's a possibility?"

"It is a two person event, so *I* can't say it's a certainty."

"Oh, it's a certainty."

"See? And you expect me to sleep?" I groan and kick my feet. "You are so cruel."

"I know." I can hear the smile in his voice.

I turn my face away and see the tour schedule taped to his locker.

Chapter 35

At first I don't really look at it, but the date 10/30 jumps out at me. The day Sam died. The day Chris was there, with me. The day, according to this paper, he was supposed to be on stage in Little Rock. It hadn't occurred to me that Chris had been with me for almost a week *before* the break. I look again. 11/1 New Orleans – I remember that one. Short Mark was jacked to be playing in the Big Easy on All Saints Day. What happened? Did Chris leave and I missed it?

I whirl back around. "What?" he asks calmly.

"What?! What! What were you doing with me before Sam's funeral?!"

"I believe I rubbed your back a lot, and I vaguely recall a fist fight."

"I mean! Why weren't you on stage in Little Rock? New Orleans?" I'm almost screaming. Okay, I am screaming.

"Sara, I'm the *bassist*, and unfortunately that means I'm not exactly irreplaceable. The shows were less than stellar, as I understand, but the guys knew I needed to be with you."

"What were you thinking?!"

"I was thinking that you needed me there."

"*That* is completely irrelevant. I can't believe you!"

"What? I don't understand why you are upset. Girls are so confusing. Wouldn't you have been upset if I hadn't been there?"

"Well, yes, of course. But Chris, this is your tour! Your band – these are your brothers, remember? How could you let them down?"

"I didn't. Sara, I never would have left them if it wasn't do-able. They would have been upset if I *hadn't* gone to be with you."

"I can't believe you did that!"

Just then Short Mark's voice yells, "FOOD!" and Chris and I both freeze.

Chris looks at his watch and I check it too. It's very hard to believe that it's not even 9 am yet, when my entire life is upside down from where it was when I woke up at Allison's this morning.

Chris looks at me. "Are you going to come down and eat something, or do I have to insert a feeding tube?"

"I... I just need a minute, okay? I'll be down in a minute." He kisses my forehead and then slides off the bed and out the tiny little door.

I can't explain my emotions, even to myself. I am sure that I could not have gotten through Sam's funeral without Chris there, but not at the expense of his band-mates. They're a family and I came between them. How am I supposed to live with the knowledge that I took Chris away when they needed him? He chose me over them. Part of me feels good, but I also feel lousy. He shouldn't have done that.

I turn my head when I feel him lay on the bed again. But it's not Chris, it's Short Mark laying next to me now. "Hey, Shorty. What's wrong?"

"Short Mark, how could you? How could you let him leave the tour?"

"How could I? Because that was where he needed to be, Sara. You needed him. You are a part of this now, and we take care of each other. Your need was greater than ours, so he went." I don't think he has ever called me "Sara" before. It sounds weird coming out of his mouth.

"He missed the Big Easy. You were so excited about that one."

"Yup, and it sucked without him. But the crowd didn't know that, not really. Please, Shorty, it's *New Orleans*, they were so damn drunk *I* could have skipped it and no one would have noticed."

"Somehow I doubt that."

"Listen to me right now, Shorty. Do not push him away for another second, you got me? Stop it. I'm not sure why you put yourself at the bottom of every list, but you do deserve him, and for God's sake, he deserves you. So stop torturing the poor man and have sex with him."

"I *tried!*"

"Ah, yes, well, I think I might prefer for you to wait at least until we are not sharing a 300 square foot space."

"Yes, that's what he said."

Short Mark gives me a hard look. "Please, Shorty. Let him love you now." He starts to get up, but stops and turns back. "And I'm supposed to tell you that he will literally force food down your throat if you don't come down and eat it of your own free will." He looks at me. "And I'll help. Get your skinny ass downstairs."

"I'm not afraid of you."

"Well, you should be. I might be short, but I carry a big stick." He waggles his eyebrows at me and I see Chris there, in his face. They could be brothers, even if it's only because they have spent so much time together that they have picked up each others' mannerisms. I push him through the door, because suddenly, I can't wait to see Chris again. "Ow! I'm going!"

I follow Short Mark down to the main room. Blond Mark is lieing back on one of the couches, one arm over his face and a can of soda next to his head. Drew is eating what appears to be a blueberry bagel with cream cheese. Chris has a bagel in his hand, but he's not eating it, he's just looking at me.

"Sare-Bear," Blond Mark mumbles from under his arm. "He's really not that important to the show. We're glad he was with you. Don't ever mention it again. You are very shrill when you are upset."

I laugh. Chris visibly relaxes and holds the bagel out to me. I take half of it from him and break *that* in half. "You're eating more than a quarter of a bagel," Chris tells me.

"Hey, you said I had to eat. I'm eating." I nibble on the bread.

Chris reaches under the counter and gets an orange juice out of the fridge. "Here, you don't want to get scurvy."

I drink the juice and eat a little bit of my bagel. Then I go and sit on Blond Mark's stomach. "Uh!" he grunts. "I don't know what they're worried about, Sara. You weigh a ton."

"Thanks." But I'm smiling. The walls are finally down. I am a part of this family now.

We have the whole day to do nothing on the bus. Which is really quite a fantastic prospect, seeing as how over the course of our friendship, Chris and I have taken the art of doing nothing to a new level. Short Mark spends a lot of time in the music room. Chris says that he is already working on music for the next album. Blond Mark spends a lot of time in his room, watching movies and listening to music. Drew spends a lot of time in the study, but I'm not sure what he's doing.

"What do you normally do?" I ask Chris.

"I don't know. Help Evans. Watch movies in my bed. Sit in here because it has the most head room." We're in the big room, sitting on a big couch.

"What do you do in here?"

"Call you. Think about you. Text you. Wonder what you're doing. Write you post cards. You know, normal, very non-stalker type stuff." He smiles at me. "What did you do with all of your time?"

"Oh, I just laid in the bed that you slept in and cried or slept."

"Ah, so you were as productive as I was."

"Yeah, so now that we're together, do we try something different or do we do our non-stalker type things together?"

He pretends to consider that. "What are our other options?"

"Hey! I just remembered something that I wanted to ask you."

"Ask away."

"Did Matt come to the show in Virginia Beach?"

Chris smiles at a memory. "Yeah, he did."

"Did you see him? Did he enjoy the sacred backstage area?"

"Um, yes and no."

"Yes – you saw him, no – he did not go backstage?"

"Right. We saw him before the show and then later at the hotel."

"Did he have a good time?"

Chris peers at my face. "When was the last time you talked to him?"

"Um, really talked? Before the funeral. But he came and picked me up from the airport after my disastrous trip to Atlanta."

"You didn't talk the whole way home?"

"No. I slept."

"Sara! You need to call him. You can ask him yourself."

"Okay, I will. But not right now. So tell me about the TV thing, because I know you want to."

"How do you know that?"

"It just seemed like it was important to you."

"Uh, it's not that." I raise my eyebrows. "You kind of came up."

"I thought we agreed that you were going to leave me out of interviews in the future?"

"We did. But come on Sara, I was sporting a black eye. They weren't going to let it go without some questions."

"I actually noticed that you could still see it, despite the stage make-up when I was in Atlanta and I saw that commercial teaser for the show. What did you say?"

"*I* didn't say anything. But Cannadiak told them that I got in a fist fight at a funeral."

"Please tell me that you're kidding."

"Um, nope, sorry. They asked and I tried to avoid it, but Evans said, 'He got it defending the honor of his not-girlfriend.' Of course they wanted details, and Cannadiak told them I 'beat the crap out of her father-in-law at her husband's funeral'."

"I bet that went over well."

"They're always looking for drama on TV. But what was I supposed to say? 'She's not my girlfriend'? Because he specifically said my 'not-girlfriend'. But I did tell them that it wasn't actually at the funeral."

"That really makes you sound like a horrible person."

"You're not mad?"

"No. As long as the world doesn't think my boyfriend lost a fight with my late husband's father, everything else can be fixed."

"So, we're back to that again."

"Yes. We are. And we should probably actually talk about it. Don't you think?"

"Yeah, we probably should."

"I have to say... as much as I want it; it's not a good idea."

"What? Being together?"

"Yeah." I can see him start to ask why, but I talk over him before he gets the chance. "I have a whole list of reasons why it's a bad idea."

"Why do I feel like you mean that literally?"

"Because I do."

"You have actually written a list?"

"Yes. I needed to be able to look at it sometimes to remind myself that we would never work so I shouldn't do something stupid like leave my husband for you." My throat catches. Sam has only been dead for a couple of weeks and I'm already talking about moving on. This is awful. I'll add that to the list.

Chris is studying my face. "Can I see it?"

"What? The list?" He nods. "What makes you think I have it with me?"

"Because I know you. And I know you do. Go get it."

"I could just tell you what's on it. I've read it often enough that I have it pretty well memorized."

"All the same, I'd like to see it. It will help keep our discussion on track."

"Okay, but I need a pen."

"Why?"

"Because I need to add something to it."

Chris looks like he's torn between laughing and crying. "Go get it and I'll get you a pen." Chris gets up and walks towards the back of the bus, to the study, I assume, but I don't actually have to go anywhere. My shoulder bag is right in front of me, so I dig through it until I find the list. Chris is back before I manage to unearth it from the depths of my crap.

I hold my hand out for the pen and write, "Sam just died. Too soon? How would we ever know if enough time has passed?" on the bottom and then I hand to him. I watch him read through the whole thing.

"Okay," he starts. "First of all, Sam is an idiot. I can't believe he let you get away so he could screw the Ice Queen. No one is as wonderful as you are, Sara. I would never find someone else more attractive, because I will never look away from your face."

"Yes, you will. Someday. It's not like Sam and I got married and he was thinking, 'I'll find someone I like better to screw on the side.'"

"Why do you think so little of yourself?"

"Not even the point. Now, start at the beginning."

"Okay. I do travel all the time – just like Sam – but you can come with me. I want you to come with me."

"What if I don't want to come with you?"

"Do you? Because if you don't, and you don't want me to go... Christ, woman, I would give it all up for you."

"Oh, no you would not. I would never let you."

"You didn't answer my question. Do you want to go with me?"

"I'm not sure yet."

"Well, when you decide we'll talk about it. Moving on, I'm sorry that I brought work with me to your house. I won't ever do it again. From now on, I will only ever work in the studio."

"That's just stupid. You don't have a job that works like that, and I know it. I was just making comparisons."

"Yes, which gets us to number three. Do you think you'll ever stop comparing us?"

"Probably not. Can you handle that?"

He smiles. "Can you? I'm pretty sure I'm coming off on top in every comparison that you make, so I'm okay with it."

"I don't know."

"What? I am not always coming off on top?"

I shove him. "No! Of course you are. It's just I don't know if I want to spend the rest of my life comparing you to a dead man."

"I don't think you will. It's still really fresh. Give it some time and then we'll come back to it someday."

"Okay."

"So, um, this one doesn't really matter anymore." He flicks the paper where it says, *Andrew doesn't want Chris breaking up my marriage.* Chris looks uncomfortable and he is pretty much whispering. "So, can we cross it off?"

I can't help it, I start to cry. "Sure." I hand him the pen, but he doesn't take it.

"Sara, I'm sorry. That was awful. I shouldn't have said that."

"Why not? It's true. It isn't an issue anymore."

"And that is not your fault."

"I know." I sniff.

"But you don't believe it."

"Not really the issue at hand. Move on."

"I —" he starts to argue, but the look on my face is enough to stop him. "Are you sure you want to do this now?" he asks.

"Nope, but it's as good a time as any, so we might as well."

He sighs. "I know you can't have kids. I'm totally okay with that."

"But your parents deserve grandchildren."

"So we'll adopt."

"They deserve Ecks."

"They'll still be Ecks. Or we can work on it for a while. I mean, I don't know the whole story, but we'll do the doctor thing together. *And* we'll adopt."

"I lied. I'm not ready to talk about this."

"Okay." He looks around for a few seconds. "Sara, I love you. That's all I need to know." He balls my list up and throws it in the sink.

I laugh through my tears. "Why the sink?"

"Because it is really hard to throw something into the trashcan from across the room when all of the trashcans are in latched cabinets."

Despite myself, I smile. "Let's just... slow down, okay?"

"I can do that." He starts to move in slow motion. When he talks it's really slow and deep. "Is this slow enough, Sara?"

"Well, if nothing else, you can always make me laugh."

He grabs me in a hug, laughing with me. "I've heard that is important in a relationship."

I inhale a deep breath. "Can I have a little bit of time to be by myself?" I ask him.

Chapter 36

I go upstairs to Chris's room, push the door closed, and lay on the bed. Then I pull out my phone and call Matt.

"Hey, stranger," I say when he answers.

"If I'm a stranger, it's only because you made me one."

"I'm not blaming you. I know I'm the one that dropped off the planet."

"Are you okay?"

"I'm getting there. How are things? Did you have fun at the concert?"

"Yeah, I thought you were going to go with me for that."

"I thought you were looking for a better option."

"I didn't find one."

"Sorry. Did you go by yourself?"

"No, I took someone; she just wasn't a *better* option than you."

"Oh, well, thanks."

"For what?"

"For saying I'm not the worst person on the planet right now."

"That was then, Sara. You might be now."

"I am hoping that you were trying to be funny."

"Trying, yes. Succeeding? Apparently not."

"Maybe not. So, did you and mystery lady have fun?"

"I don't think it was what she was expecting."

"What was she expecting?"

"To spend the night hanging out with Evansgate."

"Chris told me they didn't give you backstage passes. I'm sorry."

"Sorry for what? They gave me backstage passes. I just didn't use them."

"What?! Why not?"

"I didn't feel right going back there with her."

"Does she have a name?"

"I don't want to tell you. Let's call her 'Jane'."

"Okay, I can play along, I guess. Why didn't you want to take 'Jane' backstage?"

"I wanted to be sure that she wasn't just using me for my connection to Evansgate."

"Survey says?"

"She was."

"Oh." I can't help it, I laugh. "I'm sorry."

"It's okay. But it was a long drive home."

"Did you at least like the show?"

"Yeah, it was good. You would think standing right in front of the stage would have been enough for 'Jane', but *no*, she needed to party with them to feel like I was cool."

"Did she meet them when you saw them at the hotel?"

"Actually, no. It's a long story that I don't feel like telling right now. But I will say that I feel vindicated."

"Someday you have to tell me the story."

"Okay, someday. So, seriously, *stranger*, how are you doing? *What* are you doing?"

"Oh! I'm touring with this really great band for a while." Matt is completely silent. "Matt? Are you still there?"

"Yes."

"What's wrong?"

"Nothing. I'm just trying to process that."

"What's to process? I ran away from home and now I'm running around with no-good rock stars who are going to corrupt my innocent soul."

He snorts. "Unlikely. I'm more worried about what is going to happen to them."

"What exactly are they in danger of?"

"Complete moral degradation."

"Really? That's your opinion of me?"

"You're not really in a teasing mood yet, are you?"

"No."

"Oh, sorry. I'm worried about you, Baby Girl."

"So am I."

"Is Chris around?"

"He's downstairs. Why? Do you want to talk to him?"

"Yeah, I do. Can you get him?"

"Um, okay." I lean over and pull the door open. "Hey, Chris?" I call out.

I jump when his head appears almost immediately. "What?"

"Geez! Were you just standing there waiting?"

"Kind of." He smiles. "What do you need?"

I hold my phone out. "Matt wants to talk to you."

Chris takes it apprehensively. I hang on his every word, trying to glean as much as I can from his side of the conversation. I don't get much. "Hello? Yeah, hey. No, she's not, but I'm working on it. Yeah, I will. Sorry. I didn't realize that she wasn't talking to you or I would have called you myself. I know, she's not eating. Why? Okay, I can do that. That's the plan, sorry." He laughs. "Not really, no. I'll make sure she sees you a lot, I promise. See ya."

Chris hands the phone back to me. "What was that about?" I ask Matt.

"Just the grownups taking care of things, kiddo."

"Oh, right. Okay."

"Hey, you scared me," Matt says quietly.

"I'm sorry."

"I know. That's why I already forgave you."

"Then why did you bring it up?"

"Because I wanted you to say you were sorry."

"Done. I'm going to go."

"Okay, but you better call me again soon. You know, to tell me all about your glamorous new life."

"I will. Love you."

"I know. What's not to love?"

I look at Chris who is staring at me expectantly. "What?" I ask him as I hang up.

"Nothing. I'm just glad you called him."

"Yeah, I am too. Now what do we do?"

"Whatever you want."

I flop back down on the bed. "I'm tired. I'm not used to moving. It's exhausting."

Chris slides in beside me. "Then take a nap."

We spend the day watching movies, playing checkers and cards, and for one scary hour dancing like fools around the big room with the Marks. Someone, Tom's assistant I think, arranges for food from a restaurant for dinner, which I find impressive. Whoever it was had to have gone to a lot of trouble to find a restaurant in the area where we would be around dinnertime, coordinate an order with them and what time we would need it, and then they had it delivered to a rest area – probably the most impressive part of the whole thing. I love Italian and it's excellent.

"I'm glad to see you eating, Shorty. You were really getting to be that ugly, scary skinny. Italian is good for un-doing that. Eat more."

"I'm trying to watch my figure now that I've gotten it where I want it."

"I don't find that funny actually," Short Mark then dumps the remaining food from his plate onto mine. He points at me with his fork. "Eat."

It feels really good to laugh. "First of all, I'm stuffed. That was more food than I ate in the last two weeks, all added up. Second, that's gross and I'm not eating your nasty cast-offs."

Chris grabs my plate and says, "I don't have a problem with it. I'll finish it."

Everyone laughs. There are four people from the crew eating with us in the band's bus: Mike, Terri (the stage manager), Aaron (a sound monkey), and William (Drew's guitar tech), and Tom, so it almost feels like a party. Chris told me that they often have different people from crew eat with them. I'm glad they do it in small groups though, because it will give me a chance to get to know more of them without it being overwhelming.

The dinner crew (as they are referred to) stays on the bus with us for the whole six hour shift and we play charades and consume a fair amount of alcohol. Well, they *are* rock stars. I guess I should be glad that it isn't cocaine or something. It's midnight when we stop again and they return to the crew bus. Drew disappears to his bed, but the Marks, Chris, and I stay up for a couple of hours longer talking. Mostly I just get to hear war stories of past tour experiences and the stupid things they have done.

I'm grateful to be so tired when we finally climb the stairs and collapse in bed. Chris just holds my hand once we are lieing there. It takes me about thirty seconds to fall asleep.

When I wake up, the first thing I notice is that the bus isn't moving. I remember that the driver told Short Mark that we would be in DC around eight in the morning. I glance at my watch. It says 9:40, but I'm not sure what time zone my watch is set for, so that doesn't help me very much. I assume we are in DC though. Chris is still passed out, and I just lay there and watch him sleep for a while. I had a lot of fun last night, and I realize that it is easier to just not think about anything. I need to just enjoy this and forget everything else. Okay, new personal policy: no thinking.

I end up falling back asleep and I wake up alone. I can hear the guys downstairs. I climb down the steps, still in my jammies, and find them eating breakfast. We're in a parking lot, but I don't have a lot of other information about our current location. It's a big breakfast spread this morning because they brought in hot food from a restaurant. I eat some scrambled eggs and toast and then take a two minute shower in the tiny little stall in the back of the bus.

It's weird coming back to DC, back to the beginning for us. Because they are playing in Baltimore tomorrow, we get to stay in a hotel in DC tonight. The crew will go on to Baltimore *very* early tomorrow to set up (like, so early it's still tonight), and we will follow later in the day. They are already working on setting up the venue for tonight. All of the buses are at the pavilion where the concert will be while they start to work.

"What should I do?" I ask Chris.

"Oh, I actually have a favor to ask of you."

"Geez, I've been on the tour for exactly one day and already I'm a minion."

"*I'm* asking, not Evans. He is the only one with minions."

"Sorry. Yes, poor minion-less man? What do you need from me?"

"I need you to ride over and pick something up for me."

"What?"

"I'll tell you later." He waggles his eyebrows.

"What? How am I supposed to know what to do if you don't tell me?"

"I'm telling you. Get in the car. Ride."

"And then what?"

"I'll tell you that part later."

Hmph. Well, if he wants to be that way, "Fine. I'll be back later." I cannot imagine what he is up to, but I climb in the back of the waiting limo. I don't have any intention of paying attention, so I lay back and close my eyes. It's hard to completely empty my brain without the distractions and I find myself wondering what I'm going to do long term. This goes sorely against my *I'm not going to think anymore* policy.

When we exit for the Dulles Airport, my curiosity is sparked. What am I doing at the airport? Is he sending me home? But he told me he wanted me to pick something up. Matt?

I have pretty much decided that I'm fetching Matthew, even though I can't figure out why he wouldn't just drive up, when I see Laura Eck standing on the sidewalk. The car isn't even completely stopped when I jump out. "What are you doing here?!" I squeal.

She smiles. Chris has his mother's smile. "I'm here to see you, of course."

"I sense a plot is underfoot."

Laura laughs. "I'm part of no plot. I'm just here to see you."

"Are we going to a concert tonight?"

"That, my dear, is totally up to you."

My phone buzzes and I look at it. It's from Chris, of course.

From Chris:
Call me later.

"I think he wants us to spend some time together," I tell her.

She nods. "So where should we go?"

I end up taking her to Toddies, because I can't think of a better place. We get lattes at the counter and sink into overstuffed armchairs in the front window.

"This is the first place I ever saw your son," I start.

"I know," she says. "I recognized the name."

"He told you?" I'm incredulous.

She laughs at my reaction. "Yes, he tells me a lot. But, I guess this place really stuck out in his memory."

"It stuck out in mine, too. My whole life changed the moment I walked in the door." I look around, reminiscing. I laugh loudly. "How is it possible to feel nostalgic about a place you've only been to once and less than six months ago, at that?"

Laura smiles. "Ah, you have no idea what nostalgia really is yet. Why do you say your whole life changed?"

"Because the moment I met the guys, I looked at everything differently."

"Good different or bad different?"

"That's a hard question. And I think it would depend on who you asked."

"I asked you."

"Laura?"

She smiles again. "Yes?"

"Why did this happen?"

Her smile vanishes. "If you are asking me why Sam died, you know I can't answer that anymore than I could tell you why your mom did. He died because that was what God wanted, Sara. Remember, all you can do is play with the cards He gives you."

I'm quiet for a long time as I think about that, but Laura doesn't push me to talk. She looks at the artwork (which has changed since the last time I was in) and people watches out the front window. I stare at my coffee like it might be holding the answers to questions I don't know to ask. "Would you think less of me if I admitted that I love Chris?"

"He's my son. I would think less of you if you didn't." She smiles.

"You know what I mean. Am I a bad person? My husband *just* died and I'm in love with someone else."

"You were in love with him before Sam died, Sara."

"Which is actually worse."

"I don't think so. You can't control these things. You never did anything to be ashamed of. You might have felt something but..." she trails off.

"But I didn't cheat on my husband?"

She nods. "But it's more than that. You and Chris both – I'm proud of you. I know that my son loves you, but he would never have willingly come between a man and his wife, so he didn't. But he was your friend."

"He is my best friend."

"I'm glad to hear that. I know I'm his mother, which makes me biased, but he is a good man, Sara. You could do worse."

"I know. I did." I blanch when I realize what I said.

"Things were not always awful for you and Sam, but I think you would never have found yourself in the situation you were in if things were right in your marriage."

"But I did find myself there. Why weren't things right in my marriage?"

"I can't tell you that. And as guilty as I know you feel, I can only say this: it wasn't all your fault."

"It wasn't all *not* my fault either."

"No, it wasn't." I know that she was not being harsh, and something I appreciate about Laura is her willingness to tell the truth, but I still feel like she slapped me. She holds her hand up, almost in apology. "It isn't ever all one sided when things go wrong in a marriage; it can't be. I'm not saying you did anything wrong necessarily, but it's a joint endeavor and when things fall apart it's because two people let it happen."

I know that she doesn't actually think that I did something reproachable, but I feel ashamed nonetheless. "Sara," she says. "I know that's why you feel guilty. But you *were* trying, and that is all anyone can ask of you."

"But it wasn't enough. I was going to leave him."

"No, he was going to leave you. He was just waiting for you to give him the opening."

"Do you really feel that way?"

"Absolutely."

"Do you think less of him for it?"

"Maybe, but I don't really know what was going on."

"Do you blame me for letting it happen?"

"No! There isn't a good way to handle these things. And, for Pete's sake! He was cheating on you!"

"I know," I say quietly.

"Sara, that was wrong. He was wrong. Something was broken, and he handled it poorly. If he was unhappy, he should have come to you – not gone to someone else."

"And I should have gone to him, not to Chris. Is that what you're saying?"

"I'm saying that you can't spend the rest of your life wondering if you could have handled it differently. The situation was terrible. But it's over. You have to let it go and move on."

"Does Andrew hate me?"

"What?! Why would he hate you?"

"It's important to him that his son not come between someone's marriage."

"He didn't. I think Anna did that."

"But he did. I would have stuck my head in the sand and lived like that forever if it hadn't been for Chris. I would never have said anything."

"Then I imagine that Andrew is grateful that you met Chris. That's no way to live." She smiles and reaches out to take my hand. "Sara, if you are asking my permission, I can't give it to you. Neither can Andrew. If you and Chris are meant to be together, and I think that you are, you will be."

"There's something important that you don't know."

"There are a lot of important things that I don't know."

I smile. "Me too, but this one in particular is relevant. I. I, uh. See. I –"

"I know. I'm sorry, but Chris told me and I'm not going to sit here and pretend like I don't know so that you have to say it."

"He told you? What did he tell you?"

"That you thought it was a bad idea for you and him to be something because you think that Andrew and I deserve biological grandchildren."

"Wow. Okay, he told you."

"Well, that's garbage, Sara. I don't deserve a damn thing. But I want. I *want* my son to be happy. And if that means you, then I want you." I'm quietly studying my coffee, fighting tears, and she continues. "Don't you think your mom deserved grandchildren?"

"I – yes! But Allison... I mean, Chris is your only chance."

"And she was your only shot at a mom, but that doesn't mean you got to keep her." When I don't respond, she says, "Listen to me. *You* are worth so much. The rest is gravy."

I smile. "Your son said that once."

"What, that you're worth a lot?"

"No, he says that all the time." She laughs. "He mentioned gravy once."

"I think I actually heard it from him."

Chapter 37

Laura and I sit in the coffee shop until they make us leave at 9:30 pm when they close. The limo collects us and takes us to the hotel. We check in at the front desk and collect room key cards. The guys are still on stage as we get in the elevator. "Did you want to go to the show?" I ask her.

"Not really. I told you: I came to see you."

Thankfully, it's Paul on door duty when we get out at our floor. I was afraid I wouldn't know the guard and we would have trouble exiting the elevator. "Hi, Paul," I wave.

"Hi, Sara. You're room is down that way." He points to the left. "All the way on the end, actually." Then he turns to Laura. "Mrs. Eck?"

"That's me!"

He smiles. "You're actually the last door that way." He points to the right.

"Was he trying to keep us far apart on purpose, I wonder?" she asks. Her eyes are bright with laughter. "I'm not stupid; I know how these things work."

I can feel the blush spread up my face, but I think Paul looks even more uncomfortable. "I – he, um, he didn't want you to be too close to the elevator because he said that he didn't want you to be disturbed when everyone came back. If you would like a different room, I can get you one." He pulls out what looks like enough cards to unlock every door on the whole floor.

"It's fine, I'm just teasing. Good night, Sara." And she marches down the hall without another word.

Paul and I stare at her retreating back for a minute. "Well, that was uncomfortable," I mutter in his direction. Paul just nods. "Um, can you actually let me into Chris's room? And then, maybe not tell him I'm in there?"

"I really shouldn't."

"Please?"

Paul looks at his watch and considers. "Okay, come on. But, if I get in trouble, I'm throwing you under the bus."

"Literally? That seems a little harsh, Paul."

We both laugh as he opens the door. "Oh, is my stuff in 'my' room?" I ask.

"Um, probably. But, I don't really know."

"I'm going to go see, and get it, if it is. Will you let me back in?"

He shakes his head. "No way. I opened it once; you're on your own."

I give him a playful shove, then flip the latch to prop the door. Chris's room is only two doors down from mine. My suitcase *is* waiting in my room, so I grab it and haul back into the hall and into Chris's room.

I've never been in one of the guys' rooms at a hotel for a show before. I know he pulled some strings to get me a suite as nice as the ones that they have, but mine wasn't fully stocked with champagne, a fruit and nut basket, huge vases of fresh flowers, and all kinds of other extras that are scattered around the room. I know Chris hasn't been in here yet as I poke through all of his stuff. I look at my watch. They should be back at the hotel around midnight, so I have some time.

I lie on the couch and think about everything Laura and I talked about. I feel like she absolved me of my guilt, just by recognizing it and telling me that I wasn't completely innocent in the situation. But, I also feel like she told me it was okay to be with her son. A warm feeling spreads from my belly. I hop up and get to work, destroying the things left by the hotel. I shred flowers so that I can throw the petals around. I rip open the fruit basket and pick out the strawberries. I bury the champagne in the ice bucket and set out two of the four glasses. In the bathroom I find a basket of assorted bath oils and things so I run the hottest bath possible and dump the entire contents of the best smelling one into the water. I leave the door to the tub open so that the smell will permeate the whole room. I turn down the lights so that only two lamps are lit, both on "nighttime".

I glance at my watch and then rush out into the hall to remind Paul that he *cannot* tell Chris that I'm there, but he needs to make sure that he comes into his room alone. The look on Paul's face tells me that I have shared way too much information, but I'd rather him know that, then have Short Mark march in with Chris.

I dig through my suitcase and find the birthday gift of lingerie my sister gave me "just in case" tucked in the bottom pocket. I smile and consider texting Allison to thank her. Maybe not. I take a quick shower and shave, and then I slide on the nightie and panties. After I change, I rush around hiding evidence: throwing out flower stems, tucking the basket back nicely, hiding my suitcase in the closet. I curl up on the bed to wait, and I don't have to wait long.

I can hear Chris in the hallway. "Just tell me tomorrow, Evans! I don't care – really. Just handle it and then tell me later." Thanks

Paul! Chris struggles with his card a couple of times and then the door opens. Now, I suppose that a lot of hotels go way out for these guys and Chris is not even the slightest bit affected by the smell or the mood lighting. I see him notice the champagne and two glasses and his head cocks to the side with a question in his eyes as he looks at it. He very slowly turns his head towards the bed.

"Hi," I say quietly. I'm almost shy all of the sudden.

Chris is freshly showered, as usual, and his face breaks into a huge smile. He drops his bag and starts towards me, then stops and returns to the door. I hear him latch the catch, and I laugh. Then he rummages in his bag. He pulls out his iPod and plugs it into the sound system, something I am sure you would not find in every room in this hotel. "It's only missing one thing," he says, and Van Morrison's voice fills the room.

"*Moondance* is a good choice," I say with a smile.

"I thought so." He smiles again. "Did you have a nice visit with my mom today?"

"Okay, now is really not the time for that discussion."

"Sorry. Did you buy those pjs just for me?"

"Better. No, actually, Allison did."

"Remind me to thank her."

"I think the best way to do that might be by never mentioning that you saw them."

"Oh, well, if you're sure."

"I am. Do you have enough room now?"

He pretends to look around. He walks around the king size bed, twice, with his arms outstretched. "I mean, I can probably make it work."

"I'm not sure what you think I'm capable of, but I think you may have grossly overestimated me."

He grabs my hand and pulls me off the bed, twirling me in a circle before pulling me into a hug. "I doubt that. You've done a very nice job here."

"Thanks. You get a lot of good stuff to work with."

"Yeah, the hotels are generous." He looks around. "Champagne?"

"Sure. So, would you have come to my room to look for me?"

"I was planning on it. Hey! How did you get in here?" He gives me a glass of champagne.

"I had to promise Paul all kinds of favors that don't merit repeating, but I only have to pay up if you say anything."

Chris spills some champagne because he is laughing so hard. "I think you may have just come up with the most fail safe way of keeping someone out of trouble."

"Oh, you mean, you aren't angry with him, or you aren't going to yell at him?"

"And you said I was diabolical." He hands me a glass. "I love you, Sara."

"I know." I look deep into his eyes for an immeasurable amount of time. "I love you too."

He smiles. "I know." He sets his glass down. "I have something to ask you," he looks very serious.

"Um, okay. I feel under dressed for a serious discussion, though."

"You're perfect." He pushes me towards the bed. I sit and he drops to one knee in front of me.

"You can't be serious."

"Oh, I'm very serious. This isn't something that I take lightly, Sara. I want to spend the rest of my life with you. I know you feel the same way. I'm not asking you to marry me tomorrow, but if I go to bed with you tonight, I want to know that you're going to be my wife."

"You can't be serious," I repeat.

"I can get you a ring first, if you feel like you need it." I just stare at him. "Sara Elizabeth Harris Clarke – because I do know your whole name," he winks. "I want you to marry me. Please?"

"Not tomorrow?" I clarify.

"Not tomorrow."

"Someday, Christopher Thomas Eck, I will marry you. I promise." He smiles and reaches for me. "Wait! Something very important just occurred to me!"

"I don't want to know what it is," he snarls.

"But,

I do!" I'm suddenly considering the possibility that he is a virgin.

"What?"

"Wait, never mind. You can tell me tomorrow." Maybe I don't want to kill this moment.

But now he is curious and he sits back. "What, Sara?"

"I said 'never mind'."

"Now I mind. What?"

"I changed my mind. I don't want to know."

He laughs. "No, it's not my first time."

"Then why?"

"Because actually falling in love with someone changed me."

"Oh."

A smile is spreading across his face. "But now I'm curious."

"No. I don't want to talk any more. You told me when you had more space. Here's more space, I'm not waiting any longer."

"You are awfully impatient."

"Well, it's not my first rodeo either, but it's been a long time."

He laughs again and stands up. He reaches for my hand and pulls me up next to him. "I love you, woman." I breathe in his smell as he leans in to kiss me, his eyes never leaving mine. This one doesn't even start sweet and gentle. I have a feeling Chris has pushed his patience exactly as far as it's going to go, and suddenly I feel like toying with him.

I pull back and watch his eyes. I can see a smile dancing in them, but I can see the hunger there too. I slide my hands under his shirt and push it over his head. I laugh because there is no chance I'm tall enough to actually get his shirt off once he has raised his arms above his head – and I'm really tall. He pulls it off and drops it on the floor behind him. I step back, because, really, Chris in nothing but jeans is a sight to behold, and I'm going to take a minute to appreciate it.

"I thought you were done waiting," he growls, and he reaches for me. I have a moment of grace that I didn't know I possessed and I step backwards up onto the bed behind me and out of his reach. I put my hands out in front of me to keep him back.

"I'm enjoying the view, if you don't mind."

"I mind."

"Well, then I guess that's too bad." I lock my elbows because he is still coming towards me, but now he is laughing. He grabs me around the knees and tackles me to the bed. "That's not fair!" I crow.

"Woman, there are other people in this building."

"Well," I say with a smile, "I imagine most of them will know what we are doing."

Then he is on top of me and he covers my mouth with his so I have to stop talking. I can feel his heat as he presses me into the bed, his entire body against mine. The weight of him is enough to push me over the edge and I can't toy with him anymore. I grab his belt loops and pull his hips tighter against me.

He pulls my hair away from my face and fans it out over my head. I feel his breath on my neck, hot and quick, when he leans in to kiss my collarbone. His fingers tickle across the tops of my shoulders and under one of my straps. He spreads his hand over my shoulder, and as his mouth catches mine again, he slides it over my breast.

He pulls back and runs both hands firmly down my sides,

shoulder to hip, and then crawls backwards as he smoothes them down my legs. He stops at my toes and smiles before lowering his mouth to my ankle. He stops to smile at me before he slides his hands back up. He catches my foot and bends my knee as he slowly returns to my belly.

His hands spread out over my belly and hips under my top, and he slides his hands up to pull it off. I can feel his eyes on me, but in a sudden burst of self doubt, I close my eyes to hide from him. "I love you, Sara," he whispers.

I press my hands against his stomach and smooth them around to his back. I can feel his breath catch and I open my eyes. His face is right over mine and we are eye to eye. All of my doubts and fears disappear.

Chapter 38

Sunday morning comes too soon. Chris and I spent the entire night in each others' arms and I'm not ready to join the world again, but we are going to meet his mom and the other guys for breakfast. I'm exhausted because we didn't sleep, but Chris seems to have even more energy than he usually does. He is already dressed and standing over me.

"Ug, how are you so chipper? I'm tired. Are you sure we can't just sleep for a while?"

"I'm guessing Evans has been knocking on your door for a while and is about to break it down because he is afraid that you have disappeared. I feel like we should at least check in."

"Fine, go tell him I'm just dandy and then come back to bed."

His eyes are bright when he says, "If you're really tired, I don't think you want me to come back to bed."

"Seriously? You had a show last night. You have to run out of energy eventually."

"What can I say?" He winks. "I'm high on life."

"Tonight is going to be a disaster if you don't get some sleep."

"Probably, but I'll take my chances. That was worth any suffering I might encounter today."

I can't help the smile that spreads across my face. "That's true."

"Then come on, get up and put on some clothes. We're already late."

I groan, but drag myself up anyway. I'm bleary-eyed and I'm sure my hair is a mess. I stretch and immediately feel Chris's hands on my sides. I open my eyes. "I thought we were late."

"Seriously, what did you expect me to do when you did that?"

"Did what? You told me to get up and get dressed. I got up."

"Yeah, that."

I shove him, but he catches me in a kiss. He wraps his arms around me and lays me back on the bed. "Oh no! Get up! You said I had to, so move it, mister."

He laughs and sits up. I grab the sheets and wrap them around myself. I point at my suitcase. "You can get me some clothes. I won't stand up naked again."

"I appreciate that." He randomly pulls some clothes, a dress and a pair of shorts, out of my suitcase and throws them at me.

"Thanks, that's very helpful. Can I have a bra?" He digs through for a second and throws me a black one that should show nicely through the pale colored dress he picked. "Keep trying."

"You are bossy, did you know that?"

"Yes." He finally tosses me a white bra and I pull it on, then the dress and get up.

"Hm," he says looking at me.

"What?"

"The clothes didn't help as much as I was hoping."

"What does that mean?"

"I'd still like to throw you back in that bed."

"Okay, well, I'm worn out. So throw me back if you want, but the minute my head hits the pillow, I'm going to sleep." I put the extra clothes back in my suitcase and find some underwear.

We brush our teeth together, and for some reason it seems more intimate that a good bit of what we did last night. I run a brush through my hair and pull it into a pony tail. Chris watches me in the mirror. "You're beautiful, did you know that?"

"You're not exactly ugly yourself. Come on, let's go."

We step into the hall, and he was right, Short Mark is two doors down, banging on my door. "Shorty! Get up!" He sees Chris first. "Hey, Eck – have you seen Shorty this morning?"

Then he sees me, coming out of Chris's room just behind him. "Oh. *Oh.* I see. Good morning, Shorty. Sleep well?"

"Ha ha. Let's go to breakfast."

"So, that's a no, you did not get enough sleep?"

"What the hell is it with you guys? How can you all be so happy in the morning?"

Short Mark throws his arm around my neck, pulling me down to his level in the process. "Come on, Shorty. You can complain all the way to breakfast. Eck, your mom is looking for you."

"Where is she?"

"I think she went downstairs. Hey, Todd. We'll be back in a little while, okay?" There is a new guy on security detail at the elevator.

Chris introduces me. "Todd, this is my girlfriend, Sara." Well, I guess that discussion is behind us. I can hear his voice shine when he says "girlfriend." He is nearly giddy. "Sara, this is Todd – he's security."

"I worked that out, thanks. Hi, Todd. It's nice to meet you."

Short Mark's eyes are bugging out. "Girlfriend? What happened last night?"

"Wouldn't you like to know?" I ask.

"Yes, that's why I asked."

Chris slings his arm around my shoulders. It's much more comfortable than when Short Mark did it.

The elevator doors open, and Laura starts to step out. "Oh! There you are! Good morning, Chris. Sara! Good morning, dear." She turns back and goes back into the elevator. We all follow her in.

"Hey, mom. Evans said you were looking for me. What's up?"

"First of all, you haven't said hello to your mother yet. I flew a long way to be here, you could at least give me a hug."

Chris pulls away from me to grab his mom in a tight hug. "What's second?" he asks.

Laura glances at me. "I don't think it's relevant anymore."

Chris follows the direction of her eyes. "Yeah, Sara and I talked last night."

"I think they did more than talk," Short Mark says.

I elbow him, but Laura smiles. "Thank you, Mark. I appreciate you sharing that with me, but I think I would have been fine without that knowledge."

I know my face is bright red, but Chris is completely unembarrassed. "It was a good night, Mom. Sara and I are going to get married."

"What?!" I am incredulous. I can't believe he just said that.

"You promised that you would marry me someday. I'm going to hold you to that."

"You just made it sound like we're engaged! I don't think I would say we're there yet."

"Semantics. Close enough."

Laura smiles. "I think that is wonderful."

Short Mark still hasn't said anything, which isn't like him so I have to turn to look. He appears to be choking.

"You okay there, friend?" Chris asks.

Short Mark nods. "Welcome to the family, Shorty," he coughs out.

The elevator opens and I can see Blond Mark, Drew, Tom and Mike standing in the lobby. "Where have you guys been?" Blond Mark asks.

"Eck and Shorty have been too busy to get out of bed and join us this morning."

Drew smiles and Blond Mark laughs. "Busy, huh?"

"Okay, I'm going back to bed. You guys are just being cruel this morning."

Blond Mark nudges Chris with his elbow. "Didn't get much sleep last night?"

"You know," I say loudly. "His mother is standing right here."

Blond Mark looks at Laura guiltily. "Sorry, Laura. I didn't think."

"It's fine," she laughs. "Mr. Evans has already spent some time making inappropriate comments this morning."

"Well, let's just say we've gotten it out of our systems and stop acting like children, okay?" I am almost belligerent.

"Yes, ma'am," Chris says. "I wouldn't cross her guys. She's got a bit of a temper when provoked." He puts his arm back around my shoulders as we exit the hotel. There is a limo waiting for us, of course, even though we're only going to a little diner.

I can barely get through breakfast. I'm so glad to get back to the hotel. I sink into bed and fall asleep almost immediately. I wake up to Chris's phone going off. Chris is next to me, *very* asleep. I'm not even sure when he came into the bed, because it was after I was asleep, but he is wrapped around me. His phone goes quiet for a moment and I'm tempted to close my eyes again, but it starts right back up. It must be important. I slip out from under Chris's arm and he stirs.

I pick up his phone. It's Short Mark. Chris is holding out one hand so I start to hand it to him, but he grabs my wrist and pulls me back next to him. "You answer it," he says sleepily.

"Hi, Short Mark."

"Hey, Shorty. It's time to go to Baltimore. Drag Eck out of bed. We're getting on the bus."

"Oh! Shit! Okay – we'll be right down." I push Chris. "Come on! It's time to go! We've got to pack our stuff!" All of Chris's energy seems to have finally evaporated and he plods around the room dropping random things in his bag while I frantically try to round everything up.

Chris grabs our luggage after I zip them shut. I rush through the room one last time, looking to make sure we didn't forget anything. I grab his iPod which is still plugged into the stereo and head for the door.

On the bus, Short Mark has a few more choice comments about what kept us, but Chris doesn't even slow down to listen. He drops our stuff in the music room, and then climbs up the stairs right away. "I think he's going to back to sleep," I tell the guys. I leave our luggage there because I'm not sure I could drag my suitcase up to the second level. I make a mental note to get a bag to put stuff in for overnight stays in hotels.

"*Back* to sleep, huh?" Blond Mark starts, but I shut him up with a look.

"Good night, gentlemen." I follow behind Chris and shut the door before I climb into his bed. He wraps his arms around me and pulls me close. I can feel the bus start to move and I fall back to sleep quickly, but not as quickly as Chris.

It's not really that far to Baltimore from DC, about an hour, so we don't get much of a nap. They have to do sound and dress, which means Chris has to get up. I get up with him, even though I don't have to. "Where's your mom? I'll hang out with her while you are busy."

"Oh," Chris says, "she left already. She flew home out of Dulles. I'm sorry you were sleeping and didn't get to say good-bye, but she said that she would see you soon."

"Hm. Well, I'll call Allison and check in." He kisses me before he leaves the bus, but it isn't our old kiss-on-the-forehead that I used to get. I think I like the change. I pull out my phone and call my sister.

She answers on the first ring. "Hey, Baby Girl. How's life on the road?"

"It's great."

"How are things with Chris?"

"Better than great."

I can actually hear her smile. "I'm so glad to hear it. Hey, where are you going to be on Tuesday?"

"I don't know, why?"

"Because some paperwork came for you from the school and you need to sign some things and send it back. I'll overnight it tomorrow to wherever you're going to be on Tuesday, but I'll need an address."

"I'll try to find Tom and figure it out."

"What are you going to do for Thanksgiving? I'll be with my in-laws, but you are welcome to come too, if you want."

"I'll probably just spend it with Evansgate. They're playing in New York all weekend, but there are plans for dinner, well lunch really, on Thursday, I think."

"Are you sure? Dad is even going to come."

"I'm sure. They're like family, Ally. I'm looking forward to it."

"Ah, I've finally been replaced."

"You, dear sister, are irreplaceable."

"Don't forget it. Well, go get me an address. I want to make sure that we take care of your paperwork, okay?"

"Yup. I'll call you in a little."

"I'm happy for you. You sound great."

"I feel great. Love you."

"Love you too."

After Baltimore, we go to Philadelphia and then it's Thanksgiving in New York. We have a great big feast with everyone – the whole crew, a bunch of family, Bethany and Angie. There's a little free time for sightseeing while we're in New York, so we hit the big sights. On Saturday they have the contest winners with backstage passes and stuff. Angie, Bethany, and I hide out in our hotel all day so that we don't have deal with them. And, by hide out, I mean we spend a lot of time in the spa.

I can't get enough of Chris. I never knew it could be like this. I loved Sam, I really did, but it was so different from what I have with Chris. Whenever we are together, he is always touching me – his arm around me, holding my hand, or resting his hand on my thigh, and we are very rarely apart. It's so different from my old life of being alone all the time. I keep expecting to get frustrated and want time to myself, but I miss him when he's not next to me. I still feel really guilty about Sam, but I am so happy with Chris that I'm dealing with it quite well.

After Thanksgiving, there are less than two weeks left in the tour. I'm surprised how easily I adjust to touring and I find myself missing it when we're done. It *is* great, though, that there are no demands on either one of us. Chris comes to Richmond with me. I've decided to sell the house; it's just too much.

We spend a couple of weeks cleaning, packing, and organizing. I don't know what I'm going to do with all of my stuff. I don't even know where I'm going to live. "You don't have to make any decisions right now," Chris reminds me. "We've got nothing but time. Put it on the market and see what happens."

"Okay, but I hate the idea of people going through my house."

"Let's put everything of yours, that's important or whatever, in storage. You can come stay in LA with me and Evans for a while."

"Then what?" I ask him, even though I know what he's going to say.

"Then we get married and buy our own place." He gives me a goofy grin.

We see Matt a lot while we are in town. "I know you're going to the west coast for a while, Sara," Matt sounds almost petulant. "Don't worry. I'll keep an eye on the place."

"I'm going to sell it, Matt."

His jaw gets tight. "I knew you would."

"Come on! It's huge! I'm just one person. It was stupid for Sam and I to keep it as long as we did."

"I'm just going to miss having you around the corner."

Chris smiles. "Come to LA. There are a lot of great places, just around the corner."

Matt finds that very amusing, I can tell, even though he is trying to keep a straight face. "I don't think that would be such a great idea. One needs a job to live."

"We'll find you one in LA," Chris says as he puts his arm around my shoulders.

"We'll see," Matt says.

Chapter 39

We have decided to spend Christmas in Portland with Andrew and Laura, so the weekend before we go to New York to see my dad. He is going to Dallas to be with Allison and Tom for the actual holiday. We've invited my sister to LA for New Years, and she's excited because she is convinced that my superstar friends can come up with something really fun to do for the occasion.

We fly to New York and take a car to my dad's house. "Hey, kids!" he calls from the porch as we get out.

"Hi, Dad. You didn't have to wait outside for us, it's cold."

He smiles. "I was just ready to see you." Dad is so happy with Chris that it's almost embarrassing. But I'm glad to see him so relaxed. I think this is a different side of Joe Harris and I like it. After everything we went through with Mom and then Sam, I think the stress was really starting to get to him, and now he is finally starting to move on. I wonder if my dad will ever marry again?

There isn't very much to do around my dad's house. It's a Harris family tradition to watch as many classic Christmas movies as possible over Christmas Eve and Christmas day, and even though we are early, we spend most of our visit in front of my dad's old TV. I miss my mom, but for some reason it's not as hard to bear as I was expecting.

Laura's house is amazing at Christmas. I notice my mom's absence so much around the holidays, but Laura seems to know exactly how to handle every situation and I find myself enjoying this more than I thought I would. We go to a candlelight service at their church Christmas Eve and then caroling with some of their friends at a hospital. I'm unusually tired by the time we get back to the house, so I gratefully climb into bed and fall asleep.

"Merry Christmas, Baby Girl," Chris wakes me early Christmas morning.

"Merry Christmas." I don't feel very good, but I try to push that away so I can enjoy the day.

"I have something for you."

"For some reason, I'm not surprised. You give me stuff for no reason all the time."

"Okay, well, I want you to open it."

I don't see anything. "Open what?"

He points towards the door. "It's under the tree, of course."

I look around some more. "Um, Chris, what time is it?" It's still dark outside.

"Five."

"How old are you?"

"What?"

"Children get up before dawn on Christmas. I think it's okay for adults to sleep a little longer."

"I'm excited. You got me up before five at the beach."

"Fine." I exhale noisily and sit up. I have a moment when I'm pretty sure I'm going to throw up and it takes me a second to get it under control.

"Are you okay? You don't look great."

"I think I might be getting a stomach bug. I don't feel great. But, it's Christmas. I'll do my best." I smile.

He holds my hand as we go downstairs. We're sleeping in a room upstairs, of course, because he won't sleep down in the basement. The tree is lit up and so pretty, I do start to feel a little better. Christmas spirit will do that to you. There is an enormous box at the back of the tree that Chris pulls out.

"Did you get me a refrigerator?"

"I think they're bigger than this, but good guess."

The box weighs almost nothing. I'm intrigued. "Don't you want to wait for your parents?"

"Nope, this is just for us."

"Okay." I rip the paper off of the giant box, which used to house a dryer. "I'm guessing there isn't a dryer in here."

"Nope, my dad got my mom a new one for Christmas. I just used the box."

It appears to be filled with tissue paper, and I'm practically inside the box trying to unearth whatever it is he has hidden inside. "What is in here?" I ask as I dig.

"You'll find it."

Then I get to the very bottom of the box and I find another wrapped box, but this one is tiny. "I know what's in there, don't I?"

"Probably. You're a very smart woman."

He taped it to the bottom, so the paper rips when I lift it out. Chris drops to one knee in front of me while I pull of the last of the paper. "I couldn't help myself," he admits.

The ring is beautiful, and huge, of course. "I love it," I whisper.

"Will you?"

"I already promised you I would."

"Is it too soon to be engaged?"

"I can't really imagine my life without you. It's stupid to wait."

"So, will you?"

"Yes, Christopher Thomas, I will."

He lifts me off the couch in a huge hug and swings me around. I want to yell at him that I'm going to drop the ring and lose it, but I can't. Suddenly I know I'm going to throw up. Unfortunately, I do. Down his back. I immediately feel better, but I also feel terrible.

"I'm so sorry! Oh, I am so sorry!"

"It's my own fault. You told me you didn't feel good." He's laughing. "I'm going to go change my shirt, okay? Did you get anything on the floor?"

I shake my head. "I'm so sorry, Chris."

"It will make a good story." He's still laughing. While he is gone changing, I consider putting the ring on my finger, but I decide to wait for him.

As soon as he gets back I hand him the box. "Did you change your mind?"

"No, I just thought I'd let you do it. You seem to really be enjoying this. I didn't want to take anything away from your moment."

"Sara, you threw up on me."

"Other than that."

"Right," he agrees and then he slides the ring on my finger. It fits perfectly. "I stole one of your rings to have it sized," he admits.

"Thanks."

"You seem to be feeling better."

"I am. Totally. I'm actually really hungry now."

Chris and I eat donuts and drink coffee in the kitchen, an Eck family tradition apparently, while we wait for his parents to wake up. Around seven, they come downstairs. "I see you started without us," Andrew says when he comes in the kitchen.

"Oh! I left paper all over the living room! I'm sorry."

Laura smiles. "It's fine. It's Christmas. That's what it's supposed to look like." She wrinkles her nose. "Chris, you don't smell very good. Were you sick?"

"No, Sara was. Sorry. I changed my shirt, but maybe I should have showered."

I hang my head. "I'm sorry. Seriously, this is awful. I trashed your living room and threw up on your son and it's only 7 am."

Andrew laughs. "You seem fine. Feeling better?"

"Yeah, actually. I think I just needed to throw up."

Laura smiles. "It was like that for me when I was pregnant with

Chris. I just had to throw up every morning and then I was fine for the rest of the day."

I freeze. Pregnant? Suddenly I realize it's been a really long time since I have had a period. I start doing some math. I haven't had a period since Sam died. Actually, I was having my period *when* Sam died. I don't usually pay attention, because what difference does it make? but I definitely remember.

I'm just standing there, dumbstruck, when Laura notices the ring on my finger. "Oh!" she breathes. "Congratulations?" she asks her son.

Chris is positively beaming. "Thanks."

Andrew is looking around trying to figure out what they're talking about, and I still haven't been able to move. Is it possible? Could I be pregnant?

"We're getting married, Dad," Chris says.

Andrew looks at me, and then Chris and Laura do too. "Are you okay?" he asks me. "Shouldn't you be a little more excited about this? It's good news, right? Are you feeling sick again?"

I'm completely stuck. I can't even nod or shake my head. There's a drug store that's open 365 days a year not far. "I have to run out for a minute. Laura, could I borrow your car?"

I can see the shock on their faces, but Laura says, "Of course, Sara. Are you okay? Are you sick?"

"I just – I'll be right back."

Chris is clearly concerned, "Where are you going? Do you want me to take you?"

"No, no. Please. I'll be right back."

I'm still in my pajamas, but I just throw on my coat and grab her keys. I'm back in less than 15 minutes and I go straight up to the bathroom. I can hear the Ecks, still in the kitchen. I know I've worried them, but I'm still numb with the idea of being pregnant. We never used protection. Why would we? I can't get pregnant.

I pee on the stick and then I shove it back in the box so that I can't watch. I did this so many times when Sam and I were trying and I know how much it hurts to see only one line. I'm already considering the possibility so much, that I'll be devastated if it's negative. It seems like an eternity, but I force myself to wait the full five minutes before I take it and look.

Two lines. I'm pregnant.

I open the door. "Laura? Can you help me with something, please?" I slide the stick back in the box and cram it in my coat pocket.

333

Then I hurry into the hall to find her.

"What is it?" she asks.

"I need a box and some wrapping paper."

"Oh! Okay. Come on." I follow her down the hall into her work room, which is still completely covered in wrapping supplies.

"Thanks, but it's a secret, so I'm going to kick you out."

She smiles. "Okay." I hear her when she goes back downstairs, "No, everything is fine. She just had a last minute gift to get, apparently." Oh, if only she knew.

I find the perfect sized box and wrap the stick in tissue before putting it inside. I wrap it up and take it downstairs. I put it under the tree, in the back, before I join them in the kitchen. I'm not sure what my face looks like, I still haven't really processed the whole thing, but Chris still looks really concerned. "Sara? Are you okay? What were you doing?"

"It's fine." I smile as brightly as I can. "Everything's great. I'm sorry. I just remembered something that I needed to take care of."

"You're an idiot, do you know that?" he asks me.

"Yeah, I know. I just agreed to marry you, didn't I?"

Andrew claps his hands together. "Okay! Let's get this show on the road!"

Oh, I hope he means open presents, because I don't know how long I can keep this knowledge to myself. I'm smiling like an idiot when we head to the living room. I'm going to force myself to wait until the very end.

It's not really the gift opening frenzy of my childhood. I'm anxious to get through, but we take our time. I fidget for over an hour, trying to pretend like I'm perfectly happy and not ready to bust out of my skin. Chris finds the pregnancy test gift before all of the other presents are opened. He picks it up, but I didn't put any tags on it. "What's this?"

"Oh, that's from me. But not yet. Let me have it, okay?"

He smiles and hands it to me. "Okay, sweetheart."

There are only a couple more gifts so I don't have to wait much longer. "Well," I say when everything else is opened, "this is kind of for all of you." I hand the box to Chris.

"Is this what you ran out to get? You're such a goofball. Nothing is so important that you needed to run out on Christmas." Chris is laughing.

"Open it and see if you still feel that way."

I watch Chris eagerly tear the paper off. He really is a big kid at Christmas. It would have been so much more fun to watch him all morning if I could have just sat back and enjoyed it without this hanging over my head. He pulls the lid off of the box and his head cocks to one side like it always does when he's confused. I feel like I could explode, I'm so ready for him to know, but I force my face into an expression of patience.

He lifts the tissue paper, but I know he's still really confused. Clearly, the man is not familiar with pregnancy tests. But Laura is. She leaps off of the couch and grabs it out of her son's hand. "Are you really?!"

I nod. I'm embarrassed because we can't hide the fact that we committed a cardinal sin from his parents anymore. I should have thought about that. I wonder if she's upset. But, no.

"Oh my! I can't believe it! Congratulations! To me too! This is wonderful!" She is practically dancing around the living room.

Chris is still really confused. "What exactly are we so happy about?"

Andrew smiles at his son. "I think you're going to be a father."

Chris looks at me. "What? Sara? You can't... I thought..."

"Um, are you...? I mean, you don't seem... I'm sorry. Maybe I should have handled that differently." Crap, he really doesn't seem very happy. I probably should have broken the news to him in private.

"What are you going on about, woman?"

"You don't seem very happy."

"I'm in shock. But I'm happy! Oh, I'm happy! I can't believe it!" He grabs me off of the couch again, but stops before he spins. "Sorry. I won't do that again." He laughs. "How?"

I look at Andrew. "I think maybe you should have had a talk with your son a long time ago."

"I must have missed something, yes."

"I'm serious, Sara. How?"

"I don't know. I honestly don't. But I hope you're happy."

"I am. Are you?"

"Do you really even have to ask?"

"Want to go to Vegas with me for New Year's? I don't feel like we should wait any longer."

"Okay." He probably has a good point.

On New Year's eve Chris and I get married. It's really small, of course, but I'm amazed at what we pulled off. It's a beautiful little chapel, and we follow all of the traditions. Allison stands up with me, Short Mark with Chris. My dad walks me down the aisle. We say our vows in front of Allison, Short Mark, my dad, Laura and Andrew,

Allison's Tom, Blond Mark and Angie, Drew and Bethany, and Matt, who flew out for the occasion. It's perfect.

I know there are a lot of things that we are going to have to work out. Like where we're going to live for instance, and how things are going to work with a baby when Chris is on tour. But, I feel like Chris and I can do anything together.

Acknowledgments

I wish that I could properly thank my favorite band for inspiring this story, but I won't actually name them in case they don't appreciate the fact that I thought of them while writing it. I *did not* base this book on them – there are not even four of them. But they still inspired my story, and for that, I thank them.

Sara: I did not intend to name my main character after you, but I'm glad it worked out that way. Thank you for reading and applying your expertise. The fact that you know about subjunctive verbs adds greatly to your awesomeness. Thanks for keeping me honest, improving my story *and* my writing, and somehow finding time to fit reading this into your schedule *twice*.

Mickey: I know that my Matt in the story isn't nearly as cool as you, but that just can't be copied, my friend. I appreciate you letting me model him off of you, nonetheless. Thanks for all of the mkm originals. What can I say? You're funnier than I am. I apologize for asking you to read something so very far outside of your comfort zone. Yes, I know you're not a fourteen year old girl.

Jax: thank you for checking my content and inking up my work. You've always had the most confidence in my abilities, even those that aren't there. Thanks for always supporting me.

I have to thank my mom and Aunt Barb for reading and telling me they liked it. I'll try to not let the naked surprise in your voices when you said that you thought it was good hurt my feelings.

Dr. K: thanks for fixing me.

I can't really thank my husband enough for tolerating me while I shut myself up to write this, even if I was sick for most of the time. Brad: thanks for taking care of everything and picking up the slack around the house (like you always do.) Thank you for celebrating all of my little victories along the way and listening to me talk about a story that you have no interest in.

My two little boys: thanks for behaving while Moma was sick – you're the best.

I also need to thank my favorite band, Van Morrison, and all the other wonderful musicians that kept me going through the whole process with their music: Of Monsters and Men, Lumineers, Gotye, fun., and Ok Go, just to name a few.

Going into print is so exciting, but it also adds to the people that I need to thank!

JP: what can I say? *No one* else would have worked on the cover. Thank you so much for spending your time standing around the airport looking like a street performer and hauling heavy things with you.

Gik: thank you so much for the time you put into helping me make this book as wonderful as possible. Thank you for the fantastic photo shoot, I hope you (and JP) had as much fun as I did. Thank you for proofing.

Sara: you read it *again*. Thanks. Your knowledge of grammar and punctuation still impresses me.

Brad: thank you for all of the effort and time you have put into making my website awesome.

Please visit my webpage for story extras and info about upcoming
books in *the six degrees of separation* series
www.beckadrum.com

www.ingramcontent.com/pod-product-compliance
Lightning Source LLC
Chambersburg PA
CBHW021444240626
47153CB00001B/281